OLYMPUS
CONFIDENTIAL

OLYMPUS CONFIDENTIAL

A PLATO JONES NOVEL

ROBERT B. WARREN

DRAGONFAIRY PRESS
ATLANTA

OLYMPUS CONFIDENTIAL

Cover design by Georgina Gibson
www.georginagibson.com

Published by Dragonfairy Press, Atlanta
www.dragonfairypress.com

First Publication, November 2014
Trade Paperback ISBN: 978-1-939452-48-1
PDF ISBN: 978-1-939452-50-4

Published in the United States of America

Library of Congress Control Number: 2014942032

To Amy,
the best literary manager in the business.

1

THE WHITE VAN PULLED INTO THE ALLEYWAY AND CAME TO a stop. Black-tinted windows hid the interior.

The panel door slid open and four men jumped out: Felix King, his father, Louis, and their associates, Marcelo and Lance. All wore black sweats and empty backpacks, and carried AK-47s. Matching ski masks covered all but their eyes and mouths.

Felix closed the van door and slapped it twice, signaling the driver to leave. The vehicle pulled off and slipped into the press of rush-hour traffic, vanishing. Felix and the others hustled to the opposite end of the alleyway and stopped near the outlet. Concealed by shadow, they looked out onto the street, past the flow of pedestrians and congested thoroughfares, at their target.

Across from them, the Bank of New Olympia towered over the surrounding buildings, its white façade stained orange by the evening sun. Humans and nonhumans trickled in and out of the entrance. Felix looked to his father, as did Marcelo and Lance. Louis remained rooted in place, his gaze fixed on his tactical wristwatch.

Exactly forty-five seconds later, Louis nodded, and the group abandoned cover, running into the open. Gasps and screams followed their progress. Chaos ensued as droves of pedestrians fled in terror, clearing a route for the masked gunmen.

Felix and his partners shoved past the stragglers and rushed across the street. They didn't have to worry about oncoming cars. A red light held the traffic stationary.

Once they reached the other side, Marcelo took point and burst through the front door. Two security guards—minotaurs, both over seven feet tall—stood on either side of the entrance. Before they could attempt to subdue him, Marcelo went on the offensive. With speed that defied logic, he kicked one of the minotaurs in the abdomen. The blow landed with a loud smack—like a cannonball striking a side of beef—and sent the guard zooming backward, smashing through the window of a consultant's office.

Marcelo whirled toward the other guard. Rifle in his left hand, he delivered an uppercut with the right that caught his opponent under the chin. Knocked several feet into the air, the minotaur flailed end over end and crashed onto the marble floor—and there he remained, unmoving, his neck twisted at a terrible angle.

The engagement lasted no more than three seconds.

Screams erupted from customers and employees alike—about thirty in all—reverberating off the bank's vaulted ceiling. Felix stepped inside, his father and Lance at his rear.

He fired three warning shots into the air. "Everyone on the ground! Now!"

When the shell casings clinked on the cold, hard floor, the screams ended. The customers complied. Most of them shivered. One woman started to cry. Two little boys, twins, lay on either side of their mother. She draped her arms over them and drew them close. A satyr pissed himself, a yellow puddle expanding beneath him.

Lance hurdled over the service counter and trained his gun on the tellers—to make sure no one activated the silent alarm.

Felix peeked through the smashed window of the consultant's office. The minotaur lay unmoving on the floor amid shards of glass and the broken remains of a desk and two chairs. His large round eyes stared blankly at the ceiling. Felix nodded at Louis.

His father returned the gesture and casually walked to the vault. He took his gun in one hand and extended the other toward the circular metal door. A metallic shriek, strident and deafening, echoed as the door tore free of its hinges.

The hostages gritted their teeth against the dissonance, but most did not cover their ears. They dared not make a move.

Once the door had been unhinged, Louis lowered his hand. The door fell forward and landed with a thump that caused the floor to tremble. Someone gasped. A muffled sound followed, as if somebody had covered his mouth to smother a scream.

Louis and Lance entered the vault and began stuffing credits into their backpacks, while Felix and Marcelo kept watch over the hostages. One of them, an elderly man, glared up at Felix, his eyes hard with defiance. As if sensing the man was about to play hero, Felix kicked him in the face, knocking him out.

The hostages jerked, cowering in their places.

After Louis and Lance had filled their bags, they traded places with Felix and Marcelo. Sirens wailed in the distance. It was unlikely that a teller had had time to sound the alarm. Pedestrians must have contacted the police. But those details didn't matter. None of the gunmen appeared to be worried, and all continued working at an unhurried pace.

When Felix and Marcelo were done, the four men regrouped at the entrance. They stepped outside to find a swarm of policemen equipped with pistols and shotguns. In front of the cops, a dozen or so cruisers formed a phalanx of black-and-white metal. Lights flashed wildly, their red-and-blue signals clashing against the glow of the setting sun.

"Drop your weapons and get down on your knees," a cop shouted through a loudspeaker. "Hands behind your heads!"

Felix and the others did as instructed. As the cops came forward to arrest them, terrified voices sounded from inside the bank. The vault door crashed through the bank's main entrance, shattering glass and tearing away chunks of white brick. It sailed like a Frisbee over the heads of the gunmen and mowed down the approaching officers. It continued to spin forward, slamming head on into the police barricade, shearing it down the middle, and carrying away several cops.

The remaining officers opened fire. Felix quickly raised his hand. An unseen force responded to his movement, erecting an invisible wall in front of the four robbers. The bullets struck the barrier, flattened against it, and fell harmlessly to the ground.

The cops hesitated, in either fear or bewilderment. They soon regained their resolve and prepared for another volley. Marcelo and Lance knelt, planting their hands against the ground. The asphalt beneath the police barricade quaked and broke apart. Cops stumbled, fell, and clung to each other, as their comrades—along with two cruisers—were swallowed whole by a newly formed fissure. Water fountained from a burst fire hydrant.

While the remaining cops struggled to regroup, Felix, Marcelo, and Lance handed their backpacks to Louis. Felix nodded at his father. Then Louis rocketed high into the air.

The surrounding din—the keening of sirens, the shouts of men and women, the hiss of spraying water—fell beneath a thunderous boom as Louis broke the sound barrier, his body engulfed by a cone of white vapor.

Felix, Marcelo, and Lance watched him vanish from sight. They dropped to their knees, placed their hands behind their heads, and waited for the police.

2

The morning after the bank robbery, Zeus, King of the Gods and President of the Olympic World Council, stood before the window in his office, gazing at the city below. New Olympia. The center of the world.

His son Hermes, the Messenger of the Gods, sat in a chair across from his desk. He wore a sky-blue suit. His long silver hair gleamed like platinum in the sunshine pouring through the skylight.

"Have you learned anything from the suspects?" Zeus asked.

"Their names," Hermes said.

"That's all?"

Zeus's question came out calmly and free of reproach. But as far as Hermes seemed to be concerned, his father might as well have been shouting at him.

"Unfortunately," he said.

"So no mention of their special abilities? How they acquired them?"

"No, sir. And they haven't exhibited any superhuman powers since their arrest."

"Perhaps they're merely suppressing them."

"It's possible."

"Do you have theories?"

"Only one comes to mind, but it doesn't explain why they allowed themselves to be taken into custody," Hermes said. "We need facts, and I'm not sure how we're going to get them."

"Have you tried torture?"

"I've employed nearly every method at our disposal."

"And still nothing?"

"I'm afraid so," Hermes said grudgingly. "These humans are remarkably strong-willed, especially the one named Felix. He seems to be their ringleader."

"What about the one who escaped?" Zeus asked.

"No word yet. But I have agents scouring the city and surrounding areas. They're bound to find something."

"And if they don't?"

Hermes offered no reply.

"We can't have gangs of superhumans running around, raising havoc," Zeus said. "We need to nip this in the bud before it becomes a larger problem."

"How do you suggest we do that?"

"By seeking outside assistance."

Hermes arched his eyebrows. "I hope you're not talking about who I think you're talking about."

"Plato Jones is the best man for the job."

"He's a peasant—an irreverent one at that."

"He gets results. Something you haven't been able to do lately."

Hermes frowned. "This is my case."

"And so it shall remain," Zeus said. "For the most part."

Hermes shook his head. "I can't believe this is happening . . . again."

"Don't be so melodramatic. Working with him won't be so bad."

"I beg to differ."

"Differ as much as you'd like. I'm not going to jeopardize national security just to appease your ego."

"But—"

Zeus turned around to face Hermes. "I've made my decision."

The King's irritation was not present on his face or in his voice. But Hermes could sense it. He abandoned the argument.

"Do you have a plan?" Hermes asked.

"I do," Zeus said. "But I'll need time to get everything in order."

"What about the suspects?"

"Keep them detained while I set up a court date."

"Anything else?"

"Yes." Zeus lowered his voice slightly. "Don't mention a word of this to your mother. I don't want a repeat of last time."

"Yes, sir."

Zeus nodded. "I'll contact you once the plan has been finalized."

Hermes opened his mouth to speak, hesitated, and then said, "With all due respect, Mr. President, don't you think it's a bit . . . unwise to put all your trust in a mortal?"

Zeus tilted his chin. "Do you, seeing as how it's Plato Jones?"

Hermes shifted in his seat. "No, of course not."

"I didn't think so." Zeus turned back toward the window.

"What if he refuses to help?"

"Then it'll be up to you to change his mind."

"How?"

"Be creative."

Hermes sighed. "I still think this is a bad idea."

"Noted." Zeus waved a dismissive hand. "Now go."

Hermes got up and walked to the door. As he stepped through, he shook his head and muttered, "Unbelievable."

3

Half-naked bodies packed the dance floor of the Golden Fleece nightclub, writhing to the beat of a dubstep song I'd never heard before and illuminated by a seizure-inducing array of multicolored strobe lights.

Most were human, with a few satyrs and minotaurs sprinkled into the mix.

I stood on the periphery of the action, leaning against one of the club's three bars, a gin and tonic in hand. Unlike most of the people around me, I wasn't here to have fun. I had a job to do.

A few weeks earlier, I had met with Francis Spencer, the dean of New Olympia University. He was having a problem with a local con artist named Antonio Petros, who had gotten his hands on some embarrassing photos featuring the good dean. I'd been hired to get them back and make sure all digital copies had been erased.

I finished my gin and set the empty glass on the bar. After three of them, my buzz had finally kicked in.

The bartender, a gorgeous brunette with mile-long eyelashes, came over.

"Want another?" she asked.

"No thanks," I said, smiling. "I'm on the clock."

"Give me a holler if you need anything."

"Will do."

The bartender cleared the empty glass and went to help other customers. I shifted my attention back to the dance floor. Petros appeared minutes later, a satyr with slick black hair, a long face, and sharp, weasel-like features. His maroon crushed velvet jacket looked too hot for the club. Too hot for this time of year. I guessed his lack of pants made up for it.

He had two human girls, one on each arm. Leggy blondes in tight black dresses.

Some guys had all the luck.

The trio headed to a staircase that led up to the bar's VIP section. A minotaur bouncer stood at the base of the stairs. His white fur glowed under the strobe lights, clashing against his horns and suit, both of which were black. He stepped aside, allowing Antonio and his ladies to pass. Not a single word had been exchanged.

Antonio had clout.

I took ten credits out of my wallet, stuffed them into the tip jar, and made my way to the staircase. Earlier that evening, I had broken into Antonio's apartment to look for the photos while he was out. I searched the place from top to bottom but came up empty-handed. I wiped the hard drives on his desktop computer for good measure. But there was no telling where else he might be storing copies of the files.

Antonio could have stashed a thumb drive in some secret compartment. Or maybe he carried the copies around with him. In either case, I couldn't afford to waste any more time. I'd decided to get the answer straight from the horse's mouth.

Or rather, the goat's mouth.

After leaving Antonio's apartment, I'd returned to my car—parked at an IHOP across the street—and fired up my trusty laptop. Never leave home without it.

In the old days, tracking down an elusive sleazebag like Antonio would have been the equivalent of a snipe hunt. But the digital age eliminated much of the guesswork. Everyone knew what everyone else was doing at all times. And when it came to bragging about the fun a person was having, I figured Antonio was no exception.

I'd logged onto Facebook and pulled up his page. We weren't "friends," and his privacy settings were limiting. But I could see that he had close to five thousand friends and just as many pictures in his photo albums—though his privacy settings didn't let me see anything but his smug profile picture. I didn't have a page at all, unless you counted the one my secretary, Emilie, had set up for the agency. Seventy-two likes and counting, baby! Plato Jones, PI, was coming up in the world.

I used one of the OBI's hacking apps to bypass security and look at Antonio's complete page. One of his friends, a gorgeous yoga instructor with nothing to hide, had left a post on his wall: "Looking forward to seeing Antonio Petros and the gang at the Golden Fleece tonight—gotta make sure he's not too hung over for 10 a.m. yoga tomorrow!"

Golden Fleece tonight. New Olympia Fitness tomorrow. Ah, the wonders of technology.

I reached the staircase. The minotaur bouncer—standing over seven feet tall and ludicrously muscled—gave me an annoyed look, as if I were a stray cat that had wandered onto his porch to beg for food.

"I need to get through," I said.

"Name."

"I don't think I'm on the list."

The bouncer crossed his arms over his chest.

"But I think my friend Poseidon is." I pulled a fifty out of my pocket.

The God of the Sea's bearded mug decorated the middle of the bill. I'll give you a guess as to whose face graced each and every C-note.

The bouncer looked at the money, then at me, then at the

money again. His expression didn't change, but he accepted the bribe and moved aside.

The second floor of the club was a long balcony overlooking the dance floor. A five-foot guardrail lined the edge, to prevent any drunken patrons from falling to an unceremonious death.

A bar spanned the back wall. Three male bartenders served up an endless stream of alcohol. Here they were referred to as mixologists. As long as they made good drinks, I'd call them whatever they wanted.

Waitresses in skimpy black unitards greeted me in passing as they moved back and forth between the bar and the twelve private booths, balancing trays of drinks and carrying buckets of champagne that probably cost more than I made in a week.

I followed one of the girls to Antonio's booth. I could just as easily have found it on my own by following the noise. The goat of the hour sat between a pair of twins, his arms around them. All three laughed raucously. At what, I had no idea. But I was willing to bet it wasn't very funny.

I hung back, near the guardrail, while the waitress served Antonio and his ladies their drinks. I waited until she left, then made my approach.

"Room for one more?" I asked.

Antonio regarded me with a bored look. He held a martini. Three olives rested at the bottom of the glass.

"Do I know you?" Antonio asked.

"No."

"Then get lost."

"But I just got here," I said, feigning disappointment. "Besides, we have business to discuss."

"What are you talking about, man?"

"I'll give you a hint. It's about blackmail."

Antonio paused, the martini glass poised near his lips.

"So that's it, huh?" He lowered the glass.

"Afraid so. Now, we can do this the easy way or the hard way. Your choice."

We stared each other down. Antonio appeared calm. But I wasn't convinced.

"Can we go somewhere more private?" he asked.

"As long as it's close by."

"Let me finish my drink." He sipped his martini.

His eyes cut toward the staircase. Too late, I realized that he planned to bolt. He threw his drink in my face.

The alcohol burned my eyes and got into my nose. One of the blondes gasped. The other let out a short scream. Through blurred vision, I saw them scramble out of the booth as Antonio sprang to his feet.

He threw the table onto its side—out of his way—and rammed his shoulder into my stomach. The air rushed from my lungs, and I doubled over.

Gasping and disoriented, I struggled to my feet. The creep caught me off guard. How embarrassing. Tears had washed away enough of the alcohol, giving me a clearer view of my surroundings. The minotaur from downstairs lumbered toward me. I looked past him. Antonio had made it to the staircase.

He was getting away!

I suddenly forgot about the bouncer and propelled myself forward. Catching the perp was the only thing on my mind. Too bad my body had other plans. It hadn't fully recovered from Antonio's attack. My legs turned to jelly after only a few steps, and I stumbled into the minotaur's open arms.

Hands the size of catcher's mitts trapped me in a crushing grip. The bouncer tossed me over his shoulder like a sack of potatoes and hauled me downstairs. I knew better than to resist. Tangling with a minotaur was dangerous enough. But going toe-to-toe with one who roughed people up for a living would have been suicide.

Bystanders gawked at me. Some of them laughed—well, most of them. But anger and frustration made me immune to their mockery. I scanned the crowd for Antonio, but the coward had gone MIA.

The minotaur carried me to the nearest exit. He kicked open the door and tossed me outside, into a dark alley that ran alongside the club. I landed hard on the pavement, bruising my ribs, right hip, and elbow. Luckily, all my body parts managed to avoid broken bottles, shattered crack pipes, and discarded syringes.

Thank goodness for small favors.

I got up and wobbled in place, my head spinning. I gripped the edge of a nearby dumpster to steady myself. The stench of rotting garbage hit my nose, adding nausea to my list of aches and pains.

The minotaur watched me from the exit. "I don't want to see you around here again. Got it?"

"Loud and clear."

"Enjoy the rest of your night." The minotaur went back inside.

The door swung closed behind him.

Well, that could've gone better.

I let my wooziness subside, then left the alley. I had parked my Thunderbird in a lot down the street. I jogged over to it, looking—in vain—for Antonio along the way. Each step roused a twinge of pain. But it was nothing that a tube of medicated ointment couldn't fix.

I drove back to Antonio's apartment complex. I didn't expect to find him there so soon after our encounter. He'd probably lie low for a while, in case the police caught wind of the fight and came knocking. Granted, it was unlikely that New Olympia's finest would waste time and resources investigating a typical bar brawl. But when a large chunk of your income is earned through illegal activities, like Antonio's, it was best to err on the side of caution.

Before getting out of my car, I grabbed my Desert Eagle from the glove compartment and concealed it under my shirt. I didn't anticipate a firefight. But it never hurt to have a little insurance.

Antonio's apartment was on the third floor. I paced down the empty hallway, hurried to his door, and took out my electric lockpick. The gadget was size of a pen. A birthday present from Emilie. She always gives such nice gifts.

I inserted the lockpick into the keyhole and pressed a button on the side of it. It made a soft whirring sound, and the lock released.

I put the device back into my pocket and eased the door open. Just a crack. A peek inside revealed only darkness. As far as I could tell, the place was empty.

I went inside and locked the door behind me. Antonio's apartment was on the small side, but housed an array of expensive items: a mounted sixty-inch flat-screen television, leather furniture, two computers, a piano, ornate vases and figurines, and an authentic chimera-skin rug, just to name a few. The first time I'd broken in, earlier that evening, I couldn't help being impressed. Then I remembered how Antonio made his living—and admiration instantly gave way to disgust.

I sat on the recliner and waited. Two hours later, I heard the door open, then a quiet click. The lights came on.

Here we go.

Antonio entered the living room and immediately spotted me. He froze. His startled expression made me feel like a Bond villain. The only things I was missing were a white suit, an eye patch, and a fluffy cat resting my lap.

"Hello again, Mr. Petros," I said, trying to sound sinister. "I've been waiting for you."

Antonio shivered and seemed to regain his wits. He turned to run. I shoved out of the chair and gave chase, tackling him before he could reach the door. As we tussled on the floor, I quickly discovered that this was a one-sided contest. My opponent had a talent for grifting, but not fighting. Within seconds, I trapped him in an armbar.

The fight was over.

"Now don't you wish you had done things the easy way?" I said.

"Go to Hades!" Antonio shouted.

I pulled down on his arm, adding more pressure to the lock, straining joints and stretching muscles and ligaments.

Antonio gasped.

"Where are the photos?" I demanded.

When he didn't answer, I gave his arm another pull. He let out a yelp.

"Where are the photos?" I repeated.

"The TV!" Petros cried. "They're behind the TV!"

I released him. Antonio rolled onto his side, groaning and cradling his left arm.

"Show me," I said.

Antonio gradually got to his feet. Beet red and breathing hard, he lurched to the living room. He removed an abstract painting from the wall. Behind it was a keypad.

"Don't try anything cute," Plato said. "I'm packing."

Antonio shot me a scowl, letting me know he got the message. He entered a five-digit code on the keypad. The TV swung open like a door, revealing a secret compartment. It contained several stacks of money, a few pieces of jewelry, and a large catalog envelope.

Antonio removed the envelope and tossed it on the coffee table. "Here."

I picked up the envelope and checked the contents. Spencer's pictures were inside. Who knew that the dean of New

Olympia University enjoyed dressing up like a toddler and getting spanked by female giants?

I put the photos back into the envelope.

"Satisfied?" Antonio asked.

I skipped over his question and asked one of my own. "You wouldn't happen to have copies of these photos, would you?"

"No," Antonio said swiftly.

I wasn't convinced. So I *persuaded* him to give me a look at his laptop computer, then his phone—and surprise, surprise. Antonio not only had copies of the pictures I'd already confiscated, but a few more. Fortunately, these didn't feature Spencer, but an assortment of equally seasoned and pasty gentlemen in compromising situations. I decided to be a Good Samaritan and asked him to delete them all, while I watched. After another powwow with the apartment floor, he obliged.

"I had better not hear about you going anywhere near my client ever again," I said. "Understand?"

"Screw him and screw you too."

I took that as a yes. "Have a lovely night, Mr. Petros."

As I prepared to leave, Antonio narrowed his eyes curiously. "Hey, aren't you that guy who used to date Aphrodite?"

4

The next evening, I collected my fee from Spencer and visited my favorite bar. In the months that followed the God-killer case, the former owner, Abas, had decided to hang up his bar towel and retire. He wanted to spend more time with his family.

He sold the Night Owl to an American named Andy, who renamed it Speakeasy. Other than that, nothing had changed. The atmosphere remained calm and relaxed, the clientele mature, and the drinks still the best in town.

Herc and I were meeting up for drinks. Our pal Geno had planned to join us, but got sidelined by a sudden case of worms—a common health problem among satyrs. I decided to make up for his absence by drinking twice as much.

The sacrifices I make in the name of friendship.

No less than a dozen paparazzi loitered near the bar's entrance, a sign that Herc had already arrived.

As always, Napoleon, the minotaur bouncer, kept the parasites at bay. He had been allowed to keep his job after the change in ownership. I was glad. The place wouldn't have been the same without him.

As I neared the entrance, a paparazzo began snapping pictures of me.

"Plato, over here!" one of them exclaimed. "Think you and Aphrodite will ever get back together?"

At the mention of the Love Goddess's name, the other photographers turned their cameras on me. They bombarded me with questions about her and me.

"Are you still in love with her?"

"Is she as kinky as they say?"

"Is it true you two have a secret love child?"

I ignored them and stepped up to the door. Napoleon nodded.

"Evening, Plato," he said. "How's it going?"

"Ask me in an hour."

Napoleon returned the minotaur equivalent of a grin. It looked more like a grimace. He opened the door for me. None of the so-called journalists attempted to follow me inside. They were a lot of things—pushy, obnoxious, disrespectful—but stupid was not one of them.

The bar was filled to capacity—a fifty-fifty mix of humans and nonhumans. "I'll See You in My Dreams" by Giant poured from unseen speakers, barely rising above the rich hum of many conversations going on at once.

All the usual suspects were present. Most greeted me with waves or hellos. One of the longtime regulars, a steelworker named Mitch, gave me a hearty slap on the back and called me an asshole.

Yep. We were one big, happy bar family.

Hercules, the half-human son of Zeus, was having a beer at the bar. One of the most powerful beings in existence, he had performed countless acts of heroism over a life that spanned several millennia. His ferocity, honor, and cunning were the stuff of legend. Most people regarded him as the world's first superhero.

To me, he was just Herc, my best friend and a cheapskate extraordinaire.

I took the seat to his left. I assumed he had saved it for me. At over seven feet tall, and weighing close to four hundred pounds, Herc seemed more mountain than man. How the barstool he sat on remained intact could have been a topic on *Unexplained Mysteries.*

"Herc," I said.

"What's up, Jonesy?"

"Nothing much, brother. I see you brought along your fan club. You should invite them in one day."

Herc frowned. "Vultures, every one of them."

"They love you."

"They can take their love and shove it up their . . ." Herc paused. "I just don't like them."

Caitlin, Andy's girlfriend and one of the bartenders, came over to take my order. She was tall and blonde, with a youthful face and a welcoming smile.

"Well, hello there," she said.

"Hey, Caitlin," I said. "How's life been treating you?"

"Not too bad. How about you?"

"I can't complain."

"What can I get you?"

"The usual."

"Coming right up." In less than thirty seconds, Caitlin whipped up a rum and Coke and set it in front of me. "Here you go, hon."

"Much obliged." I handed her my debit card.

"Keep it open?"

"You know it."

Caitlin got on the cash register and opened a tab for me. She then glanced at Herc's half-empty beer bottle.

"Almost ready for another?" she asked him.

Herc killed his drink. "I am now."

Caitlin trashed the bottle and grabbed a fresh beer from the cooler. "Here you go."

Herc nodded. "Thanks,"

"If you guys need anything, let me know." She left to check on the other customers.

Herc drank some beer and looked at me. His blue eyes possessed the same unearthly glow as his father's.

"What's bugging you?" he asked.

"Nothing," I said. "Didn't you hear what I just said to Caitlin?"

"I heard what you said. I just don't believe it."

"And why is that?"

"Because I can tell when you're upset."

"Is that your godly insight at work . . . or demigodly?"

"Nope. Just plain old intuition. So come on, Jonesy. Rap with me."

"Herc, never say that again."

"Okay, okay." Herc chuckled. "But seriously, you should get whatever's bothering you off your chest. It'll make you feel better."

"Nah."

"Did something happen between you and Bellanca?"

I didn't respond.

"That's it. Isn't it?" Herc asked.

Like the question that had come before, this one also went unanswered. I chugged my rum and Coke in one long pull, and waved my hand in the air to get Caitlin's attention. When she noticed me, I pointed at the empty glass.

She smiled and nodded.

Herc stared at me as though waiting for an explanation. He must have realized it would never come because he opened his mouth to speak. But Caitlin's arrival forestalled him.

She served me another rum and Coke. "You must be thirsty."

"Absolutely parched."

Herc waited until Caitlin had gone before speaking. "What did Bellanca do?"

I sampled my drink. It had a stronger bite than the first. I suspected I might need it.

"Did she cheat on you?" Herc asked.

"You're not going to drop this, are you?" I asked.

"Nope. So let's get it out of the way early."

"Fine," I sighed. "She didn't cheat on me. She dumped me."

"What?" Herc seemed surprised. "When did this happen?"

"Three weeks ago."

"And you didn't tell me?"

"There was no point," I said. "Talking won't bring her back."

"Did you love her?"

"I don't know. I guess."

"Damn." Herc shook his head. "I'm sorry, Jonesy."

"Don't be. I'm growing accustomed to bad relationships."

That was the most honest thing I had said all night. I thought back to Alexis and Calais's wedding. They looked so happy—my former wife and the man she now loved. Throughout the ceremony, the jealousy bug had not only been nipping at me; the damn thing had burrowed into my heart and laid eggs.

I'd thought Zeus's personal assistant, Chrysus, could help me forget my troubles and give me a fresh start. Those aspirations died less than a month after the God-killer case—two weeks before I began dating Bellanca exclusively. Chrysus and I realized things would never work out. Our personalities just didn't mesh. She loved structure and order, and I was a habitual rule-breaker—especially where the Gods were concerned. But at least we parted amicably.

I wish I could say the same about Aphrodite. Ours was the relationship that never was. Only no one told her that. She still seemed interested in me—in jumping my bones, to be specific.

Every now and again, she would send gifts to my apartment: flowers, designer clothes and watches, high-end electronics, stuff like that. Now if she got me a copy of *Detective Comics* number twenty-seven, I might be inclined to give her a shot. One thing confused me, though. She could have anyone she wanted, yet she chose me. Why?

"Because she's a God, and Gods are weird" seemed a fitting explanation.

And then there was Lamia. Out of the whole bunch, she was the one I thought about the most. The night she died would haunt me for the rest of my life. The night I was forced to kill her. Though it sickened me to admit it, I still had feelings for her. Sometimes I wondered how things would've played out had she not been a murderous sociopath.

I didn't have an answer.

"Who'd she leave you for?" Herc asked.

"Collin."

"Her ex?"

"That'd be the one."

"Why him?"

"She said that I was the better man," I said, "but Collin had her heart."

"What a load."

"Tell me about it."

"Don't worry about her," Herc said. "If she's dumb enough to go running back to that asshole, you're better off without her."

One day I might believe that. For now, the best I could do was pretend.

"Yeah," I said. "You're probably right."

"Of course, I'm right. Now, how about a few shots, on me?"

"On you?" I asked dubiously. "Did I just hear right?"

"Yes, your ears do not deceive you."

"Hey, Caitlin," I shouted toward the opposite end of the

bar. "You didn't slip any psychoactive drugs in my buddy's drink, did you?"

"Not today, hon," Caitlin said.

"Can we get four shots of Patron?" Herc chimed in.

"You sure can."

Andy emerged from the storage area near the back of the bar. Tall and thin, he wore a black, short-sleeve button-up with the bar's name stitched onto the pocket, and a pair of jeans. Strands of brown hair slipped from beneath the red baseball cap he wore backward.

"Hey, Andy," Herc yelled. "Wanna have a shot with us?"

"I don't see why not," Andy said.

"When did you become such a big spender?" I asked Herc.

"What do you mean?"

"You know very well what I mean, Scrooge McDemigod."

"Hey, there are things in this world that I care about more than money."

"Like what?"

"Like my best bud."

Caitlin brought over our shots as Andy joined her behind the bar.

"That'll be six credits," she said.

Herc gave her seven. "No change."

Caitlin smirked. "You're so generous."

It was then that I noticed the chalkboard behind the bar. It displayed the daily specials. "One dollar Patron shots, all night!" was written in yellow at the very top.

I should have known.

"More important than money, huh?" I said, jabbing my thumb at the board.

Herc returned an unapologetic smile. Looking at him, I felt a grin tug at the corners of my mouth. I fought to suppress it, but it was a battle I couldn't win.

Herc raised his shot glass. "A toast."

"To what?" I asked.

"To you, Plato Jones. One of the greatest guys I know."

Andy shook his head. "You two are so lame."

No one disagreed with him.

After six more rum and Cokes, and an untold number of shots, my stomach said, *No more!* I stumbled to the men's room, on the verge of throwing up. It was empty. I entered the nearest stall and started puking my guts out. Between heaves, I heard a voice. The last voice I wanted to hear.

"Good evening, Jones. Would you like me to hold your hair?"

Hermes.

"What's with you sneaking up on people in bathrooms?" I asked, then spewed another stream of vomit.

"I like to see people in moments of weakness. It warms my heart."

"Whatever you want, the answer is no."

"Who said I wanted anything? Perhaps I just want to talk."

"Has anyone ever told you, you suck at lying?" I retched two more times before I was finally done.

I pulled myself up off the floor and staggered to the sink. Behind my haggard reflection stood the Messenger of the Gods. His pristine cream-colored suit made me glad my stomach was completely empty.

"Feeling better?" he asked.

"I will as soon as you leave me alone." I turned on the faucet and splashed my face with cold water.

"I don't think I'll ever understand mankind's obsession with alcohol."

"I'm sure your pal Dionysus can enlighten you on the subject."

Hermes offered no rejoinder. Score one for Plato Jones!

I turned off the faucet. Hermes handed me a paper towel.

"Thanks," I said automatically.

"The Gods have a proposition for you."

Here we go again.

I dried my face and tossed the towel into the wastebasket. "What is it this time?"

"I'm not at liberty to say. Not here."

"Worried that someone might be listening in?"

"Yes."

"Don't be. I can assure you that absolutely no one is listening to you right now."

Hermes frowned. "Must you be so stubborn?"

"I'm a mortal. Stubbornness comes with the territory. Now if you'll excuse me, I have a date with Johnnie Walker, and I don't want to keep him waiting."

"Very well, Mr. Jones. We'll resume this conversation when you're sober."

"Not happening." I left the restroom and returned to my seat.

"You okay?" Herc asked.

He'd had just as much to drink as I did, but didn't appear drunk. His superhuman metabolism burned off the alcohol before it had a chance to settle into his bloodstream. He could chug everything in the bar without getting so much as a buzz. I didn't know whether to envy the guy or pity him.

"I'm fine," I said. "But guess who I saw in the bathroom. I'll give you hint. He spends most of his time glued to Zeus's backside."

"Hermes?"

"Ding, ding, ding!"

"I didn't see him come in," Herc said. "You think he's been hiding in there the whole time?"

"Your guess is as good as mine."

"What did he want?"

"I didn't stick around to find out."

"Want me to go and have a chat with him?" Herc asked.

"And by chat, you mean punch his lights out, right?

"More or less."

"As tempting as that sounds, I'm going to use my better judgment and decline. Besides, I think I'm done for the night."

Herc frowned at me as I searched for my phone to call a cab. Remember: Never drink and drive unless you're a God, demigod, or other supernatural being with a hyper-accelerated metabolism. I couldn't tell if Herc was upset over my leaving, or because I denied him the opportunity to rough up Zeus's errand boy. Maybe it was a combination of the two.

"How about one last shot," Herc asked, "for the road?"

"You still paying?"

"Of course."

"Then let's make it two."

5

Zeus had given me a hefty reward for solving the God-killer case—enough credits to purchase a condo on a nice side of town. It wasn't much bigger than my old place, but it had a private balcony that offered a breathtaking view of Empusa Gardens, a sprawling park located in New Olympia's financial district. Herc had tried to talk me out of buying it, said it'd be a waste of money. His wife, Hebe, on the other hand, had given me her full support.

Majority rules.

I'd had enough cash left to replace the Lotus Hera's goons helped total. But I decided not to. I'd take having a beautiful account balance over a beautiful car any day. Besides, I still felt guilty about abandoning my Thunderbird. But she forgave me—and all it took was a wax job and a bouquet of flower-scented air fresheners.

When I got home, I went straight to the bedroom to crash. I turned on the lights—so I wouldn't bump into anything—and discovered my cat, Mr. Fancy Pants, sleeping belly up in the middle of my bed.

"Really?"

At some point, the little jerk figured out how to open and close doors. He cracked his green eyes and regarded me with something that resembled annoyance.

"Look, pal," I said. "I'm really not in the mood for this."

Mr. Fancy Pants closed his eyes and went back to sleep.

I sighed, too exhausted to argue, too proud to lie beside him. I left the room, closing the door behind me, and trudged into the living room.

"What kind of cat sleeps on his back?" I mumbled.

I set the alarm on my cell phone—since I had to go to work in the morning—and plopped on the couch. That night, I had a dream. Or rather, a flashback. It was about the time my older brother, Socrates, got jumped by a group of bullies. I'd instinctively jumped in, but my inclusion made little difference. We were still outnumbered five to two. Things went about as well as you'd expect. The good news was that our coach and his assistant had broken up the fight before the bullies could finish handing us our asses. The bad news was that we all got suspended for two days.

Later that night, as Socrates and I lay awake in our beds, he revealed the reason behind the brawl. The bullies had been picking on a female satyr. He had stepped in to put a stop to it, and one thing led to another. He apologized for getting me involved. I told him there was nothing to apologize for. Helping him had been my decision. Besides, brothers had to stick together.

I could see Socrates smiling at me in the dark. The dream ended on that smile, shattered by the sound of my alarm. Then one of the worst hangovers I'd ever had welcomed me back to full awareness. My head throbbed, my stomach churned, and a sour taste coated the inside of my mouth.

I peeled myself off the couch and shuffled, zombielike, to the bedroom. Sunshine slipped through the spaces between the blinds, throwing bars of light across the now vacant bed.

There was no question as to where Mr. Fancy Pants had gone. I entered the bathroom, drew the shower curtain, and found him sitting in the tub with his legs tucked under his body. He looked up at me with an expression that was bland even by cat standards.

"Okay, you know the drill." I gestured for him to leave.

Mr. Fancy Pants remained in the tub.

My headache intensified. "I'm serious."

Mr. Fancy Pants yawned.

"For the love of . . ." I picked him up and set him on the floor.

He jumped right back into the tub. I could have put him out of the bathroom and locked the door. But pain and rational thought rarely occupy the same space.

"Okay, we'll do things the hard way." I reached into the tub and rested my hand on the cold-water knob.

Mr. Fancy Pants sat unfazed.

"You must think I'm bluffing." And I was.

Mr. Fancy Pants must have realized it. He refused to budge.

"Are you really willing to risk it?" I asked.

Mr. Fancy rose as if to leave. He stretched his back, flexed his paws, and sat down again.

Why you . . .

I turned the knob, enough to get the pipes stirring. Water dripped from the faucet.

Mr. Fancy Pants climbed out of the tub and strode out of the bathroom, taking his sweet time.

"That's what I thought," I called after him.

Plato Jones, one. Dumb cat, five hundred.

I was gaining on him.

I skipped breakfast and went straight to work. My stomach couldn't handle anything bolder than Jell-O—and I was fresh out of the stuff. Maybe I'd feel better by lunch. Probably not, but a guy can dream.

Emilie had a bottle of spring water and a bottle of antacids waiting for me on my desk. I hadn't even told her about my night of drinking. A sweetheart and a mind reader. That little lady was full of surprises.

I took a couple of antacids with some spring water. I felt marginally better. But one key element was still missing from my hangover kit. Coffee.

"Duccio!" I shouted from my desk.

Silence.

"Duccio!"

Still no answer.

"For the love of . . ." I got on the intercom. "This is Plato calling Duccio. I repeat, this is Plato calling Duccio. Duccio, do you read? Over."

My personal assistant's voice issued from the speaker. He sounded nervous.

"I read you loud and—I mean yes, sir, Mr. Jones."

"Don't call me Mister."

"Yes, sir, Mist . . . I mean Jones."

"Don't call me that either."

"Okay," Duccio said. "What should I call you?"

"My first name would be nice."

"Plato?"

"Yes, Duccio."

Goodness, gracious.

Clearly, Duccio had never been on a first name basis with an employer. I appreciated the respect, but not so much that I'd let him call me Mr. Jones. Only older people could get away with that—and Emilie, but that was only because she insisted. Certainly not some bright-eyed twenty-something. It made me feel every bit of my age and then some.

"What can I do for you . . . Plato?" Duccio asked.

"Mind bringing me a cup of coffee?"

"Of course! I mean no. I mean . . ."

"Relax," I said. "Take a breath."

I heard Duccio inhale and exhale.

"Feel better?" I asked.

"Yes. Yes, I do. Do you want it in your special mug? Your coffee, that is."

"I would. Thank you, Duccio."

"No trouble at all. I'll get it to you as fast as I can."

"You do that." I turned off the intercom only to turn it right back on. "Don't go too fast. Scalding coffee plus recklessness equals work-related accidents."

And work-related lawsuits.

"I'll be careful," Duccio said. "You can count on me."

"That's what I like to hear. Plato out."

I shut off the intercom again and got to work, going over the notes from one of my recent cases. It involved a minotaur named Roland. For over a month, his house had been repeatedly tagged with racial slurs: cud-eater, milk bag, pink slime, and a host of other derogatory terms. He hired me to find the culprit, or culprits.

I uncovered the truth in less than a week. Three teenage boys had been responsible. Humans. I shared my findings with the police. The punks were charged with trespassing and vandalism. Each of them received 250 hours of community service, while their parents were forced to pay for the repairs to Roland's house. To top things off, the judge awarded Roland an additional two thousand credits for emotional distress.

Not too shabby.

Personally, I would've handed them over to Roland. The parents, too, for raising such lousy kids.

Five minutes after I started working, Duccio brought my coffee. He stood around five-seven, with blond hair and a compact build. Freckles dusted his cheeks, and his blue eyes shone with youth. He was every grandmother's dream. He was also Calais's nephew. I only hired him as a favor to Alexis. So far, he was performing well . . . enough. But time would tell if I'd made the right decision.

"Here's your coffee, Mr. . . . I mean Plato." Duccio placed the steaming mug on my desk.

It was a Ninja Turtles mug modeled after Michelangelo's head. My mom bought it for me when I was kid. Mikey had a huge smile on his green face, even though the top of his skull was missing, and his brain had been replaced with hot coffee. Now that's what I call optimism!

"Thanks," I said.

"My pleasure."

I tried the coffee. Bitterness hit my taste buds, acrid and overwhelming. I put down the mug.

"Duccio," I said calmly. "Why is there salt in my coffee?"

Duccio's eyes widened. "Salt?"

"Yes, salt."

"I thought it was sugar."

"It's not sugar. Tell me; how did you screw up something as simple as a cup of coffee?"

Duccio hesitated. "Um, well, you see there are two shakers beside the coffee maker. They both look the same, so . . ."

I held up my hand. It had been an honest mistake. But it raised an important question. Why was the saltshaker next to the coffeemaker?

"It's fine," I said.

"Can I make you another cup?" Duccio asked.

"Good idea."

I slid the mug toward him. "And while you're at it, label the saltshaker. Put a strip of duct tape on it or something."

"Duct tape, got it. Is there anything else?"

"Not at the moment.

"Okay." Duccio picked up the mug and started to leave.

He paused at the door and turned around. "I'm really sorry about this."

"All is forgiven."

"Are you sure you're not angry?"

"Duccio," I said, indicating the door.

"Oh, sorry . . . again. I'll be going now." Duccio scurried out of the office.

Kids.

I got back to work. The taste of salt still lingered in my mouth. Putting a saltshaker near a coffeemaker. Who came up with that idea? Not me. And Duccio's apparent shock ruled him out. That left only one suspect.

I activated the intercom. "Emilie?"

My secretary promptly answered. "Yes, Mr. Jones?"

"We have a bit of a problem. It seems that someone put a saltshaker near the coffeemaker, a saltshaker that happens to be identical to the sugar shaker. You wouldn't know anything about that, would you?"

"Yes, sir, I would."

I waited for her to elaborate. She never did.

"Care to tell me why?" I asked.

"I enjoy salt in my coffee."

"I see. That'll be all."

"Yes, sir."

I was about to turn off the intercom, but didn't. "Hey, Emilie."

"Sir?"

"You're a very odd woman."

"Thank you, sir. By the way, Mr. Hermes just arrived. He'd like to speak to you."

"Tell him I'm not in."

Jackass's voice issued from the speaker. "You do know I can hear you, right?"

"Obviously."

"Let's not turn this into an issue, Mr. Jones."

Realizing there was nothing my staff or I could do to stop him, I said, "You've got five minutes," and switched off the intercom.

Hermes came into my office wearing a ridiculous red suit. He carried a file folder in his right hand.

"Fire truck couture," I said. "Nice."

"Good morning, Mr. Jones." Hermes tossed the folder onto my desk.

It bore the OBI's official seal: an uroboros—a snake eating its own tail—that formed a circle around an eagle. The words *Olympic Bureau of Investigation* lined the circle's inner edge.

"You're looking terrible," Hermes said as he took a seat.

"And you look like a strawberry Twizzler."

"I'll have you know that this suit cost more than you make in a year."

"I'm sure it did. You must have done a great job cleaning Zeus's bathroom, washing his windows, mopping his floors, feeding and watering his wife, taking her to the groomer's . . ."

"That's not very nice, Mr. Jones."

"You're right. I apologize. Let me make it up to you. How about some coffee?"

"That would be nice, provided you don't spit in it beforehand."

"Now, would I do something like that?" I asked, pretending to be offended.

Hermes said nothing.

I pressed a button on the intercom. "Duccio?"

"Yes, sir?"

"Could you bring Hermes a cup of coffee?"

"Sure," Duccio replied excitedly. "Cream and sugar?"

I glanced at Hermes.

"Sugar," he said. "A fair amount."

"You heard the man," I said to Duccio. "Oh, and use the shaker you just labeled. You did label it, right?"

"Yes, sir, but I thought . . ."

"No back talk. Hop to it."

"Yes, sir."

I deactivated the intercom. "Kids sure can be a pain sometimes."

"True," Hermes said, looking mildly annoyed.

He might have been thinking about his own children. His son Pan, in particular. I could almost understand why—*almost* being the key word, since I had no kids of my own.

A ten-foot tall, satyr-like creature, Pan resembled Granny Hera more than his actual father. He lived as a hermit in the woods of southeastern Greece, dabbling in illegal narcotics, pretty much every one you can think of. Centuries of substance abuse had turned his brain into mush. He now believed himself to be the living embodiment of nature, a forest spirit.

That wasn't even the dumbest part. That honor went to the morons who actually bought into his drug-induced fantasy. Every year, hundreds of humans and nonhumans made pilgrimages to his woodland cabin, seeking "enlightenment," which equated to tossing back cocktails of hallucinogenic substances and running, naked and screaming, through the forest.

But like most things nowadays, enlightenment wasn't free. Pan's services carried a substantial price tag.

I imagined Papa Hermes wasn't too happy about his son being a drug dealer; Mom either, for that matter, whoever she was. Of the countless women Hermes had bedded over the course of his life, one of them, Driope, seemed the most likely candidate, given that she had been pregnant shortly before Pan—as a big, hairy baby—appeared on the scene.

Driope was a nymph. I wasn't sure what kind, since she

looked completely human. She had also been the wife of Odysseus—the ancient king of Ithaca, who had a well-known series of wacky adventures on his way home from the Trojan War.

I wonder how Driope reacted to her husband showing up ten years late for dinner.

"I never thought I'd see the day when we agreed on something," I said.

"Nor I," Hermes allowed. "Let's see if we can agree some more."

"I doubt that's possible, but I guess we can give it a shot."

"Have you heard about the recent bank heist?" Hermes asked.

I had. According to reports, four robbers, all resembling humans, used godlike abilities to murder two security guards, injure a dozen police officers, and cause extensive property damage. Three of them had been captured but no longer displayed superhuman powers. The fourth escaped by flying away, taking the entire haul with him—over a million stolen credits.

"Yeah," I said.

"Then you know how important it is for us to handle this before it becomes a bigger issue," Hermes said.

"What's the matter? You and Daddy Dearest afraid of being overthrown by a few puny humans?"

Anger flashed in Hermes's eyes. I was still too hung over to care.

"Excuse me?" he said.

"You heard me. Humans have been pushed around by the Gods from the very beginning. And it's not just us; it's other races too. Minotaurs, satyrs, giants, anything that walks, crawls, swims, or takes a dump. We've all had enough of your crap."

Hermes grinned unexpectedly. "That's borderline heresy, Mr. Jones. But considering what you've been through, I'll give you a pass, this time."

"What are you talking about?"

"About you and Ms. Stone, of course. Oh, I'm sorry. *Mrs.* Stone."

I wasn't surprised that Hermes knew about my relationship with Bellanca. Spying on me seemed to be one of his favorite pastimes. Being a prick came in a close second.

Duccio appeared in the door with Hermes's coffee and mine, but didn't pass through. I motioned for him to come in.

He avoided eye contact with Hermes as he set the white mugs on my desk—though Jackass seemed oblivious to the kid's presence. Duccio's hands trembled noticeably, and sweat glittered on his forehead.

"Thanks," I said to Duccio.

"Y-you're welcome," he replied, his voice cracking. "Is there anything else I can get you?"

"That's all for now."

Duccio returned a jerky nod and scurried out of the office.

Without so much as a thank you, Hermes picked up the mug closest to him and sipped. His expression turned sour.

I almost chuckled. "How is it?"

"Strange."

"It's a new brand."

"I'm sure."

Good job, Duccio. Someone could expect a bonus at the end of the month.

"Enough dallying." Hermes put down the mug. "Let's get down to business, shall we?"

"Sure." I checked my watch. "You've got exactly five minutes, starting . . . now."

Hermes opened the file folder, removed several sheets of paper, and spread them across my desk. Criminal records belonging to the captured robbers.

Hermes pointed out two of the three records. "Marcelo DeSilva and Lance Price. Both are career criminals with offenses that range from vandalism and petty theft, all the way up to murder and cyber-terrorism. Their rap sheets are almost identical."

I examined the pictures. Marcelo looked to be in his early to mid-forties. The stereotypical tough guy: a square-shaped head, hard eyes, and short brown hair. Not the type of customer you'd want to encounter in a dark alley.

Conversely, Lance had the look of a man who'd run from a fight rather than start one. Thick, blond curls topped a relatively narrow head, which in turn, was connected to an even narrower neck. Pimples and acne scars marred his face, and his blue eyes glimmered with intelligence.

The nice guy appearance didn't fool me. Over the course of my career, I'd seen plenty of stone-cold killers with bright eyes, bifocals, and baby faces. Only seeing a person for who he or she appears to be can have deadly consequences. Particularly in my line of work.

"If these men were so dangerous, why were they on the street and not behind bars?" I asked.

"They were part of a prison break that happened a little over a year ago. You're familiar with the Atlantis incident?"

"I know a little something about it."

Actually, I'd heard a lot about it. The Atlantis penal colony was Europe's answer to Alcatraz, except the facility had been constructed underwater. It was supposed to be inescapable. But a small group of inmates dismissed that claim—Marcelo and Lance among them.

Authorities still hadn't figured out how they managed to escape. But their plan was rumored to have involved a roll of masking tape, rubber tubing, and several empty soda bottles. Love it or hate it, criminal ingenuity could be downright impressive at times.

"At some point, DeSilva and Price joined up with this man." Hermes indicated the third record. "Felix King."

I inclined my head forward. Felix had been listed as being six-two and 190 pounds. He had a long face and angular features, roughened by a thin layer of beard stubble. He wore his black hair in a mohawk made of long, thin braids. I suspected the braids were tied off at the nape—with a rubber band, perhaps—to form a ponytail.

The hair was a distinguishing feature to be sure. But to me, his eyes stood out the most. Whereas Lance's suggested intelligence, Felix's betrayed something that resembled—for lack of a better term—bat-shit craziness. Large, dark, and wild, they seemed to pop out of the photo.

The eyes of someone who was not only willing to kill, but enjoyed it.

Other than Felix's physical description, the only information the OBI had on him came from the robbery and his subsequent arrest. Unless details had been purposely left out, this guy hadn't existed before the heist.

"Is this all you have on him?" I asked.

"For now," Hermes said.

"You think he was involved in the prison break?"

"It's possible."

"Where did he come from?"

"We're not sure," Hermes said. "But we believe he's the leader of the three."

I took another look at Felix's file and pushed it away.

"So what does all this have to do with me?" I glanced at my watch. "You're almost out of time, by the way."

"We want you to go undercover and find out how King and his friends acquired their special abilities."

"But King is in jail."

"Yes, he is."

I held up my hand. "Hold on. Let me get this straight. You want to send me to jail to make friends with a potentially dangerous criminal and his equally dangerous accomplices?"

"Of course not, Mr. Jones."

"Good. For a second there, I thought you'd lost your mind."

"We want to send you to Tartarus."

"Tartarus? *The* Tartarus?"

"Correct."

I let out a humorless laugh. To call Tartarus Maximum Security Penitentiary the most dangerous prison on Earth would have been completely inaccurate. That's because it wasn't located on Earth, but in another dimension, only accessible by one of Hades's magical portals. The facility housed some of the worst criminals of all time. Monsters beyond redemption.

"You know, I take back what I said about your losing your mind," I said. "Because I see now that you've clearly gone bananas. I should've known it from the moment you walked in. Only a crazy person would wear a suit like that in public. Can I offer you another cup of coffee?"

Hermes ignored both the insult and the offer. "King and his associates will be going to trial soon. They *will* be convicted, they *will* be sent to Tartarus, and you *will* be right there beside them, becoming a member of their inner circle."

"And what if I say no? Which I *will* most certainly do."

"Refusal would be ill-advised."

"Ill-advised, huh? What are you going to do? Hold my ex-wife hostage again? Blackball her new husband?" I paused. "On second thought, you guys can have a field day with him. But leave Alexis out of this."

"No one's going to be held hostage, Mr. Jones."

"Then it looks like you don't have anything to threaten me with." I checked my watch. "Oh, would you look at that. It seems we're out of time. I even gave you two additional minutes. Aren't you lucky?"

"Stubborn as usual." Hermes slid the reports into the folder and stood up. "But I'll change your mind."

"Whatever you say, chief. Now if you don't mind, I have work to do."

"I respectfully advise you to cooperate."

"And I respectfully decline."

"Have it your way, Mr. Jones. I'll be in touch."

Hermes left.

I knew that he and Zeus wouldn't give up until they'd gotten their way. What did they have in store for me this time, now that threatening my loved ones was no longer an option—unless Jackass lied to me? I didn't want to think about it. But I knew one thing: Kicking and screaming was the only way I'd ever go to Tartarus.

6

The next day after work, I stopped by the ATM to make a withdrawal. For the past few months, Mr. Fancy Pants had been using my recliner as a scratching post. Last night he finally finished it off. When I told Herc about it, he suggested I visit a furniture warehouse aptly named the Furniture Warehouse.

The creativity was awe-inspiring.

Herc gave me one of their flyers. The prices were lower than Hera's breasts, but the store only accepted cash or money orders. No credit cards. I couldn't help wondering if the merchandise was hot—or at least some of it. I decided to take a chance regardless. I couldn't pass up such great bargains.

The recliner I wanted cost two hundred credits. I withdrew three hundred, lest the store tack on any unexpected charges. I counted the money and slipped it into my wallet. The machine printed my receipt. A quick glance at it led to a double-take. The balance showed a hundred million credits in my account. I had no idea where they had come from. This had to be a mistake.

I swiped my card again and selected the option to check my balance. The ATM printed me another receipt. It said the exact same thing as the first. A little voice in the back of my head told me to make a massive withdrawal and go on a shopping spree—the natural reaction to seeing that many zeroes in your account. I forced myself to ignore it.

The bank was closed, so I'd have to wait until tomorrow to sort things out. I suspected Hermes had a hand in this. He might've been trying to bribe me into going on his suicide mission, though I doubted it. That would have been too simple. I tried calling him several times on the way home, but only got voicemail. I left him a series of messages, each one ruder than the last. I thought that with enough insults, I could bait him into returning my calls—Jackass loved trading insults almost as much as he loved sucking up to his father. It turned out to be a waste of time.

I decided to go over Hermes's head and contact Zeus. But he wasn't in his office. How convenient. I called Herc and asked him to give his dad a ring on his home phone—to tell him that I needed to speak with him ASAP.

I would have called him myself, but I didn't want to take the chance of Hera's answering the phone. Knowing her, she'd use it as an excuse to send her cronies after me. Herc asked me why I wanted to get in touch in touch with Zeus. I promised I would tell him the whole story after I got home and had a chance to sit down.

When I stepped into my apartment, Mr. Fancy Pants greeted me with a series of long meows. Complaints. I learned that from an Animal Planet special on cat behavior.

"I suppose you're ready for dinner," I said.

Mr. Fancy Pants returned a low meow—a grumble that sounded vaguely human.

"Let me show you to your table." I went into the kitchen, Mr. Fancy Pants fast on my heels.

I took a can of King Kraken cat food from the cupboard. The most expensive brand on the market, and Mr. Fancy

Pants's personal favorite. He liked it so much in fact, that he refused to eat anything else. Prima donna.

The label depicted a cartoon fish that seemed awfully happy about the idea of being mashed to bits and stuffed in a tin can. To each his own, I guess.

I opened the can and dumped its contents into Mr. Fancy Pants's stainless steel food bowl. With the lord of the manor taken care of, it was time for me to find something to eat. I grabbed a beer and two slices of leftover pizza from the fridge. I popped the pizza in the microwave. Thirty seconds later, I took my dinner to the kitchen table. I hadn't even started eating before Herc called.

"What's up, brother?" I said. "Were you able to get ahold of Zeus?"

"Nope. I called him a dozen times. He's not answering."

"That's not good."

"You're telling me. I'm nearly out of minutes."

"You still use a prepaid phone?"

"You bet your ass I do," Herc said. "Those contracts are deathtraps."

I shook my head. But I couldn't criticize him too harshly. I still used a flip phone while everyone around me had switched to smartphones. I guessed Herc and I were the friends that time forgot.

"Did you leave a message?" I asked.

"Yeah, a bunch. I can keep trying if you want."

"That's okay. But thanks anyway."

"No sweat. So, are you gonna tell me what's going on? I thought you didn't want anything to do with Zeus."

"I don't. I just have a question for him."

"Concerning?"

"Concerning the hundred million that mysteriously showed up in my bank account."

Herc was silent for a moment. "I fail to see the problem."

"The problem is I don't know where it came from. Either the bank screwed up or someone deliberately put it there. I'm leaning toward the latter."

"Who do you figure is responsible?"

"You know who." I drank some beer.

"The Gods?"

"Bingo."

"You think it has something to do with your chat with Hermes?" Herc asked.

"I don't think. I know."

"Have you talked with him since the other night?"

"Yes, unfortunately," I said. "He showed up at my office yesterday and offered me a job. I refused, of course."

"Let me guess. He wanted you to investigate that bank robbery."

"Yeah, but that's not all. He also wants me to make friends with the three men who were captured, find out the secret behind their . . . special abilities."

"But those guys are in jail," Herc said.

"And headed to prison," I added. "Tartarus, to be specific."

Herc cursed under his breath. "Has Dad lost his mind?"

"He must have, if he thinks I'll ever set foot in that place."

"This is unbelievable. What are you gonna do?"

"For starters, I'm going to hand the money over to the bank."

"You're gonna give it all back?"

"Yes, Herc. I'm giving it all back."

Herc sighed wistfully.

"After that, I'll pay Zeus a visit," I said. "He seems to have forgotten I don't work for the OBI anymore."

"I'm coming with you."

"I don't think that's a good idea."

"Why?"

"Because it's my problem, not yours."

"Come on, Jonesy. You don't expect me to just sit on my ass and do nothing, do you?"

"It'd be nice if you did."

"Sorry, but no dice," Herc said. "I'm going whether you like it or not."

I knew that arguing would be a waste of energy. As was the case with Hermes, I couldn't stop Herc from doing as he pleased. It'd be like trying to stop a rampaging elephant with a water pistol. Besides, he had a better chance of talking Zeus out of this crazy plan than I did.

"Okay, Herc," I said. "Have it your way."

"Glad you're seeing things my way. What time are you heading to Olympus?"

"Depends on what time I leave the bank," I said. "I'm guessing around eleven."

"Did you want to meet up somewhere?

"I guess."

"How about the bank parking lot? Sound good?"

"Sure."

"Don't worry, Jonesy," Herc said. "We'll get to the bottom of this."

"I hope you're right."

"I'm always right."

"That's debatable."

Herc chuckled. "Anyway, I gotta make a run."

"Where to?"

"Victoria's Secret."

"Picking up something for Hebe?" I asked.

"Just the opposite—returning something she bought. That woman and her shopping. It wouldn't bother me as much if she used her own money."

"Aw, cut her some slack."

"I will, as soon as she stops cutting checks. See you tomorrow."

"Take it easy."

After dinner, I sat on the couch watching reruns of *Popeye the Sailor.* I'd found a half-finished bottle of Jack Daniel's in the freezer and used it make a Jack and Coke. Mr. Fancy Pants snoozed beside me. He almost looked cute, but not quite.

I had finished my drink and gotten up to make another when I heard a loud bang. The front door swung open. Startled, I dropped my plastic cup as a SWAT team stormed my apartment wielding assault rifles and shotguns. So this was how it would go down. They wrestled me to the floor and handcuffed me.

"What's going on?" I demanded. "Get off me!"

"Plato Jones, you're under arrest for grand larceny," said one of the officers.

"You're making a mistake."

The officers pulled me upright. I glimpsed Mr. Fancy Pants on the edge of my vision. He was still lying down. His eyes opened a crack then closed.

Traitor!

7

The cops took me downtown and tossed me into a brightly lit interrogation room. The detective who interviewed me spelled out what I was being accused of: stealing a hundred million credits from the Olympic Treasury.

Surprise, surprise.

The interrogation lasted over three hours. Once the investigator realized he wasn't going to get a confession out of me, I was charged and thrown into a holding cell. My cellmate, a satyr who lay snoring on the floor, reeked of booze.

Eventually, the cops allowed me to make a phone call. I asked Emilie to hold down the fort until I figured a way out of this mess. I also asked her and Duccio to look after Mr. Fancy Pants. I made sure to mention which brand of cat food he would insist upon, when he would demand to be fed, and the spots where he typically hid his favorite toys.

Because of the severity of my "crime," the judge refused to set bail. That meant I had to remain in jail until my court date.

During that time, the only person allowed to see me was Geno, whom I had convinced to represent me at the trial. He still had worms, so I felt bad about asking for such a big favor. But he was the only lawyer I trusted.

I told Geno about my recent encounters with Hermes—that he wanted to hire me for a case. When he asked for details, I said I had refused Jackass's request before he could give me the specifics. I hated lying to a friend, particularly one who was trying to keep me out of prison. But the issue with Felix King and his accomplices was one of national security, and there was no telling how the Gods would react if I went public with the truth.

I'd say badly.

Geno swore to do his best. But we both knew I wouldn't be leaving the courtroom as a free man.

Lucky for me, the case was accelerated for undisclosed reasons, and I didn't sit in jail for long. On the morning of the trial, I was led into the courtroom wearing an orange jumpsuit and handcuffs and seated at the defense table.

Geno sat next to me sporting a fitted gray jacket, a lavender dress shirt, and a matching silk tie. His hair was expertly cut and styled. He easily held the title of best-dressed satyr in New Olympia.

My family and friends showed up to lend their support: my mom and her boyfriend James, Uncle Magus, and Herc. Even Alexis came. It was a nice gesture. I would have appreciated it a lot more if she'd left Calais at home.

The one person I didn't expect to see was Aphrodite. The Goddess of Love sat in the back of the courtroom between two minotaur bodyguards. She wore a black, one-button jacket with nothing underneath, and a large hat that wasn't unlike something you'd see aliens piloting. Huge sunglasses hid her eyes.

More than once, I caught myself glancing at her. Each time, she returned a smile that grew increasingly seductive. Red lipstick emphasized her full lips.

My groin began to swell as I thought back to the make-out session she and I had had during the God-killer case. Hers were still the softness lips I had ever kissed. No one else even came close. I had to force myself not to look at her as the trial commenced.

"All rise," said the bailiff—a fifteen-foot giant with a hundred tiny yellow eyes crammed into the middle of his face. "The honorable Judges Minos, Rhadamantys, and Aiakos presiding."

A bizarre figure took a seat behind the podium. Robed in black, and of average height and build, it appeared human from the neck down. But its head was abnormally large and contained three evenly spaced faces—one in the center and two on either side—all wrinkled and bearded. They shared the same pate of thinning gray hair, which had been styled in the least convincing comb-over I'd ever seen.

So these were the infamous judges of the underworld. I'd heard of them but had never seen them in person—or persons. They spent most of their days in Hades, where they judged the souls of the recently deceased. Good souls went to the Elysian Fields, while evil souls were condemned to eternal damnation. The only times they ventured into the world of the living were to preside over the highest-profile cases.

Didn't I feel special?

Originally, the judges existed as separate individuals who, at some point, decided to fuse themselves into one being. How they did it was a mystery. Maybe they invented a do-it-yourself fusion kit or something. Or just a plain old needle and thread. But I think the better question was why did they do it?

All three judges regarded me with the same sour expression.

"Friendly-looking bunch," I whispered to Geno. "But where are their ears?"

Geno ignored my question and leaned toward me. His eyes were glazed over, and he swayed in place even while seated. The effects of the deworming medicine he'd been taking.

"When you speak to the judges, address them as Your

Honors," he said, his voice slurring noticeably. "That's Honors with an *S*. They don't consider themselves to be a single individual."

"What happens if someone does," I asked, "treat them as one person?"

"Watch this." Geno waved at the bailiff.

The giant smiled and returned the gesture. I glimpsed something on his palm.

"Was that a face embedded in his hand?" I whispered, shocked.

"A human face," Geno said. "The judges enjoy coming up with new and creative ways to punish those they deem disrespectful. So remember, judges with an *S*."

"Got it."

Geno poured himself a glass of water. His coordination seemed to be off, causing him to spill some on the table. Looking as if he might curse, he pulled a handkerchief from his pocket and wiped it up.

"Hiring me was a big mistake, Plato," he said. "This medicine's got me all spaced out. I feel like I'm on the moon."

"That's all right," I said. "Just promise not to float away."

Geno shook his head.

From the corner of my eye, I noticed Alexis moving to the front of the spectator's gallery. I turned in my chair to meet her.

Alexis had always been a looker, but now that she and I were no longer together, she seemed more beautiful than ever. Her blue eyes contrasted the thick red hair she'd tied into a bun. A small mouth combined with full lips gave her a sort of perma-pout. Her navy pantsuit, worn with black heels, hugged the slight curves of her slim figure.

As she placed her hand on the wooden railing, I caught sight of her wedding ring and quickly looked away. It was smaller than the one I'd bought her, but I found little consolation in the fact.

"I'm so sorry about this," she whispered. "I somehow feel responsible."

"Go with that feeling," I said. "If we're lucky, we can convince the judges to lock you up instead of me. Better yet, we can convince them to lock up Calais."

"This is no time for jokes, Plato."

"I disagree, seeing as how this so-called trial is nothing but a farce."

"What do you mean?"

I shook my head. "Nothing. Look, don't worry about me. I'll be fine. Just go back to your husband. It's almost time for his bottle."

"Calais is only a few years younger than me, unlike the love of your life."

"I assume you're talking about Aphrodite."

"What did you ever see in her? She's a whore and an airhead. And she's not even that cute to be honest."

"I'm not sure if you're aware, but Olympians have superhuman hearing."

She glanced at Aphrodite, who smiled politely at her. Alexis's face paled.

"I'll be going back to my seat now." She gave me a quick pat on the shoulder. "Good luck, Plato."

"Thanks." I was going to need it.

Hermes sat at the prosecution table, whispering to the prosecutor, a stern-looking woman named Abigail Russo. After he finished speaking to her, he came over to the defense table.

"How are you doing, Mr. Jones?" he said with a grin.

"Good, actually," I said. "I woke up with the sun, did a few push-ups, had a decent breakfast. You know, jail food isn't as horrible as people say. It's still bad, mind you. But it's not total garbage."

"Prison food is worse. That's where you're going. Prison."

"I see you've got jokes. Bad ones."

Hermes disregarded the insult. "Stealing from the Gods. You're either the boldest mortal I've ever met, or the dumbest."

"Says the guy who steals cows," I said, referring to the time when Hermes, as a kid, stole cattle from his half-brother Apollo.

Hermes frowned. "I wish you the best of luck, Mr. Jones. Though I don't think it'll do you any good. I'll make sure to visit you in Tartarus."

Hermes returned to the prosecution table and the proceedings began.

Geno gave me with a look that said: *We are so screwed.*

The prosecution wasted no time in trying to establish me as the scum of the earth. They presented a video of me breaking into the Treasury in the dead of night and tampering with a computer there. The person in the video was either some CG puppet or a guy with an extremely convincing makeup job. He even moved like me.

Later, the prosecution introduced Chrysus as a surprise witness. It came as no surprise to me, however. No doubt Zeus and Hermes put her up to this—and she dared not disobey the President and his idiot son.

Chrysus avoided looking at me while on the stand. As usual, she was working the sexy librarian look. Her thick blond hair was up, her glasses in place. Her black skirt suit emphasized some very impressive curves.

Russo replayed the video and paused on a shot that featured my doppelgänger staring directly into camera as if on purpose. The handsome devil even had the nerve to smile.

"Ms. Chrysus," Russo said. "Are the defendant and the person in the video one and the same?"

"It looks like him," Chrysus said, her voice calm and even.

Russo smiled, apparently satisfied with Chrysus's non-answer. Her reaction reinforced my belief that this trial was nothing more than a sham.

"Is it true that you and the defendant used to date?" Russo asked.

"Yes," Chrysus said.

"For how long?"

"Three months, two weeks, six days, four hours, and twenty-seven minutes."

"So you got to know him fairly well?"

"Correct."

Russo paced back and forth in front of the witness stand. "Given what you learned about the defendant, do you believe him to be capable of the crime for which he stands accused?"

"Everyone has the capacity for evil," Chrysus said, staring at Hermes.

He smiled at her.

"And is it possible that he only dated you to gain access to the Olympic Treasury?" Russo asked.

"Anything is possible."

While the prosecution continued to question Chrysus, Geno gestured for me to come closer.

"I tried to have the video evidence dismissed before the trial," he whispered, "but the judges weren't having it."

"That's not me in the video."

"I believe you. The problem is getting the jury to believe you."

I glanced at the jury and found most of them glaring at me. To Geno, I said, "I don't like our chances."

When the prosecution finished tearing me a new one, Geno put me on the stand. He hoped to salvage what remained of my reputation. As he questioned me, he leaned when he could—on his chair, on the defense table, and even on the witness box—attempting to disguise his poor balance as part of his courtroom performance. His slurring didn't help. The judges asked him if he had been drinking before the trial. Geno must have been embarrassed to tell the truth, merely saying that he felt a bit under the weather.

The judges seemed unconvinced, but allowed him to continue.

"You're a model citizen who not only loves his country, but spent years defending it as an agent of the Olympic Bureau of Investigation," Geno said to me. "The thought of you harming this wonderful nation—the one you care so much about—is preposterous, isn't it?"

"Objection, your Honors," Russo said. "He's leading the witness."

The three judges all answered at once. "Sustained."

Geno sighed inaudibly. Instead of rephrasing his question, he skipped to the next one.

"Is it true that prior to your arrest, you spoke with Hermes, son of Zeus?"

"Objection, your Honors," Russo said. "That question is irrelevant."

"Sustained."

"Oh, come on!" my mother shouted from the gallery.

The judges gaveled for order. "One more outburst like that and we'll find you in contempt."

Hearing those three bozos reprimand my mom sparked a flame of anger in my heart. I fought to keep quiet.

"Mr. Crowne," the judges said. "Is there anything else you'd like to ask the witness?"

Geno glanced at me. I shook my head. We'd done enough damage for now.

"No, your Honors." Geno looked to Russo. "Your witness."

Snickers rippled through the jury and spectator galleries as Geno staggered back to his seat. The judges allowed it.

Russo approached the stand. "Mr. Jones, I'd like to speak to you about the video evidence."

"Okay."

"I think it's safe to say you bear a striking resemblance to the person in that video. One could even say you two are identical. So I have to ask: Who is it, if not you?"

"I don't know," I said, "but he's one sexy beast."

Laughter erupted in the courtroom.

The judges banged their gavel. "I advise you not to try our patience, Mr. Jones."

"Sorry, your Honors." It was a lie.

"I'll ask you again," Russo said. "Are you the man in the video?"

"No. And for the record, your so-called video evidence is a load of fabricated crap."

"Fabricated crap. Mr. Jones, do you think everyone here is a complete idiot?"

"Not everyone." I gestured at Hermes. "Just the clown in the tacky suit."

Hermes scowled at me as my supporters chuckled, along with a handful of other men and women in the audience. Everyone else remained silent, probably afraid to laugh at a God of Olympus.

For some miraculous reason, the judges let the comment pass.

"If what you say is true," Russo began, "then explain to the court how a hundred million credits ended up in your bank account."

"Space magic?"

A venomous smile spread across Russo's face. "No further questions."

As the trial drew to a close, the judges addressed Geno. "Does the counsel for the defense have any closing arguments?"

"Yes, your Honors," Geno said.

He slowly stood up and turned toward the jury. To steady himself, he grabbed the wooden railing in front of the gallery. No one laughed, but I saw plenty of smiles in the jury box.

"Your Honors, ladies and gentlemen of the jury," Geno began. "I realize the evidence against my client is strong, but it doesn't prove he's guilty. It doesn't remove all doubt. I ask that you question the authenticity of the video footage, the time it was recorded, and the unnatural speed with which authorities responded to the theft. It is sketchy, almost as if the events were scripted . . . perhaps by someone who has a personal vendetta against my client. Someone intent on ruining his life. I've known Plato Jones for years. He's my friend. He's also one of the most honest, dependable people I've ever had the pleasure of knowing. I'd trust him with my life—and my money. Thank you."

Geno sat down. Silence pressed upon the courtroom. The members of the jury exchanged glances, outwardly conflicted.

I patted Geno on the back. "Good job."

He smiled, but the smile was sad.

The judges called for a recess while the jury deliberated. Three hours later, a decision had been reached. The foreman, a tall, thin man with silvery hair stood up. He read the verdict from an index card.

"We of the jury find Plato Stealth Jones guilty of grand larceny."

Cries of outrage rang out from the gallery.

Herc shot out of his seat. "You can't be serious! How stupid *are* you people?"

The judges slammed their gavel repeatedly, but the chaos continued. Hermes and Russo sat grinning at the prosecution table.

Herc pointed at the jury. "Change the verdict before I break you!"

The jury members shrank with fear.

"Hercules, Son of Zeus, we find you in contempt of court!" the judges shouted.

"I don't give a damn about you or your court!"

"Remove him!" the judges shouted to the bailiff.

The giant hesitated.

"Now!" the judges yelled.

The bailiff approached the gallery with notable reluctance. I couldn't blame him.

"Stay back, unless you want a hundred black eyes," Herc warned.

The bailiff came to an abrupt halt.

"Order, order!" The judges banged their gavel.

Their commands went unheeded.

The courtroom doors boomed open and in rushed a swarm of police officers. They demanded that everyone settle down, threatening them with tasers and cans of pepper spray—everyone except Herc, from whom they kept a distance. They probably would've done the same for Aphrodite had her bodyguards not whisked her away once the cops showed up.

The bailiff didn't join the fray. Instead, he ushered the jury into the conference room. He gestured for the judges to come along, but they shook their head. I guessed they planned to go down with the ship.

As the situation grew increasingly volatile, Geno ducked under the table. I climbed on top of it and stood. This had to end before someone got hurt.

"Everyone stop!" I shouted as loud as I could.

The audience ignored me. It took three more attempts before I finally reached them. The noise dwindled to silence as everyone turned their attention to me.

"I need you all to calm down," I said.

"Calm down nothing!" Herc argued. "Come on, Jonesy, we're getting outta here."

"I can't do that, brother."

"You can and you will. I'm not gonna watch you go to prison!"

"Neither will I," my mom said.

Tears ran down her face. James pulled her close to him. She buried her face in his chest. In that instant, I forgot how much I disliked him.

I hopped off the table. "I'll be fine guys. Trust me."

"I suggest you all listen to him," Hermes said, still seated.

Russo had disappeared. She'd probably gone with the jury.

Herc pointed at Hermes. "You and me are gonna have words later. For now, keep your mouth shut!"

Hermes raised his hands in mock surrender, smiling.

The gesture seemed to exacerbate Herc's anger. "Forget later. I'm gonna wax your pompous ass right now!"

He stalked toward the defense table. The police made no attempt to stop him. Hermes stood up and unbuttoned his jacket.

"Herc," I said. "This is only making things worse."

Herc paused. His blue eyes burned with a warrior's rage. "But you're innocent."

"Doesn't matter."

Herc opened his mouth to respond and immediately closed it. Sadness and frustration replaced the anger in his face. He hammered his fist against the gallery railing, snapping it like a twig. Everyone started—except for me, Hermes, and the judges.

I ran my eyes across the audience. My mom hadn't stopped crying. Alexis and Calais appeared distraught.

"Thanks for coming out to support me, guys," I said. "But I'll be fine. Really."

No one uttered a word. My mom's sobs grew louder, the only sounds in the room.

A dull ache arose in the middle of my chest. I refused to let her suffer another second of this madness. I faced the judges.

"Hurry up and sentence me so I can get out of here."

8

I RECEIVED LIFE IN PRISON WITHOUT THE POSSIBILITY OF parole. I had to admit, Zeus and Hermes got me good. Now I had no choice but to play their game. Otherwise, I'd spend the rest of my days in Tartarus.

The morning after the trial, seventy-eight other convicts and I boarded a prison barge that transported us to Departure—a small, manmade island in the middle of the Mediterranean. The barge crew handed us off to a team of corrections officers whose ranks were equal parts human and satyr. They did a headcount then loaded us onto a white prison bus bound for Tartarus. Metal grating covered the shatterproof windows.

To avoid interspecies conflicts, each race rode a separate bus. Those conflicts would come after the cell doors closed.

We all had assigned seats, with two to each. People next to each other on the bus would be cellmates. Marcelo and Lance sat on opposite rows near the back of the bus. Felix shared a seat with me. Coincidence? I think not.

As the bus started to move, I struck up a conversation with him. "'Sup?"

Felix ignored me.

I tried again. "My name's Plato Jones."

Felix jerked his head toward me, his eyes wide and dark. "Did I ask for your name?"

His aggressive pitch caught me off guard. I fumbled for a response.

Felix suddenly smiled. It looked more maniacal than friendly.

"Just kidding," he said. "Didn't make you piss your pants, did I?"

He spoke at a breakneck pace, and his voice carried an accent I couldn't place. It sounded Germanic but not quite.

"No," I said. "But you came pretty close."

"I must be losing my touch. I'm Felix. Felix King. But you can call me 'sir.'"

"Okay."

"That was a joke," Felix said. "You do know what a joke is, right? I say something odd or nonsensical, you scratch your head, trying to figure out just what in the world I'm talking about, and then *bam*, I hit you with a punch line. We both laugh, ha, ha, ha. Good times."

I pretended to laugh. *Is this guy serious?*

"You nervous, Plato Jones?" Felix sniffed the air. "You smell nervous."

"Nervous, no. Terrified, yes."

"That's good. That's real good. Fear keeps you on your toes."

"What about you?" I asked.

"What about me what?"

"Are you nervous?"

"Nervous? Me?" Felix chuckled. "That's a good one, Plato Jones. You should do stand-up. You have a gift for comedy. "

"So, I'm guessing that's a no."

"You guessed right. You're very perceptive, you know that?"

"Thanks."

"You're not welcome."

I didn't respond. I didn't know how.

"That's another joke," Felix said. "You seriously need to lighten up."

“Maybe you’re right.”

“I’m always right, even when I’m wrong. But yeah, to me, fear is a four-letter word. After all, we’re only going to the worst prison of all time. What’s there to be nervous about?”

The mad look in his eyes made it hard to tell if he was kidding or not. I was leaning toward not.

“What are you in for?” Felix asked. “Jaywalking?”

I had never been to prison before, but I possessed a basic understanding of the culture. In the pen, it’s considered rude to inquire about another inmate’s crime. Surely, Felix knew this as well and was just being a tool. I answered his question nonetheless, in hopes of getting on his good side—provided he had one.

“I stole a hundred million credits from the Olympic Treasury.”

“Nice,” Felix said. “How’d you do it?”

“I took a job with the OBI to learn how the Treasury worked. After I got all the information I needed, I quit and devised a plan of action. I also had some help from the treasurer.”

Revealing my connection with the OBI had been a big risk. But in prison, the walls have ears and secrets don’t stay hidden for long. It was better to tell the truth now than to be caught in a lie later.

If Felix took issue with my past, he gave no indication. “The treasurer was in on it?”

“Yeah. But she didn’t realize it until it was too late.”

“Stealing from the Gods.” Felix slowly nodded. “I can respect that.”

“How about you? You must have done something pretty bad to end up here.”

“You don’t watch the news much, do you? I can’t blame you. Ninety-nine percent of the stories are lies disguised as the truth. The other ten percent is padding. Sports, entertainment, the pet of week. Trivial shit.”

"I like the pet of the week."

"You look like you would. Let me guess. Cat person, right?"

"Reluctantly."

"I hate cats."

"I'm sure they hate you, too."

"Again with the jokes," Felix said. "I'm liking you more and more, Plato Jones. Anyway, the news is a total crock. They want to paint me as the villain, when I've done nothing wrong."

"Who are *they*?"

"The government, the media, the self-righteous assholes who do everything they can to keep the little man down. They're the real crooks. Not me."

"So you stole something?"

"I took something back. Did you hear about the incident at the Bank of New Olympia?"

"The robbery?"

"Yes, though I wouldn't call it a robbery. It was more like an act of liberation. I liberated the Gods' money from their pockets."

"That was your handiwork?"

"You're impressed, aren't you? I can see it."

If that's true, you might need to consult Lens Crafters.

"I heard some strange stories about that rob—I mean, act of liberation," I said.

"Such as . . ."

"Such as you taking down a pair of minotaurs with your bare hands."

"That wasn't me. That was my pal, Marcelo."

"My mistake."

Felix shook his head. "What else did you hear?"

"I heard that one guy ripped open the vault door with his mind, while another used the same trick to send it flying at the cops."

"That was my dad," Felix said. "Both times."

"Talented fella."

"You don't know the half of it."

We sat in silence for an interval. During that time, I tried to come up with more questions to ask Felix, questions that seemed innocent enough but would provide me with tidbits of useful information. I needed to find out how he and his partners acquired superpowers.

As if he'd read my mind, Felix said, "I can tell you want answers. You've already got the *who*s, the *when*s, and the *where*s. Now you're looking for the *how*s. How does a human become more than a human? Did I hit the nail on the head?"

"Yeah, you did."

"And you thought I was kidding about being right all the time," he said. "Can I tell you something?"

"Shoot."

"When I found out I'd be sitting next to you, I wasn't sold. You looked like the type of person I wouldn't get along with. I said to myself, 'I'm gonna end up killing this guy. He's gonna piss me off somehow and before you know it, I'll have another life sentence on my hands.' But you seem like a decent sort. Uptight, but decent. So I'll cut you a break."

"Lucky me."

"Want to hear my philosophy?"

"Why not?"

Felix shifted in his seat until his body was almost facing mine. "I've always believed that life is more exciting when you don't have all the answers. Is Felix going to smother me in my sleep? Is he going to shank me in the shower? Is he going to cave my skull in with his fists? It's mysteries like those that inspire us to live life to the fullest. Because you never know. You could be walking down the street, minding your own business, and then *bam*, you're dead!"

I was sure the *bam* had been intended to startle me. It had, but I managed not to flinch. Felix seemed impressed.

"You've got balls, Plato Jones," he said. "Big, gigantic bowling balls. I like that. Stick with me and maybe I'll help you live your life to the fullest. What do you think?"

I try not to. I shrugged. "Fine by me."

Felix extended his hand. I willed myself to shake it.

9

The one and only entrance to Tartarus lay within a military installation known as the Ark Facility. Enclosed by an electric fence, it consisted of two dozen dormitories, warehouses, and medical facilities. A chateau on the southern edge of the base acted as the administrative building. Sniper towers rose from all four corners, and foot soldiers patrolled the grounds.

The guards herded us to the center of the base. Beneath a massive stone arch, the silver portal to Tartarus rippled like a silk sheet. As far as I knew, this was the only interdimensional gate in the entire world. It was magical in nature, maintained by Hades's power. The God of the Underworld seemed to be one of the few people who knew how it worked—though it was unclear if he actually created it. The area was under twenty-four-hour surveillance, with teams of guards alternating every twelve hours.

We entered the portal two at a time. Felix and I were the eighth pair to go through. A booking station lay on the other side. Judging by the ancient stonework and gothic architecture, the prison might have once been someone's home.

A bloodthirsty warlord perhaps.

Guards in black uniforms lined either side of the room, their eyes and assault rifles trained on us—and what they didn't see, the security cameras would. I heard a rustle of movement behind me. A prisoner had recoiled, shuffling backward. I knew why.

Revenants—zombies—comprised the entire prison staff, withered corpses with grayish-purple skin. Some had hair resembling Spanish moss. Others were completely bald. Orbs of milky light glowed dimly in their eye sockets.

In life, they had been warriors, heroes who perished in combat. As a reward for their valor on the battlefield, Hades tasked them with watching over the Tartarus for all eternity. I would have taken the consolation prize instead. On the plus side, revenants were immortal, as well as impervious to pain. You could burn them, shoot them, chop them into pieces—it didn't matter. They'd always pull themselves back together.

Once all the inmates had crossed over, an alarm sounded. Yellow caution lights danced crazily throughout the room. Then the portal vanished.

There was a security booth at the far end of the space. "Gate Control" was painted in bold white letters above the viewing window. Through the glass—or plastic—a guard could be seen working at a computer station.

After being booked, strip-searched, and sprayed with fire hoses, the other prisoners and I put on the traditional black-and-white-striped uniforms. The guards guided us to an auditorium akin to a medieval arena complete with a sandpit, stadium-style seating, and a private box.

The surroundings gave me flashbacks of my last visit with Hades.

We stood in the middle of the sandpit, waiting. For what, I couldn't say.

As the minutes passed, nonhuman prisoners filed into the auditorium: satyrs, minotaurs, cyclopses, and giants. Oh, my! There were even a few centaurs—quadrupeds that were human from the waist up and horse from the waist down.

Soon enough, the pit overflowed with what had to be at least five hundred inmates. The air grew hot and dense, fouled by the stench of sweat, wet fur, and . . . urine? I guess some people couldn't hold it in. Or they were marking their territory.

Sweat rolled along my skin. Some got into my eyes. I wiped it away with the bottom of my shirt—the only part that wasn't damp.

To my left, Felix hummed "Everybody Wants to Rule the World" by Tears for Fears. Sweat cascaded down his face, at odds with his calm expression.

The warden, Achilles, appeared in the private box above the arena, decked out in a white suit and tie so sharp he had could have pulled it straight from Hermes's closet—after digging through all the skeletons. Two guards stood on either side of him.

A hero of the Trojan War, Achilles was one of the greatest, if not *the* greatest, fighter to have ever lived. When he was a child, his mom tried to endow him with immortality by dipping him into the River Styx. But she had neglected to get his heel.

That small oversight cost Achilles his life when Paris, the Prince of Troy, tagged him with an arrow to that one weak spot. The Muhammad Ali of the ancient world taken out by a kid who would have come out second best in a shadowboxing match. What a way to go.

The only things to rival Achilles's proficiency in battle were his good looks. But those days had ended long ago.

"Greetings," Achilles said, his voice deep and commanding. "Allow me to welcome you to Tartarus Maximum Security Prison. I am Achilles, your warden. You are here because you are scum of the lowest order, a cancer upon society that must be cut out before it spreads.

"We have rules here, rules that each of you will abide by. Your cell is your new home. I expect you to treat it as such.

Keep it clean at all times. The same goes for the rest of this facility. Pick up after yourselves. You are required to work in one of the prison workshops. We allow you to have up to two jobs. Two. Not three. Not five. Two. Understand?"

Several people nodded, but no one spoke.

"Maintaining order is my top priority," Achilles continued. "That means you will not eat, sleep, or shit without permission. There is no fighting, no stealing, no fucking, no drug use, no gambling. Anyone who breaks the rules will answer to me. Believe me, you don't want that.

"On the outside, your names may have carried some weight. But in here, you're nothing. Remember that and you'll be fine. Any questions?"

He received no response.

"Before we wrap things up, I'd like to give a brief demonstration, show you what happens when an inmate refuses to conform." Achilles snapped his fingers.

The guard on his right jumped into action. He stood close to seven feet tall and had an impressive build for a zombie. His hair and beard reminded me of broom straw. I had a hunch that he was Ajax—Achilles's cousin, who had fought alongside him during the Trojan War.

The large revenant exited the box and returned shortly with a human inmate bound with handcuffs.

The man seemed on the brink of passing out. He had scraggly brown hair and beard, and was so emaciated his rib cage could've doubled as a xylophone. Cuts and bruises mottled his shirtless torso. His ripped pants were bloodstained and smudged with grime.

"This maggot thought the rules didn't apply to him," Achilles said. "He thought he was special. I gave him an opportunity to straighten up. But he continued to misbehave."

Without being prompted, the large guard trapped the inmate in a rear bear hug. The man put up a weak resistance.

He muttered incoherently. His tongue must have been cut out.

"Now, pay attention, everyone." Achilles grabbed the inmate's head with both hands and pulled.

The man screamed, unable to move, as skin and muscle tore with a wet rip.

Achilles gave one final yank, wresting the inmate's head from his body. Blood sprayed, splattering against his clean suit. He didn't appear to care.

The large guard released the inmate's body. It crumpled to the floor and out of sight.

Achilles raised the severed head by its hair so everyone could see it. The inmate's eyes were closed. His mouth hung open.

"This is the price of disobedience!" Achilles tossed the head into the crowd.

Those who had enough space to move from its path did so. The head bounced off a satyr's chest and hit the ground with a thump. Those closest to it stared in shock and revulsion.

"Do we understand each other?" Achilles asked.

No one responded.

"Do we understand each other?" Achilles repeated more loudly.

This time, most of the inmates either nodded or said yes. I did both. Felix smiled. I asked myself again: *Is this guy for real?*

"Good," Achilles said. "Now get out of my sight."

Tartarus had twenty cellblocks, ten for men and ten for women. The women's blocks were housed in a separate building accessible by an underground shuttle system.

Before being shown to our new home, we prisoners were each presented with what the guards called care packages.

Aw, they shouldn't have.

Each package contained the same items. Atop a folded blanket and a pillow rested a selection of toiletries: a toothbrush, a small tube of toothpaste, an even smaller stick of deodorant, a bath towel that felt more like a Brillo pad, shower sandals, a comb, a roll of toilet paper, and a bar of soap—which to my disappointment, didn't come with a rope.

Those of us who wanted to shave would be given one razor per week. As a safety precaution, we were expected to return it by the end of the day, at which point they would all be counted. I wasn't sure what the penalty was for losing a razor—accidentally or otherwise—but after the show Achilles put on, I didn't plan on finding out.

Cellblock D was where I'd be spending my little vacation. One of the convicts in my group informed the rest of us that it was one of the roughest areas in the prison. Fights were commonplace. But the murder rate had recently fallen from three a week to only one. I saw it as a silver lining, no matter how tarnished it may have been.

In keeping with the medieval motif, the area had the appearance of a dungeon. A clean dungeon, but a dungeon nonetheless. I guessed Achilles was serious about keeping the facility spotless.

The walls and floors were stone. Six stories of cells rose on either side of a large common area, where groups of inmates—divided by species—carried on conversations, played cards and checkers, and had rap battles. High above, two guards monitored the activity from a guard station.

The cells on the ground floor were enormous, reserved for cyclopses, giants, and centaurs. None of them had doors. The prison must have used energy barriers rather than bars, barriers that could be activated remotely from the guard station.

All eyes turned on the other new prisoners and me when we entered the common area. Then came the taunts, whistles, and catcalls. My legs were wooden as the guard led us through the middle of the floor toward a staircase leading to the upper levels. I tried to look tougher than I felt, but not so tough as to invite trouble.

Felix, on the other hand, apparently had a death wish. He hadn't stopped smiling since we left the auditorium. His cheerfulness garnered a lot of attention. Inmates threw up gang signs, issued threats, and called him names so offensive they would've made Hades himself blush.

Felix moved closer to me and whispered, "This is gonna be fun."

I pretended not to hear him.

Four minotaurs blocked the base of the stairs, bulging with muscles that bordered on grotesque.

"Out of the way," said one of the guards.

The minotaurs complied without comment, albeit slowly. As we passed by, the biggest among them, a behemoth with black hair and horns as long as my arm, winked at me.

I shivered.

Yeah, real fun.

Felix and I had been assigned to cell number 215. It featured all the luxuries of your finest four-star penitentiary: a set of bunk beds, a sink, a toilet, a storage chest, and a shelf that was part of the wall. Well, almost all the luxuries: This space lacked a window. In a normal prison, I might've been upset. But this was Tartarus.

Beyond the cell walls lay a scorched wasteland plagued by electrical storms and air that was toxic to most mortal races. But the dangers didn't stop with the climate. Lost souls, furies, and the Hecatonchires were said to haunt the nightmarish landscape.

Not something you'd want to wake up to every morning.

Felix put his belongings on the top bunk. "You don't mind if I take this one, do you? I mean, I am the top dog and all. It only seems right."

"Be my guest," I said.

"You're too kind, Plato Jones. You need to work on that. In a place like this, kindness can get you killed."

"Thanks for the advice."

"That's what I'm here for. Well, that and the whole bank thing. But that's in the past. It's time to focus on the future."

"The future's looking pretty bleak from where I stand." I placed my pillow at the head of the bed, and set the rest of my stuff on the shelf.

"So glum. You should meditate. Or do some Pilates. Get those endorphins fired up. I know! Let's mingle with the locals. Sound like a good idea?"

"No. No, it doesn't. In fact, I'd go so far as to say that it's a terrible idea."

"There's no such thing as a terrible idea," Felix said with a dismissive wave of his hand. "Just terrible execution."

I couldn't say why, but something about that statement seemed profoundly stupid.

"I'll take your word for it," I said.

"Does that mean you're not coming with me?"

"Not this time." I lay down on my bed. The hard mattress would have given Iron Man a backache. "You go on ahead, though. Have a blast. And while you're at it, try not to get yourself killed."

"Your concern is heartwarming, Plato Jones. It really is. But don't worry about me. I'm good at watching my own ass, and the asses of beautiful women. You got a woman on the outside?"

"Nah. You?"

"Of course. I mean look at me. Sadly, I had to leave her—them—back at home."

"And where is home?"

Felix dodged the question. "You know what we should do?"

"No, but I'm sure you're going to tell me anyway."

"We should sneak into one of the female cell blocks, get a little boom-boom bang-bang, then slip back in here before anyone notices we're gone. What do you think?"

"It's a lot better than your last idea."

"I thought so too. But we'll talk later. After the old meet and greet. You sure you don't want to come?"

"Yeah, I'm good."

"Okay. I'll be back later. Don't get violated while I'm out."

I gave a thumbs-up. "You got it."

Felix left.

I lounged for a few minutes, then got up. I deposited my toiletries in the storage chest at the foot of the bed. There was only one, meaning Felix and I would have to share. I hoped he'd have the courtesy not to rob me blind.

I unfolded the blanket and spread it across my bed. Considering the prison's sweltering heat, I'd probably never use it. But draping it over the bed would make sleeping a hair more comfortable. I paced back and forth for about a minute, then settled onto the bed again. As I stared at the bottom of Felix's bunk, sounds from the common area drifted into the cell.

My mind drifted to my loved ones on the outside. I already missed them, even Mr. Fancy Pants and his penchant for destroying furniture. I imagined they were begging Zeus to pardon me. I wasn't optimistic. The President and his son had gone to a lot of trouble setting this up. They were in it for the long haul, and so was I, whether I liked it or not.

Hermes probably expected a status report ASAP. I noticed a pay phone in the common room—and the long line of inmates waiting to use it. I disliked the idea of calling him in front of everyone, but I saw no other option.

The longer I reflected on my predicament, the more frustrated I became. I needed something else to occupy my mind. Building prison muscles seemed as a good a distraction any. I got up and started doing pushups and sit-ups.

I had been working out for a little over an hour when a buzzer sounded, signaling the end of the day. Sweaty and winded, I rose from the floor and sat on the edge of my bed.

The chatter in the common area dwindled to silence, replaced by the thunder of myriad footsteps. Soon, inmates moved single file down the walkway that ran alongside our cells. As they passed, a few of them regarded me with blank expressions. The rest either glared or ignored me completely.

I wondered how many of these men were like me—blamed for a crime they didn't commit. It seemed unlikely that everyone here was guilty. That would imply that the law is never wrong.

And we all know better than that.

"Headcount," a voice shouted over the loudspeaker.

I got up and stepped out onto the walkway. Inmates stood quietly on either side of me, waiting. Felix soon joined me, still smiling.

"Have fun mixing and mingling?" I asked.

"I had a blast, Plato Jones, an absolute blast. Didn't do too much mixing though. None, to be specific."

"What's that mean?"

"Exactly what it sounds like. I'm not too fond of . . . you know, nonhumans."

Crazy and a racist—what a charming fellow.

"The Gods are the worst of the bunch," Felix said. "They treat us like ants, stepping on us just because they can. But one day, all us ants are going to band together and ruin their picnic. I guarantee it."

"War?" I asked.

Felix didn't comment, but his eyes told me everything I needed to know. His opinion of the Gods was the first and quite possibly the only thing we would ever agree on. Mankind had been at the mercy of Olympus for as long as anyone could remember. It was about time someone stood up to them—and the bank heist had established Felix and his crew as legitimate threats to Zeus's reign.

But an all-out war between superpowered beings would bring about untold destruction. Civilians would be caught in the crossfire—and unfortunately, neither faction seemed to care much about collateral damage. I wanted to see Zeus dethroned just as much as the next guy, but not at the cost of innocent lives.

For their sakes, I had to make sure Felix's plans never got off the ground.

After everyone had been accounted for, the guards ordered us into our cells. Barriers of glowing red energy appeared in the entrances, just as I had expected. I was familiar with such fields. Similar ones were used at OBI headquarters, designed to shock and immobilize rather than kill.

No sooner had Felix and I brushed our teeth and gotten into bed than a voice blared from the loudspeaker.

"Lights out!"

The lights shut off with a loud boom and the block fell silent. For the next few minutes, I lay wide-awake, bathed in the red glow of the barrier. Not for the first time, I wondered exactly how he and his friends intended to take down Olympus. Brute force wouldn't be enough. Only the Claw of Erebus could kill a God. Otherwise, they were invincible.

No one bothered to tell me what Zeus had done with the Claw after Ares and I had recovered it. I imagine that—rather than being returned to the vault—it had been moved to a more secure location.

I wondered if Felix knew about the Claw. I hoped not. A weapon like that would take their chance at victory from being nonexistent to extremely possible.

As if he sensed I was thinking about him, Felix whispered, "Hey, Plato. Plato Jones. You 'sleep?"

"Nope."

"Yeah, me neither."

Clearly.

"Can I ask you something?" Felix asked.

"It's a free country, relatively."

"What do you think of the Gods? I mean, what do you *really* think of them?"

"Not much. All day, they sit in their ivory towers, thinking up new ways to make our lives miserable."

"By *our*, you mean mortals."

"Yeah."

Felix was silent for a moment. "You remember what I said earlier, about all the ants coming together?

"Yeah. Were you serious?"

"I'm always serious, Plato Jones."

"Even when you're not, huh?"

"That's right."

"Challenging the Gods." I chuckled softly. "If I had doubts about your being crazy, you've effectively removed them."

"I'm not crazy, Plato Jones. Well, maybe a little, but that's not the point. The point is I'm tired—tired of Zeus being in the driver's seat. Controlling our lives. Telling us what to think. How to feel. I say it's time we take back what's ours. We should be the masters of our own destinies, not the Gods."

"No arguments here."

"Good. I'm glad we're on the same page."

"So, how do you plan to do it? Overthrow the Gods? That's a tall order, even with superpowers."

Felix snickered. "I have my ways, Plato Jones. I have my ways. Maybe, if you're lucky, they can become your ways too."

10

THE PRISON CAFETERIA WAS THE SIZE OF A SOCCER FIELD. Humans, satyrs, and minotaurs sat near the front of the room while the larger races dined in the back.

Breakfast began at seven sharp every morning, at which time the cafeteria doors were locked. The menu consisted of disgusting brown slop, disgusting green slop, disgusting beige slop, chunks of mystery meat floating in oily slime, and fruit cocktail. Fancy schmancy. Equally impressive was the vast beverage selection: cartons of milk, water in Styrofoam cups, and juice that came in tiny bottles shaped like wine barrels.

Oh, Olympic prison system, you spoil me.

Felix and I found a table near the middle of the cafeteria. In less than ten minutes, an argument broke out between a giant and a cyclops.

The incident started when the cyclops accused the giant of looking at him the wrong way. I couldn't help wondering which of the giant's hundred eyes had been the offending one. Their quarrel immediately drew attention.

"This should be interesting," Felix said.

The two behemoths—and their entourages—rose from their seats and met in the space between tables. Onlookers began banging their trays. War drums. I didn't join in. Neither did Felix. He seemed content to just sit back and watch the show.

Two guards intervened.

"Sit down," one of them demanded.

The opponents refused to back down. The banging of trays became deafening.

The guards didn't issue a final warning. They drew stun batons. Black and glossy, the weapons looked like miniature baseball bats. Sparks of electricity pulsed on their tips, bright blue.

One guard hit the giant in the back of the leg. His partner struck the cyclops in the kidney.

The opponents roared in pain and fell to their knees. Their crews tossed angry curses at the guards. A chorus of boos joined the incessant banging.

The cyclops quickly recovered. He lashed out with a backhand. The blow struck one of the guards with a boom like thunder. The revenant flew ass over teakettle through the air, crashing onto the serving counter.

Cheers erupted.

Before the other guard could react, the giant seized him by the waist and pitched him across the cafeteria. The revenant bounced off the wall and landed face first on a table of satyrs. He didn't get up.

With no one left to interrupt them, the two factions turned on each other. The floor quaked under their immense footfalls. As the fight moved through the cafeteria, nearby spectators abandoned their food and scrambled clear.

An alarm sounded.

A team of guards wielding stun batons burst into the cafeteria—through the now unlocked door—and joined in the scuffle, only to be swatted away like gnats. Zombie gnats.

Two more guards entered, larger than the rest. They wore

black riot gear and visored helmets, wielding shotguns loaded with what I assumed to be nonlethal ammo.

A siren moved between them, making this only the fourth time I'd seen one in real life. I wished I had camera. Sirens were semiaquatic creatures that lived on remote islands scattered throughout the world. They rarely ventured inland—so a person could go his entire life without ever seeing one.

This particular siren stood around six feet tall, rail-thin, with skin like porcelain and long black hair that she wore in a bun. She had eight squid-like tentacles in place of legs—using them to pull herself along—and brownish-gold eyes that were spaced far apart. The riot vest that protected her upper torso was less padded that those of her companions, and she carried no visible weapons. Something that resembled a breathing mask covered the bottom half of her face.

The siren and her companions remained at the head of the cafeteria. The guards trying to break up the fight abandoned their efforts and gathered behind her as she removed her mask.

The gangs continued to brawl while the rest of us covered our ears. Sirens were regarded as having the most beautiful voices in the world, which they used to draw hapless sailors to their islands—for the purpose of devouring them. But when tuned to specific frequencies, that same voice could be turned into an offensive weapon. They'd make a literal killing at a karaoke contest.

The siren handed her mask to the guard on her right. She had two thin slits where a nose should've been, and a wide, lipless mouth.

"Here it comes!" Felix shouted.

The siren's mouth opened like a black hole, releasing a shrill wave of sound. Imagine squeaky hinges and screeching tires combined with nails raking across a chalkboard. Then multiply it by a thousand.

The dissonance bore through my hands and assaulted my eardrums. I gritted my teeth, crippled with agony. My head felt like it might explode. The other human inmates seemed to be in the same boat as me. But the nonhumans, with their enhanced hearing, had to have been in even more pain. Satyrs and minotaurs fell out of their seats and crashed onto the floor, their cries of pain drowned out by the siren's scream.

The fight came to an end as the giants and cyclopses doubled over, vigorously shaking their heads, their hands pressed over their ears.

The siren stopped screaming, and the guards removed everyone who'd been involved. No one resisted. Less than minute later, a buzzer marked the end of breakfast.

Later that day, Felix and I were lifting weights in the gym. I spotted him as he finished the last few reps of a three-hundred-pound bench press. He performed the lifts smoothly, despite the weight. I might've thought he was suppressing his powers so as not to draw suspicion. But his flushed skin, sweat, bulging veins disputed that notion.

He was strong, but not superhumanly so.

I racked the bar and Felix sat up on the bench, breathing hard. "That shit at breakfast—pretty wild, huh?"

"Wild and painful. My ears are still ringing."

"You know, this place is already starting to grow on me. I like the vibe."

"In that case, the next two centuries should just fly by."

Felix grinned and stood up. "Your turn."

I didn't even think about trying to match Felix's bench press. I knew my limits. I removed two twenty-five-pound plates from the bar. Felix didn't give me a hard time about it. A pleasant surprise.

As I set the plates aside, Marcelo entered the gym. He and Felix exchanged nods but no words. He glanced at me on his way to the dumbbell stand. Mistrust clung like frost to his face. He grabbed two fifties and started doing curls.

I leaned back onto the bench and did a set. I'd just finished when a guard showed up.

"Plato Jones," he said.

"Need something, officer?"

"You have a visitor."

I stood up, using the bottom of my shirt as a face towel. When it came to visitors, inmates were allowed two fifteen-minute visits per week, or one thirty-minute visit—but only after filling out several forms. I hadn't completed a single one. Whoever had come to see me had pulled some serious strings.

Gee, I wonder who it could be.

I followed the guard to one of the visiting rooms. It was small and dark, containing a single plastic chair and a large, round lens embedded in the middle of the floor—it appeared to be made of glass, black and glossy.

As a rule, only guards, inmates, and high-ranking government officials could physically enter Tartarus. Everyone else had to use the Ark Facility's holographic projection system.

I sat down in the chair. The guard left the room, shutting the door behind him and leaving me in near-total darkness. The lens began to glow neon blue, and the image of a man I'd never seen before flickered into existence. He appeared almost transparent, surrounded in pale light.

He fit the mold of your typical businessman: a suit, glasses, and expertly cut hair. The only thing missing was a briefcase.

"Good morning, Mr. Jones," the man said, his voice even, his smile friendly. "You are Plato Jones, aren't you?"

"Last I checked. Who are you?"

"Easton Green. Nice to meet you."

"Likewise. So, to what do I owe the honor of your visit?"

"I'm here on behalf of Hermes. He has a few questions for you."

"Okay."

Easton shut his eyes and reopened them.

"Hello, Jones," he said. "So nice to see you alive and well." Easton's voice hadn't changed. But the words he spoke weren't his own.

"Hello, Hermes."

"How is prison life? Have you been deflowered yet?"

"No, and I plan to keep it that way."

"Good for you."

"So, this is your newest puppet," I said. "Where'd you dig him up?"

"Easton here works in the accounting department on Olympus. He wanted to make a little extra money."

I shook my head. The Gods' ability to control mortals through telepathy was common knowledge. But their influence was limited to those who willfully allowed their minds to be taken over, and individuals suffering from severe mental illness. Easton seemed to fall into the first category, which came as relief. Taking advantage of the mentally ill was low, even for a creep like Hermes.

"How much does he know?" I asked.

"Only that I wanted to speak with you," Hermes said.

This was one of those rare occasions where I actually believed him. But knowing Jackass, he'd probably erase Easton's memory later on, just to be on the safe side.

"Have you found anything out yet?" Hermes asked.

"Yeah. Felix and his buddies seem to be part of a resistance group. Their goal is to bring down Olympus."

"That much is obvious. Give me something I can use."

"How about a new stylist? That suit you wore to the trial." I sucked air through my teeth.

"Stow the wisecracks, Jones. I'm not in the mood. Have you discovered the source of their powers?"

"Not yet."

Hermes frowned and moved on to the next question. "How do they plan to overthrow the government from prison?"

"I'm not sure. But I'm trying to find out."

"I'm disappointed in you, Jones. I thought you'd have at least one piece of new information."

"I just got here!"

"Just have something for me the next time."

"When will that be?"

"One week from today. Is that satisfactory?"

"I don't know. I'll have to check my schedule."

Hermes's frown turned into a scowl. Even though it was Easton's face, the expression was quintessentially Hermes. "Goodbye, Mr. Jones. Try not to get yourself killed. At least until the mission is over."

"Ciao," I said. "Oh, by the way, did you and Herc ever have that little chat?"

My question arrived a second too late. Easton had reassumed control.

"Are we done?" he asked.

"Yep."

"Excellent. Again, it was nice meeting you."

"Ditto."

The hologram vanished, and the lens stopped glowing. I exited the room and returned to D-Block. The meeting with Hermes could've gone better. But at least he hadn't forgotten about me.

When I returned to the weight room, I expected Felix to grill me about my visit. But he never brought it up. We resumed our workout as though nothing had happened.

The rest of the day passed without incident. No fights, rapes, or murders. Everyone seemed at ease. Everyone except me. This moment of reprieve, I realized, was an illusion. A curtain to mask the dark clouds gathering overhead.

A storm approached.

I could feel it in my bones.

11

The next morning, Felix and I—along with several other inmates—were given a tour of the prison to check out the jobs Achilles had mentioned.

We visited the kitchen, the infirmary, the craft shop, the greenhouse, and the sulfur mines that ran deep below the prison.

After the tour, the guards led us outside. In the yard, prisoners conversed, shot hoops, smoked, played cards and dominos, and engaged in group exercise. A clear dome covered the area. Beyond, the wastes of Tartarus stretched endlessly in all directions. Blood-red clouds pulsed with trapped lightning above the cracked earth. There were no animals, no plants. Nothing. We might as well have been on Mars.

I sat alone on a bench near the basketball court, where a team of humans played against a team of satyrs. Felix had ventured to the opposite side of the yard to have a word with Marcelo and Lance. When he finished, he came over to me.

"Behold, the king of Tartarus," he said. "The alpha male, the undisputed champion of badassery, come to grace the common folk with his presence."

"Thanks for the compliments," I said.

"Compliments? I was talking about me."

"I stand corrected."

Felix sat down beside me. He pulled a pack of cigarettes out of his pocket and held it toward me.

I shook my head. "No thanks."

"You don't smoke?"

"Never." That wasn't exactly true. I occasionally used to smoke as a teenager, but not tobacco.

Felix removed a cigarette and put the pack back in his pocket. "What are you, a Boy Scout?"

"Used to be, when I was kid."

Felix put the cigarette between his lips, sparked it using a stinger lighter he'd made out of double-A batteries and other ordinary items. He took a drag, blew a cloud of smoke into the air.

"Now that I think about it, I can picture you in that little green uniform," he said. "With that necktie-thing, showing off all your little merit badges."

"Believe it or not, I still have all that stuff."

"Oh, I believe it." Felix took another pull. "You seem like the sentimental type. But that's cool. I like sentimentality."

"I'd never have guessed."

"There's a lot you don't know about me, Plato Jones. There's more to me than just a handsome face and a perfect physique. Deep down—deep, deep, deep down, I have the soul of poet."

"I'll bet."

"I heard you and Aphrodite used to be an item," Felix said unexpectedly.

Wonderful. Even in another dimension, everyone knew my business.

"She thought we were," I said.

"So, you weren't together?"

"Nope."

"What about all those pictures in the tabloids?"

I sensed that Felix was trying to catch me in a lie. He'd

probably Googled my name in the prison's computer lab to make sure I was legit.

"We went out twice," I said. "I was never interested in being her boyfriend—one of her boyfriends."

Felix stared at me, smoke coiling from the tip of his cigarette. "You see this look on my face, Plato Jones? It's confusion. I don't like being confused. Makes me feel icky."

"Look, I dated her to get information on the Olympic Treasury—its security measures. I thought I could trick her into giving me what I needed. But she knew about as much as I did. Business and economics weren't her thing. On the plus side, she paid for our dates."

Felix pointed at me as if to say *good job.* "Did you smash?"

"If I did, do you think I'd be sitting here right now, having a coherent conversation?" I asked, referring to the rumor that any mortal who had sex with Aphrodite would lose his mind and become dangerously obsessed with her.

Some even went as far as to commit murder or suicide just to prove their love for her.

"No, I don't, Plato Jones," Felix said. "I just wanted to see if you'd try to bullshit me. You passed the test. Congratulations."

"Three cheers for me."

Felix finished his cigarette, flicked away the butt, and pulled a fresh one from the pack. "I also heard you're buddies with Hercules. Any truth to that?"

"Yeah. He's my best friend, actually."

Felix raised his eyebrows, as though surprised by my honesty. "How'd the two of you meet?"

"He and I went to the same gym when I worked for the OBI," I said. "We just started talking one day and realized we had a lot in common. The rest is history."

I omitted the part where Herc saved me from being strangled to death by a weight bar. I had to protect my reputation as a tough guy, after all.

"That's sweet," Felix said with a wry grin. "Real sweet. So, you two had some things in common, huh? Like what?"

"MMA, alcohol, junk food," I said off the top of my head. "And he's not too fond of the Gods."

That was mostly true. Herc viewed his father with a certain level of respect—and he seemed to be on friendly terms with Aphrodite. The rest of the Gods he either flat out despised or merely tolerated.

"Did he know about your plan to rob the Treasury?" Felix asked.

"Of course not. Don't get me wrong. Herc is like a brother to me, but at the end of the day, he's still a demigod."

Felix nodded. He took another pull from his cigarette and tapped the end. Ashes drifted to the ground, glowing white in the red-tinted air.

"You decided where you want to work?" he asked.

"Not yet."

"Good, because you're gonna be working with me in the greenhouse."

"Do I have a choice?"

"There's always a choice, Plato Jones. But with choices come consequences. Getting shanked in the stomach, for example."

"Well, since you put it that way . . ."

"Just kidding. You can do whatever you want. But I highly suggest you work with me. Humans have to stick together, right?"

I saw right through Felix's ploy. He wanted me to join his resistance movement. But he needed to know he could trust me. To do that, he had to stick to me like whiskers on Hera's chin. That suited me. I'd do just about anything to escape this nightmare.

"Right," I said.

"Good man." Felix clapped me on the shoulder. "This is going to be fun, a nice bonding experience."

12

Felix and I moved along the breakfast line. Lance worked the buffet as part of his new job. He plopped a generous portion of mystery glop onto our trays. Intuition told me that Lance's kitchen job would play a part in whatever scheme Felix was devising.

I wondered where I fit in.

Not long after Felix and I had started eating, we were approached by the minotaur who'd winked at me the day before, and his band of circus clowns. I knew this would happen sooner or later. But why, out of all the potential bullies in this prison, did mine have to be a minotaur? I guessed it could have been worse. It could have been a giant or a cyclops.

"Morning, gentlemen," said the minotaur, his voice low and even. "How are you settling in?"

Felix paid him no mind. I did the opposite. Unlike him, I preferred to keep all my teeth.

"Just fine, thanks," I said.

"My name is Reave." The minotaur indicated his posse. "These are my associates."

"Nice to meet you, Reave." I nodded at the other minotaurs. "Associates."

They didn't respond.

"What are your names?" Reave asked.

"Plato."

Felix remained silent, still eating.

"What's up with your friend?" Reave asked me.

I'd been trying to figure that out ever since I'd met him.

"Nothing's up with me," Felix said. "I just don't like filthy, dirty beast-men."

Reave seemed to brush aside the insult. His companions tensed. One snorted. But no one made a move.

"I'm not here to cause trouble," Reave said. "In fact, I'm here to help you. I'm a businessman."

"Don't you mean business-cow?" Felix said.

One of the minotaurs stepped forward. Reave stopped him with a glance. Around us, guards and inmates began rubbernecking, anticipating a fight.

"I'm extending an offer of protection," Reave said. "Tartarus can be a dangerous place. Especially with no one to watch your back. For a modest fee, my associates and I can guarantee your safety."

"Go fuck yourselves," Felix said.

My heart nearly stopped.

Reave gave the minotaur equivalent of a smile. "If money is the issue, I'm sure we can make *other* arrangements."

The implication sent a chill down my spine.

"When I told you to fuck yourselves, I meant it figuratively," Felix said. "This time, it's the real deal. Go fuck yourselves."

The breath in my lungs froze. I stared at Felix, mortified. I knew he was crazy, but how far down did the well reach?

By now, we had the attention of the entire cafeteria. Reave's expression appeared serene, his muscles relaxed. But his associates huffed and snorted. Their bodies trembled in what might have been anticipation.

"Sit down, all of you," a guard shouted from the front of the cafeteria.

The minotaurs headed back toward their seats without a fuss.

"Move along there, Bessie," Felix called after them.

The minotaurs paused.

"Don't even think about it," the guard said.

Grudgingly, Reave and his crew sat down.

"And you," the guard said, pointing at Felix. "Zip it!"

Felix gave a small salute. Gradually, the chatter fell silent and everyone returned to their meals. Everyone except Reave and his gang, that is. They watched us as we ate, like a pack of hunters studying their prey.

"Six new enemies in one day," I said. "That tops my previous record."

"Mine too," Felix said.

"Somehow, I doubt that."

"You scared?"

"What do you think?"

"I think you need to relax."

"Relax? You do realize they're going to kill us?"

"They'll give it their best shot," Felix said.

I stared at him, amazed that someone this stupid existed beyond the realm of cartoons. "Can I ask you something?

"You can ask me anything. Doesn't mean I'm going to answer. But we'll see. What's your question?"

"Did you sniff Magic Markers as a kid?"

Felix laughed. "That was a good one, Plato Jones. Grade A material. You know, we should enter you in the prison talent show. You can do a stand-up routine. I'll even help you come up with a few zingers. What do you think?"

"Whatever."

"Come to think of it, does this place even have talent shows?"

Suddenly feeling exhausted, I mentally checked out of the

conversation. I no longer had an appetite, but I forced myself to pick at the tasteless mush on my tray. I'd need all the strength I could muster for the days ahead.

13

Working in the greenhouse almost made me forget I was in prison. I supposed that was the point—to make us long for the freedom we had lost by offering an illusion of the outside world, a fragment of serenity, a cruel joke to keep us miserable and easily controlled. If that assumption rang true, then mission accomplished. White glass panels covered the walls, emitting rays of artificial sunlight that fed a vast assortment of flowers, vegetables, fungi, and herbs.

Considering the garbage in the cafeteria, it seemed unlikely that anything here would ever find its way to Tartarus's kitchen. Instead, it was likely being sold back in the outside world, resulting in more money lining the Gods' pockets.

Tending the plants in relative comfort, I wondered why more inmates hadn't applied for this job. There were only ten of us in all. Then I found out how much it paid compared with the other gigs. Mystery solved.

Near the end of our shift, I noticed Felix covertly picking various herbs and stuffing them into his pants. Verbena, white sage, and an anti-inflammatory called cherub's breath were the ones I recognized. I suspected he planned to whip up some sort of narcotic substance.

Here's hoping he doesn't offer me a sample.

* * *

After work, Felix stashed the smuggled herbs in our cell.

When I asked what he intended to do with them, he merely smiled and said, "You'll see."

Provided you live that long was the part he left out.

Afterward, we headed to the shower room. The previous night, I had fashioned a wristband for my bar of soap using a shoelace. Not the greatest example of prison ingenuity, but it would serve its purpose.

Given the option, I wouldn't have taken one single shower for the entirety of my sentence. All 457 years. Regrettably, Tartarus's strict stance on cleanliness applied not only to the facility itself, but also to the prisoners living within its walls. The system had stripped us of our most basic rights—even the right to smell like week-old roadkill.

There were three shower rooms in our block. One for humans, satyrs, and minotaurs, one for giants and cyclopses, and one for centaurs. Ours had gray tiles and stainless steel fixtures. Water hissed from the showerheads, and white steam clouded the air.

There were only five other inmates present, humans. Reave and the funky bunch were nowhere in sight. As I lathered up, I almost let myself believe that my luck had finally changed.

Silly me.

Reave and three of his friends entered the shower room, stark naked. They immediately spotted me and came over.

I pretended not to notice them. Beside me, Felix scrubbed away without pause, whistling the theme to *The Andy Griffith Show.*

They say ignorance is bliss. I wondered if that applied to insanity as well.

The minotaurs stopped a few feet away from us.

"You two are either the bravest humans I've ever met," Reave said, "or the stupidest."

I said nothing. I didn't fool myself into believing that words could diffuse the situation. The incident in the cafeteria had destroyed any chance for diplomacy.

Only blood would resolve the issue.

"I'm talking to you," Reave said.

Felix stopped whistling and glanced over his shoulder. "Hey, there, cowboy. Didn't see you come in. While you're here, would you mind scrubbing my back?"

"You know why I'm here," Reave said.

His words were directed at Felix more than me.

"Isn't that cute?" Felix asked, turning around. "The prey thinks it's a predator."

Reave chuckled. "I was planning to just rough you up a little. But now I'm going to tear you a new one, figuratively and literally."

Felix gave a fake gasp. "Oh, no! Not *literally.* Please, anything but that."

Reave's muscles tensed. He seemed on the verge of attacking. I had to step in. Felix was my only means of escaping Tartarus. He must survive.

"No need to get excited," I said, stepping between Felix and the minotaurs. "My friend here is only kidding."

"I am?" Felix asked.

"Wait your turn," Reave said to me.

"Can't we discuss this later, when we're all fully clothed?"

Reave shoved me aside with enough force to send me flying across the shower room. I landed on my back with a wet smack. The air burst from my lungs. I slid across the floor, tripping up two inmates before slamming against the wall. Laughter echoed around the room.

I got up, disoriented, struggling to find traction on the

slippery tiles. Through a chaos of spinning imagery, I saw Felix and Reave staring each other down.

Okay, I thought. *On to Plan B.*

"Is that all you got?" I said. "Are those water balloons you call muscles just for show?"

The insult earned me an *Oooooh* from the onlookers.

Reave jerked his head in my direction. "You seem determined to take your friend's beating for him. So be it."

He and the other minotaurs moved toward me.

Felix looked as though he might come to my aid. I shook my head. He arched his brows dubiously. I returned a quick nod.

Felix seemed to get the message. He leaned against the wall between two showerheads, his arms crossed.

Physically, I was no match for a minotaur, let alone four. I needed to make this a one-on-one contest—and hope the commotion would attract the guards.

"Four against one," I said. "What's the matter, Reave? Can't fight your own battles? Or are you afraid of getting whooped by a human?"

Reave called a halt. "Stand back, boys. I've got this."

His cronies backed away.

Reave came to stand before me. I only came up to his chest.

"Take him down, Plato Jones," Felix said. "I'm in the mood for steak."

Will you please shut up?

"You're pretty ballsy for a human," Reave said to me. "I'll tell you what. You can have a free shot."

"I don't want to fight you."

"This isn't going to be a fight," Reave said. "Go ahead. Hit me."

I didn't have much of a choice. I reared back and took a swing at Reave's face. It was like hitting a wet brick wall. Pain shot from my knuckles to my elbow, so intense it nearly stole my breath.

Reave's hand shot out. Thick, hairy fingers closed around my neck, lifting me off my feet. I struggled, unable to breathe.

Through the pounding of blood in my head, I heard Felix's voice. "Do something, Plato Jones! You're embarrassing yourself!"

Reave pulled me close and whispered, "The pain you're about to feel is nothing compared with what I have in store for you and your friend later."

In desperation, I shoved my bar of soap into Reave's eyes.

The minotaur bellowed in pain, releasing me.

I landed with a splat. Coughing and gasping, I pushed to my feet. My head throbbed, and white spots flashed before my eyes.

Around me, the spectators cheered.

Reave thrashed about, his hands pressed over his face. I kicked him in the crotch with everything I had, nearly breaking my foot in the process. The minotaur gasped. He fell over and curled into a ball on the floor, moaning. Everyone stood in shock.

In typical action movie fashion, a guard showed up only after the conflict had ended. He glanced at me, then at Reave.

"What happened here?" he demanded.

"Reave and I were having a friendly game of charades," I looked down at Reave. "You're a nutcracker, right?"

The minotaur groaned.

The guard appeared less than convinced. But he didn't press the matter.

"You maggots had better cut out the horseplay," he said to all of us. "Understand?"

No one responded. Reave moaned louder.

"Someone take him to the infirmary," said the guard.

Reave's friends helped their leader to his feet and guided him out of the shower room. The guard left afterward. I resumed my shower sans soap. The other inmates congratulated me on my victory with words, smiles, and nods.

Felix said nothing. He rinsed off, grabbed his towel, and strolled out of the bathroom, once again whistling the theme to *The Andy Griffith Show.*

14

I SPENT THE REST OF THE EVENING IN BED, TRYING TO KEEP a low profile. It'd probably be some time before Reave returned from the infirmary. But I wasn't taking any chances.

Felix came into our cell with a bag of pale orange liquid. Prison wine, a.k.a. hooch. A rubber band secured the mouth of the bag, which had a drinking straw sticking out of it.

"I come bearing gifts," Felix said.

I carefully sat up, my body aching. "How'd you sneak that past the guards?"

"Easy. I made sure they didn't see it."

"Ah."

Felix sat on the toilet. It made me wonder where he'd gotten the water for the hooch. I was probably better off not knowing.

"I want to thank you, Plato Jones," Felix said. "What you did earlier took guts. I mean, I could have soloed Bessie and his crew. Easy. But you saved me the trouble of getting my hands dirty."

"No problem."

Felix offered me a drink. "First sip is yours."

"You didn't pee in it, did you?"

"No, but the thought did cross my mind."

That must have been a short journey.

I took a sip. The hooch tasted like cheap wine that had

been filtered through a trash can full of rotten fruit. Even so, it wasn't the worst drink I'd ever had. That honor went to a concoction Herc stirred up during a barbecue he and Hebe had thrown, using only the finest bottom-shelf liquors.

"Pretty good, huh?" Felix said. "It's my own recipe. The key ingredient is cinnamon. Don't tell anyone, or I'll have to kill you."

"Your secret is safe with me." I passed the hooch back to Felix.

We drank in silence for the next minute or so. I was already buzzed. Felix still appeared sober.

"I like you, Plato Jones," he said. "You seem genuine. I think it's time for us to take our relationship to the next level."

I leaned back, my eyes narrow. "I don't think I'm ready for marriage. We just met, after all."

"No, nothing like that." He chuckled. "Besides, you're not my type."

"I'll drink to that." I took a sip.

The bag was nearly empty. I handed it back and let Felix finish off the rest.

"Me and my friends are putting together an operation," he said. "You want in?"

"What kind of operation are we talking about?"

"We're busting out of here."

"Out of Tartarus?"

"Yes."

"And I thought *my* comedy routine needed work."

"It does. Your shit's on life support. But that's beside the point. There's a war coming. Mankind has been at the mercy of Olympus for too long. It's time for us to rise up and fight back. Show Zeus how powerful we really are. So, are you in?"

Hmm. I could either join this nut on his suicide mission or I could decline and spend the rest of my life as Reave's personal beat-up toy.

The decision was clear.

"Sure." I leaned back on my bed, resting my hands behind my head. "I've got nothing better to do."

15

In the morning, I called Hermes and left a message with his assistant, letting him know I had big news. Within the next few hours, I was sitting in one of the visitation rooms, across from a hologram of Easton Greene. Jackass spoke through him.

"This had better be good, Jones. I was in the middle of an important meeting."

"Getting fitted for another ugly suit?"

Hermes frowned. "Do you have something for me?"

"Do I ever. It turns out Felix and his friends are planning a jailbreak."

"When?"

"He didn't say. But something tells me he's going to act sooner rather than later."

"How did you get this information?"

"Straight from the horse's mouth. He asked if I wanted in."

"Did you accept?"

"I didn't really have a choice."

"This could be just the break we need," Hermes said. "I want you to make sure at least one of them makes it out of there alive. Then I want you to stick to him like flies to dung."

"Or your nose to Zeus's backside."

Hermes's frown deepened, but he offered no retort. "Keep

working to gain his trust. We need to know everything about him and his organization. How large it is, how far it reaches, everything."

"I'll try my best."

"Don't try. Do. Now, is there anything else?"

"Just one more teeny-tiny little thing. Assuming this breakout is a success, and Felix and I become good chums, what am I supposed to do about the tens of thousands of cops that'll be out for our blood?"

"We'll take care of them. You just do as you're told."

By *we*, I figured Hermes meant the OBI.

"I always do as I'm told," I said, "whether I want to or not. So, what happens to me once the mission is over?"

"You'll be given a presidential pardon as well as a modest financial reward."

"Sounds good. Can I make a special request?"

"If you must."

"After we've taken down Felix's gang, I want an apology . . . from you."

Hermes's right eye narrowed. "An apology?"

"Yes, an apology."

"For what?"

"For all the crap you've given me over the years."

Hermes laughed scornfully. "Absolutely not."

"Don't worry. It doesn't have to be public. It doesn't even have to be in person. You can do it over the phone if you'd like. But no letters and no e-mails. I want to hear your voice when you say it. I want to savor the moment."

"You're out of your mind." Hermes chuckled. "I won't disgrace myself by apologizing to a mortal."

"What if Zeus told you to do it?"

The laughter ceased.

"You wouldn't . . ." Hermes said.

"Go over your head? You bet your ass I would."

Hermes's right eye twitched. "This exchange is over. Contact me when you have more information. And don't drop the soap."

"I've already got it covered," I said.

But the hologram had already vanished. Leaving the visitation room, I suddenly remembered something. I'd meant to ask Hermes if Herc ever caught up with him for a private smackdown.

Oh, well. Next time.

When I returned to my cell, Felix was lounging on his bed. Marcelo leaned against the opposite wall, his clothes covered in soot. He must've taken a job in the mines. The two of them had been talking before I arrived. Their conversation died the moment I showed up.

"Well, if it isn't the man of the hour. Plato Jones," Felix said, "I'd like you to meet Marcelo Sandoval."

"Nice to meet you." I extended my hand toward Marcelo.

He looked at it.

Oookay.

"Don't mind Marcelo," Felix said. "He's just trying to preserve his tough guy image. Deep down he's a softy, all warm and cuddly—like one of those giant teddy bears you get at the carnival."

"You sure about this guy?" Marcelo asked Felix.

"Without a doubt. Plato Jones is one of the good guys. Like us."

Marcelo gave a slight shrug. "You're the boss."

"That's right. I'm the boss, and the boss says play nice with the new guy. Make him feel like part of the family."

"Whatever you say," Marcelo said unenthusiastically.

"Hey, since I'm part of the club now, do I get a super-secret decoder ring?" I asked.

Marcelo closed his eyes for a long moment.

"You'll get a lot more than that," Felix said. "Once we get out of here."

I wasn't optimistic.

Marcelo glanced at the cell entrance. "We'd better do this quick, before the guards notice."

"Right. Plato Jones, do me a favor and keep watch."

"Okay." I stepped outside and leaned against the railing, facing my cell entrance.

Marcelo took off his left shoe and removed something he'd been hiding under the insole. A clump of bright blue moss. I remembered seeing a lot of it during my tour of the mines. It grew in abundance on the cave walls.

Marcelo handed the moss to Felix, who hid it under his pillow.

I gathered he planned to use it in conjunction with the smuggled herbs. Whatever concoction he planned to cook up would play a role in the escape. Of that, I was certain.

Marcelo put his shoe back on. "I'll see you later."

"Make sure to tell Lance about our newest recruit," Felix said.

"Yeah." Marcelo left the cell.

He walked past me without a word, or even a glance.

"Pleasant fellow," I said as I reentered the cell.

"I know, right?" Felix said. "Wherever he goes, rainbows and butterflies are sure to follow."

I claimed the spot Marcelo had previously occupied. "What did he give you?"

"Moss of the rarest variety. It's called spriggan bush. Tartarus is the only place it grows."

"What does it do?"

"Nothing by itself. But when mixed with the right components, it's one bad mother."

"So, it's a drug?"

"It's *the* drug. Actually, it's more like a potion. Harmless to humans, but man, does it do a number on other species. Minotaurs, satyrs, centaurs, giants, cyclopses. Makes them go berserk, and makes them more resistant to pain."

Felix's potion sounded like a disaster in a bottle—and all the ingredients were right here in Tartarus. The prison staff couldn't have known about it, or else the mines and greenhouse would have been off limits to inmates.

My inner Boy Scout urged me to blow the whistle. Criminals or not, no one deserved to have his mind taken away. But stopping Felix wouldn't eliminate the problem. His father was still out there somewhere. I had to see this through to the end.

"This potion," I said, "how did you learn to make it?

"I'll tell you after you've passed the initiation. Maybe."

"Initiation? Getting my ass handed to me by an angry minotaur wasn't enough?"

"Nope. But I appreciate what you did all the same. Anyway, we'll cross that bridge when we get to it, if we get to it. Right now, we need to focus on getting out of this cesspit."

"Cesspit? I thought this place was growing on you."

"It was. But I think it's giving me a rash."

"Come on, Felix. Can't we stay just a little longer? I was so looking forward to getting shanked."

"If it makes you feel better, I'll shank you once we're outside."

"Sounds like a plan."

Felix grinned.

"And speaking of plans," I began, "you haven't told me ours. That might be some useful information to have, don't you think?"

"Indubitably. That's my word of the week: indubitably. I've been trying to expand my vocabulary."

"Good for you. Now about the plan."

Felix sat up in bed. "Check this out. We're going to create a distraction and slip out during the chaos, like ninjas."

"It'll have to be a pretty big distraction."

"Oh it will be, Plato Jones. We're going to kick-start the biggest riot this prison has ever seen. It's gonna be a lot of fun."

"And this is where your potion comes in."

"Yessiree. We'll slip it into everyone's breakfast, then sit back and watch the fireworks."

"Interesting plan," I said. "But what's to stop the bloodthirsty hordes from tearing us to bits?"

"Your legs, Plato Jones. You know? That pair of toothpicks attached to your pelvis. When the shit hits the fan, run, run, and keep on running."

"Run to where? The portal closed after we came through. And even if we manage to open it, there's still the tiny problem of being on an island full of armed guards."

"You worry too much, Plato Jones. That's not good for you. It could shave years off your life. Years. It's true. I read about it in a magazine."

"Funny. I could say the same about your plan."

"Relax, amigo," Felix said. "I have everything under control."

"I'll take your word for it."

"A smart decision."

"What else is on the agenda? Besides escaping?"

"That's classified information."

"Look, I just want—"

"Classified information," Felix said, cutting me off.

I opened my mouth to argue but decided against it. It wouldn't have done any good. Felix seemed hardwired to be as nebulous as possible, whenever possible.

"When does your plan go into action?" I asked.

"In two days."

"Why two days?"

"Elementary, my dear Plato Jones. That's when the stars align."

Felix and I went to work the following morning. By the time our shift ended, Reave had returned to general population sporting a noticeable limp. He and his gang gave me my space. But I knew things weren't over between us. Once his crotch healed, he'd come after me. With any luck, I'd be long gone by then.

Later on, Felix gave me a juice bottle containing a blue-green liquid. The potion. He asked me to deliver it to Lance while he made a phone call. The plan was to spike tomorrow's breakfast. I hated being a part of this—something so fundamentally wrong. But it was my only means of escape, and of preventing the worst war since the Titanomachia.

I stuffed the bottle down the front of my pants and went to Lance's cell. Posters of nude women and rock bands covered the walls. Lance sat on the edge of the bottom bunk, reading a book on self-improvement.

I cleared my throat.

Lance looked up from his book. Unlike Marcelo, he seemed sociable.

"Salutations." Lance put down his book and stood up. "I don't think we've been properly introduced. I'm Lance."

"Plato."

We shook hands.

"Got something for me?" Lance asked.

"Yep." I gave him the bottle.

"Thanks." Lance put the bottle under his pillow. He didn't seem to mind that it had been in my pants.

"No problem. I have to say, it's nice to finally meet someone who doesn't look like they want to kill me."

"You must be talking about Marcelo. Don't worry about

him. He's like that with everyone. Trust issues. Me, on the other hand, I like to give people the benefit of the doubt. Besides, Felix seems to trust you. That's good enough for me."

I nodded. "So, what's the deal with this plan of ours?"

"What do you mean?"

"Getting out of here isn't our only objective. What's Felix really after?"

"I'm not supposed to tell you. Sorry."

"Why not?"

"Because Felix said so," Lance said. "I've never been one to challenge authority."

"Fair enough."

"I suggest you get plenty of rest. Tomorrow's going to be a busy day."

"I can imagine. Anyway, I'd better get going. It's nice meeting you."

"The pleasure was mine," Lance said. "Oh, and welcome aboard."

16

On the morning of the escape, Felix and I were having breakfast in the cafeteria. Nervousness had destroyed my appetite, but not his. He scarfed down his food with all the manners and etiquette of a junkyard dog.

Reave and his gang had been eyeballing me the entire time. I made a conscious effort not to look in their direction. Maybe Felix would follow my example. I didn't get my hopes up.

"You gonna eat that fruit cocktail?" Felix asked.

"Help yourself."

Felix grabbed the cup from my tray and peeled back the aluminum cover. He picked out two whole cherries and smiled. Probably not a good sign.

"Watch this," he said.

"Whatever you plan on doing, don't," I said.

Felix snubbed my request and turned around in his seat, so that he faced Reave's table. He held the cherries high, one in each hand, holding them between his thumbs and forefingers. He made sure the minotaurs could see them clearly, then crushed them.

I almost cursed.

Reave snorted so loud I could hear him over the surrounding conversations. He and the other minotaurs shot out of their seats and started making their way to our table.

"Now why'd you go and do that?" I asked.

"Just watch."

The minotaurs had almost reached our table when all five froze in place. Their eyes grew large and vacant. Their mouths hung open. Around them, other nonhumans fell into the same motionless daze. The cafeteria fell silent as humans and revenants looked around in confusion.

Felix removed two king-sized pieces of bubblegum from his pockets—I assumed he'd gotten them from the commissary. He offered me one. When I held up my hand in refusal, he arched his eyebrows as if to say, *I insist.*

I took the gum in spite of myself. Felix unwrapped his piece and popped it into his mouth. He chewed it for a few seconds, removed the pink lump from his mouth, then pulled it into two equal portions, which he shoved into his ears. The reason behind his actions seemed obvious. I followed his example. A guard confronted Reave and his gang. "Sit your asses down."

His order went unheeded. The minotaurs seemed oblivious to his presence.

"I said sit down!" The guard drew his stun baton.

When implied threat of violence failed to yield results, the guard resorted to actual violence. He jabbed his baton into Reave's ribs. The minotaur trembled but remained standing. He didn't even blink.

The guard furrowed his brow, outwardly baffled. He struck Reave again. This time, his attack incited a reaction, though probably not the one he had expected.

Reave let out an enraged bellow. He grabbed the guard with both hands, lifted him overhead, and ripped him apart at the waist. Blood rained down on him, black and viscous. He dropped the revenant's lower half on the floor, and flung the torso full-out across the cafeteria.

Then all Hades broke loose. Fights erupted throughout the cafeteria as nonhumans lashed out at anyone in their vicinity. The alarm sounded. The remaining guards jumped into action. But with their stun batons rendered useless, they were quickly overrun.

Bodies sailed overhead, swatted into the air by minotaurs, giants, and cyclopses. Felix and I took refuge under our table. The floor trembled beneath us, and even with my makeshift earplugs, I could still hear the sounds of battle: screams and grunts, the crack of bone, the squelch of flesh being ripped.

Felix beamed like a kid tearing open a birthday present.

The cafeteria doors boomed open, admitting a flood of reinforcements in padded armor. Most of the guards carried assault rifles or shotguns. The rest wielded pistols and riot shields. The siren slithered among them, their greatest weapon.

The guards with shields formed phalanxes in front of the exits, while shotgunners and riflemen fired nonlethal electric rounds into the crowd. At first, the lack of lethal weapons surprised me, until I saw a guard go down from an electric round. I guessed there were enough fights here that they wanted to avoid killing all their guards with friendly fire. The rounds had no visible effect on the nonhumans. But several human prisoners stiffened and fell, their bodies mercilessly trampled.

The siren took position at the front of the cafeteria. She removed her mask and released an earsplitting shriek. Every human—save me and Felix—collapsed, their hands pressed over their ears. Their screams of pain were rendered mute by her cry.

A terrible pressure built in my head. I gritted my teeth. The earplugs succeeded in blocking out some of the noise. Not much. But enough to prevent me from passing out.

A giant charged toward the head of the room, bowling over anything in his path. He leaped at the siren. She tried to move out of the way. But her tentacles were suited to water, not land. Too slow to escape, she braced herself.

The giant smashed into her. His momentum sent them both crashing through the buffet and into the kitchen.

The shrieking stopped.

The pain in my head diminished within seconds, but my ears rang. I shook my head, trying to clear it. Felix nudged me with his elbow and gestured for me to follow him.

We scrambled from beneath the table and made for the nearest exit, shoving through the masses and steering clear of the larger nonhuman inmates. Felix attacked a guard whose back was turned. He disarmed the revenant and knocked him out with the butt of his own rifle. In such close quarters, he used the gun as a melee weapon, bludgeoning anyone who tried to engage us.

Straight ahead, the guards' phalanx had broken. Felix and I rushed through the door and into the hallway. The fight had spilled beyond the cafeteria, spreading cancerously through the cellblock's warren of halls and corridors.

We pressed forward and down a long stairwell. It ended at a metal door that read: "Maintenance. Authorized Personnel Only." Felix knocked on the door. Two slow knocks, three fast, and one more slow.

Marcelo opened the door, holding a rifle. "I thought you'd never get here."

"Better late than dead," Felix said.

Marcelo let us inside and locked the door. We stood in one of the prison's boiler rooms. It looked as though it had started life as a cave, enormous, with walls of rough, jagged stone and standing puddles of water. Halogen lights flickered in the dimness, while catwalks crisscrossed overhead, casting deep shadows across heat exchangers, vats, and pumping units. The damp heat clung to my skin, breathtaking.

Lance greeted us with a smile. Like Marcelo, he had a rifle. Two guards lay unmoving at his feet. A third hung over the edge of a catwalk, blood leaking from a nasty gash in his head.

Felix and I removed our earplugs.

Marcelo picked up a rifle lying near the two guards and tossed it to me. I checked the magazine. It was full, thirty rounds in total, all nonlethal. Good. Too many people had died already. I didn't want to add to the body count.

"Okay, gentlemen," Felix said. "Time for phase two."

"What's phase two?" I asked.

No one replied. Surprise, surprise. Using the stairs, we made our way to double doors at the end of the highest catwalk. An alarm wailed on the other side. Marcelo took out a ring of keys, which he likely had confiscated from one of the guards. He picked out one and slid it into the lock.

The doors opened into a large storage room. Tools and various mechanical components filled the shelves, neatly arranged.

Marcelo took point as we exited the room and entered an empty hallway. A single camera was mounted on the ceiling. He fried it with an electric round. He seemed to have expected it. They all did. Had they gotten their hands on the prison's schematics? And if so, how?

Marcelo led us to a restroom near the end of the hall. Felix watched the door while the rest of us checked the stalls for potential threats.

"Clear," Marcelo said.

Lance entered one of the stalls and stepped onto the toilet seat. He removed a tube of toothpaste from his pocket. Only it wasn't toothpaste. He unscrewed the top and squeezed a large, white glob onto the ceiling.

"You might want to step back," he told me.

I took his advice.

Marco fired a round at the paste. It exploded on impact. We covered our faces against flying debris. The dust settled to unveil a hole in the ceiling.

"Homemade C4," I commented.

"My own special recipe," Lance said.

"Don't you mean *my* special recipe?" Felix said from the door.

"Of course." Lance looked at me and mouthed the word *no*.

I grinned in spite of myself. Marcelo slipped his rifle onto his back—our weapons had nylon slings—and climbed through the hole. Lance went next.

"Your turn," Felix said to me. "I'll be right behind you."

The hole led to the prison's ventilation system. The darkness was absolute, and the tight quarters forced us to crawl on all fours as Marcelo navigated the maze of metal shafts. I imagined a hunk of cheese waiting for us at the end.

We eventually reached a ventilation grille. Bars of white light shone through the gaps. Marcelo removed it with a shank that doubled as a screwdriver and went through the opening. The rest of us followed, stepping out onto the floor of a hallway.

The hall stretched before us, made of white stone and polished to a mirror finish. I estimated the ceiling to be around fifty feet high.

There was a vault door at the end of the hall, which was so huge a giraffe could have passed through without bumping its head. A camera sat above it. Marcelo disabled it as he had the other one.

Beside the door was a security panel. Marcelo pried off the cover with his shank and manipulated the wire and circuits underneath. The door made a clunking sound as it inched outward.

When it had opened just a crack, Lance pulled a juice bottle filled with white liquid out of his pocket. He gave it a few shakes and tossed it into the room beyond.

There was a loud pop, followed by a long hiss like steam from a teakettle. An alarm sounded, but no one seemed surprised. Once the door had opened a quarter of the way, we slipped through and into another enormous hallway.

Two heavily armed guards lay incapacitated beneath a

blanket of thinning white mist. The air smelled of harsh chemicals. The bottle of liquid had been a gas grenade, likely crafted from various cleaning solutions and other inconspicuous items.

Door hacking, potions, and now homemade grenades. These guys didn't mess around.

Another vault door lay ahead, identical to the first. But this time, Marcelo didn't bother destroying the camera mounted above it. There was no point. It had already seen the guards being taken out. Soon, we'd be swimming in revenants. We picked up the pace.

The security panel beside this door was more advanced than the previous one, containing a numeric keypad, a thumbprint scanner, and a built-in microphone—presumably for voice recognition. I found the increased security unsettling. Achilles had gone through a lot of trouble to keep this area secure. But why? Everyone seemed to know except me.

"Hey, guys," I said. "I don't mean to nag, but will someone please tell me what's going on?"

"Remember that distraction we talked about?" Felix said.

"Yeah."

"It's a two-parter." Felix picked up one of the guard's assault rifles and gave it to me. He claimed the other for himself.

I examined the weapon. It appeared to be a modified version of the gun I already carried. It weighed more and featured a red dot reflex sight. The magazine contained live ammunition.

Osmium rounds.

My unease evolved into fear. The Gods had only two weaknesses that I knew of. The Claw of Erebus and osmium.

Plato, what have you gotten yourself into?

Felix patted down the guards and confiscated two magazines. He gave one to me and kept the other.

At the security panel, Lance took something out of his pocket—a clump of what looked like red gelatin, likely pilfered from the cafeteria, which had been molded into the shape of human thumb. He pressed it against the thumbprint scanner. The machine beeped.

I had an idea about whose thumb the gelatin had been modeled after. "How'd you get the warden's prints?"

"One of the janitors who cleans Achilles's office," Lance moved away from the panel, allowing Marcelo to take his place. "He pulled the print off a doorknob."

"I can't imagine he did it out of the goodness of his heart."

"I arranged for him to have a conjugal visit with my sister. I had to pull a few strings, have some documents forged, on account of her being a little underage. But it all worked out in the end."

"A bit of a dick move, don't you think?"

"She doesn't mind."

Disgusted, I checked out of the conversation.

Marcelo entered a combination on the keypad. The panel beeped again.

"Done," he said.

Felix stepped forward. He cleared his throat and pressed a button on the panel.

"Open this door before I skin you alive," he said in the microphone, perfectly mimicking Achilles's voice.

The panel beeped for the third and final time. The locks released in a procession of cold, metallic snaps, and the door grinded open.

"Neat trick," I said to Felix as we went through.

"Ain't it, though?"

A brightly lit corridor extended to a huge pair of elevator doors. There was no camera mounted above them, but an automated turret gun. Small red squares covered the white walls, shining like glass. Motion sensors?

The shredded remains of two revenants twitched on the floor, riddled by hundreds of bullet holes. Black blood seeped in stark contrast to the white surroundings.

Felix attempted to move forward.

I caught his arm. "Call it a hunch, but I don't think going in there would be in your best interest."

Felix grinned at me, like a parent whose child had just said something silly. "Relax, Plato Jones. You do know the definition of relax, right? I think we've talked about it before. We really gotta work on improving that memory of yours."

"No need to soil yourself, Jones," Marcelo said. "I disabled the laser grid. After I commandeered that gun and well . . ."

He gestured at the guards.

Felix pulled free of my grip and stepped into the hallway. He took several paces, stopped, and turned around. "See? Nothing to worry about."

If this were a movie, this would have been the point where the gun suddenly activated and ripped Felix to pieces. But nothing happened. That still didn't stop me from cringing as I entered the corridor. As we moved on, the vault door closed behind us. I could no longer hear the alarm. This hall must have been soundproof.

"How did you do it?" I asked Marcelo.

"Do what?"

"Disable the security measures."

Marcelo sneered and didn't answer.

Lance spoke in his stead. "He sneaked into one of the security offices through the air ducts, took out the guard on watch, and hacked into the automated defense system."

Marcelo frowned at Lance. "Thank you, Captain Exposition."

"Anytime."

"I would've done more," Marcelo said. "Shut down some of those damn cameras. But time wasn't exactly on my side."

"Don't be so hard on yourself," Felix said. "No one's perfect. Except for me, that is."

"Riiiight," I said.

Marcelo and Lance searched the guards—what was left of them—for anything useful. The turret gun destroyed the revenants' weapons and radios. But the keycards they carried had survived.

"Nice," Marcelo said. "Saves me the trouble of having to hack the door."

There were two card readers on either side of the elevator. Marcelo and Lance swiped their keycards at the same time. A bell chimed and the doors slid apart.

Going through, I discovered that this was no normal elevator, but a funicular—an elevator on steroids configured to move along an incline. Twice as big as my condo, the cabin featured seven rows of stadium-style seating and a common area with couches and a full-service bar. Steven Tyler was rumored to have once lived in an elevator. If it was anything like this one, I could see why.

There was another pair of doors at the head of the cabin, bordered by long windows. Through the glass, a dimly lit tunnel sloped downward into darkness.

The control panel had only two buttons. Up and down. Marcelo pressed the down button. As the doors closed, I had a flashback of Ares and me venturing down into Chrysus's wine cellar. Once again, I was headed into the dragon's den.

I guessed that made Felix my new Wiglaf.

17

The funicular descended faster than Garfield the Cat scarfing down a pan of lasagna. Marcelo, Lance, and I remained standing. Felix lazed in one the chairs, his feet propped on the seat in front of him.

Felix must have sensed my unease. "You look scared."

"*Moi*?" I said. "You must be mistaken."

"Then why are you trembling?"

"Excitement. Isn't it obvious?"

Felix chuckled. "You're not a very good liar, my friend."

Better than you think.

I peered through one of the windows. Beacons of light marked the end of the shaft, growing larger and brighter.

"We're almost at the bottom," I said.

Felix stood up, and we all checked our weapons.

"Pucker those assholes, ladies," he said. "When those doors open, we're going to be face to face with some heavily armed, highly trained deadheads. Chances are they know we're coming, so I want you all to come out swinging—or shooting, whichever you prefer. I'd suggest shooting."

We paired up and crouched on either side of the door, planning to use the walls beneath the windows as cover. Felix and I took the right. Marcelo and Lance handled the left.

The games were about to begin.

The funicular stopped. Light shone pale white through the windows. The bell chimed, and the doors slip open. A voice echoed in the room beyond, angrily pitched.

"We know you're in there. Drop your weapons, and come out with your hands up."

Felix craned his neck to peek through the window and returned to cover.

"How many?" I asked.

"Just five," Felix said. "All carrying assault rifles."

I asked, my brows raised, "*Just* five?"

"Calm down, Plato Jones. They may have the numbers, but we have the talent."

"We're doomed." I sighed.

The voice called out again. "This is your last warning, Give yourselves up or we will open fire."

"I have a better idea," Felix shouted. "Why don't you clowns give up instead, spare yourselves some pain and suffering."

His suggestion was met with a hail of gunfire that peppered the funicular's metal exterior. The windows shattered. We covered our heads against the shower of broken glass as bullets whizzed into the cabin. Chairs in the seating area burst into clouds of white stuffing.

When the barrage ended, we returned fire. Marcelo, Lance, and I raised our rifles overhead, shooting blindly though the broken windows. But Felix went full-on Rambo. He popped in and out of cover, firing three-round bursts, then retreating when the guards shot back. Of the four of us, only he and I used live ammunition.

The shootout lasted only a minute but felt much longer. It might as well have been. With every passing second, our chance of escape got cut in half. This had to end.

Steeling my nerves, I blind-fired until my gun clicked empty. I realized revenants were essentially walking corpses, but they still looked human. I tried not to think about that part.

I'd just replaced the magazine when a grenade sailed through the window. It bounced off one of the mangled chairs, rolled across the floor, and stopped at my feet. My breath caught.

Oh crap!

I snatched the grenade and tossed it back through the window—and not a moment too soon. A resounding bang issued from outside the funicular. The enemies stopped firing.

Felix peeked through the window and beamed. "Good job, Plato Jones."

We left the funicular one at a time. The space we entered was the biggest I'd seen so far—almost the size of a football stadium, with a domed ceiling and large white tiles covering the walls and floor. The room was empty except for a single control panel near its center.

And the guards we took out . . . I took out.

The grenade hadn't even left a dent in the floor. But the revenants had been reduced to chunks of dark, quivering flesh. Black blood spread across the white tiles. The scene resembled some maniac's art project.

Looking at it soured my stomach. Fighting zombies felt no different from fighting someone with a pulse, and inspired just as much guilt.

Felix clapped me on the shoulder. "That's a quintuple-kill. You get bonus points for that, my friend."

I looked away from the carnage. "What is this place?"

"A containment chamber."

"Containing what?"

"I'll show you," Felix said.

Marcelo got on the console while the rest of us kept an eye on the funicular—in case someone summoned it. On the edge of my vision, I glimpsed one of the guards beginning to stir. I turned toward him. His body had been ripped in half, and his right hand was missing. His left held something. A radio or a remote control. Or a detonator.

"Hey!" I rushed over and wrestled the device out of the guard's hand.

"You're too late," he wheezed, blood pouring from his mouth.

I checked the device. Gray and the size of a standard flip-phone, it had two black buttons. A small green light flickered on top of it.

Felix and Lance jogged over to me. Marcelo remained at the console.

"Problem?" Felix asked.

"I think so." I tossed him the remote control. "He did something. I don't know what. I tried to stop him but . . ."

Felix briefly examined the remote then passed it to Lance. "Do something with this."

Lance adjusted his glasses. "I don't even know what it is."

The wall panels on either side of the chamber began to shift.

"What's going on?" Marcelo had stopped working, his fingers poised above the keyboard.

"Never you mind," Felix said. "Get back to work. Chop, chop!"

Marcelo returned his attention to the console. The wall panels continued to move, revealing two compartments—slightly smaller than the vault doors and filled with darkness too deep to penetrate.

The guard laughed weakly. "You're all dead."

Felix stomped on the revenant's head, crushing it in a burst of blood, bone, and brain matter. "And so are you . . . again. You know, I always wondered how that works. If you're already dead, can you still be killed? A gold star for anyone who can give me the answer."

"Do you ever shut up?" I asked.

"Not while I'm awake."

I almost threw my hands up in frustration. "Lance, please give me some good news."

"I wish I could," Lance said, staring at the remote control. Sweat gleamed on his forehead and upper lip. "But I'm kinda stumped here."

"Then get un-stumped, or no dessert after dinner," Felix said. "Marcelo. Progress report."

"I'm close," Marcelo replied, typing more furiously than ever.

Thunderous footsteps grabbed our attention. We jerked our heads to the right as a Cerberus the size of a small elephant emerged from the compartment. Packed with muscle, it had light-brown fur with black spots. Its three heads were those of hyenas. Drool poured from its mouths.

Fear plunged like a cold dagger into my stomach. Lance dropped the remote control and raised his gun, along with me. Marcelo glanced at the beast, cursed, and quickly got back to work. Felix, however, appeared perfectly calm, even as a second Cerberus lumbered from the adjacent compartment.

"How cute," Felix said as the creatures slowly converged on us. "I wish I had Milk Bones. Six of them."

"I'm sure they won't mind using your bones as a substitute," I said.

Next to me, Lance appeared to be hyperventilating. His glasses had fogged up, and the rifle trembled in his hands. He began muttering incoherently.

"Lance," Felix said, his tone reproachful. "You're going to piss them off."

"They already look plenty pissed off to me," I said. "How's it coming, Marcelo?"

"Almost there. And . . . got it!" Marcelo hit one last button on the console.

The walls of the chamber started flashing red, and a caution alarm sounded.

Lance opened fire on the Cerberus to our right. The sound and change in lighting must've startled it.

The Cerberus charged through the nonlethal barrage, seemingly unaffected. Felix and I dove in opposite directions as the creature descended on Lance.

Three sets of snarling jaws tore him apart. He had no time to scream. His right hand, severed at the wrist, dropped from one of the creature's mouths.

The rest of us broke for the funicular. The other Cerberus gave chase. We'd almost reached the cabin when Marcelo's body suddenly went rigid. He fell flat on his face, one of Lance's electric rounds sticking from his calf. I paused, planning to help him. But Felix seized my arm and forced me to keep running.

I looked over my shoulder and saw Marcelo pinned beneath one of the Cerberus's forepaws. Completely paralyzed, he could nothing as the beast devoured him whole.

When we reached the funicular, I rushed to the back of the cabin and reached for the up button.

Felix caught my wrist. "Not yet. We still need to do what we came here to do."

I snatched my arm free. "What? To get ourselves killed and eaten? If that's the plan, then I'd say mission accomplished!"

"Let me handle this." Felix stepped out of the funicular.

The Cerberuses turned toward him, their muzzles covered in blood. Rather than running, Felix walked forward to meet them.

"What are you doing?" I shouted. "Get back here!"

Felix paid me no attention. He cast his gun aside and outstretched his arms.

"You wanna challenge the alpha? Bring it! Let's see if we can fit six heads up two asses!"

His bravado spurred the Cerberuses to run, chewing up the distance between them. Minutes ago, I'd almost envied Felix's insanity. It lent him unnatural courage. Not anymore. This wasn't bravery. It was suicide.

I guessed I'd have to save this moron from himself. But before I could make a move, the Cerberuses came to an unexpected halt. Their clawed feet skidded against the floor.

"Yeah, that's right," Felix said, nodding.

The Cerberuses hunkered down, heads low, fangs bared, tails between their legs. Growls rumbled from all six mouths, but neither creature pounced.

"I'm the alpha, the pack leader," Felix lowered his arms. "You belong to me. Understand? Now, sit."

The Cerberuses refused to submit any further.

"Sit!" Felix snapped.

The Cerberuses started. The growling stopped, and both creatures lowered onto their haunches. The bloodlust in their eyes had died. Their tongues lolled to the sides.

I blinked hard, opened my eyes, and blinked again. Over the course of my professional career, I'd seen crazy things—things that would've made ghost boy Danny Phantom go a shade paler. There weren't many situations that truly surprised me. But this one didn't just surprise me. It knocked my socks off.

"Good boys." Felix picked up his rifle and turned to me, leaving his back exposed. "Okay, Little Red Riding Hood. You can come out now."

It took a second for his words to register. Cautiously, I exited the cabin. The Cerberuses growled at me.

Felix glanced back at them. "Hush."

The creatures complied.

"How?" I asked, in complete awe.

"I watch *The Dog Whisperer,*" Felix said.

"Bull."

"You don't believe me?"

"No?"

"Why not?"

"For starters, hyenas aren't dogs," I said. "Secondly, I've never seen anyone control a Cerberus that wasn't theirs. Tell the truth. How did you do that?"

"Ancient aliens."

"Never mind. Just do what you came here to do, so we can get out of here."

Felix and I approached the control panel, the two Cerberuses trotting behind us, panting happily. The next thing you knew, they'd be rolling over for belly scratches.

The alarm stopped after we reached the console. But the walls continued flashing. At some point, the floor tiles in front of the console had spread apart to unveil a circular pit.

I peered over the edge and saw nothing but bottomless dark. As I continued to watch, I caught sight of something ascending from the blackness. I stepped back as a huge, cylindrical glass tank rose from the pit. Built into the base was a console with thick black tubes attached between it and the tank.

The walls stopped flashing.

Suspended in clear liquid was an enormous humanoid. Roughly twenty-five feet tall, it was heavily muscled with black skin that had the appearance of stone. Intricate symbols—reminiscent of crop circles—covered the creature's entire body, carved into its flesh. Humanlike teeth the color of tarnished nickel filled a wide, lipless mouth. It had no eyes, no nose, no ears, no body hair, no genitals.

It appeared to be in a state of suspended animation, presumably unaware of our presence. But that did nothing to stem the chill spreading through my body. Behind me, the Cerberuses growled low and deep. Glad I wasn't the only one shitting bricks.

"What *is* it?" I asked.

Felix rested his hand on my shoulder.

"Plato Jones," he said. "Meet Cronus, King of the Titans."

18

CRONUS. *THE* CRONUS. KING OF THE TITANS. FATHER OF ZEUS, Poseidon, Hades, and Hera. He was here, right in front of my eyes. Yet my mind rebelled against the notion.

Before the rise of Olympus, the Titans—beings of immense power—ruled over mankind with Cronus as their leader. His strength and ferocity in battle had become the stuff of legend, as had his cruelty toward his subjects.

According to legend, Gaia—Cronus's mother and the earth Titan—told Cronus that his sons would overthrow him. To remedy this problem, the king decided that eating his children would be the best course of action.

I wish I were making this up.

Zeus had been the only sibling not to take a tour of his dad's intestinal tract. Apparently, Cronus's wife, Rhea, didn't approve of her husband's new diet—so when it was Zeus's turn to be devoured, his mom replaced her bouncing baby boy with a rock . . . and the trick worked.

Did I mention that Cronus was supposedly highly intelligent? I guess you can't believe everything you hear in stories.

He was also depicted as having a humanlike appearance. It seemed that a few ancient scholars played fast and loose with the facts—though he and Hera did share a few similarities, particularly in the nose area.

To make a long story short, Zeus grew up, rebelled against Cronus, and overthrew him. During the process, he managed to free his siblings from their father's stomach, and the four of them forged a new empire.

I'd heard that after getting their collective asses kicked, Cronus and the other Titans—the ones that didn't go into hiding—had been banished to the pits of Tartarus. I'd never have expected to find him within the prison walls.

"Your mouth is hanging open," Felix said to me.

I tried to respond but couldn't find my voice.

Felix pressed a series of buttons on the tank's control panel. The Cerberuses growled louder, and I regained my wits.

"Don't tell me you plan on letting him out," I said.

"Okay, I won't," Felix said. "*You're* going to let him out."

I recoiled. "What?"

"You've done a lot for me since we met. It's only right that you do the honors." Felix stepped away from the controls.

The message on the computer screen read: "RELEASE? YES or NO."

"Go ahead," Felix said. "You've earned it."

"No thanks."

"I insist."

I shook my head. "Nah."

"Come on."

"No."

"If you don't, you're out of the club. And if you're out of the club, you're an enemy. And if you're an enemy, I'll have to kill you. But to be fair, I'll let you decide how you die. I can shoot you in the head, or I can let Fido and Rover use you as a chew toy. Then I'll let handsome here out myself."

Though Felix wore a smile, the laughter had gone from his eyes, supplanted by something dark and threatening. I could tell he was serious. At that point, I had two choices. I could either die by his hand—thus failing the mission—or I could free Cronus. My chance of survival would be as slim as Aphrodite's waistline, but I'd have one.

Working for the Gods—the very definition of a divine comedy.

"You do know there's a good chance he's going to attack us, right?" I asked.

"Relax, Plato Jones," Felix said. "I have everything under control. Now take your balls out of your mommy's purse, and do what I tell you."

I cursed him in my head and looked down at the control panel. The NO button seemed to stare me in the face, beckoning me not to do the dumbest thing I'd ever done in my life—the dumbest thing anyone had ever done. Why couldn't the Gods ever handle their own problems? Laziness wasn't completely to blame. Stupidity played an equal role.

"Do it," Felix said.

I gritted my teeth.

"Press the button!" Felix commanded.

"Damn it!" I shouted and pushed YES.

Jets of steam hissed from vents on the bottom of the tank, and the liquid began to rapidly drain.

What have I done?

Felix patted me on the shoulder. "That'll do."

Behind me, the Cerberuses laughed frantically like the hyenas they resembled. As the last of the liquid drained away, the jets of steam weakened and died. Cronus revived at once. He went down to one knee and remained stationary for some time. When he raised his head, he looked directly at me. Though he had no eyes, I could still feel his gaze upon me.

Felix and I kept our guns pointed down as Cronus stood up.

"Hey, big fella. My name is Felix, and this is my friend Plato."

Cronus said nothing. He *stared* at me. Blindly. My heart hammered against the inside of my ribcage. I fought the compulsion to look away. Rule number one when encountering potentially dangerous mythological beings: Show no fear. It's like candy to them.

"Say something," Felix whispered to me.

"Hi," I said. "We come in peace."

Cronus tilted his head slightly to the side, similar to a confused animal.

"Not much of a talker, is he?" Felix said. "Must be shy."

"Or maybe he just can't hear us. I don't see any ears, do you?"

"Hmm, I hadn't noticed that."

"I guess that goes to show," I said. "You have to make sure a person is trustworthy before lending them your ears."

The bad joke, I realized, was a coping mechanism to deal with the fear. It didn't work.

"We're here to bust you out," Felix said to Cronus. "You can return the favor by tearing this shithole apart, brick by brick. How does that sound? A fair deal if you ask me. Don't you agree, Plato Jones?"

"Sure."

Cronus continued to stare at me. Sweat rolled down my face, trickling into my eyes. I blinked it away. That moment, the Titan clenched his teeth angrily, and the markings on his body began to pulse with neon-blue energy.

"I think we made him mad," I said.

The Cerberuses' laughter grew louder and more manic, but the creatures didn't flee.

"Strategic retreat?" Felix said.

"I think that would be best."

Before we could flee, Cronus opened his mouth and released a roar unlike any I'd ever heard before—a twisted union of mechanical and organic noises, deafeningly loud. The force it produced shattered the tank, unleashing a sandstorm of glass fragments.

The backlash sent us—and the Cerberuses—flying. We landed near the funicular. Felix and I struggled to rise, laced with scratches. Bits of glass glittered on our clothes and in our hair. Nearby, the Cerberuses scrambled to their feet. They whirled in Cronus's direction and took defensive stances. The floor shuddered as the Titan stalked toward us.

Felix and I had both managed to hang onto our rifles. We opened fire on Cronus. He slowed down and covered his face as the osmium rounds punched into his flesh. Blood spattered across the floor, bright blue. We moved backward, toward the funicular, pumping round after round into the Titan. We ran out of ammo just as we reached the cabin.

Cronus recovered instantaneously and charged.

"Sic him, boys!" Felix shouted to the Cerberuses.

The creatures obeyed without hesitation. Either they didn't want to anger their new pack leader, or they were just doing what they'd been bred to do: prevent the King of the Titans from escaping—an impossible task. I couldn't help but feel sorry for them.

I hit the up button. Felix didn't stop me this time. As the doors closed, I caught a glimpse of Cronus and the Cerberuses rolling across the floor, locked in combat. The funicular started to move.

I fell into a chair that was still mostly intact. My face, arms, and neck stung as sweat seeped into my cuts. Felix paced back and forth at the front of the cabin, grinning profusely.

"Woo!" he said. "Now that was exciting!"

"So, this is why you let yourself get arrested."

"Looks like the secret's finally out."

"Why?" I said. "Why do something that stupid?"

"Every army needs a secret weapon. Who better to fill that role than the one person . . . thing . . . monster . . . whatever . . . that hates the Gods more than anyone else?"

"Makes sense. But did you ever say to yourself, 'Hey, there

are plenty of Titans I could recruit for my war—ones that aren't locked up in the worst prison in existence? Maybe I should track them down instead?'"

"I did. But convincing them to join the cause is another matter. If anyone can make them fall in line, it's Cronus."

"Nice plan. Too bad no one told him about it."

"He'll come around. He's just a little grouchy right now. We did wake him from his nap, after all. Sooner or later, he'll remember what we did for him and return the favor."

"We shot him multiple times and sicced two Cerberuses on him."

"Details, details."

"You are truly amazing, Felix."

"Why thank you."

Amazingly idiotic.

As the funicular slowed to a stop, I switched out the empty assault rifle with the nonlethal tranquilizer gun, strapping the former across my back. No guards awaited us in the corridor, besides the ones that had been taken down by the turret gun.

We moved into the next hall. The alarm still wailed, and the chemical smell of Lance's gas grenade lingered in the air. The guards had yet to regain consciousness. There was no else around.

I allowed myself a moment of relief, only to have it snatched away as Achilles appeared at the end of the hall.

19

We pointed our guns.

Achilles gave a half-smile. Blood covered nearly every inch of his white suit. Red blood. Not black. In his hands, he carried an LMG—light machine gun. A gold wedding band gleamed on his ring finger. Five heavies with assault rifles assembled behind him. The one I believed to be his cousin Ajax stood among them, towering over his leader by a head.

"Gentlemen, gentlemen," Achilles said. "If you wanted a complete tour of the facility, you should have just asked."

No doubt Achilles had seen us enter the funicular via the security feed and came to confront us. But was he also aware that Cronus had been set free? Judging by the heat he and his men were packing, it was a strong possibility.

The warden's casual demeanor might have suggested otherwise, had his skill on the battlefield not been packaged with an ego bigger than the Trojan Horse. But if he believed himself to be a match for Cronus, Felix may not have been the craziest person in Tartarus.

"Any ideas, fearless leader?" I asked.

"Just one," Felix said.

"Let me guess. We fight our way out."

"How'd you know?"

"I'm psychic." I gave a barely audible sigh. "At least we'll go out in a blaze of glory."

"Trespassing in this part of the facility carries an automatic death sentence," Achilles said. "Surrender and I guarantee your end will be quick and relatively painless. Or you can open fire . . ."

"Is there a third option?" I asked.

"Last chance," Achilles said.

"Buzz off, pretty boy," Felix said. "We own this prison now."

Achilles tilted his chin imperiously.

"What are you doing?" I hissed at Felix.

"Evening the odds."

"Shoot their kneecaps." Achilles said.

His men took aim. My muscles tautened. My trigger finger twitched.

"Why don't you take us on yourself, pretty boy?" Felix asked. "Traded in your sword and shield for a pink tutu and pointe shoes?"

Achilles raised his hand, halting his men.

"Are you sure this is wise?" I whispered. "Wait a minute, what am I saying? Of course, you're not. Being wise would make too much sense."

"You got a better idea?"

I thought about it. "I guess not."

"Then chill out and let me work my magic." Felix gave me that damn wink again.

Stupid move in three . . . two . . . one . . .

"How is that heel of yours, by the way?" Felix said to Achilles.

The warden chuckled. He addressed his subordinates. "At ease, men. I'll handle these worms personally."

"But sir . . ." said the biggest of them.

"It's fine, Ajax. This won't take long."

Achilles handed his gun and wedding band to Ajax. I wondered whom he was married to. Briseis, the princess of Lyrnessus, seemed the most likely suspect. She'd been his main squeeze during the Trojan War.

"Tartarus is my home, gentlemen," Achilles said, cracking his knuckles. "I strive to be a gracious host. But even I have my limits. Now I'm going to show you what happens when you piss on hospitality."

As Achilles walked toward us, I suddenly grasped Felix's plan. He was stalling. Defeating the warden wasn't our goal—as if we could. We just needed to survive until Cronos showed up. With any luck, the Titan would go after him instead of us, giving us a chance to slip away. Not an ideal plan, but we didn't have the luxury of being picky.

Felix put his gun on the floor. I did the same, against my better judgment

"Wanna go first?" Felix asked.

"No," I said. "Do you?"

"No."

"We could always double-team him," I suggested.

"That wouldn't be very fair."

"Forget fairness. We're talking about the greatest warrior of the ancient world. And when did you develop a sense of honor?"

"A few seconds ago."

I felt the urge to slap my forehead. "Fine. But I'm not going first."

"Neither am I."

"Well, we're going to have to figure out something, fast."

"Rock, paper, scissors?"

I shrugged. "Why not?"

Felix and I spoke in unison. "One, two, three, shoot!"

I chose rock. Felix went with paper. He grinned.

Great. I trudged forward, as if heading toward the guillotine. Achilles and I met in the middle of the hallway. He and I were almost the same height. His glowing eyes seemed to look right through me. A nervous lump formed in my throat.

Felix shouted encouragement from the sidelines. "Don't let him intimidate you. Just remember—you're a lion. A lion!"

"Is it too late to surrender?" I asked Achilles.

He grinned. I took it as a yes.

"Okay then." I sucker punched Achilles with a left jab, followed up with a right cross, and ended with a left hook. The blows had no visible effect.

"Not bad," Achilles said.

I threw a left kick at his shin. Achilles raised his leg, avoiding it. I didn't give him an opportunity to counterattack. I launched a flurry of punches, kicks, and elbows. He blocked them all. Undaunted, I threw a left cross. He caught my fist in his hand and squeezed. I gasped, paralyzed with pain.

"You have good technique," Achilles said. "But not good enough, I'm afraid."

He struck me in the chest with a palm strike I didn't see coming. The blow knocked the wind out of me and sent me reeling backward. I lost my balance and fell at Felix's feet.

He looked down at me, holding out his hand. "Tag me, tag me!"

I slapped it away, gasping and coughing.

Felix rushed at Achilles. Smacks and grunts rose seconds later.

I pulled myself off the floor and saw Felix flying toward me. I had no time to react. He crashed into me and we both went down. Achilles and his men laughed.

Felix and I slowly got up. We planted our hands on our knees, sweating and panting.

"I think we need to come up with a new strategy," I wheezed.

"Down for a little two-on-one?" Felix asked.

"What happened to your code of honor?"

"He knocked it out of me."

"Had enough, gentlemen?" Achilles said.

We rushed him without answering.

"Cowards!" Ajax shouted.

But neither he nor the other guards stepped in. They didn't need to. We hurled punches and kicks at Achilles in rapid succession, aiming for organs and pressure points. Felix's speed and technique rivaled my own, and like me, his fighting style incorporated moves from various forms of martial arts. Had we faced a normal opponent—or even a group of them—the fight would have already been over. But the warden was as far away from normal as you could get.

He blocked, dodged, and countered our attacks with ease. Any gap in his defense closed before it could be exploited. Rarely did he strike back—he was toying with us. But when he did, his blows always landed.

My head swam, and bursts of pain ricocheted through my body with every hit I received. I struggled to breathe. Fatigue sizzled in my limbs, and my movements became increasingly slow. Felix fared no better. We couldn't keep this up for much longer. Delirium made me actually look forward to the moment when Cronus would burst into the room like the Kool-Aid Man.

Felix threw a haymaker, seemingly near the end of his strength. Achilles trapped his arm in the crook of his elbow and delivered a hammer strike that sent his adversary to the floor. In what could only have been an act of desperation, Felix wrapped his arms around the warden's ankles.

Achilles wobbled, caught off balance and by surprise. I saw my opening and surged forward with a lunging kick to the chest. The attack hit its mark with a resounding thump. The warden sailed backward and landed hard on his back.

His men seemed shocked. But no one helped him up. To

do so would imply that he was incapable of finishing the fight. It was part of the warrior's code. But I wasn't a warrior. Just an average Joe. I offered Felix my hand and hauled him to his feet.

"Good job, Plato Jones," he said.

We high-fived. It seemed like the thing to do. But our celebration was short-lived.

Achilles sprang to his feet and went on the offensive, bouncing back and forth between us as he unleashed a maelstrom of crushing attacks. His speed made evasion impossible—and blocking only served to leave other parts of my body exposed. Felix was the first to fall, tagged by a short hook. A kick to the stomach sent him skidding along the floor. Then it was my turn.

Achilles caught me with a headbutt. Pain exploded in my face. The next thing I knew, the warden had hoisted me overhead. With a grunt, he tossed me across the hall. I hit the floor rolling.

Felix, having recovered from his stint as a hockey puck, helped me up. I shook my head, trying to orient myself. Everything hurt. I was surprised my pain receptors hadn't gone on strike.

"That could have gone better," I panted.

"We're not out of this yet."

"Another strategy, huh? This'll be Plan C, right?"

"I think so," Felix said. "What's plan C?"

"You tell me. You're the mastermind behind this fubar operation."

"I'm just pulling your leg, Plato Jones. I always have a plan. How do think we got this far?"

"I'd go with dumb luck. Now, this plan of yours? Is it something that might actually work?"

"Watch and be amazed."

"I have to commend you two," Achilles said. "No one has

been able to land a hit on me in centuries. I hope you enjoyed it."

"School's not over yet," Felix said "There's still show-and-tell."

I shook my head, embarrassed for both of us. But bad jokes aside, I shuddered to think what was going on in Felix's head. Would he finally reveal his true power, as he should have done from the start? Or was this plan of his just more of the topnotch buffoonery I'd come to expect? I'd put my money on choice number two.

Across from us, Achilles and his men were all smiles. At least someone was having fun.

"You've piqued my interest," Achilles said. "Show me what you can do."

"You sure?" Felix asked. "Once this ass-whooping starts, there's no turning back."

Achilles gestured for him to go ahead.

"Okay, pretty boy," Felix said. "But remember, I gave you a chance to walk away. Now, I'm gonna have to go all Wolverine on you. Stand back, Plato Jones. This is going to get nasty."

Oh boy.

Before Felix could get himself killed, a thunderous boom shook the corridor. We all looked to the back of the hall. The vault door lay on the floor, knocked off its hinges. Cronus stepped through.

20

"CRONUS," FELIX SAID. "GLAD YOU COULD JOIN THE PARTY."

The King of the Titans came barreling toward us.

"New plan," Felix said. "Run!"

That was the first good idea he'd had all day. Achilles and his men didn't try to stop us as we rushed past. Instead, they engaged Cronus head on. Ajax tossed the warden his LMG, and the whole squad opened fire. The osmium rounds would slow the Titan down, but not for long. Cronus would eventually get his hands on them and pour on the hurt.

Felix and I escaped to the main corridor. No sooner had we squeezed into the air duct than a group of guards hurried past. They moved in the direction of the vault. More action figures for Cronus to break and toss aside.

We scrambled through the ventilation system until we reached the restroom. From there, we hotfooted it back to the boiler room and returned upstairs. The fighting in the halls had not only persisted; it seemed to have gotten worse. Some of the inmates wielded guns, suggesting they'd broken into the armory. The alarm wailed, barely rising above the din of battle.

Felix took point as we fought our way to the main lobby, striking enemies with the butts of our assault rifles and stepping over the bodies of the fallen. The fighting had reached this room as well. Through gaps in the crowd, I saw that the portal was inactive. The control room appeared to be empty. The reinforced glass window bore myriad scratches and scuffs.

Felix and I made our way to it. I tried the door. Locked. Naturally.

Felix produced a keycard, seemingly out of nowhere, and swiped it through the reader. The device beeped and the door opened. We rushed inside. The door closed behind us and locked automatically.

"Where'd you get that?" I asked, referring to the keycard.

"Off the warden," Felix said. "He really shouldn't carry around something this important, particularly if he's going to be fighting in close quarters."

I grinned. "Sly dog."

I doubted that pickpocketing Achilles had been part of his original plan. He'd probably intended for Marcelo to hack the door to this room. If that was the case, our running into the warden had been a stroke of luck. Who'd have thought that getting thrashed by a living—or undead—legend would be a good thing? Not me.

Felix got on the console. A blue password screen appeared on a monitor in the center of the console. He typed something. The letters on the screen appeared as white asterisks.

"INCORRECT PASSWORD" appeared on the screen. Felix reentered the password. It was still a no-go.

"This is new," he said.

"What's wrong?"

"Password doesn't work. Achilles must've had it changed recently."

"Is there a way to override it?"

"Why, yes. Yes, there is."

"Then hurry up and do it."

"I said there's a way to override the system, Plato Jones—not that I knew how to do it."

"Unbelievable." I shook my head, sighing in exasperation. "What other options do we have?"

"If you're feeling lucky, we could try to guess the password," Felix said as a chair bounced off the reinforced window separating the control room from the main lobby. "Do you feel lucky?"

"Not especially. But we don't have a choice."

"Any guesses? Get it right within three tries, and get the grand prize. No pressure, though. But keep in mind that the whole place will go on automatic lock-down after five incorrect passwords. Again . . . no pressure."

I took a second to think. It stood to reason that Achilles had come up with the new password. This was his prison, after all. It was probably something important to him.

"Try Myrmidon," I said.

Felix keyed it in and mimicked the sound of a game show buzzer. "That's a negative, good buddy."

"How about horse?"

Felix made another buzzer sound. "Oh, I'm sorry. Horse is not the answer. Last try."

I thought hard. Achilles's wedding ring flashed in my head.

"Briseis," I said.

Felix entered the name. The password screen vanished, replaced by the portal access menu. "Congratulations. You win the grand prize: the satisfaction of a job well done."

"No trip to Hawaii?"

"Maybe next time." Felix pressed several buttons on the console.

Warning lights flashed. The portal blinked into existence a second later. The chaos resumed as inmates clambered over one another toward freedom. The guards could do nothing to stop them, crushed beneath the wave of bodies.

We left the control room. Felix smashed the card reader with the butt of his gun to make sure no one closed the portal before we escaped. Then we joined the flow of inmates, hurling ourselves into the shimmering void.

Sunlight stabbed my eyes, momentarily blinding me. Someone crashed into me from behind, knocking us both down. I felt dirt against my cheek, under my palms. Warm as a hug from mom. I wanted to cry out in joy. I'd made it.

I was back on the outside.

I stood up as my eyes adjusted to the light back on the island of Departure. Once my vision cleared, I discovered that one roadblock still barred my path to freedom—a slew of guards with automatic weapons.

Most of the inmates—humans and satyrs—who had gone through the portal had their hands up. The rest lay dead or dying, riddled with bullets.

"Drop your weapons and raise your hands!" one of the guards shouted, looking directly at me and Felix.

We complied, slowly. No sudden movements.

"I'm guessing you have a plan for this too?" I whispered to Felix.

He smiled.

Suddenly the guards' faces paled. They backed away, their eyes fixed on the portal. One of them tripped and fell—over what, I couldn't tell. Felix, the other inmates, and I turned around, lowering our arms. Cronus loomed over us, gnashing his teeth. His markings burned with blue light.

"And Cronus for the save," Felix said.

The Titan released a roar that sent inmates and guards alike running in terror. Felix and I scooped up our rifles as we fled. An alarm horn sounded, its wail interspersed by screams, shouts, and cracks of sniper fire from the watchtowers.

Felix and I ran as hard as our legs would allow. Guards spilled from the surrounding buildings and opened fire on Cronus. They completely ignored us. With the King of the Titans back on Earth, we ceased to be a concern.

Felix headed toward a warehouse. As we neared the entrance, a shadow passed over us. I glanced up and saw Cronus leaping through the air. He crashed into one of the watchtowers, bringing the whole thing down. I realized, with a sinking feeling, that the feat was just a taste of the Titan's true power. The thought of what he'd do once he reached New Olympia terrified me. It also reminded me that I had been the one to let him loose. I had to fix this—I *would* fix this.

Wooden crates filled the warehouse, stacked to the ceiling. There were no workers present. The poor stiffs had probably gone into hiding. I followed Felix up a stairwell that took us to the roof. There, we found a large transport helicopter preparing to take off—the bay door still hung open. Nearby, a pallet stacked with crates sat on a driverless a forklift. The letters TMSP—Tartarus Maximum Security Prison—were stamped in black on each crate.

I now understood why Felix chose today to execute his plan—to coincide with the prison's delivery schedule. Clever.

A single guard with an assault rifle covered the delivery crew as they made their escape. He noticed us too late and received a stun round to the thigh, courtesy of Felix.

We skipped claiming the guard's weapon and sprinted forward, just as the helicopter door began to close. With running leaps, we caught the edge of the bay door, pulled ourselves over the edge, and spilled into the cargo area. Our entrance startled three crewmembers.

Felix and I went on the attack before they regained their senses, knocking out two of them with the butts of our guns. The third, a guy who looked like he'd just graduated from high school, raised his hands in surrender.

"Hi," Felix said.

The kid trembled, his breathing shattered.

"This is the part where you take us to your leader," Felix said.

With our guns pointed at his back, the kid led us to the cockpit, where the two pilots were still prepping for takeoff.

"Uh, guys," said the kid, his voice cracking. "We got a problem."

The pilots turned in their seats. Both wore gray flight suits and white helmets with tinted visors. They started in alarm.

"Hey, flyboys," Felix said. "Mind if we join you in first class?"

One of the pilots reached under his seat for something.

"Uh-uh." Felix pressed the muzzle of his gun against the back of the kid's head. "Get up, both of you."

The pilots rose without having to be asked twice. We directed them to the entrance of the cockpit.

"Face the other way," Felix added.

The hostages did as they were told, turning away from us. Felix sat in the pilot seat.

"If one of them moves," he said to me, "you know what to do."

"Can you fly one of these things?"

"I can do a lot of things."

"Most of them illegal, it seems."

"Those are the best kind."

As we took off, I kept my gun trained on the hostages. I glanced through the cabin window. On the ground, more guards had arrived to fight Cronus. From this altitude, they looked like ants assaulting an action figure.

The Titan charged through them, then sprang skyward, propelling himself hundreds of feet into the air. He soared across the Mediterranean, growing smaller and smaller until he disappeared on the horizon.

Wonderful.

In a single day, I'd started a full-scale prison riot, freed a convicted psychopath, and unleashed one of the most destructive forces the world had ever known. Did I still qualify as one of the good guys?

21

We landed on a small, uninhabited island in the middle of the Mediterranean. I booted the crew off the helicopter while Felix disabled the vehicle's satellite tracking system. So they wouldn't starve, I instructed them to unload all the crates containing food and water. I also let them keep one cell phone to call for help—I'd removed the battery and flung it into the woods bordering the beach. Now they'd have to find it before calling in their backup, giving us more time to escape.

I then joined Felix in the cockpit. He was speaking with someone on the radio. I assumed he had finished deactivating the tracking system.

"Head to the meeting place," he said. "Bring the new recruit with you."

A man's deep voice crackled from the radio. "Roger that."

"And pick me up three Slim Jims, a Faygo Red Pop, and a pack of candy cigarettes."

"Candy cigarettes were banned years ago."

"Damn." Felix snapped his fingers. "Just get me a bag of gummy bears then. Wait, no. Gummy worms. You got all that?"

"Loud and clear."

"See you soon." Felix ended the transmission and looked at me. "I'm sorry. I didn't ask if you wanted anything. How rude of me. Can you ever forgive me?"

"Give me one of those Slim Jims and I'll consider it," I said.

"Deal."

I sat in the copilot's chair. I'd learned how to fly a helicopter while in the military. But I hadn't done it in ages. It made me glad Felix knew what he was doing.

"Who was that on the radio?" I asked.

"Danny. He's been with us for a little over two years now. Sharp kid. Really sharp. I'm sure you two will become fast friends. Don't get on his bad side though. He once bombed a bunch of hospitals just to get back at the Goddess of Childbirth. Danny's a real asset to the cause, but he's got a quick temper."

He sounds even crazier than you are. "You mentioned a new recruit. Who is it?"

"Some college boy. Wants to make a difference. Blah blah blah. You'll meet him soon enough."

We set a course for Jason's Respite. A backwater town about seventy miles away from New Olympia, it was so small and rural that it made Boreasville look like Times Square.

On the way, Felix told me about his organization, the Mortal Liberation Front, or MLF, a band of nut jobs who aspired to cleanse the world of all nonhumans, starting with the Olympians. With the Gods out of the way, the other races would roll over. But he never mentioned how they planned to achieve their goals—or the threat Cronus now posed. I doubted he and the other Titans would be too keen on a human-run government. A pretty big oversight.

Felix also detailed a number of terrorist attacks the MLF had been responsible for: temple bombings, cyberattacks on government websites, nonhuman lynching, and so on. I remembered hearing about some of them on the news. The idea of participating in similar activities didn't sit well with me, to say the least. I hoped I could shut them down before it came to that.

* * *

We reached Jason's Respite and landed in the middle of a grassy field. There were no houses in sight, no power lines, just grass, grass, and more grass—and beyond that, trees. A black Hummer with tinted windows sat parked several feet away. A man leaned against it.

He appeared to be Asian. Tall with a bodybuilder's physique, he wore a black wife-beater T-shirt, black track pants, and sneakers. His dark-brown hair was short and spikey. Tattoos covered thick, veiny arms. Seeing him reminded me of a Sherman tank.

"Danny," Felix said. "Looking good, man. You've been working on your shoulders. I can tell."

"Where are Lance and Marcelo?" he asked, ignoring Felix's banter.

"Dead. Eaten alive by Cerberuses. Very nasty."

Danny received the news with indifference. He had the look of a man well acquainted with death and violence. Thick callouses covered his knuckles.

He glanced at me but spoke to Felix. "Is this him?"

"Sure is. Plato Jones, this is Danny Zhou. Can you guess what he does for a living? Get it right on the first try and I'll give you half of my red pop." Felix switched his regard to Danny. "You did remember my red pop, didn't you?"

"It's in the car," Danny said.

"Splendid!" Felix returned his attention to me. "So, what does he do? The clock is ticking."

"Wet work," I said with certainty.

"And you are correct!" Felix looked at Danny. "I told you he was good."

Danny appeared unimpressed.

I held out my hand. "Nice to meet you."

Danny said nothing. But he did shake my hand. His handshake was strong, borderline painful. It sent a clear message. This was not a man to be taken lightly.

"We should get going," he said.

"What about the chopper?" I asked.

"A crew will come by later and junk it."

Felix pressed his face against the Hummer's backseat window, attempting to peer through the tinted glass. "Where's the new guy? You didn't kill him on the way here, did you?"

"I dropped him off at the safe house so I wouldn't have to," Danny said. "He doesn't know when to shut up—like someone else I know."

"Hey, be fair," Felix said. "You've only just met Plato Jones."

Danny offered no rejoinder. Felix grinned. I pretended to be invisible.

We loaded into the Hummer and traveled down a dirt road that wound through the forest. It emptied us onto the highway.

The safe house Danny had spoken of was our destination. It acted as a temporary home for recruits going through the initiation process. The gauntlet, as Felix called it, included a number of tests—mental and physical evaluations designed to weed out the weak. Because of my participation in the prison break, he allowed me to skip to the final test. I wouldn't find out what it was until later.

A large military tent acted as the safe house. A second black Hummer was parked outside, as well as a 1969 Cadillac convertible. The Caddy reminded me of my own ride. The beige paint and black leather interior oozed style. A car for the car enthusiast.

Inside, six cots lined the tent's sidewalls. Shelter lights ran along the ceiling, casting artificial lights on coolers, portable generators, and a collection of large, metal storage boxes.

A sinewy man with unkempt brown hair worked on his laptop. A guy to his right fiddled with a smartphone. He had slick black hair, beard stubble, and a muscular build.

A third man played solitaire, the cards arranged neatly in front of him. He was at least several years younger than anyone else here. He looked athletic, with fluffy blond hair and a baby face. His blue polo and khakis were dingy—as if he hadn't changed clothes for the past few days—but still screamed Ivy League.

This must have been the other new recruit.

"Everyone can relax," Felix said. "Your king has returned."

"Woo-hoo," muttered the man with the phone.

"Nice to see you alive and well, your highness," said the one on the laptop. "I would bow to you, but I can't. Bad back."

"You two clowns are lucky I like you," Felix said. "Otherwise, I would've sent you to the gallows a long time ago."

The kid playing solitaire seemed to be in a daze, his blue eyes wide, as if he sat in the presence of a celebrity.

"Hey . . . you," Felix said.

The kid started like a dreamer that had been jerked awake. He shot to his feet, disarranging the cards on the floor.

"H-hello, sir," he stammered. "It's good to see you again. You're looking well."

Danny sighed. The man on the laptop grinned. The other shook his head.

"Words of wisdom, Grasshopper," Felix said. "Nobody likes a suck-up."

The kid blinked. He opened his mouth, to apologize most likely, but Felix cut him off.

"Except for me, that is. I love compliments. They're like crack to me. Keep them coming."

The kid hesitated, apparently at a loss.

"Just sit down," Felix said.

The kid started again and quickly obeyed.

Oh brother.

"I can see why you dropped him off," Felix said to Danny.

"You must be Plato Jones," said the man on the laptop, his face illuminated by the glow of the monitor. "I've heard a lot about you."

"Most of it good, I hope."

He didn't comment on that. "I'm Eric MacDougal. The weasel over there is Stavros Venizelos."

The man on the phone gave a casual two-finger salute.

Eric inclined his head toward the kid. "And this fine specimen here is Claude Sanders."

At the mention of his name, Claude dropped a handful of cards—he had been in the process of gathering them. He flashed white teeth in a smile that made him look even younger.

"Hi, Mr. Jones," he said. "I've seen . . ."

Again, Felix interrupted him. "Are we forgetting our manners? Or did you grow up in the wilderness, like one of those feral children you see in the tabloids?"

Claude shook his head brusquely. "N-no sir."

"Then get over here and shake his hand."

Claude jumped up. He nearly slipped on his playing cards as he hurried over.

"Where did you find this guy?" Felix asked Danny. "Please don't say Craigslist."

"It's a real honor to meet you, Mr. Jones," Claude said, vigorously shaking my hand.

His eyes sparkled with youthful enthusiasm. In a way, he reminded me of Duccio—a good kid but too eager to please.

"Right back at you." I tugged my hand free. "And call me Plato."

"Okay, Plato. Sorry if I seem a little nervous. I've never met anyone famous before."

"I think you have me confused with someone else. I'm no celebrity."

"Well sure you are. I see your commercials all the time."

The commercials.

I'd purposely forgotten about those. Last year, Emilie convinced me to make a series of television ads, said it would bring in more business. They were similar to those law firm commercials that run between soap operas and court shows. The ones where the ultra-serious lawyer stares directly into the camera and lists the services his or her firm offers. I felt silly while filming them, and even sillier reviewing them. The deadpan stare, the robotic delivery. Yeah, the camera and I have never been the best of friends. We simply tolerate each other.

"I hope my bad acting didn't scar you for life," I said.

"No, not all," Claude insisted. "I liked them. They were funny."

Funny hadn't been my intention, but a compliment is a compliment. "Thanks."

"You're welcome. I hope you don't mind me asking, but . . ."

"Yes, Aphrodite and I dated for a while," I interrupted, "and no, she and I never had sex."

"There you go again, using those psychic powers," Felix said. "We need to get you to Vegas, stat. You'd clean house. Mental note. Plan . . . trip . . . to . . . Vegas."

"You're weird, man," Eric said.

Stavros chuckled.

"Find something funny, old chum?" Felix asked.

"Yeah," Stavros said. "You."

Felix shook his head. "You see what I have to deal with, Plato Jones? No respect at all."

I shrugged. "What are you gonna do?"

"What, indeed. Eric. Be a pal and rustle up some dinner while I have a heart to heart with my new deputies."

"Whatever you say, sheriff." Eric stood up. "Got a taste for anything in particular?"

"Surprise me. But be creative. That means no burgers, no hotdogs, and absolutely no pizza. Stavros, you go with him and make sure he doesn't screw up."

"Do I have to?" Stavros moaned.

"Afraid so," Felix said. "I'd let you stay, but my hands are tied. Sorry."

"Yeah, yeah."

"Be back in a few," Eric said.

He and Stavros left the tent. I heard an engine start. One of the Hummers.

Felix clapped his hands together. "Before I give you guys the rundown, I could use a shower. And so could you, Plato Jones. You smell like a moose's scrotum on a hot summer day."

"How would you know what a moose's scrotum smells like?" I asked.

"Funny story. Maybe I'll tell you about it someday. But probably not. Let the past stay in the past. That's my motto. Danny, be a sport and grab the shower gear. Oh and, Claude, you're coming with us. Leaving you and Danny alone . . ." Felix sucked air through his teeth.

Danny opened one of the metal storage boxes and removed three contraptions that looked like showerheads, but with small motors attached. A long, rubber tube protruded from the bottom of each one, wrapped tightly around the handle. I recognized them from an infomercial. A portable shower for the outdoorsman. It pulled in water and purified water from any available source. Pretty nifty. Danny gave one to each of us, along with a bar of soap and a towel.

"No bath salts?" I asked. "We really are roughing it."

"Hey, Danny," Felix said. "Be an even bigger sport and set up the presentation while we're gone."

Danny nodded. "Sure."

Claude and I followed Felix out of the tent and into the neighboring woods. I took in everything: the musk of tree bark, the rustling of leaves, evening light filtering through the canopy. This place, nature, it was the antithesis of Tartarus. The physical manifestation of freedom. Bliss in its truest form. I could have spent all day just walking.

A ten-minute hike saw us to a shallow creek. As I finally shed my filthy prison uniform, I felt like bursting into song. I almost did when the icy jets of water hit my skin. High notes.

As the three of us showered, I asked Claude a question that had been bugging me since we met. "Hey, Claude, you seem like an okay kid. How in Hades did you get hooked up with all these killers and lowlifes? No offense, Felix."

"None taken."

"I wanted to make a difference," Claude said. "I got tired of watching the Gods treat humans like second-class citizens. So I dropped out of college, moved to Greece, and here I am."

"Where are you from, originally?"

"Connecticut."

"You're a long way from home."

"Yeah," Claude said somewhat wistfully.

"What was your major in school?" I asked.

"Philosophy."

"Philosophy?" Felix interjected. "You mean you paid—oh, I'm sorry, Mommy and Daddy paid—someone to teach their little overachiever how to be a professional bullshitter? And you went along with it? I guess stupidity is hereditary."

Claude's head sank.

To Felix, I said, "Give him a break." *Jerk.*

"You ever kill anyone?" I asked Claude.

He blinked. "Who me? Never! I'm not even sure I could."

Poor kid. He had no idea what he was getting himself into. I wanted to tell him to go home and get back in school. In fact, I intended to. Just not in front of Felix and the others. Convincing one of their newest recruits to pack up and leave probably wouldn't go over too well with them.

"Looks like we got our work cut out for us," Felix said. "But we'll show you the ropes. Isn't that right, Plato Jones?"

I forced myself to agree. "Yeah."

"Before it's all said and done, you'll be a stone-cold killing machine, one that pisses fire, craps chainsaws, and . . . Help me out here, Plato Jones."

"Jaywalks," I said.

"Not the kind of answer I was hoping for, but it'll do," Felix said. "So, Clodhopper, does that sound like fun? See what I did there, don't you? Claude plus grasshopper equals magic."

Claude hesitated. "Uh . . ."

"Ignore him," I said. "He's is only half as crazy as he seems."

Felix started humming "Tracks of My Tears" by Smokey Robinson while swaying in place and holding the showerhead close, as he would a woman.

"Okay," I said. "A little more than half."

Not much later, we returned to the tent with our towels wrapped around our waists. There were fresh clothes in one of the storage boxes. Bringing them to the creek would have been more convenient, but hey, what do I know?

The selection was . . . retro. Straight out of the 1980s—an era defined by questionable fashion choices. I picked out a red and yellow Hawaiian shirt and a pair of khaki slacks. I'd been spying a faded black shirt with Inspector Gadget on it, but Felix beat me to the punch. Claude opted for a green velour shirt and a pair of acid-washed jeans. We looked like extras from *The Breakfast Club*.

Danny had set up a portable projector screen while we were out. Claude and I sat down on separate cots.

Felix stood beside the screen. "The show is about to begin."

Danny hit the lights and started the projector. For the next ten minutes we were treated to what Felix referred to as an educational slide show. It touched on the aspects of being a full member of the MLF.

The presentation consisted of twenty crudely illustrated slides, all hand drawn by Felix himself using what I assumed were the best markers, colored pencils, and crayons money could buy—and set to some ragtime piano song that got old within seconds.

Each slide featured a cartoon version of Felix engaging in various illegal activities: bomb-making, robbing a bank, and so on. The show was narrated by the man himself.

Slide number eleven depicted him having doggy-style sex with a large-breasted brunette. It seemed to serve no purpose to the overall presentation, and Felix didn't comment on it.

Classy.

The last slide depicted Felix kicking Zeus in the crotch. The president's eyes were popping out of their sockets while a bolt of lightning shot out of his rear end. It was my personal favorite. Disappointingly, none of the slides showed Felix performing any superhuman feats.

When the show ended, Danny turned the lights back on.

"Did you guys enjoy my presentation?" Felix asked, grinning widely.

"Yes, sir!" Claude said, clapping. "It was one of the best I've ever seen."

"I thought so too," Felix concurred.

Someone shoot me now.

"What did you think of it, Plato Jones?" Felix asked. "Is it Oscar-worthy?"

More like Razzy-worthy.

"Sure, why not," I said.

"Now, onto the next order of business," Felix said. "The last part of the gauntlet. But first, roll up one of your pants legs. Right, left, the choice is yours. I love variety."

Claude and I did as he asked. Danny opened one of the metal chests and took out a pair of ankle monitors. I suspected they were something more. He strapped one to my right leg.

The other to Claude's left. He then took out his smartphone and pressed a few buttons. The bracelets beeped once. He handed the phone to Felix, who slipped it into this pocket.

"I'm sure you're both wondering—what is this thing on my leg?" Felix said. "Any guesses?"

"An ankle monitor?" Claude guessed.

"You're absolutely correct. Good job."

Claude smiled excitedly.

"It is, in fact, an ankle monitor," Felix said. "It lets me know where you are at all times. If you go to grocery store, I'll know. If you go for a relaxing stroll through the park, I'll know. If you go to a strip club, I'll know . . . and probably join you. Oh, it's also a bomb. Almost forgot to mention that."

"Bomb?" Claude and I cried in unison.

"Don't soil your britches," Felix said, "After you pass the final test, the bombs will be removed and we can all celebrate, have a barbecue or something. And speaking of barbecue, where's my dinner? I'm wasting away here."

"Mind telling us what this test is all about?" I asked.

"Not at all, Plato Jones. It's just a simple exchange. Easy as can be. There's a guy, a collector, who deals in rare and unusual items. He's got something for us, something that's worth a lot of money. Tomorrow morning, two of his boys will be in a motel in Larissa. I want you to go there. If the product is legit, pay them. If you can do this without fucking up, you'll be full-fledged members of the MLF. Got it?"

Claude gave a jerky nod. "Yes, sir."

"Who is this collector?" I asked. "And more importantly, what is he selling?"

"Don't know," Felix said. "He and I have never spoken face to face. As for the item, it's not for me. I have no clue what it is."

I found no deceit in Felix's eyes. But that meant nothing. Certain gestures are synonymous with deceit: fidgeting, avoidance of eye contact, excessive hand movement. Seasoned liars could suppress them. Felix belonged in that category. Regrettably, so did I.

"Let me get this straight," I said. "You want us to meet with two black market goons to buy some mystery item, while wearing bombs on our ankles?"

"Exactly," Felix said. "Is there an echo in here? Oh, and pro-tip: Don't tamper with those bombs. I think you know why."

This mission is getting better all the time.

I heard a car pulling up outside.

Felix threw up his hands. "Finally!"

Eric and Stavros came inside, each with a large, paper grocery bag. Stavros carried something extra with him: a twenty-four-pack of beer.

Felix sniffed the air. "Is that pho I smell?"

"Nothing but," Eric said.

He and Stavros set the bags on the nearest cot and began removing plastic containers filled with broth, rice noodles, and a variety of meats and herbs.

"Did you remember the Sriracha?" Felix asked.

Stavros pulled a bottle of the red chili-based sauce out of his bag and held it up.

Felix put his hand over his heart. "My heroes."

"We try," Eric said.

Danny broke out the plastic bowls and we all sat down to eat. The Vietnamese noodle soup was the first satisfying meal I'd had in weeks. The beer made it that much better.

After dinner, we all did our own thing. Eric fired up his laptop, Stavros messed around with his phone, and Felix sat cross-legged on the floor with his eyes closed. He appeared to be meditating. Trying to center a mind like his must have been a Herculean effort. But at least it kept him from talking.

Claude and I had a friendly game of Scrabble. His anxiety about tomorrow's mission was apparent. He didn't finish his dinner, and he had stopped smiling. In an attempt to bolster his confidence, I let him win the first two games. It didn't work.

I challenged him to a final rematch. Third time's the charm. This time, my loss seemed to lift his spirits a bit. That was good enough for me. I conceded defeat and retired for the night.

As I drifted into slumber, visions of Cronus flashed in my mind. I could almost hear that terrible roar. I had to get in touch with Hermes soon. The authorities still had my cell phone—and stealing one from Felix and friends carried too great a risk. All they'd have to do was check the call record and my cover would be blown. For now, I was trapped.

22

I WOKE BEFORE SUNRISE. THE FIRST THING I SAW WAS FELIX'S smiling face hovering over me. He sat in a crouch next to my cot, his dark eyes glittering with madness.

"Good morning," he said.

"Hi. Thanks for the nightmare fuel."

"No sweat. Ready to do this?"

"I guess."

Felix patted me on the shoulder and moved away from my cot.

I sat up and tried to orient myself. Eric was on his laptop, making me wonder if he had gone to sleep at all last night. Stavros sat on the edge of his cot, cleaning his gun, using one of the metal boxes as a table.

I recognized the firearm. A USP semiautomatic pistol. I'd given one to Alexis as a surprise gift, along with a membership to a local shooting range. I was with the OBI at the time. The nature of my work had left me extremely paranoid and equally as protective. I wanted her to be able to protect herself while I was on assignment. As far as I knew, she still had it.

Claude was the only person still asleep.

Felix grabbed a bottle of spring water from one of the metal boxes and poured the entire thing on the poor kid's head. "Wake-up call!"

Claude jerked awake, coughing and sputtering. I couldn't say for sure why Felix enjoyed picking on Claude. My guess was because he could. I wanted to step in. But doing so might've damaged the pseudo-friendship he and I were forming.

"Move it, ladies," Felix yelled. "Move it, move it, move it! I don't have all morning!"

Claude scrambled off his cot and crashed onto the floor, his blanket twisted around his legs. Eric and Stavros chuckled.

"You're coming with us?" I asked Felix as I stood up.

"Obviously," he said. "You didn't think I was going to let you crazy kids go off on your own without a chaperone, did you? That's just common sense. Now, get your shit together. We leave in five minutes."

Felix tossed a suitcase containing fifty thousand credits in the trunk of the Caddy. Payment for our mystery purchase. He got behind the wheel while I slid into the passenger seat. Claude got in the back.

We took the same dirt road from yesterday and got on the highway. From there, Felix let the top down and found a radio station that played all '80s music all the time. He turned up the volume as loud as it would go.

He seemed to be making a conscious effort to draw attention. Luckily, there were few cars on the road. The music, coupled with our clothes, gave me the impression of being stuck in a time warp.

It took us an hour to reach our destination, the Exquisite Inn. The owner should've been sued for false advertising. The small, two-story motel appeared on the verge of collapse, with chipped paint, missing roof shingles, and no pool. A sign hung on the door of the manager's office. It read "OUT TO LUNCH," despite its being only half past nine.

There were two vehicles in the parking lot: an old, red

truck with four flats and more rust than paint, and a black 1977 Firebird in pristine condition.

Felix parked on the side of the complex, as far away from the manager's office as possible. He killed the engine but left the radio on. "Broken Wings" by Mr. Mister blared from the speakers. He lowered the volume to a reasonable level.

"Time for a pop quiz," he said. "Can either of you tell me what you're supposed to do?"

Claude seemed to consider the question. "Meet with dealers and make sure their product is authentic. If it is, give them the money."

"And what else?"

Claude hesitated. "Bring it back to you?"

"There may be hope for you yet."

"How are we supposed to check the authenticity of whatever it is they're offering?" I said.

"I'm glad you asked." Felix opened the center console and removed something that resembled a supermarket price gun, only smaller, about the size of a toy water pistol. He handed it to me.

Claude leaned forward for a better view.

"What's this?" I asked, examining the device. "Some kind of alien ray gun?"

"Can the jokes, Plato Jones. Alien technology is to be feared and respected. But to answer your question, no, it's not a ray gun. It's a scanner. Point it at the item and hold down the trigger. If it's legit, the scanner will make a beeping sound, like this: Beeeeeeeep. If it's a fake, it'll make an angry sound." Felix made a sound reminiscent of a joy buzzer.

"Seems simple enough." I put the scanner in my pocket. "What do we do if the item is bogus? Or if these potentially dangerous criminals . . . I don't know . . . start acting like dangerous criminals?"

"Like us?" Felix said.

"Like you," I corrected him.

"I brought a few party favors, in case the negotiations turn sour. Check the glove compartment."

I did. Inside were two handguns, FN Five-sevens, modified with compact integral suppressors.

"Party favors, huh?" I claimed one of the guns for myself and handed the other to Claude.

He accepted it with shaky arms, eyes wide as he stared at the weapon.

"And here I was, hoping for streamers and confetti," I said.

"Sorry to disappoint you," Felix said. "I'll do better next time. If there is a next time."

I checked the ammo. Osmium rounds. Nineteen in the magazine and one in the chamber. I wondered if this was standard ammunition for MLF members, in case they happened to run into a God while in the field. Or were these dealers something other than human?

"What's the room number?" I asked.

"Eleven," Felix said.

"My lucky number." I looked into the backseat at Claude. "Ready?"

He had been checking his ammo as well. He reinserted the magazine. The corners of his mouth twitched as he smiled and said, "Good to go."

Claude and I stepped out of the car and hid the guns in our waistbands. At the smalls of our backs rather than our abdomens. I always did this with new guns—if I lacked a proper holster—as some seemed more prone to accidentally firing than others. Besides, I'd take getting shot in the ass over getting shot in the crotch any day. Claude seemed to agree.

"Good luck, boys," Felix said.

"Thank you, sir," Claude said. "We'll make you proud."

"Yeah, swell." Felix let his seat back and propped his feet on the dashboard.

I grabbed the briefcase from the trunk. Then Claude and I walked to the front of the building. His movements were stiff, his breathing audible. If he didn't relax, he might spook the dealers. Never a good thing. I decided that now was as good a time as any to talk some sense into the kid, convince him to give up this mindless crusade—as far as I could tell, our ankle monitors didn't contain listening devices.

"You said you were from Connecticut, right?" I asked.

"Yeah," Claude said. "My folks moved there from Holland when I was six. Dad got a new job."

"Parents still together?"

"Twenty-five years come November."

"Any brothers or sisters?"

"One brother and one sister. I'm the middle kid. You?"

The question made me think of Socrates, a subject that always put me in a bad mood. But I learned how to hide my emotions long ago.

"No siblings," I lied.

"Only child. Must have been nice."

"Yeah."

When we reached the stairs leading up to the top row of apartments, I came to a halt.

"Why are we stopping?" Claude asked.

I ignored the question and posed one of my own. "Do you love your family?"

Claude appeared confused. "Well, yeah."

"Then go back to them, once we're done here."

"What?"

"Look, you're a smart kid. Too smart to get mixed up in all this. Go home and get back in school. Live your life. Enjoy it."

Claude smiled uncomfortably. "I appreciate what you're trying to do, Mr. Jones, but . . ."

"Don't worry about what Felix and the others might say," I said. "I'll keep them off your back."

"How?"

"I have my ways."

I recognized that if Claude quit, the MLF would come after him. Though slim, his knowledge of the organization made him a liability. The best course of action would be for Hermes to place him and his family into protective custody until this operation was over.

"I can't just leave. For the first time in my life," Claude argued, "I feel like I'm making a difference."

"If you want to make a difference, volunteer to feed the homeless, start a community outreach program. This isn't for you."

Claude's face crumbled. I felt bad about crushing his dreams. But he'd thank me later.

"Come on," I said. "Let's get this done."

Claude returned a half-hearted nod and followed me upstairs.

We stopped in front of room eleven. The blinds were closed, but I could hear the TV playing. I knocked on the door. It creaked opened and Claude gasped.

A harpy stood across from us, barely five feet tall, sinewy with pale, leathery skin. His head was bald, his ears pointed, and his large, black eyes shone like marbles. He had a hooked beak in place of a mouth, the same color and sheen as his eyes, and bony, claw-tipped fingers. He wore an olive-green T-shirt and gray sweatpants. Glossy black wings sprouted from holes in the back of his shirt, folded so as not to get in the way. Something, probably a gun, bulged at his waistline.

Harpies usually kept to themselves, living in secluded mountain villages. Since they rarely ventured outside their communities, seeing one was a rare occurrence. Seeing a male was even rarer. Physically, they looked almost identical to females, the only difference being a yellow growth on the base of the male's beak.

Females comprised ninety-eight percent of the harpy population. The other two percent—males—were considered mutants, freaks of nature. Most were either killed at birth or abandoned in the wilderness to die. In the latter situation, their wings were chopped off to minimize their chance of survival—and since female harpies can produce eggs asexually, their absence carried no consequences. How this one had escaped death and kept his wings was a wonder. But their presence raised another, equally baffling question.

If Felix hated nonhumans, why was he consorting with them? Maybe he told the truth about never having met them. Or maybe he was willing to put aside his racism for the sake of money.

The harpy glanced at me and Claude, then at the briefcase, then back at us. I saw my reflection in his eyes but nothing else. No emotion. He let us inside and locked the door.

Trepidation had already begun to set in, like a spider crawling up my back. I played it cool. I hoped Claude could keep it together, too.

The hotel room had a king-size bed, a table and chair, a nightstand, and an ancient TV. Stains and burn marks dotted the carpet, and the air was stale with the lingering odor of cigarette smoke.

Another male harpy sat on the edge of the bed, watching *Mister Ed* on TV. He wore a brown T-shirt and denim shorts. He glanced at Claude and me, then returned his attention to the show. As was the case with his partner, his eyes and beak made it impossible to gauge his mood. Because he was seated, I couldn't tell if he had a gun. But there seemed no reason why he wouldn't.

The harpy who answered the door walked to the opposite end of the room and leaned against the wall. Both were barefoot. Their feet resembled hands tipped with black claws.

Claude stood completely still, his eyes bugging out. Fear

rolled off him in waves, almost tangible. If I could sense it, surely the harpies could too. It didn't seem to bother them, though. I guessed they were used to getting funny looks.

Because of their appearance—and reclusiveness—harpies were often feared and discriminated against. I considered them no different from any other race. They weren't bloodthirsty monsters with a taste for human flesh. They didn't steal children from their beds in the dead of night. They were just people trying to get by.

But like all people, there were good ones and bad ones.

For a time, no one spoke. No one moved. The only sounds in the room came from the TV. The harpy on the wall stared at us. The other continued to watch his show. I waited for one of them to say something. When that didn't happen, I took the initiative.

"Afternoon, guys. I'm Plato and this is my friend Claude."

"Hi," Claude said.

Miraculously, his voice didn't crack.

Neither harpy responded. Had I known breaking the ice would be this hard, I'd have brought along a jackhammer.

"And you are . . ." I said, gesturing for them to respond.

"I am Damianos," said the one on the wall. "This is my brother, Linos."

His voice was shrill and high-pitched, the auditory equivalent of chewing tinfoil. It also carried an undefinable accent. I recalled harpies having their own language. Harpish. It consisted of screeches, cries, and whistles delivered at various frequencies. I'd heard that in the 1950s, recordings of harpies arguing were used to get confessions during police interrogations. It certainly seemed plausible.

"Nice to meet you," I said, and nodded at the harpy on the bed. "Linos."

Linos ignored me.

"You have the item?" I asked Damianos.

He looked at the briefcase. "Is that the money?"

"Yeah."

"Show me."

I placed the briefcase on the table and opened it. Credits filled the interior, arranged in neat stacks.

Damianos came over to get a closer look. "Is this all of it?"

"Fifty thousand," I said. "Right down to the last credit."

Or I hoped it was. I trusted that Felix didn't intend to shortchange the dealer. Trusting Felix—now that was a scary thought.

Damianos stepped back.

I closed the briefcase. "I've shown you mine. Now it's your turn."

"First, we need to confirm your identities."

Translation: We need to make sure you're not cops.

"Fair enough." I lifted the front of my shirt to show I wasn't wearing a wire.

Stashing my gun at my back served a dual purpose. In addition to keeping my manhood out of harm's way, it could also lead unwary criminals into thinking I was unarmed. Unless they asked me to turn around.

Claude followed my example, albeit stiffer and unnatural. His every movement seemed designed to incite suspicion.

I maintained a calm expression, clenching my teeth behind closed lips. *Get it together, kid.*

The harpies watched Claude in silence, their eyes impossible to read.

I let down my shirt. "Satisfied?"

Damianos and Linos looked at each other. Something seemed to pass between them, an unspoken line of communication.

"Almost," Damianos said.

"What more do you want?" I asked.

"We need to conduct a more thorough search."

"If by thorough you mean a strip search, you can forget it."

Damianos and Linos glanced at each other again. Though their faces gave no indication of it, I could sense their annoyance. But I didn't care. I'd sooner have an arm wrestling match against Atlas than have the harpies' clawed fingers poking around my privates. It was a matter of principle.

"If you refuse, the deal is off," Damianos said.

Claude glanced intermittently between me and the harpies, his brow creased in concern—concern over what Felix might do to us if this deal didn't go through. I wasn't worried about myself. But I couldn't let the kid get hurt. I only hoped the harpies wouldn't force us to drop our pants. The ankle bracelets would definitely become a topic of conversation.

"I guess we really don't have much of a choice, do we?" I said.

The harpies didn't respond.

"Fine." I began removing my shirt.

"No." said Damianos.

I paused.

He tipped his head in the direction of the bathroom. "In there. One at a time."

"Why?" I asked.

"Just a safety measure."

Safety measure, huh? Right. If I learned anything in the OBI, it was to never get separated from your partner. In the field, a lone wolf usually ended up a dead one.

"You know, I think I'm gonna have to pass on that," I said. "Situations like these usually end with someone kissing the business end of a chainsaw."

Claude glanced at me in confusion.

"*Scarface* reference," I said.

Claude's eyes widened. "Ah."

"Then we have nothing more to discuss," said Damianos.

Claude spoke up before I had a chance to respond, his voice even and resolute. "I'll go first."

"No, you won't," I said.

"It's all right," Claude said, "I know what I'm doing."

"You really don't."

"I'll be fine." Claude gave me a reassuring smile and walked into the bathroom.

Damianos followed.

"Mind leaving the door open?" I asked just as the bathroom door closed shut.

I cursed inwardly.

Linos continued to stare at the TV, the light reflecting off his eyes.

"So," I said. "How about them Bears?"

Linos said nothing. Maybe I should have gone with, *What's the deal with airplane food?* On TV, in an old rerun, Mr. Ed was performing a song called "The Empty Feed Bag Blues."

"Talking horses," I said, pointing at the television. "People sure were creative back then."

Still nothing.

That instant, Claude cried out from behind the door. "It's not what you—!"

His words were cut short by an unsuppressed gunshot. Linos and I locked eyes. Before I could go for my gun, he had already beaten me to the draw—he pulled a pistol from under his shirt and pointed it at me. He slowly stood up.

I raised my hands.

The bathroom door opened. The sound seemed to distract Linos. He glanced in its direction. That lapse in his attention, though brief, was all I needed. I didn't bother reaching for my weapon. It would've taken too long. Instead, I shifted left, clear of the enemy's line of fire. I grabbed the top of the gun, pushed the barrel parallel to his forearm, and ripped it from his hand.

The gun fell to the floor. Holding Linos's wrist, I pulled him close and, upon release, wrapped my arm around his neck, trapping him in a standing rear choke, and turning him into a human shield—or in this case, a harpy shield.

I completed the sequence just in time. Another crack of gunfire rang out. Linos's body jerked as a bullet slammed into his stomach. He screeched in pain. His wings flared out, knocking over the TV, and inadvertently providing me another layer of cover.

Across from us, Damianos stood with his gun pointed at us. His face betrayed no emotion. But he stood motionless, presumably in shock over shooting his brother.

I took advantage of his hesitation. I released Linos and shoved him hard in the back. He crashed into Damianos, causing the latter to drop his gun. They both fell in a heap of twisted limbs and flapping wings.

I drew my Five-seven and rushed forward to press the attack. I knocked out Linos with a kick to the head and pointed gun at Damianos's head.

The harpy froze. His gun lay close by. I kicked it away. It slid toward the bathroom and stopped just outside the doorway.

"Get up," I demanded.

Damianos didn't move.

I lowered my gun and fired a round. It punched into the floor, right between the harpy's legs. He flinched.

"Now," I said.

Damianos slowly rose, his hands in the air.

"Turn around," I said.

He did.

I smacked him in the back of the head with my gun. Damianos collapsed, unconscious. My heart racing, I slipped the Five-seven back into my waistband and collected the harpy's guns. I removed the magazines, emptied the chambers, and tossed the useless weapons aside. I stuck the ammo in my pockets for safekeeping.

I checked the bathroom. Claude lay on his back. Blood flowed from a bullet wound in his chest. He still had all his clothes on. His fingers were wrapped loosely around the handle of his gun.

He must've tried to disarm himself, to show Damianos that he was willing to play by the rules. The harpy probably mistook his compliance as an act of aggression. It made sense. When someone pulls a gun on you, you assume they're going to use it. At that point, it was fight or flight. Damianos chose to fight.

Claude had already started to turn pale. I checked his pulse. He was still alive, barely. Damn it! I promised myself I'd get him through this. Maybe there was still time.

Carrying him all the way back to the car—clear on the other side of the building—would've been too slow and risky. Someone might come along, get suspicious, and call the police. Felix's help could speed up the process.

"Hang on, kid." I left the bathroom.

No sooner had I cleared the door than a weak groan stopped me in my tracks. Claude had regained a flicker of consciousness. His eyes were half-open.

"Don't leave," he whispered, reaching for me.

I knelt beside him, took his bloody hand into mine. His grip was weak.

"Hey, buddy," I said. "How're you feeling?"

"Tired."

"Try to stay awake. We're gonna get you out of here. Get you patched up."

Moisture glittered in Claude's eyes. "Am I going to die?"

"Not today."

Claude seemed not to hear that. Tears rolled down his colorless cheeks.

"I don't want to die," he whimpered. "I'm not ready."

I felt a tearing pain in the middle of my chest. "I'm going for help. Just sit tight until I get back. And don't fall asleep."

I left the bathroom. Damianos was still out. Linos might've been dead. A pool of blood had spread beneath him, soaking into the carpet. I briefly imagined putting bullets in both their heads, but I pushed the thought from my mind just as quickly. I was a lot of things, but cold-blooded killer wasn't one of them.

I hurried out of the apartment and down the stairs. A white '64 Mustang was parked near the manager's office. The sign in the window had been taken down. Suddenly, I became aware of the blood on my shirt, hands, and forearms.

I ran to the side of the building where Felix had parked. Both he and the Caddy were missing. Maybe the manager's arrival forced him to find another hiding spot. I did a lap around the complex and found nothing but empty parking spaces.

He ditched us! That bastard ditched us!

I headed back to the room—to keep out of sight and try to come with a plan. I also wanted to keep an eye on Damianos and Linos, in the event they woke up and finished off Claude. When I reached the stairs, I heard music. "She Drives Me Crazy" by Fine Young Cannibals. I looked left and glimpsed a car approaching from the highway.

Felix.

He pulled into the parking lot and around the side of the building. I raced over.

Felix killed the engine. "Howdy, pilgrim."

"You're a dick," I snapped.

"Whoa! What's with all the hostility, Plato Jones? You're starting to make me think that we aren't really friends."

"Where were you?"

"Picking up a few necessities," Felix said.

Two large cases of beer sat in the backseat.

"You left us to get beer?"

"I got beer for all of us, Plato Jones."

"It's scary how stupid you are."

"I can see you're upset, Plato Jones, so I'll let that one slide." Felix reached into a plastic grocery bag sitting on the passenger seat and pulled out a king-size box of Nerds candy. "Check it out. I even got something special for the schoolboy. Where is he, by the way?"

"Still in the hotel room. He's been shot."

"Ah, so that explains the blood. I was wondering about that."

"I need your help getting him out of there."

"What about the item?"

I arched my brows. "Did you hear what I just said?"

"I did. But I seemed to have forgotten. Maybe the item will refresh my memory."

"Fine, I get it. I'll be right back. Don't go anywhere."

"You've got my word."

Whatever that's worth.

I dashed back to the room. The harpies were still out. I checked on Claude. His eyes were closed. He wasn't moving.

"You okay in there, kid?" I asked.

No answer. I had to find that item fast. I checked the most obvious hiding spot. The closet. Inside, I found a large duffel bag with shoulder straps. I picked it up. It had to have weighed close to a hundred pounds.

I carried it to the bed and removed a black orb the size of a carnival balloon. It was shiny and leathery to the touch, like a medicine ball. I had no idea what it was, and I didn't have time to speculate. I used the scanner on it. The device beeped, confirming its authenticity.

"Just hold on a bit longer," I said. "Okay, Claude."

Silence.

I put the orb back into the duffel bag and slipped it on my shoulder. As I reached the door, I glimpsed the briefcase of money. I grabbed it and brought it to Felix.

"The money *and* the merchandise," he said. "You're on the ball today, Plato Jones!"

I slapped my hand against the car's trunk.

Felix popped it. "Did you make sure it's real?"

"Yeah." I deposited the bag and suitcase, and closed the trunk. "I did what you asked. Time for you to return the favor."

"Right you are." Felix took out the smartphone Danny had given him.

My heart all but stopped. "What are you doing?"

"Keeping my word."

Before I could stop him, Felix pressed several buttons on the phone.

A deafening boom shook the air as room eleven exploded in a ball of fire. Chunks of wood, metal, and stone scattered in all directions, caught in a wave of superheated air.

I crouched and covered my head. When I straightened, the center of the complex was completely gone. Fire crackled, clouds of black smoke billowed skyward, and charred debris littered the parking lot.

Felix gazed in amazement at the smoldering ruins, then at the smartphone. "I told the boys in R&D that I needed stronger explosives. They listened. They definitely listened."

"You maniac!" I shouted.

Felix disregarded the insult. "Come to think of it, that might've been a little excessive. I'll tell them to dial it back just a pinch."

"Claude was still in there," I said.

"Duh! Otherwise the bomb wouldn't have gone off from inside the room. You seem like a pretty smart guy, Plato Jones, but sometimes I just don't know."

"You promised to help him!"

"And so I did." Felix grabbed the plastic bag from the passenger seat and tossed it into the back. "Hop in."

It took every drop of willpower I had not to shoot him then and there.

On the side of the complex, a tall man with a beer belly rushed out of the manager's office. He seemed to be in a panic. He took out a cell phone, presumably to call the police.

I jumped into the Caddy, and we screeched off. I stared at the rearview mirror, watching the smoke rise until it vanished beneath the horizon. A small, naïve part of me imagined Claude stumbling out of the wreckage covered in soot and ash, his hair sticking straight up but otherwise unharmed. Felix's voice brought my reverie to an end.

"Grab me a beer, will you?"

"Get it yourself."

"Oh, all right." Felix let go of the wheel and turned around in his seat.

The car veered to the right.

"Hey!" I caught the wheel and kept us on course.

"*Gracias, señorita,*" Felix said as he reclaimed the wheel, a bottle in his hand.

Psycho.

Felix pried off the cap with his teeth, spit it on the floor, and extended the bottle out the window.

"This one's for Claude." He tilted the bottle downward, pouring beer on the highway. "He was all right."

The gesture seemed a mockery. I struggled to collar my rage.

"Congratulations, Plato Jones," Felix said. "You're one of us now."

I didn't respond.

"I hate seeing you like this. I really do," Felix said. "Is there anything I can do to make you feel better?"

"Actually, there is. It involves a long jog and a short cliff. I'll let you figure out the rest."

"Don't tell me this kind of stuff gets to you."

"What? Killing kids?"

Felix sighed. "Look, Plato Jones. Friend, buddy, *amigo*, *tomodachi* . . . uh, what else, what else . . . Ah, yes! Comrade! Listen to me, and remember what I say. Sometimes, the only difference between the good guys and the bad guys is perspective. To accomplish certain goals, you occasionally have to blur the lines even further."

"Which ones are we, Felix?"

"The good guys, of course."

"I see. Thanks for clearing that up."

"That's what I'm here for."

"You're full of it," I sneered.

"Awesomeness? Yeah, I know. It's both a gift and a curse. Grab me another beer, would you. And get one for yourself too. You look thirsty."

Too weary to argue, I did as he asked. For the first time in months, I found myself in no mood to drink. But I needed the alcohol. It wouldn't erase the memory of what happened today, but it'd make it easier to deal with.

I passed one of the bottles to Felix. "Where are we going?"

"The safe house. We'll eat and finish off these beers. We can even build a campfire and tell ghost stories, if you want."

I opened my beer and took a sip.

"No ghost stories, huh? That's cool. It'll be something for another day." Felix finished his beer in one gigantic pull and tossed the bottle out the window. It shattered against the road. "Tomorrow, I'll introduce you to the rest of the gang. They're gonna love you."

23

Felix removed my ankle bracelet once we arrived at the safe house. I'd almost expected him to leave the thing on as a sick joke. We gave the orb to Danny, who left to deliver it to MLF headquarters. I still didn't know what it was—this thing that cost Claude his life. Felix did. Of that, I was sure. But I couldn't prove it.

I washed up at the creek then changed clothes. As it turned out, one of the metal boxes contained garments that were more modern than the ones I'd been wearing. I suspected Felix had been aware of this the entire time. Why he wanted us to dress like cosplayers at a Miami Vice convention was anyone's guess.

While we were out, Eric had picked up dinner: a large tray of pastitsio from The Nomad Café. I'd never heard of the place. The food tasted great. But I didn't have enough of an appetite to truly enjoy it.

As we ate, Felix made no mention of Claude's death—and neither Eric nor Stavros seemed interested in his whereabouts. I found the lack of concern sickening. What they did do, however, was congratulate me on passing initiation. I pretended to be happy about it. But in truth, the achievement was as hollow as a bamboo flute.

By the time we finished our meals, we'd gone through

an entire case of Felix's beer. He tore open the other, and we continued to drink.

With alcohol in their systems, Eric and Stavros seemed more at ease around me. They even shared details about their pasts. Both used to be soldiers in the Grecian army until they were discharged. They didn't say why. Probably not a good sign.

After being booted out of the service, they formed a mercenary group with three of their buddies. They did a little bit of everything: security, murder, kidnapping, extortion. The quality of their work had established them as the best in the business, and eventually caught the attention of the MLF. At no point during the story did they mention the Gods. I got the sense they were more concerned with making money than liberating humanity.

But their story did shed some light on the MLF as an organization. Felix's dad, Louis, was the brains behind the operation. I also learned that this wasn't some small, rinky-dink outfit. It was global and operated like a legitimate military organization.

In addition to free room and board, members were provided a monthly allowance as well as bonuses based on performance—and judging by the cars parked outside, the MLF had serious financial backing. But where was the money coming from? Bank heists? I doubted it. Though the means were probably just as illegal.

No one questioned me about my past. I surmised that Felix had already told them everything they needed to know. And what they didn't know could be found on the Internet. Modern technology. Never before has spying on a person been so easy and so discreet.

We finished the last case of beer and turned in for the night. The last thing I remembered before falling asleep was looking at Claude's empty cot.

* * *

MLF headquarters was in New Olympia. Not the ideal location for a criminal organization bent on toppling the government. Felix's dad must've had that hide-among-your-enemies attitude. To his credit, the base was located on the edge the city, in the former industrial district. Once a bustling hub of industry, the area had devolved into a hodgepodge of condemned factories, crumbling warehouses, and gutted dormitories, all consumed by wild vegetation. The entire area was a no man's land, devoid of police presence, and a hotspot for New Olympia's ne'er-do-wells, some of whom were undercover lookouts for the MLF.

With all the spies around, I should fit right in.

I'd never seen this part of the city in its prime, but according to a faded billboard, it was still a great place to work. The fact that the Gods never tried to clean the place up came as no shock. As long as a problem didn't affect them directly, it might as well have not existed. So what if there were women and children squatting in abandoned buildings, eating out of dumpsters, and being terrorized by thieves and murderers? Hera and Hermes needed their daily mani-pedis.

An old warehouse contained the entrance to the base. We rode to the back of the building, to the loading area. The garage door was down. Felix whipped out his phone and entered a security code.

The garage door opened. Felix drove up the cargo ramp and into the warehouse. The interior was pitch black. He turned on the headlights, illuminating piles of rubble, shattered glass, old tires, broken crates, and stacks of rotting wooden pallets. Everything lay under a mantle of dust and cobwebs. The hot, dry air made breathing difficult.

I noticed tire tracks in the dust. They extended to the

center of the building, ending at a metal platform, the kind you'd find in an auto garage.

Felix coasted onto the platform and stopped. He entered another code on his phone. With a hiss of steam and a groan of metal gears, the platform descended down a metal shaft.

A secret elevator. Nifty.

The ride lasted over a minute. I wondered how far down we had traveled. If I had to guess, I'd say around two hundred feet. Felix drove off the platform. It immediately began to ascend. A manmade tunnel stretched before us, brightly lit. It ended at a massive blast door with a camera mounted above it. Felix and the others weren't kidding about the MLF being well funded. Following the paper trail would almost certainly lead to a number offshore banks and front businesses.

Felix stopped before the blast door. A red light on the camera blinked three times then turned green. Facial recognition software. The door slowly swung open. We drove through, into an underground parking garage.

Vehicles of every make and model filled the spaces—zippy little sports cars, wallet-busting exotics, vintage classics, motorcycles, trucks. Felix pulled into a space and cut the engine. I followed him to an elevator at the back of the lot. The complex had six levels. We were at the top. I noted a keyhole beneath the button panel. I assumed it served some kind a maintenance purpose.

Felix pressed the button for the fourth floor. It brought us to an area that once might have been part of a subway station. Now it more closely resembled a newsroom—a vast field of workstations separated by metal support beams and hemmed by walls of reddish-brown brick.

Cameras positioned overhead monitored every inch of the floor. Dozens of men and women engaged in organized chaos: having phone conversations, working on computers, and sifting through towers of paperwork. With all these people hovering, gathering clues was going to be more of challenge than I had anticipated.

Felix announced his presence as only he could. "Hear ye, hear ye! You can all breathe easy. Felix the Great has returned from his noble crusade."

Most of the people appeared too busy to acknowledge him. The rest didn't seem particularly happy to see him. I was sure his charming personality had something to do with that.

"We're like one big, happy family," Felix said to me. "Can you feel the warmth?"

"Sure can. Makes me wish I'd packed swim trunks."

Felix led me up a flight of stairs that led to an office overlooking the floor. A one-way mirror stood in place of the front wall, and there were no decorations to speak of. The only furniture came in the form of a metal desk and chair.

Two people occupied the space. Danny sat behind the desk, working furiously on a laptop. I'd never seen the other man before. He stood gazing out the window, his hands behind his back.

When he turned toward us, the wildness in Felix's eyes gave way to something resembling awe—and beneath that, a sliver of fear.

"I'm back," Felix said.

The man regarded him with hard, amber-colored eyes. He stood around six-three, bald, and jacked like a pro-wrestler. He had strong, blocky features, further harshened by a layer of beard stubble. A hideous scar ran down the side of his head, ending at the corner of his mouth. He wore a sleeveless flak jacket with a T-shirt underneath, tactical pants, and combat boots.

This must be Louis.

"This is Plato Jones," Felix said. "The guy I told you about. Plato, this is Louis King. My dad and the leader of our organization."

Louis moved forward and stopped less than a foot away from me, smelling of gun oil and boot leather. He looked me over, his gaze like a surgeon's scalpel. It made various incisions, searching for what made me tick. I resisted the urge to back away.

"So, the little man is the great Plato Jones," Louis said.

His voice arrived low and gravelly, as though he had smoked an entire cigarette factory. It also had the same unidentifiable accent as Felix's.

"Glad to be aboard." I held off trying to shake his hand. He didn't seem like the hand-shaking type. More like hand-breaking.

"Show him around," he said to Felix. "And set him up in a room."

"Sure thing." Felix motioned for me to follow him.

I could feel Louis's eyes on me as I left the room. Foreboding prickled my skin, like a brood of centipedes crawling over me. I couldn't get away from him fast enough.

"I think he likes you," Felix said as we reached the bottom of the stairs.

"Yeah, that's the vibe I was getting." I made no attempt to mask my sarcasm. "So that's the boss man, huh?"

"That's him. Word of advice. Don't piss him off."

"Noted."

"Ready to start the grand tour?"

"Let's do it."

Felix guided me down a path that ran through the center of the room. "This is our intelligence department. Pretty sweet, huh?"

"Not too shabby."

"This is where we gather dirt on our enemies and use it to make their lives miserable. Fun times. There's another on the floor below us just like this one. The techies there do the same thing as the techies here."

Back at Tartarus, I suspected that Felix had somehow obtained the prison blueprints. If my assumption rang true, I now knew where he got them. With this many hackers all working together, there weren't many secrets the MLF couldn't uncover given enough time.

Felix and I took a peek at the second intelligence department, then headed for the sixth floor—Research and Development, where the MLF's resident mad scientists came up with all sorts of crazy gizmos and doodads. He informed me that the Chief Science Officer was Dr. Daedalus.

I recognized the name. In ancient times, Daedalus had been a brilliant inventor, architect, and craftsman. Under the order of King Minos of Crete—one of the three idiots who presided over my trial—he built a mazelike dungeon called the labyrinth that was used to house the first minotaur in recorded history.

For some reason, Minos had decided to keep the minotaur as a pet—a violent, uncontrollable pet that craved human flesh—and locked it in the labyrinth. Whenever feeding time came around, the king's enemies were on the menu, along with anyone he suspected of being an enemy.

When the minotaur was eventually killed, Minos blamed Daedalus for the death of his prized pet. As punishment, he tossed the architect and his son, Icarus, into the labyrinth. Daedalus and Icarus escaped, but they were still trapped on the island of Crete. Using sticks, wax, twine, and bird feathers, Daedalus MacGyvered two sets of wings, one for him and the other for Icarus.

As the pair soared across the sea toward freedom, Daedalus warned Icarus not to fly too close to the sun, lest he draw the attention of the sun God, Helios. But like a lot of kids, Icarus did the exact opposite of what his parent told him.

This is where the story gets hazy.

Some people suggest it was the heat of the sun that melted

the wax on Icarus's wings. Others believe it was Helios being an ass. Whatever the reason, the result was the same. Icarus's wings failed, causing him to plummet into the sea, presumably killing him.

Maybe I'm biased, but I believe that creep Helios was to blame.

Since Daedalus had been a mortal, I doubted the one working for the MLF was the genuine article. Still, I didn't rule out the possibility entirely. I learned long ago that few things in the world made sense, and even fewer things were impossible.

The brick walls of the R&D lab had been painted white, the floor tiles too. The aesthetics likely doubled as a safety precaution, ensuring that spills, hazardous or otherwise, could be easily spotted.

The place was a warmonger's wet dream. To the left, behind a wall of glass—reinforced no doubt—researchers worked on computers, peered through microscopes, and examined the contents of petri dishes, all under the scrutiny of two security cameras positioned on either side of the room. They all wore the same getup: a clear plastic smock over a white lab coat, hairnet, goggles, surgical mask, and blue latex gloves. I assumed they were developing bioweapons.

The other, larger portion of the lab seemed to deal with conventional weaponry: guns, grenades, rocket launchers, and everything else that goes boom. Fifteen long tables were arranged in rows of three, covered with research materials. A small army of researchers milled around.

Felix and I approached a man with thinning brown hair and small-rimmed glasses. He stood near one of the tables. Staring at the data pad in his hand, he seemed unaware of our presence.

Felix picked up a thick book from a nearby lab cart and slammed it against the table. The impact echoed throughout the department.

The researcher jumped, almost dropping his pad. His coworkers froze. Someone cursed.

The researcher glowered when he discovered the source of the disturbance. "Felix."

"Hello, Chuck. How are we doing today?"

"Just fine. Are you here to change that? Or do you actually want something?"

"You scientists can be so rude. No social graces whatsoever. This is what happens when you don't get out enough. Or don't get laid enough. And speaking of which—"

"What do you want?" Chuck interrupted.

"Respect would be nice. Not a lot. Just enough to whet my appetite."

"Dream on."

"You know, Chuck. One of these days, me and you are gonna have a chat about the price of insubordination. Because if things between us stay as they are, I may end up ripping your intestines out through your eyeballs. Is that something you want?"

"Please. If you were going to kill me, you'd have done it by now."

"Good point. Anyway, this is Plato Jones, our newest member."

"Nice to meet you, Plato."

"Same here," I said.

Chuck put aside the data pad, and we shook hands.

"Have the boys upstairs assigned you a job?" he asked.

"If they did, they haven't told me."

"Don't worry. They'll find out what you're best at, and then stick you in a position where it'll be of no use."

Felix leaned in and whispered in my ear. "Chuck's dream was to become the MLF's first and only go-go dancer. But he didn't have the legs. So sad."

Chuck must have heard the joke because he shook his

head. "It was nice meeting you, Plato. Sorry I can't be more social, but I have to get back to work. These unstoppable death machines aren't going to build themselves . . . yet."

"I understand."

"Hold on a second," Felix cut in. "We're not done here."

"What is it now?" Chuck sighed.

"Plato Jones is on pins and needles to meet Dr. Daedalus." Felix clapped me on the shoulder. "Isn't that right?"

"If you say so."

"Do your old pal Felix a favor and fetch him."

"If I do this, do you promise to get out of my hair?" Chuck asked.

"I can promise you whatever you want," Felix said.

Chuck mumbled something under his breath. He took a smartphone out of his lab coat and shot the doctor a text. The phone, I noticed, was the same model Felix carried. Maybe they were standard issue for MLF members.

Not ten seconds later, Chuck's phone chimed. He glanced at it and put it back into his pocket.

"The doctor is on his way."

"Super," said Felix.

"Can I get back to work now?"

"In a minute. First, we need to talk about those baby nukes you guys gave me."

"The ankle monitors?"

"Yes, the ankle monitors."

"You asked for something with more of a kick," Chuck said.

"I know, but jeez."

Chuck shrugged as if to say, *What do you want me to do about it?*

"Let's take a walk. I want to have a heart to heart with you and the other eggheads, make sure you know the difference between boom and kaboom."

Chuck frowned but didn't argue.

"I'll be right back," Felix said to me.

He and Chuck exited the area through an automatic door on the right side of the room. Left alone—with nothing to do until the doctor arrived—I put my hands in my pockets and started humming the theme to *The Andy Griffith Show.* Now Felix had *me* doing it. Fantastic. I guess crazy is contagious.

"Mr. Jones?" said a small voice.

I turned around to see a little boy who couldn't have been more than twelve or thirteen years old. He had curly brown hair, large brown eyes, and round cheeks dusted with freckles. He wore a lavender dress shirt and khakis under a white lab coat.

You've got to be joking.

"Hi." The boy extended a tiny hand toward me, smiling. "You must be Plato."

"*You're* Daedalus?" I said, shaking his hand.

"Guilty as charged. Welcome to my little slice of Elysium. If you can think it up, we can build it."

Okay, maybe this isn't a joke.

"I'm sure you're wondering how a child became head of this entire department," Daedalus said.

"Well, yeah."

"It's because I'm not a child. This body is almost completely synthetic. Only my brain is organic."

"Who made it?"

"I did."

Looking at Daedalus, I would never have pegged him a cyborg. The level of realism was downright frightening. Before his death, Hephaestus had been considered one the best inventors of all time. It seemed the doc was right up there with him.

"I have to say, I'm impressed."

"Thank you," Daedalus said. "I modeled this unit after my son, Icarus. Perhaps you've heard of him."

"Everyone's heard of him. I'm sorry, by the way."

Daedalus nodded. His smile remained in place, but his eyes dimmed slightly. "It still hurts, even after all these years. The body helps to ease the pain. Whenever I want to see my boy, all I have to do is look in the mirror.

The admission was sad, endearing, and creepy all rolled into one. But we all have our own coping mechanisms.

Daedalus looked around. "Where's Felix? I thought he came with you."

"He went somewhere with Chuck, said he'd be right back."

Relief settled over Daedalus's face. I assumed he was no fan of Felix either. It seemed that not all the MLF members were crazy.

"For Felix, 'right back' could be anywhere from an hour to next week." Daedalus chuckled. "In the meantime, how about I treat you to a tour of the lab?"

Before I could answer, Daedalus had already started walking. I fell in behind him. First, he introduced me to his team of key researchers: Johnny, Ralph, and Bobby.

Afterward, Daedalus gave me the rundown on some of his favorite toys. Spy drones, ridiculously large guns, ridiculously small guns, EMP-hardened electronics, and contact lenses that protected against gorgon stares—I could have used those back at Prometheus's torture party.

The more Daedalus talked about his inventions, the more excited he seemed to become, and soon his eyes had taken on a strange glow—a gleeful madness. His exuberance peaked when he showed me one of his newest creations: the locust egg. Three of them sat in a glass display. They resembled frag grenades but were filled with over a million nanobots. The little suckers had insatiable appetites for all things metal. According to the doctor, they could now consume structures as large as the Eiffel Tower in under an hour—since he had figured out a way expand their one-minute lifecycle.

Finally, Daedalus took me to the genetics lab—the portion used to house live specimens. He was itching to show me another of his crowning achievements. An extremely rare specimen, he called it. I had no idea what to expect. But that was the story of my life. Leaving my expectations at the door had almost become second nature.

The entire area was stark white, in keeping with the rest of the department. Glass holding cells lined either wall, six on each side. All sat empty save one, which housed a tiny goat. The animal had reddish-brown hair with patches of gold here and there. It stood motionless in the middle of the cell, staring at nothing.

From across the room, I could see the various posters and calendars that decorated the back wall of the goat's cell: mountains, seaside vistas, puppies, kittens, rainbows, and butterflies—every relaxing and happy cliché in the book. There were also a few posters of Storm from the X-Men. I guess even livestock has its favorite superheroes.

"What's with the goat?" I asked.

"This is the specimen I mentioned." Daedalus grabbed me by the arm and tugged me toward the cage. "I'll introduce you."

The goat turned her head in our direction, regarding us with those large, soulless eyes that most goats seem to have. The ones with those freaky rectangular pupils. Just thinking about them gave me the creeps. Actually seeing them made my skin crawl.

"This is GS124-26534," Daedalus said. "We call her Gabby for short. Gabby, this is Mr. Jones. He's the newest member of our organization."

The goat stared vacantly at us.

Daedalus looked at me, his brows arched, as though waiting for me to say hello to Gabby the goat. The doctor seemed like a nice enough guy—albeit a bit kooky—so I decided to humor him.

"Pleased to meet you, Gabby. I'd shake your hand, but you don't seem to have any."

Daedalus gave a chuckle that sounded forced. Gabby had no reaction whatsoever. Everyone's a critic.

"So, what's so special about Gabby here?" I asked.

Daedalus' face lit up, "I'm glad you asked. Through genetic engineering, we've turned her into the world's smartest goat. Her intelligence rivals that of our most talented researchers. She may even be brighter than I."

"I'm sorry. My ears are getting bad in my old age. Did you just say you genetically engineered a goat—this goat—to be smarter?"

"That's right."

"Why?"

"Why not?" Daedalus said with a shrug.

Touché.

"She just looks like a regular goat to me," I said.

"Ah, but looks can be deceiving. And she's a pygmy goat, by the way."

"My mistake."

Daedalus shook his head as if to say, *That's all right.* "Gabby has a master's in psychology and is working toward a PhD. She's also an accomplished writer and poet."

I pretended to be impressed. "How about that."

Daedalus must have seen through my ruse. The light in his eyes dimmed. It somehow made him look even younger, to the point where I almost forgot he wasn't a real boy.

"You're not convinced," he said.

I suddenly felt like a heel, despite the fact that this doctor—this man of science and reason—was trying to convince me that I, Plato Jones, supersleuth, was dumber than a goat. Nevertheless, I decided to appease him. After all, Dr. Daedalus was better company than Felix. With him, I didn't have to worry about getting shot, stabbed, or blown to pieces. Besides, what did I have to lose other than the tattered remains of my dignity?

"Glasses," I said abruptly.

Daedalus narrowed his eyes, outwardly confused. "Glasses?"

"Yeah. Glasses. She needs a pair."

"I'm afraid I don't understand."

I gestured for Daedalus to come closer, and lowered my voice to a whisper, in the unlikely event that Gabby the supergoat might overhear, let alone comprehend, the wisdom I was about to impart upon the good doctor.

"Glasses are the universal symbol of intelligence, always have been," I said. "If you want people to take Gabby seriously, just slap a pair on her. Instant genius."

"So, with the addition of glasses, you would be more inclined to believe that Gabby is, in fact, a genius?"

"I wouldn't go that far, but it'd be a start."

Daedalus nodded, his gaze thoughtful. Then a smile spread across his face—one of those self-indulgent grins intellectuals get when they're about to prove someone wrong.

"I believe I have something better than glasses," he said.

"What's that?"

"Just wait. You're going to love this."

Oh boy.

Daedalus removed a small notepad and pencil from his coat pocket. He slipped the pad into Gabby's cell via a small rectangular slot. It landed on the floor with a soft smack. The goat slowly approached it.

"Gabby, I want you to write Mr. Jones a stirring sonnet," Daedalus said while holding a pencil through the slot. "A feast for the senses, a taste of your genius."

Gabby inclined her head forward. She sniffed the pencil, took it into her mouth . . . and ate it.

Daedalus went completely still, as did I—but for completely

different reasons, I'm sure.

After Gabby had swallowed the pencil, she started in on the notepad. With each crunch of paper, Daedalus's face grew increasingly flushed—further blurring the line between organic and synthetic—and I came closer and closer to bursting with laughter.

Only a true scholar could eat paper like that!

Once Gabby was done feasting, Daedalus seemed to have regained his composure. He straightened, cleared his throat, and offered me an apologetic smile. For my part, I tried to keep the laughter out of my eyes.

"I'm sorry about this," Daedalus said. "Gabby's usually very well behaved."

"It's all right," I said, struggling not to smile.

Daedalus shook his finger at Gabby in reproach. "That wasn't very nice of you. No after-dinner sugar cubes for a week."

Gabby met his disappointed gaze with her own vacuous stare. Then she began to urinate.

For the second time in less than five minutes, both Daedalus and I froze in place. This time the doctor's mortification wasn't evident on his face—his expression was unreadable. I, on the other hand, teetered on the edge of hilarity. My stomach trembled, the corners of my mouth twitched, tears welled in my eyes. Somehow I managed not to double over with laughter.

For almost a minute, the only sound in the entire room was the patter of Gabby's urine stream splattering against the cell floor. Her bladder empty, she turned, walked to the back of her cell, and commenced staring at the wall of posters and calendars.

Daedalus gaped at the puddle of goat urine for a time. When he finally spoke, he did so wearing a smile too bright and cheery to be real.

"I believe this concludes our tour. We should probably get back. Wouldn't want to keep Felix waiting."

24

Next, Felix took me to the recreation center on the fifth floor. I wondered why we had skipped this level to visit the R&D department instead of going in sequence. I guessed Felix wanted to save the fun stuff for last.

The rec center offered all the amenities you'd find in an exclusive health club: weight room, basketball court, shooting range, pool, running track. There was even indoor rock climbing and a movie theater. To sum it up, the place was a dream.

The boxing gym was our last stop. It was everything a gym should be. No high-tech training equipment. Just the essentials. Two rings, some punching bags, some jump ropes, and not much else.

There were three people in the gym. Two men traded blows in the ring. But it was the third person who grabbed most of my attention—a woman hammering taped fists against a heavy bag. Her form was flawless. Her blows landed with enough force to send the bag swaying. To call her good would have been a gross understatement. Amazing seemed a better fit. The same went for her looks.

She appeared to be in her late twenties or early thirties, wearing a white tank top, red shorts, and sneakers. She possessed a lean build that reminded me of a fitness model. Her mahogany skin glistened with sweat, and wavy black hair bounced around her shoulders with each perfectly executed strike.

I stared at her without realizing it. Felix put his hand on my shoulder, snapping me out of my daze.

"Nice, huh?" he said. "Come on. I'll introduce you."

We approached the woman from behind.

"Whoa, whoa," Felix said to her. "Calm down, champ. I think he's had enough."

The woman delivered a three-punch combo to the bag before turning to face us. Breathing hard, she wiped several strands of wet hair from her face.

"What do you want?"

Her voice was soft but confident, with an undertone of aggression. She had a British accent.

"I just stopped by to introduce you to our newest member," Felix said. "This is Plato Jones, part-time do-gooder, full-time badass. He also moonlights as a comedian."

Large brown eyes acknowledged me with indifference that bordered on disdain.

My muscles tensed, and a nervous lump formed in my throat. *Keep it together, superspy.*

"Nice to meet you." I offered her my hand. "And you are?"

The woman answered my question, but ignored my hand. I was batting five hundred.

"Helena," she said. "Helena Smirnov."

I watched her lips as she spoke. They were full and smooth. I wondered if they were as soft as they looked.

"Your last name," I said. "It's Russian."

"I'm aware of that."

Why did I just say that?

My cheeks burned with embarrassment, and retaining a calm demeanor became a battle of attrition.

Felix mercifully jumped in. "Helena works in the research department with the other eggheads. She can hack like nobody's business. And she does a little wet work from time to time. No sexual innuendo intended."

"Sounds like you're pretty talented," I said. "Emphasis on the *pretty*."

I'd done it again! Two brain farts in a row. It was as though my mind and mouth had joined forces to make me look like an idiot. If I kept this up, *People* magazine would have to add *Most Awkward Man Alive* to their list of countdowns.

"It was nice meeting you," Helena said with brevity.

"Yeah. Maybe we'll see each other around."

Helena resumed her assault on the heavy bag.

With that bit of humiliation out of the way, Felix introduced me to the men in the ring. Claus and Piertro. Both had been members of Eric and Stavros's mercenary group. Like their comrades, they seemed to have joined the MLF primarily for the money.

Then we started the last part of the tour. Leaving the gym, I took a final glance at Helena. She drank from a black squeeze bottle, a towel draped over her shoulder. She caught me looking. I instinctively turned my head.

Smooth, Plato. Real smooth.

As we walked to the elevator, Felix gave a long whistle then mimicked the sound of an explosion.

"Crash and burn."

"What are you talking about?" I asked, playing dumb.

"Oh, I think you know, Plato Jones."

"I think you give me too much credit."

"If you want to get to know Helena better, I can order her to go out with you. One of the perks of being the boss's son. I could even set you up with an ear piece, so I can feed pickup lines from afar."

"My own personal Cyrano de Bergerac."

"Who?"

"Never mind."

"So, what's it gonna be?"

I considered Felix's offer and immediately felt guilty about it. "I'll pass."

"No dice, huh? We can always go the traditional route."

"What's that?"

"Writing her a love note. At the bottom, you can put: 'Do you like me? Check yes or no.'"

"Fourth grade dating advice. I've hit a new low. Besides, who said I was even interested in her?"

"You did. Just not with words."

I could feel my face flushing.

"How sweet," he said. "My little boy is growing up."

"Shut up."

We traveled to the fourth floor, where the barracks, cafeteria, and armory were located. All the members of the MLF, with the exception of Louis and Felix, lived here. Felix didn't mention where he and his father kicked their feet up. Probably for security reasons.

The barracks was split into two parts, one for men and the other for women. The rooms were private, though friends and couples had the option of shacking up. In fact, they were encouraged to do so—to make space for new recruits like me. The halls were mostly empty, since everyone was hard at work.

I wondered what my assigned job would be. The last thing I wanted was to end up as part of a wet team. I'd seen enough death in the past few weeks to last a lifetime.

The armory offered the standard fare: handguns, assault rifles, shotguns, grenades, night-vision goggles. Not so standard were the crates upon crates of osmium ammo. The metal was rare, expensive, and highly regulated. It seemed unlikely that the MLF had acquired it through legal channels. They were either being supplied by black marketeers or had a secret mine somewhere. I'd have to look into that.

After leaving the armory, we swung by the cafeteria. I

suddenly realized I'd skipped lunch. With that realization came the question of what to eat.

On offer were a staggering number of dishes from all corners of the globe. In the mood for a hot dog? They had you covered. Curry on your mind? There it was. Monfongo? No problem. Kimchi? Help yourself. There was something for everyone. But one dish perplexed me. Something called salad jelly—basically, a gelatin mold filled with all the veggies you hated as a kid. I hoped to one day meet the person who came up with that vile concoction and ask him why. Just *why*?

Felix and I loaded our trays with mostly meat. My colon was going to hate me. Tomorrow, I'd apologize with a green salad. We grabbed a table near the buffet line, as men and women from the various departments filed in for dinner. I kept an eye out for Helena. When she didn't show, I felt slightly disappointed. Plato Jones, master detective, crushing on a woman I'd known for less than a day.

Strangely, interacting with Helena brought up memories of my marriage. The first time I saw Alexis, I'd been in awe, not only because of her beauty, but also because of the aura that surrounded her. It was warm and inviting, the kind you want to bask in for the rest of your life.

Helena's was different. Hers had an air of mystery. Bright and ominous at the same time, like a rumble of thunder on a sunny day. It was the potential for danger that I found captivating. Trying to find out why could've been the subject of a case study.

Our tour ended in the dorm's east corridor, where my room was located. I'd asked Felix if the unit had belonged to Marcelo or Lance. He assured me that it hadn't. The news came as a relief. I wasn't afraid of ghosts or anything like that. It's just that moving into someone's spot so soon after his death seemed inappropriate.

Felix pulled a plastic card out of his pocket and held it up to the scanner beside the door. The machine beeped, and the lock disengaged.

Felix pushed the door open. "Welcome to your new abode."

The room was an efficiency apartment, roughly eight-hundred square feet, fully furnished with a kitchenette, a walk-in closet, and—be still, my beating heart, do I even dare to dream?—a private bathroom. Finally, I could take showers without fear of being shanked or violated.

Score one for me!

It had beige walls and hardwood floors. Between two nightstands sat a full-size bed, draped with white covers that matched the couch and armchair. The desk and coffee table had a sleek appearance, very nouveau chic. But my favorite feature had to be the mounted flat-screen TV. Fifty inches of high-def, 3D-capable perfection.

"You like?" Felix asked.

"I love."

Felix handed me the keycard. "I'll let you settle in. If you need anything, or someone murders you in your sleep, don't hesitate to scream into the intercom over there."

He tipped his head at an intercom near the bed.

"Thanks for the tip," I said. "But how will I scream for help if I've been murdered?"

Felix narrowed his eyes in thought, then laughed. "That's why I like you, Plato Jones. You're not afraid to ask the tough questions. Anyway, I'll see you later. Got a few things to do. Debriefing. My dad's a stickler for details. One bullet equals one page of paperwork."

"Then it's a good thing we didn't use miniguns during the escape."

"Truer words have never been spoken."

"Have fun."

Watching Felix leave, I felt like a great weight had been lifted from me. I'd only known him for a short time and already he was plucking my nerves like banjo strings. How could the other MLF members deal with him on a daily basis? Maybe they'd grown accustomed to his particular brand of crazy. Still, it was nice to know at least one person more than just by name. In the company of strangers, you gravitate toward anything that's even remotely familiar. That was my experience, at least.

I sat on the couch for several minutes, in case Felix or someone else came knocking. When no one did, I got up and searched through the cabinets and drawers, pretending to take stock of the essentials I'd been provided: silverware, cleaning supplies, hygiene items. In truth, I was checking the room for bugs. Hidden cameras. Listening devices.

As far as I could tell, the place was clean. But apart from tearing down the walls, I couldn't be absolutely sure. After all, these MLF guys had been living in Zeus's backyard for years and were just now getting his attention. For them, hiding an impossible-to-find bug should've been the easiest thing in the world.

That's why I had to be aware of my movements at all times. Being a double agent is like trying to walk on ice while wearing dress shoes. One misstep, one lapse in concentration, and you'll end up flat on your back.

Permanently.

25

The next morning, I awoke to the sound of someone knocking on my door. I cracked open my eyes, slowly, so as not to expose them to too much sunlight too soon. Then I remembered my room had no windows.

I turned on the lamp and rolled out of bed. My body still ached from the can of whoop-ass Achilles had opened up on me the other day. The warden and his men probably fared worse. I knew Cronus had put the hurt on them. The only question was how bad. Luckily for them, getting ripped apart posed only a minor inconvenience for revenants.

I wrestled my clothes on and answered the door to see Felix's smiling face. Why couldn't it have been Helena's? Now there was a face I wouldn't mind waking up to.

"Good morning, Plato Jones," Felix said. "You look like fricasseed shit."

"Thanks."

"I got you a birthday present." Felix held up a bright-orange gift bag with a picture of a cartoon dog on it. It was licking its own balls.

"I appreciate the gesture," I said. "But you're a few months too early."

"Au contraire. Today *is* in fact your birthday. The old Plato Jones is dead. He died back at that hotel. You've been reborn as an MLF operative."

"Oh, okay."

Felix handed me the bag. It was fairly heavy. He sat in my armchair while I took the couch. I placed the bag on the coffee table. A little card attached to one of the handles read, *To Plato Jones. You're all right.*

The bag contained a Five-seven—likely the same one I carried back at the motel—two magazines filled with osmium rounds, a black smartphone identical to Felix's, and a phony driver's license. I spread them out across the table.

I recognized the headshot on the license. It had been lifted from my company website and Photoshopped to make me look edgier, with a buzz cut and beard stubble. The background, a still of the New Olympia public library, had also been altered, changed to a featureless shade of light blue. The signature on the back was a perfect forgery. The name, not so much.

"Brick O'Hardhat?" I said dubiously.

Felix grinned. "Mine is Willy McRambush."

I shook my head and moved on to the smartphone. I clicked the power button. The screen turned red.

"That's not a normal phone," Felix said.

"Is it a bomb?"

"It's *the* bomb, Plato Jones. Press your thumb against the screen."

"Okay, but if this thing explodes in my face, you had better hope it kills me."

Felix pretended to shiver. "Ooooh!"

I touched the screen. It turned green and the main menu popped up, displaying tons of icons, some familiar, others completely alien.

"Your phone has a built-in biometric sensor." Felix rose from his seat and came over to sit beside me. "You're the only person who can use it. Well, you, me, and my dad. Security measures. You understand."

"Sure," I said, wondering how R&D had gotten my fingerprints. I was probably better off not knowing.

"Let me show you what this sexy mama can do." Felix gestured for me to give him the phone.

He showed me all the features and how to access them. His earlier assessment rang true. This wasn't a normal phone. It was a superphone, even better than those used by OBI operatives, loaded with apps that no self-respecting spy should be without: a facial recognition scanner, various hacking programs, a particle detector, and an electronic jammer just to name a few. It was EMP-hardened as well, like the models in Daedalus's lab, and had a self-destruct mechanism, in case it fell into the wrong hands. But best of all, it came preinstalled with Angry Birds and its sequels. Cutting-edge tech. Gotta love it.

The phone was also the only means of activating the lift in the warehouse. Sort of like a garage door opener. All you had to do was enter the passcode on your phone and presto, you're on your way to MLF headquarters.

Felix returned the phone. "What do think? Cool, huh?"

"Very," I said. "Thanks."

"No thanks necessary, Plato Jones. You're part of the family now."

"Aren't I the luckiest boy in the world?"

"Damn right." Felix rose to his feet. "Now hurry and wash up. We've got things to do."

"What kind of things?"

"First, we grab some breakfast. It's crepe day in the cafeteria."

"And after that?"

"We hit the mall. The MLF is the hottest thing going these days. If you're gonna be working with us, you've got to look the part."

"Sounds great. But I'm a little short on cash. The authorities still have my wallet."

"I've got you. That's what friends are for. Besides, the guys in the records department are setting up your company account. They should be finished by tonight. Tomorrow morning at the latest. You can pay me back then."

"What about the cops?" I asked.

"What about them?"

"Don't you think that two criminals on the run, moving around in broad daylight, might attract a little, I don't know, attention?"

"You worry too much, Plato Jones."

"One of us has to."

"You haven't seen the news, have you?"

"Can't say that I have. TV doesn't seem to have cable."

"That's no good," Felix said. "I'll make sure someone gets on that right away."

"You're too kind. What were you saying about the news?"

"Oh, yeah, the news! I watched it last night, to see if we made the headlines."

"Did we?"

"Nope. They didn't mention us or the breakout. I was kinda disappointed. There's nothing more exciting than life on the lam. Being an outlaw on the run. Having your own wanted poster hanging outside the local saloon. Just like in the movies."

The lack of media coverage suggested the Gods were trying to cover up the incident. If the public knew that two dangerous criminals had not only escaped from an inescapable prison, but also had freed Cronus in the process, there'd be panic in the streets. On the plus side, I now had some wiggle room. Not a lot, though. I was still the new kid, and under close surveillance. For this first week, I wasn't allowed to leave the facility without a chaperone. A probationary period.

"That doesn't mean people aren't looking for us," I said. "Did you forget about the OBI?"

"The OBI is too busy looking for Cronus to worry about us. We're small potatoes. Well, you're a small potato. I'm a superstar."

"A superstar with zero media coverage."

"The coverage is coming, Plato Jones."

"After we win the war, right?"

Felix pointed at me. "I'll see you in the cafeteria. Don't take too long getting there. We run out of crepes pretty fast."

"Gotcha."

I remained on the couch after Felix had gone, trying to figure out how to contact Hermes. Using my new phone was out of the question. It was probably bugged—and the fact that Louis and Felix could access it whenever they pleased didn't help either. I wasn't very likely to happen upon a pay phone inside MLF headquarters, and finding a pay phone on the street these days was almost as unlikely. A prepaid cellular would work, if I could manage to get hold of one. In the end, I'd do whatever the situation demanded.

After breakfast, Felix and I rode the elevator up to the garage. Helena waited for us near the Caddy. A welcome surprise.

She wore a white tank top, jeans, brown riding boots, and a beaded bracelet that might have been jade. Her hair was pulled back into a short ponytail, accenting her eyes and cheekbones. If she wore any makeup, I couldn't tell. Not that she needed any.

"Looks like we're ready to get this show on the road." Felix glanced at me. "I almost forgot to tell you. Helena will be joining us. I thought we could use a woman's perspective. They do love to shop, after all."

Helena rolled her eyes.

I suspected the decision to come hadn't been hers. But it gave me a chance to redeem myself after our awkward first meeting—and it might give me more insight on how the MLF operated.

I nodded at Helena. "Good morning."

She returned neither the gesture nor the greeting. Getting on her good side was going to be a challenge. But defying the odds happened to be one of my specialties.

Felix hopped in the driver's seat. Helena and I took the back. I'd intended to do the gentlemanly thing and propose she ride shotgun, but Felix had other plans.

"Sit in the back with Helena," he said. "Keep her company."

Helena sighed but complied.

I convinced myself it was a good sign.

We rode the lift to the surface and headed east, through the ruins. When we hit the interstate, Felix turned on the radio. He stopped on a station that played nothing but old school R&B love songs. It appeared my unofficial matchmaker was trying to set the mood.

His plan worked. But probably not the way he had intended. I found myself glancing at Helena from the corner of my eye, as she sat motionless, gazing out the window, to a soundtrack of sexually charged tunes.

The situation reminded me of the time my mom drove my date and me to the junior prom. She made humiliating me her top priority, bringing up the most embarrassing moments from my childhood. Tantrums, bedwetting, crying over boo-boos, the whole shebang. Milestones of humiliation. She thought they were cute. I'd never been so mortified in all my life. Until now.

But why? Why did I feel more awkward now than I did back then? I rarely cared what people thought of me, especially people I barely knew. But there was something about Helena, something that had worked its way inside my head. It made me want to impress her. I couldn't explain it. Maybe Felix's insanity was rubbing off on me.

We traveled to Chimera's Crossing—a small settlement that walked the line between village and hamlet. Time didn't move slowly here. It was at a standstill. Everyone knew everyone, and the crime rate was in the negative. Sometimes I forgot that places like this still existed. A true community.

Chimera Shopping Centre sat just off the interstate ramp, a hub of activity peppered with bored teenagers waiting to move away after high school. It had four department stores and a movie theater connected by a central courtyard.

Felix pulled into a parking space and turned in his seat. "Well, I'm afraid this is where we part ways."

"Where are you going?" I asked.

"The sporting goods store. I need to pick up a new baseball bat. My old one's broken."

I had a theory about how that happened—one that involved bruises and broken bones.

"You two can go wherever you want." Felix handed me a wad of credits. "Helena will help you pick out something nice. Isn't that right, Helena?"

Helena gave an unenthusiastic thumbs-up.

We entered the mall via the food court, where Felix left Helena and me to do his own thing.

"So," I said, when we were alone. "Where should we start?"

Helena shrugged. "It's your shopping trip."

We headed to Bahari's—one of the four department stores—and hit the men's section. I sifted through the racks, glancing intermittently at Helena, who stood off to the side with a bland expression on her face. Things were off to a pretty shaky start. But there was still time to turn it all around.

"You like to shop?" I asked.

"According to Felix, every woman does," Helena said without humor.

"And we both know he's never wrong."

Helena's mouth twitched, almost becoming a smile. It

appeared I was making progress. I kept the ball rolling.

"Got any nicknames?" I asked. "Or do you just go by Helena?"

"Helena."

"I've got a quite a few. Most of them are only four letters long."

Helena didn't laugh. Maybe Felix had been right about my comedy routine needing work. I grabbed a random shirt from the rack. A white button-up with blue schooners and palm trees on it.

"What do you think of this one?" I asked.

"Looks fine."

I couldn't tell if she was being honest or just trying to shut me up. Ever the optimist, I chose the more favorable possibility. I folded the shirt over my forearm and continued to shop. The garment wasn't my style, but I planned to buy it anyway. I wanted to show Helena that I valued her opinion.

"How long have you been on the team?" I asked.

"A little over a year."

"You like it?"

"Sometimes," Helena said.

The conversation deflated into silence. The dull, forgettable department store music filled the void.

"What did you do before?" I asked after a minute.

"You have to earn the right to ask those kinds of questions," Helena said.

"Sorry."

Helena shook her head but appeared more irritated than before. Time for some damage control. I picked out a plain black button-up.

"How's this one?" I asked.

"It's better than the last," Helena said.

I sensed she was being honest this time, and swapped out the shirts.

In addition to helping me build a new wardrobe, her opinions also gave me insight into her personality. With clothing, she favored simplicity and cleanliness. Pieces that looked nice but didn't call too much attention to themselves. Maybe the same applied to people.

I picked out some more shirts and several pairs of jeans, and went to try them on. Helena waited outside the entrance to the dressing rooms.

I showed her six outfits in total. I received five nods and one head shake.

After everything had been paid for, Helena and I stopped by the shoe department—a place I hadn't been in a very long time.

As I tried on different pairs of shoes, I noticed Helena glancing at the women's section. Her eyes seemed drawn to a particular display: a high-heel sandal with an ankle strap that came in six different colors.

"Something tickling your fancy?" I asked.

Helena shifted her gaze from the display to me. "Not at the moment."

Ouch.

"Are you almost done?" Helena asked.

"Yeah, I think I'm good."

I bought five pairs of shoes: two pairs of sneakers, two pairs of dress shoes, and a pair of those sneaker-dress shoe hybrids. Helena called Felix to let him know it was time to go. But there was still something I needed to do.

"Nature's calling," I said. "You go on ahead."

"I'm sure Felix will be here right away."

"I'll be quick."

"You'd better."

Helena walked away without offering to carry the bags to the car. I was hoping she would have. Then I could have done the gentlemanly thing and said no, convinced her that I was every bit the courtier I appeared to be. Oh, well. There was always next time.

The restrooms were located in the customer service department. I left my bags with the clerk—a blonde satyr working behind the counter—and entered the men's room. I was alone.

I hid my smartphone behind the toilet in one of the stalls, waited two minutes, and returned to the customer service desk. The clerk reached for my bags, which sat on a shelf behind her.

"Sorry, but can I use your phone?" I asked, smiling apologetically. "I seem to have misplaced mine, and I need to remind my uncle to take his medicine. He's a touch senile."

The clerk said nothing but handed me a cordless phone, her expression bland.

"Thanks," I said. "This call won't be monitored, will it? My uncle doesn't want people to know about his . . . condition."

"No, sir," the clerk said monotonically.

I dialed Hermes's private number. I needed to let him know that I had survived the breakout—if he wasn't already aware—and that things were going according to plan. Whose plan, I wasn't quite sure. As the phone rang, I turned around and leaned against the edge of the counter. That way, I could be on the lookout for Felix and Helena.

Hermes picked up. "Who is this?"

"Why, it's your loveable nephew."

"Jones." Hermes didn't say my name so much as spit it out.

"That's right. Have you taken your antidiarrheal today? You remember the mess you made last week. The maid is still cleaning it up."

"You've got a lot of things to answer for."

I realized he was referring to Cronus. "It'll have to wait."

"Where are you?"

"Chimera Shopping Centre. It's in Chimera's Crossing."

"I know where it is, you simpleton. What are you doing there?"

"Shopping. About to head home in a few minutes."

"Where is that?" Hermes asked.

The question gave me pause. At present, revealing the location of HQ carried too great a risk. Knowing Jackass, he'd come sniffing around the industrial district. His presence could compromise the entire operation.

"I'm not at liberty to say," I said.

"Are you being watched?"

"I don't think so. But that could change at any moment."

"I knew this was a bad idea from the start."

"Great minds think alike."

"Don't flatter yourself," Hermes said. "When will you be able to speak openly?"

"I don't know. Soon, I hope. But look, I gotta go. I'll contact you again when I get the chance."

"You'd better."

"Oh, and don't call this number looking for me."

Hermes didn't bother asking why, but cursed under his breath.

"Talk to you later, Unc," I said. "Make sure to steer clear of greasy foods, and check your underwear regularly."

Hermes hung up.

I handed the phone back to the clerk. "Thanks again."

"Mm-hm."

Before she could go for my bags, I softly smacked myself on the side of the head. "Now I remember where I left my phone. I can be such a dummy sometimes."

The clerk smiled. It looked insincere.

"Back in a second."

I retrieved my smartphone then grabbed my bags. I made one last stop at the shoe department to pick up the heels Helena had been eyeing. I bought a green pair that almost matched her bracelet. Judging by her height and build, I estimated her to be a seven or seven and a half. I picked the latter. With everything taken care of, I finally left the mall. Felix and Helena waited for me in the car.

"Glad to see you're alive," Felix said. "Helena told me that you had to use the can. We were starting to wonder if you'd fallen in. I was about to call the coast guard."

I chuckled.

"He's serious," Helena said.

Felix nodded in affirmation.

Okay, then.

I loaded my bags into the trunk, on top of a baseball bat that looked brand new. A sticker on the side claimed it was unbreakable. Now Felix could bludgeon his enemies senseless without fear of damaging his weapon.

I held off giving Helena her gift. I preferred to do it in private. I realized that pursuing her romantically was a bad idea. If I accomplished my mission, she'd either end up in prison, dead, or on the run. Not the best foundations for a relationship. I almost wished she'd tell me that I had no chance. That would have made things much easier.

Worse yet, I failed to get any information out of her about the MLF. But I guessed it made sense. I still had to prove my loyalty. Felix seemed to trust me to an extent. But I had my sights set on bigger fish. If I managed to get on Louis's good side—provided he had one—I'd be set. It was like dominoes. Knock over the first one and the rest will follow.

26

Back at HQ, I went by Helena's place to drop off her gift. Finding it had been easy, thanks to the sliding nameplate on each apartment door. They saved me the trouble of having to ask Felix for the room number, then explaining why I needed it.

Helena answered the door, looking surprised to see me. "Need something?"

"I just stopped by to give you this." I held out the plastic bag containing the shoes.

"What is it?"

"Look, and find out."

Helena accepted the bag with notable reluctance, and removed the shoebox. I took the bag from her, crushed it into a ball, and stuffed it in my pocket.

Helena removed the lid and her eyes widened. She shook her head. The reaction appeared to be automatic.

"I can't . . ." she began.

"Sure you can."

"No, really . . ."

"I noticed they were the same color as your bracelet."

Helena glanced at her wrist. She still wore the bracelet.

"Almost," I added.

Helena frowned. For a moment, it seemed as though she might hand the box back to me. But she just sighed and said, "Don't make a habit of this, buying me things."

"Okay."

We stood in awkward silence for a moment.

"I should be going," I said.

"Yeah."

"I guess I'll see you later, yeah."

"Yeah."

"Bye."

"Bye." Helena slowly closed the door.

I walked away, feeling the sting of rejection. A feeling I was all too familiar with. She hadn't wanted to accept the gift. That much had been obvious. She likely did it out of pity. As I contemplated throwing in the towel, I heard a door open behind me.

"Plato."

I turned around to see Helena standing outside her door. She smiled at me. "Thanks."

I smiled back. "My pleasure."

"Don't get too comfortable, though."

"With what?"

Helena shook her head and changed the subject. "A few of us are going clubbing tonight."

"Am I invited?"

"I should hope so. It's in your honor, for passing your initiation. Felix came up with the idea while we were waiting for you."

"Are you coming?"

"I said 'us' didn't I?"

"Yeah, I suppose you did."

"Anyway, I've got a few things to take care of. I'll see you later tonight."

"Later."

Helena closed the door. As I walked down the hall, I felt a burst of glee. I jumped in the air and clicked my heels.

A woman rounding the corner caught me in the act and gave me a strange look.

"Don't mind me," I said. "Just working out a few kinks."

Felix and I jumped in the Caddy and headed to a nightclub called the Ferryman. Louis, Helena, and Danny would meet us there. The place was located in a predominately human neighborhood, and the clientele reflected this.

It also had the reputation of being a popular police hangout. The type of establishment hardened criminals might want to avoid—under normal circumstances. But nothing about the past few weeks had been normal.

According to Felix, Louis had an army of crooked pro-human cops on his payroll. I planned to share that tidbit of information with Hermes. Maybe he'd cut me some slack over the whole Cronus situation, as if I didn't already feel bad about it. I seriously doubted it. But it was worth a shot.

Before leaving HQ, I shaved my hair close to the scalp but left a five o'clock shadow untouched. I wanted to look less like my police mug shot and more the picture on my counterfeit license. Felix had suggested I bring my Five-seven in case we ran into trouble. His advice proved unnecessary. Sadly, carrying a concealed weapon had become part of my daily routine.

The Ferryman was a chimera of sorts: part jazz lounge, part bar, and part restaurant. It attracted an older crowd. You would've been hard pressed to find anyone there under twenty-five. Everyone seemed to know Louis, and people greeted him with the kind of enthusiasm usually associated with fear.

The doorman escorted us to a private booth at the back of the club. The booth had a single, curved bench. I sat next to Felix and across from Helena and Danny. Louis sat in the middle. A waitress appeared at our table. The thin brunette didn't look old enough to be selling alcohol.

I asked for a gin and tonic. Felix and Danny each had a bourbon and Coke. Louis ordered a pint of mead. I'd never tried the stuff. I'd never even been to a place that served it. Out of everyone, Helena went the most traditional route with beer.

There was something down to earth about a woman who drank beer. Something attractive. Though there was nothing about Helena that I didn't find attractive. As we drank, Louis told me about the club's clientele.

"The people here are like us," he said. "They've been wronged by the Gods. Had things taken away from them. Livelihoods, opportunities, loved ones. They're tired of it."

Listening to him, I realized that I still didn't know what the Gods had done to piss him off. It must have been pretty horrible if it inspired him to start a rebellion. Felix had refused to shed light on the subject. It'd probably be the same case with his dad. If I wanted the truth, I would have to get it from an unrelated secondary source.

Helena, maybe.

"Most of these men are cops," Louis continued. "A few are ex-cons. But in this place, none of that matters. Here, we're all brothers. We look out for each other."

Cops, ex-cons, and freedom fighters, all in the same bar. There was a joke in there somewhere.

"Looks like you have friends in high and low places," I commented.

"There are no such things as friends," Louis said. "Not for us. These people, every one of them is capable of betrayal. They can be bought, sold, or coerced into fighting against their own kind. To trust them is to invite ruin."

"How do you keep everyone in line?"

"I think you already know the answer."

I did. "Fear."

Louis nodded. "The most powerful force in the universe."

"Has anyone ever turned against the organization?"

"Two people."

I didn't have to ask what happened to the deserters. Louis's gaze told the violent story.

"Conspiring with the Gods is a crime against mankind," Louis said, peering at me with those hard eyes. "One that should never go unpunished. Wouldn't you agree?"

"Completely." *Unless it prevents innocent blood from being spilled.*

"Everyone has an agenda," Louis continued. "Their own vision of the future. Anyone who doesn't share ours is an enemy."

"I'll remember that."

Louis went back to his mead. But his eyes remained on me. The scrutiny filled me with unease. But I think that was the point. He wanted me to know someone was always watching—he was always watching—ready to put the screws to me if I ever wandered astray.

Across from me, Helena polished off her beer, making her the first person to finish his or her drink. Ten points for her. She flagged down the waitress and ordered another.

The girl vanished into the crowd and resurfaced in less than a minute. Someone bumped into her as she approached our table. She dropped the beer. The bottle shattered against the ground.

Helena mumbled an expletive. "I'll be at the bar."

"You should go with her," Felix said to me. "Keep her company."

"Sure." I downed the last of my drink and got up.

Louis, Felix, and Danny remained in the booth. They'd probably talk about me while I was gone. Here's hoping they had only good things to say.

* * *

Helena and I found two vacant stools near the middle of the bar. The bartender, her tank top full to bursting, tossed her black hair back over one shoulder as she picked up a tray and took our orders. Instead of getting another beer, Helena asked for a Tom Collins. I stuck with my gin and tonic.

I reached for my wallet, intending to pay for both our drinks.

"That won't be necessary," said the bartender. "Mr. King is handling everyone's tab."

By everyone, it sounded to me like she meant the entire bar. The generosity made sense. Fear as a form of control was more effective when coupled with random displays of altruism. "No need to let Louis have all the fun." I stuffed a twenty into the tip jar.

"Thanks, sweetie," the bartender said with a smile.

After our drinks arrived, I started a conversation with Helena.

"Where are you from originally?"

"Africa," Helena said.

"How'd you end up here?"

"It's a long story."

One she didn't feel like sharing, apparently.

"I'm from Skiathos," I said. "Ever been there?"

"No."

"Any siblings?"

"None that I know of."

"It looks like we have something in common," I said.

"Your file said you have a brother."

"You read my file?"

"I read everyone's file. I like to know who I'm working with."

"Gotcha. Yeah, I have an older brother. But we haven't spoken in years. I don't know where he is or what he's doing. To be honest, I don't care."

We were quiet for a time.

"Want to have a shot with me?" Helena asked out of the blue.

"Sure."

Helena raised her hand to get the bartender's attention. "Two shots of ouzo."

The woman poured our drinks.

"Cheers," I said.

We toasted to nothing. Helena took her shot as easily as I took mine.

"Not even a flinch," I said. "Impressive."

"I've had practice."

Something else we had in common. When it comes to drinking, there are three types of people: those who do it for fun, those who do it to forget, and those who simply love alcohol. I wondered which category Helena fell into.

"Up for round two?" I asked.

"Always."

"Let the good times roll." I summoned the bartender, who made us two more shots. "Cheers, again."

We had another toast and swallowed our drinks. This time, mine went down the wrong pipe. My throat tightened painfully. My expression turned sour. I tried to hold in a cough but failed.

A sly grin crept onto Helena's face.

"What?" I asked, clearing my throat.

"Nothing."

"It went down the wrong pipe, that's all."

"Whatever you say."

"You think I can't handle my liquor?"

Helena gave a slight shrug. "I didn't say anything."

"You don't have to. Your eyes say it all, which are very nice, by the way. Your eyes. Even when they're glazed over."

"You're not trying to change the subject, are you?"

"Now why would I do that?"

"Maybe to distract from the fact that you can't hold your liquor." Helena's smile broadened.

"Care to partake in a wager?"

"What kind of wager?"

"A friendly one," I said. "Four shots for each of us. Whoever finishes first is the winner."

"What do I get when I win?"

"*If* you win, you get a prize of your choosing. Anything you want."

Helena pursed her lips thoughtfully. I imagined kissing them.

"And if you win?" Helena asked.

"You have let me take you out."

"On a date?"

"Yep."

Helena seemed to consider the offer. "Let's make things more interesting. Five shots. One-fifty-one."

"Uh oh, we've got a badass on our hands." I called over the bartender and ordered ten shots of Bacardi 151.

The woman didn't bat an eyelash. Maybe she thought we planned to share our shots with Louis and the others. Or maybe she was just used to seeing people exceed their limits.

"Ready to lose?" I asked Helena.

"Only if you are."

I stood up and arranged the shots in a horizontal line across the bar. Helena did the same. During my college years, I discovered that drinking shots in rapid succession was better done while standing up. Improved leverage for improved performance.

Bystanders started looking in our direction. They must have sensed the imminent showdown. Surrounded by criminals and crooked lawmen, I felt like I was in a cowboy movie. But instead of a six-shooter, I carried a semiautomatic.

"On your mark," I began, "get set, go!"

Cheers erupted as the contest began. I finished four shots. Already, I felt sick. But I ignored what my body was telling me and downed the last one, defeating Helena by a hairsbreadth. My head spun and my stomach burned. I didn't care. I slammed the empty glass against the bar.

My victory was met with thunderous applause.

Helena looked half-angry, half-impressed. Her eyes gleaming with drunkenness. Letting her win might've been the chivalrous thing to do. But she was no damsel in distress. She exuded strength and self-sufficiency—the kind that remained evident whether she was in a T-shirt and jeans or a ruffled ball gown. Indulging her solely on the basis of gender seemed demeaning.

"Looks like I won," I slurred as we sat down.

"So you did," Helena said, her voice deep and husky.

"You know what that means."

"Yes. One date."

"That's right. And who knows? One date might turn into two. Two into three. Three into . . ."

"Let's just focus on getting through the first one."

"Absolutely," I said, nodding.

The movement caused Helena to spawn a pair of semi-transparent clones. Beautiful illusions.

The bartender put two more shots in front of us.

"What's this?" I asked.

"Your friend said you both could use one more." The bartender tilted her head toward Louis's booth.

I turned around on my barstool and saw Felix grinning at me.

I should have known.

I turned back around. To Helena, I said, "Good for one more?"

She raised her glass without a word.

* * *

I had planned to crash as soon as I got back to HQ, but Felix pestered me into to staying up with him. We sat in the movie theatre in the barracks, eating junk food and watching *The Explorers*—one of my favorite alien flicks of all time. Empty soda cans and candy wrappers lay at our feet.

"You believe in aliens?" Felix asked.

"Sure," I said. "The universe is a big place. Has to be something out there."

"Ever seen one?"

"Just Hera. I keep hoping that one day she'll return to her home planet, and take the rest of the Gods with her."

"Fucking-A," Felix agreed, raising his soda can in approval.

"How about you? Ever had any close encounters of the third kind?"

"Plenty. In fact, I interact with extraterrestrials on a daily basis. You, for instance. No mere human is able to outdrink Helena without passing out immediately after."

"I was on my way there. Trust me."

"She's more than just a pretty face, and a nice ass, and perky . . . you know what I'm saying."

"Yeah."

Felix tossed his empty drink can on the floor and cracked open a new Sprite. "But don't get on her bad side. She'll rip your nuts off and use them a Baoding balls."

"Speaking from personal experience?"

"Nah. I just read her file. She's ice cold. You're welcome to take a peek. I mean, I can't give you access to all our personnel files. Security purposes. Classified information and all that. But Helena's is fine. With you being sweet on her and all."

It was an attractive offer. Gathering information on Helena might prove valuable to the case. However, the idea of invading her privacy in such a way didn't sit well with me. I'd rather get the info straight from the source. Sure, it was a bad idea. But bad decisions were the building blocks of my career.

"I'll pass," I said. "But thanks for the offer."

"If you change your mind, let me know."

"Okay."

"I'm glad you're here, Plato Jones. We're going to bring about a new era. Mankind is crying out for a new world. And the MLF will deliver. The Gods, their time is up."

"That'll be a great day," I said.

I probably should have felt guilty for agreeing with him. But I didn't, at least where the Gods were concerned. Getting rid of them would not only benefit the human race, but every race—and that was where my ideology differed from the MLF's. Uplifting humanity was their only concern. No one else mattered. If Louis's dreams came to fruition, humans would become the new Olympians. Nothing would change. The cycle of hatred and injustice would continue in perpetuity. I refused to let that happen.

"Before I forget." Felix took a card out of his pocket and gave it to me. "A gift from me to you."

"And it's not even my birthday." I examined my new debit card or, rather, Brick O'Hardhat's debit card.

It was clear, with white lettering and a silver magnetic strip. The account was with a bank I'd never heard of, Pollux & Castor. Probably just a front, masquerading as a legitimate business. Gangland tactics at their best.

"You get a monthly allowance of twenty thousand credits," Felix said.

My breath caught. Twenty thousand credits. I hadn't even made that much when I worked in the OBI. No wonder the MLF had such a dangerous recruitment process.

"My dad put in a little extra for what you did back at Tartarus," Felix went on. "I did too."

"Thanks." I put the card in my wallet. "Can I ask you a personal question?"

"I don't know. I'll have to think about. Okay, I've thought about it. Fire away."

"How in the world are you and Louis paying for all this?"

"We have a business venture on the side. Very lucrative."

"What kind of business venture?"

"I guess you could say we're procurers of rare and valuable items."

More cryptic bullshit. But at least I had a something new to think about. No doubt the black orb counted as one of those rare and valuable items. It must have been important if Louis and Felix were willing to do business with nonhumans. I wondered what other shady activities the two of them were involved in.

"On another note," Felix said. "We've figured out what to do with you."

"Have you now?"

"Oh yes. You're going to be a field agent. That means you get to do all the fun stuff."

"Like what?"

"Spying on people, gathering information, sneaking behind enemy lines, things like that."

I hoped my duties didn't include assassination as well.

"You'll also be acting as my personal bodyguard," Felix said.

"Need me to fend off your army of rabid female fans?"

"Exactly."

"In that case, it should be an easy job. I won't have to do much of anything."

Felix chuckled. "I'm not going to sugarcoat things, Plato Jones. The coming days are going to be rough. A lot of our teammates won't live to see the new era. Just an unfortunate reality of war. But you, me, we're warriors. We'll survive. We always do. And we always come back for more."

27

In addition to the twenty thousand credits in my account, Louis and Felix had each deposited an additional five hundred thousand. I, Plato Jones, was officially a millionaire. It felt like a dream—and it might as well have been one. Once the mission ended, the OBI would confiscate my assets. It was standard procedure for all undercover operations. Faced with that realization, I decided to live it up while I could.

I bought three passes to Shangri-La—one of the most expensive resorts in Europe. I invited Felix, hoping to get more information out of him. I also invited Helena. When she tried to refuse, I reminded her about our bet. She kept her word and agreed to come. Ten points for her.

Shangri-La sat atop a floating island. How it stayed aloft was explained in the brochure. Something to do with particle manipulation. Not my area of expertise, but impressive nonetheless.

The resort had a futuristic aesthetic. Lots of smooth, white architecture and mirrored windows. The morning sun gave each structure an ethereal glow.

Upon our arrival, Helena made a beeline for the health spa. Felix and I checked out the largest of the resort's ten pools. The crowd was a mix of races—humans, minotaurs, satyrs, and even a few water nymphs.

We lounged poolside, tossing back mojitos and swapping stories about our love lives. Mine fell into the horror category. Felix bragged about a foursome he'd had with three Swedish supermodels. I questioned the authenticity of his claim.

The conversation inevitably touched on my pseudo-relationship with Aphrodite. I saw it coming and had prepared a lovely revision. Now, instead of discussing her husband's death over dinner—which is what actually happened—she and I met at an OBI function hosted by Zeus. Hermes had brought her along as a date, only to have me steal her from under his nose.

"So, you never banged her?" Felix asked.

"Nope."

"You didn't put it in? Not even a little?"

"Read my lips. I did not have sexual relations with that Goddess."

"Do you regret it?" Felix asked.

"Not one bit. Just kissing her almost took me under. I don't want to think about what might've happened if we'd gone further."

"How were you able to resist?"

"Willpower."

Felix grinned. "Plato Jones, you are a God among men, and Gods. But don't take that literally, or I'll overthrow you too."

"We wouldn't want that to happen."

A trio of bikini-clad women walked past us. Felix winked at one of them—a blonde. She smiled provocatively. Maybe he hadn't been lying about that foursome.

"You never told me how you and your dad got into all this," I asked, after the women had passed.

"I know." Felix sipped his mojito.

"Feel like sharing?"

"Not right now. I don't mix business with pleasure, unless stabbing, shooting, or maiming is involved."

I had thought bringing Felix here would've loosened his tongue. That's what I get for thinking. But this trip didn't have to be a total waste.

The girls that walked past us had grabbed a table near the bar. The blonde stared at Felix while her friends carried on a conversation.

"If that girl stares any harder, you might get a concussion," I said to Felix.

He looked at her. "Can't say I blame her."

"You should talk to her. Buy her a drink or something. If you're lucky, she might be willing to look past that gruesome face of yours and see that you're not such a bad guy . . . ten percent of the time."

That seemed to be all the motivation Felix needed. "You know what, Plato Jones? I think I'll do that. Want me to set you up with one of her friends? The brunette looks like she'd be dynamite in the sack."

"I'll pass."

"Oh yeah, I almost forgot. You only have eyes for Helena."

I neither confirmed nor denied that statement.

"Do what you have to do," Felix said.

"I always do." *Occasionally to my detriment.*

I exited the deck while he introduced himself to the girl. I wouldn't think he'd try anything funny with her, not with so many people around. He wasn't that crazy.

I ditched my smartphone in my cabin and bought a prepaid cell from one of the resort's gift shops—one with easily avoidable security cameras. I used the last of the money Felix had lent me the other day. Using my debit card would have created a paper trail for the MLF to follow. I'd have had a tough time explaining why I needed another cell phone when the one I had was already top of the line.

I went into a nearby restroom. There were three people

inside. I hung out near the sinks, pretending like I had something in my eye, until they left. Then I dialed Hermes's number.

"Who is this?"

"This is your father," I said in my best Darth Vader voice. "Have you finished buffing my floors yet?"

"Hello, Jones."

"You'll never guess where I am."

"Hades?"

"Nice guess, but no," I said. "I'm at Shangri-La."

"The resort?"

"Nothing but."

"How did you . . . ?" Hermes didn't finish the question.

I could finish it for him though. He wanted to know how a schmuck like me could afford to be in a place like this. He must've realized the obvious—that I was on the MLF's payroll.

I spent the next few minutes telling him about my experience with the MLF up until that point. This time, I risked revealing the location of HQ. I also told him about the crooked cops, Pollux and Castor, Louis's mysterious business venture, and the black orb.

"Any information on the source of their powers?" Hermes asked.

"Not yet. No one's even mentioned it. They don't fully trust me."

"Then make them trust you."

"I'm working on it."

"Work harder."

I had sensed Hermes's anger from the second he answered the phone. It seemed to be intensifying. I knew why.

"Any luck finding tall, dark, and gruesome?" I asked.

"No."

"Sorry to hear that."

"This was a mistake," Hermes said. "Hiring an idiot like you for something this important."

"I didn't get hired. I got drafted. So who's the bigger idiot? The idiot who screwed up on the job, or the idiot who hired him in the first place?"

Hermes let the insult slide. "You think they planned on Cronus joining their ranks?"

"Yeah, but not just him. Louis figured that if Cronus teamed up with the MLF, the other Titans might jump in as well."

"Has King mentioned any of the other Titans?"

"Only that the best way to get them involved is to get Cronus to convince them. But that seems impossible now that Cronus himself isn't on board. Funny thing, though. Felix doesn't seem too broken up over Cronus not playing ball. I guess he figures the big guy will keep the OBI busy while he sets up the next stage of his master plan?"

"And that would be?"

"I haven't found out yet," I said. "But I'll let you know the second I do."

"Anything else to report?"

"That's it for now. By the way, there are lookouts posted throughout the industrial district, posing as beggars, squatters, drug dealers, and the like, so don't go snooping around the area. I'd rather not have my cover blown."

"Are you implying that I don't know how to be discreet?"

"Only when it comes to wearing ugly suits that attract a lot of negative attention. Oh, before I forget. Has Herc pounded you into the ground yet?"

"Goodbye, Jones." Hermes hung up.

I dropped the phone onto the floor and stomped it until it shattered. I flushed the smaller pieces down the toilet. The rest I tossed in the trash. Keeping the phone would have been too dicey. I'd buy another once my probation ended—and I was allowed to leave HQ without a babysitter.

On my way back to the pool, I ran into Helena in the

hallway. Her tank top and very short shorts put more of her dark skin on display than I'd seen up to that point. I'd been looking forward to seeing her in a bathing suit, but beggars can't be choosers. Besides, she could've worn a potato sack and made it work.

"Fancy meeting you here," I said. "Have a good time at the spa?"

"It was okay."

"Where are you going now?" I asked.

"The gift shop."

"How about that? That's exactly where I was headed."

Helena smirked in what might have been amusement. "I suppose you want to go together."

"Well, since you brought it up . . ."

Helena's smirk inched toward becoming a smile. "Fine. But don't even think about buying anything for me."

"If you insist. If you want to buy me something, though, I won't stop you."

Helena laughed softly, flashing perfect teeth. "Come on."

We went to a gift shop on the third floor. It wasn't the one I had visited earlier. That one had been similar to a drugstore. This one catered to the big spenders. It had everything: designer clothes and jewelry, high-end electronics, and even a small selection of exotic automobiles.

While Helena hunkered down in the women's clothing department, I drooled over the cars. A red Ferrari Spider in particular. The dealer on hand was Chet—a man with shiny black hair and one of the most artificial smiles I'd ever seen. He descended like a vulture the instant he spotted me and spent half an hour giving me the usual salesman shtick, relaying the manufacturer's history and listing the car's numerous features. He was getting around to the most important bit of info—the price—when Helena came over with two garment bags.

"What have you got there?" I asked.

"Clothes."

I expected her answer to be a tad more specific, but it didn't matter. Whatever was in those bags, she'd look good in it.

"Want me to take those off your hands," I asked.

Helena shot me a look that said *you can't be serious.*

I figured she'd shoot down my attempt at chivalry. But it showed my capacity to be a gentleman. That had been the point.

Chet stepped toward her, beaming.

"You must be the wife." He extended his hand toward Helena. "Chet Stevens."

She made no effort to shake it.

"Be nice," I said to her.

Helena sighed and shook Chet's hand.

"Naomi Douglas," she said, using an alias. "We're not married."

"Nice to meet you, Naomi," Chet said. "Plato and I were just talking about this beautiful piece of Italian engineering."

He gestured at the Ferrari.

"Not bad," Helena said. "A little flashy, but not bad."

"Well, now that we've gotten the little lady's seal of approval," Chet said, and looked at me, "the only one that's left is yours."

I laughed uncomfortably. I almost told him that the car, while beautiful, was out of my price range. Then I remembered all the zeroes in my back account—and my plan to live it up while I could.

"I'll take it," I said.

Chet clapped his hands together. "Excellent!"

I thought I saw cartoon dollar signs flash in his eyes.

28

I WAS LOOKING FORWARD TO BREAKING IN MY NEW RIDE after the vacation ended. But it would have to wait. Felix received an assignment from Louis. I was obligated to join him—as his bodyguard. Imagine my excitement.

Louis owned a secret airfield in rural Boreasville. From there, we traveled to India by private jet. Our goal was to broker a deal with someone named Majit. As usual, Felix skimped on the details. I didn't know what we were after or why, just that it was secret to all but the highest ranking MLF members. Could it be connected with the superpowers Felix and the others displayed during the heist? Fingers crossed.

We landed in Himachal Pradesh in Northern India. Restaurants, tenements, and open-air markets lined the crowded streets, resplendent with bright colors and decorations. Snowcapped mountains loomed in the distance, dotted with similar settlements. The humid air smelled strongly of spices and car exhaust.

We rented a jeep and drove into the neighboring jungle, following a series of trails that wound through the underbrush. At length, we came to a stronghold contained by a towering wall of stone. It looked old, perhaps something left over from the British occupation. Snipers—human and minotaur—watched us approach from the ramparts with their weapons trained on us.

Four guards met us at the front gate. They wore jungle fatigues and carried AK-47s. After confirming our identities, they let us pass. A collection of silos, storage buildings, and housing units lay within the curtain wall. We parked in a small lot beside a warehouse.

As we hopped out of the jeep, a golf cart pulled up. A guard sat behind the wheel. The person I believed to be Majit occupied the passenger seat.

During the plane ride, Felix had told me a little about the guy—how he had been working with the MLF since its inception, and how their continued partnership was integral to our success. Unfortunately, he didn't offer any specifics. He also failed to mention Majit was a wood nymph.

The cart came to a stop and Majit stepped out wearing a tan leisure suit and sandals. He stood around five-six, frighteningly thin, with skin like tree bark. His yellow eyes glowed eerily, and he had moss in place of hair.

Another nonhuman with connections to the MLF. What was going on here?

"Welcome, gentlemen," the nymph said with a heavy Indian accent. "I trust you're doing well."

He and Felix shook hands.

"Very well, Majit," Felix said. "What about you, Plato Jones? Are you doing well . . . as well?"

"Just peachy," I said.

The fact that Felix used my real name implied that he trusted Majit on some level.

"Plato Jones," Majit said, "I don't believe we've met."

"Yeah, I'm the new kid in town." I shook his hand.

It felt as rough as it looked.

The three of us got into the golf cart. The driver took us

to a Spanish-style villa on the northern edge of the courtyard and dropped us off at the front door.

The house could have been one of Oprah Winfrey's summer retreats. Three stories high, it had huge windows and a roof shingled in terra-cotta. Vines snaked up walls of pure white, bursting with flowers.

"Welcome to my humble abode." Majit led us inside.

Stone floors and walls of polished wood gave the interior a warm, lived-in feel. Everywhere I looked, I saw something expensive: rugs, paintings, tapestries, antiques, and other symbols of opulence.

We ascended marble stairs to a third-floor patio that overlooked an orchard, where a team of humans and satyrs—wearing loincloths—toiled in the subtropical heat. Right away, I noticed something unusual about the trees being tended. They were all dead.

We sat at a wicker table. Three human butlers in white livery had pulled out our chairs. A parasol shielded us from the sun.

"Can I offer either of you a drink?" Majit asked.

"I'm cool," Felix said.

"So I am," I said. "Thanks though."

Majit nodded. "So, Mr. King. How is business?"

"Booming," Felix answered curtly.

"That's good to hear. I wish I could say the same. This season has been particularly rough. Monsoons."

"I hope this doesn't affect our deal. That would put a real damper on this entire trip. And if there's one thing I can't stand, it's dampness."

"No need to worry. Our agreement still stands."

"Awesome."

Majit got on his cell phone. "Bring it out."

A male satyr with red hair entered the patio. He wore

the same white uniform as the human servants. He carried a metal briefcase. Alongside him walked two armed guards, minotaurs with black-and-white-spotted fur.

The satyr placed the suitcase on the table, bowed his head, and exited the patio. The minotaurs remained—I guessed in case Felix or I tried anything cute.

Majit pressed a button on his phone. The lock on the briefcase released. The lid slowly opened. Inside, a vacuum pack containing around ten seeds—the size of apple seeds—rested in a foam indentation. Their translucent shells contained motes of glowing yellow light. I'd never seen anything like them.

Felix took out his smartphone and started one of the scanning apps. Which one, I wasn't sure. He held the device over the seeds for several seconds.

"Is everything satisfactory?" Majit asked.

"Looks that way," Felix said.

Majit closed the briefcase. The lock reengaged.

"Shall we settle up?" Majit asked.

"Let's," Felix said.

Majit tapped his thumb against his cell's touchscreen. Felix's smartphone chimed. He pressed a button on his phone, and the briefcase's locking mechanism disengaged. He closed the lid before it had a chance to fully open, resetting the lock.

He and Majit put away their phones.

"Thank you very much, Mr. King," Majit said.

"No, thank you, Mr. . . ." Felix paused. "You know, I don't think I ever learned your last name."

Majit smiled, his eyes glowing. "We all have our secrets."

His comment made me wonder if Majit was his real name or just an alias. I wasn't about to ask.

"Well, as nice as this get-together has been, I think it's time we hit the old dusty trail," Felix said. "You ready to get outta here, Plato Jones?"

"Lead the way," I said.

"Then let's hurry." Felix pushed out of his seat. "I want to pick up a few orders of lamb curry before we head home. You can't visit India without getting some authentic, tongue-torching curry. State law."

"I do enjoy a good curry." I stood up and grabbed the suitcase.

Felix pointed at me while speaking to Majit. "I love this guy. Very professional, but still takes time to enjoy the little things."

We returned to the front of the house and loaded ourselves into the golf cart. As we moved through the courtyard, I noticed a scuffle to our right. Two human guards struggled to restrain a satyr—a field worker judging by the loincloth. Felix and Majit ignored the commotion.

As I continued to watch, the satyr wriggled free and broke into a sprint. There was a crack of gunfire. He collapsed.

Crouched atop the rampart, a sniper had his rifle trained on the satyr. He kept it there as the two guards removed the body.

Anger and revulsion forced me to look away. I wasn't sure which one sickened me the most: the fact that someone had just been gunned down or the lack of reactions from Felix and Majit. For the first time, I couldn't wait to speak with Hermes. If the OBI didn't burn this place to the ground, I'd do it myself.

We reached the parking lot. Majit accompanied us to the jeep. I deposited the briefcase in the backseat and got into the passenger side.

As Felix started the engine, Majit offered us a few parting words. "It's always a pleasure doing business with you, Mr. King. I hope to see you again soon. You too, Mr. Jones."

"You'd see us a lot more if you cut down on your prices," Felix said. "Give us a loyal customer discount or something like that."

Majit disregarded the comment.

"Farewell, gentlemen," he said. "Give your father my regards."

We left through the main gate. The compound soon became lost in the foliage.

"I hate that guy, don't you?" Felix said.

"Well, I only just met him, but yeah. I hate him."

"He's lucky he has something we need. After we win the war, he's mulch."

"Speaking of the war," I said. "Are those seeds part of the battle plan?"

"We wouldn't be here if they weren't, Plato Jones. You ask the silliest questions."

"I have to keep you on your toes, make sure you keep giving me silly answers. Consistency is a virtue."

"That it is."

"You gonna tell me what they are?"

"Not until you're a member of the inner circle with me and my dad . . . and Danny . . . and Helena . . . and Eric . . . and Stavros . . . and all the rest."

"You forgot the Professor and Mary Ann."

Felix chuckled. "Just keep doing what you're doing, and you'll be playing with the big dogs in no time."

"Can you give me a little something to go on in the meantime?"

"The most I can say is that those seeds are the future of mankind. Building blocks for a new world. A better world. So long as they stay in the right hands."

"Our hands," I said.

Felix pointed at me as if to say *bingo.*

29

My probation ended while Felix and I were in India. When we returned, I decided to celebrate by taking my Ferrari for a spin. I would've invited Helena to come along, but that would have to wait. I needed to contact Hermes first.

I left the base—*accidentally* leaving my smartphone behind—and got on the highway. My new wheels garnered a lot of attention from my fellow motorists, as well as a few cops. But with Hermes and Louis working behind the scenes, I had little to fear from the authorities.

The MLF was another matter. They might have planted a bug in my car while I was away. I treated the notion as truth. Better safe than dead.

Owl's Creek was a small town east of New Olympia—a place I hoped was under the MLF's radar. I stopped by an ATM and took out some cash, which I used to purchase another prepaid cell phone. Pretty soon, I was going to have to start buying them wholesale.

My next stop was a green space called Owl Park. I parked behind the rec center and crossed the grass to a restroom facility. There was no one inside. I called Hermes, who wanted to speak with me in person—to make sure I wasn't an MLF imposter and I hadn't been indoctrinated. We agreed to meet in the arcade of a nearby mini-mall. The noise would mask our conversation.

The mini-mall was a ghost town. I wouldn't have been shocked to see tumbleweeds rolling by. You could have counted the number of shoppers on one hand, and there were more empty spaces than stores. I found the sight to be bit depressing.

The arcade sat between an empty storefront and a rug shop that was going out of business. A lanky teen with a blond mop top and severe acne stood behind the counter, messing around on his phone. He and I were the only people there.

Retro titles filled the game cabinets—*Pac-Man*, *Galaga*, *Donkey Kong*, and so on—and the trinkets in the prize case looked as though they had been there since the Pleistocene era. I bought some tokens and played *Kung-Fu Master*, beating the game in one clean run.

Yep. I've still got it.

I went to the other end of the arcade to play some skee ball. I finished one round and was about to start another when Hermes—as Easton—showed up.

"Mind if I join you?" he asked.

"Depends on how bad you want to lose."

I slipped two tokens into the skee ball machine. It lit up and made a series of digitized noises tailored particularly to annoy parents.

"A new look," Hermes said.

I realized he was referring to my haircut. "Like it?"

"Not at all."

"In that case, I think I'll keep it for a while," I stepped away from the machine. "After you."

Hermes grabbed a wooden ball from the dispenser and rolled it up the slick incline. It sailed into the topmost hole—the smallest hole, worth fifty points.

"You've played this before?" I asked.

"Once."

"It's not nice to lie."

Hermes grinned and moved aside. "What do you have for me?"

"New information." I grabbed a ball. "Something important, I think."

"We're not paying you to think. We're paying you to get results."

"I don't recall you paying me at all. Unless you're talking about that little deposit you put in my bank account."

I rolled the ball. Fifty points. Hermes seemed slightly impressed. I was too. I guessed Jackass brought out the competitor in me.

Hermes and I continued taking turns at the machine, as I told him about Louis's private airfield, the compound in India, and the bronze seeds. By the time I finished speaking, we were still tied. Neither of us had rolled anything under fifty.

"Bronze-colored seeds," Hermes said as if talking to himself.

"Yeah. You familiar with anything like that?"

"No." He rolled another fifty.

"Sure about that?"

Hermes frowned at me. The Olympians had a thing about being asked to repeat themselves. They considered it beneath them. But as always, Jackass's ego was the least of my concerns.

"Don't even think of pulling the same crap you did during the last case." I matched his roll and turned to face him. "If you know something, tell me."

"You forget yourself, mortal."

"I haven't forgotten myself. But apparently you have. If you planned to intimidate me, you should have worn a different suit, Easton."

Hermes's expression darkened. The muscles in his jaw jumped noticeably.

I glanced at the skee ball machine. "You're up. Or are you throwing in the towel?"

Hermes rolled without lining up his shot. The ball missed its mark by a hair and slipped into the bottommost hole, which had no value.

"It seems I'm the victor," I said.

"The only reason you won is because of this body," Hermes argued. "It lacks coordination."

"The old it's-not-my-body excuse, huh? Surely you can do better than that."

Hermes gave no response.

"Let's try this again," I said. "Do you know anything about those seeds?"

"For the last time, no," Hermes replied, anger clinging like frost to his voice.

Stubborn goat.

"I'm not sure who's worse, you or your mom," I said. "I'd probably give you the edge, though. You've never sent hired guns after me. If you wanted to kill me, I'm sure you'd prefer to do it in person."

"You know me better than I thought," Hermes said.

"Are we done here?"

"Yes. Unless you have something else for me."

"I'm tapped out for now. But I do have a request. Don't shut down Majit's operation until I give the go-ahead. And if you plan on doing recon, please stick to satellite surveillance."

"I know how to run an operation."

"Yeah. Right into the ground."

Hermes tilted his chin. "After this is over, we're going to have a discussion about respect."

"Mutual, I trust."

Hermes scoffed.

"For now, I'll keep playing nice with Felix and the others," I said. "I think I'm close to joining he and Louis's inner circle."

"Keep me posted."

"Sure thing. By the way, have you made any progress on your end?"

Hermes's suddenly looked weary. He must have realized I was talking about the hunt for Cronus. "We're still following leads."

I had hoped for a different answer. Cronus posed an infinitely greater threat than the MLF. If he managed to rally the other Titans, it would be only a matter of time before they marched on Olympus. The destruction would be unimaginable.

"I'm rooting for you," I said.

Hermes nodded. As we prepared to go our separate ways, I caught him glancing at the skee ball machine.

"Have time for a quick rematch?" I asked.

Hermes returned a grin.

I put my last two tokens into the coin slot.

30

HERMES'S UPDATE ON THE CRONUS SITUATION HAD GIVEN ME a case of the jitters. It only got worse after I arrived at HQ. I hit the weight room to burn off my nervous energy. There, I found Helena performing a 180-pound bench press without a spotter. I blinked hard to make sure I wasn't seeing things. Nope. This was the real deal.

I waited until she had finished her set before approaching. "Is there anything you can't do?"

Helena sat up on the bench, breathing heavily. Sweat ran down her face, arms, and chest, dampening the front of her blue tank top.

"If there is, I can't afford to know about it," she said.

"What do you mean by that?"

"Nothing." Helena stood up.

I followed her to the treadmill area. It seemed we had yet another thing in common—mixing resistance exercise with cardio. The bigger the muscles, the more oxygen they need to perform efficiently—to go the distance. Without stamina, they might as well be beach balls.

Helena stepped onto one of the treadmills. She picked the medium setting, which simulated a brisk jog. I got on the one to her left and chose the same speed. As we ran, I struck up a conversation.

"What do you like to do for fun?" I asked.

"Exactly what I'm doing right now."

"Besides this."

"I don't have time for much else."

"You don't have any other hobbies?"

Helena sighed loudly. "Singing."

"Really? Are you good at it?

"I'd like to think so."

"I'm a pretty good singer, too. But only when no one's listening."

Helena cracked a smile.

"Anything else?" I asked.

"Hacking."

"So I guess being here is like a dream come true. Getting paid to do what you love."

"Yeah, it's pretty fulfilling," Helena said.

Though her voice and expression gave no indication, I still felt she wasn't being completely honest.

"How about you?" she asked. "What do you like to do besides ogling me?"

"I don't ogle. I admire. There's a difference."

"Sorry. I wasn't aware."

"I'll forgive you just this once," I joked. "But yeah, I have a wide range of hobbies and interests. Karaoke, martial arts, video games, long walks along the beach, candlelit dinners, romantic comedies. You know. Guy stuff. Do you like movies?"

"Who doesn't?"

"In that case, we should catch one sometime."

"Maybe."

"Anyone special in your life?" I asked after a short period of silence.

"No."

"No significant other?"

"I don't have time for one."

"That's a shame," I said. *Not for me, though.*

"What about you?" Helena asked.

"I'm single."

"And looking, right?"

"More like waiting."

"For what?"

"For the right one."

Helena glanced at me as I glanced at her. Then she quickly looked away. "I see."

"When it comes to love," I said, "I haven't had the best of luck."

"I can relate."

"Had your heart ripped out too, huh?"

Helena didn't reply. Her silence was telling.

"I was married once," I said. "Things didn't work out."

"I remember reading about that in your file. But it didn't go into what actually happened between you two."

"Things got in the way."

"Which is exactly why I prefer to be alone," Helena said.

"Think you'll ever change your mind?"

"It's possible, if the right person comes along."

"Someone once told me that finding the one is fifty percent place, fifty percent time. I've dated a good bit since my divorce. But I haven't been able to find anything real. My approach might be to blame. I guess I'm a little rusty, having been out of the game for so long."

"Rusty?" Helena almost laughed. "You dated Aphrodite. If that's you in a funk, I wouldn't want to see your A-game."

Aphrodite again? I thought I had cleared all that up.

"She and I went on dates," I said. "We never dated."

Helena shot me a sly look. "There's a difference, huh?"

"Yes, there's a difference."

"Right."

"Why doesn't anyone believe me?" I groaned.

"Who said that I didn't believe you?"

"Your expression. It's shouting at me. It's deafening."

Helena fought to keep her smile from getting any bigger.

"Well, now that I've finished spilling my guts, it's time for you to do the same," I said. "It's only fair, wouldn't you agree?"

"If you say so. I guess you want to know about my past relationships."

"Only if you don't mind discussing them."

"I do mind. But it doesn't matter. Sooner or later, Felix will let you take a peek at my file."

"He already made the offer. I declined."

"Why?"

"Because I want to get to know you without taking any shortcuts."

"I'm not sure you do, Plato," Helena said.

It was the first time she had spoken my name. I didn't know if it meant anything. I liked to think it did.

"Try me," I said.

Helena was momentarily silent. "I've always been unlucky in love."

"Ever been married?"

"Yes. It was good for a while. But nothing lasts forever. I haven't been in a relationship since then."

"Have you dated since?"

"Occasionally. But they all wanted more than I was willing to give."

"And what was that?"

"Don't make me say it."

Love.

"Sounds like you might have some trust issues," I said.

Helena gave a humorless laugh. "You don't know the half of it. Let's just say people aren't always who they seem to be."

Hearing that, I felt a pang of guilt. Some small, irrational part of me wanted to tell her the truth about me. Tell her to run before things got ugly. But Helena didn't strike me as the running type. She'd likely go straight to Louis, who would interrogate me before blowing my head off. Or she might just kill me on the spot. There was no scenario that ended with me walking away, unless someone decided to do a reenactment of *Weekend at Bernie's.*

"Think you'll ever find it?" I asked. "That word you don't want to say?"

"Not looking for it."

"That's the thing about love. It sneaks up on you when you least expect it."

Helena increased the speed on her treadmill. I did the same.

"Felix is hitting a club tonight," Helena said, clearly trying to change the subject. "He plans to invite you."

"Another club? I'm starting to feel like I'm in college again. Who else is coming?"

"Danny, I think."

"My number one fan," I said. "What about you?"

"Probably not."

"You should. It'd be nice to have at least one sensible person around. And I enjoy your company."

"You're going to keep bugging me until I say yes, aren't you?"

"Yep."

"Fine," Helena groaned. "But this isn't a date."

"Of course not."

"I must be going crazy."

"This is the MLF. Crazy is in the job description."

31

Three days later, I received my first field assignment. It was exactly the type of mission I'd hoped never to get—an assassination.

The target, a human named Manuel Hernandez, had been a high-ranking member of the MLF—one of the two traitors Louis had mentioned back at the Ferryman. He and another operative went on the run after they'd been caught selling secrets to the OBI. Hernandez escaped. His coconspirator hadn't been as lucky. The nature of these secrets wasn't mentioned during the briefing. Strange.

Intelligence had tracked Hernandez to São Paulo, Brazil. I was going solo, since Louis wanted to see how I operated without backup. Every MLF operative was expected to be self-sufficient, he had told me. He also wanted to know that I was willing to pull the trigger in the name of the organization.

I had no plans to kill Hernandez. But I couldn't let him run free. If I returned to HQ claiming the target had been neutralized, only to have him pop up on the MLF's radar again . . . Well, that wouldn't look too good on my performance report.

Also, the secrets he carried intrigued me—even more than that, the fact that he'd tried to sell them to the OBI.

I took Louis's jet to his private airfield in Brazil. Seriously, how many of these airfields did he have? The area lay outside the city, fenced off with warning signs posted everywhere. They were in Portuguese and all said the same thing: "KEEP OUT! VIOLATORS WILL BE SHOT."

The sun blazed in a cloudless sky above a heat-smothered landscape. A jeep awaited me at the security gate. I loaded my one suitcase into the back and hopped in. The driver, a burly man with a nose like a potato, took me to downtown São Paulo. He didn't speak for the entire trip.

Downtown resembled any other modern metropolis, but somehow seemed brighter and livelier. Skyscrapers rose all around, interspersed with cafés, storefronts, and structures left over from the city's colonial era. Palm trees, store signs, and billboards provided splashes of color, breaking up the monotony of stone and metal.

The name of the hotel where I'd be staying translated to the Golden Arms. It was one of the area's pricier establishments. My room featured a hot tub and a minifridge and complimentary room service. The bed and room safe were all I needed. After settling in, I called my contact, an undercover operative named Blindside.

The voice that answered spoke in Portuguese. It was also artificially distorted, so I couldn't identify the speaker's gender. I had the same app on my smartphone.

"*O que é isto?*"

I confirmed my identity with a passphrase Felix had given me. "I love this town."

Blindside responded in Greek. "The women have such nice asses."

Felix. Always keeping it classy.

"Welcome to Brazil, *Senhor* Jones."

"Thanks for having me."

"Shall we get down to business?"

"By all means."

Blindside gave me directions to a nearby restaurant called Faísca. I jotted them down on a pocket-size notepad.

"Meet me in the alley behind the restaurant in exactly one hour," Blindside said. "I'll be waiting." He ended the call.

To pass the time before my meeting with Blindside, I enjoyed some Brazilian TV. The reality show I watched featured seven strangers, one human and six nonhumans, all racists, living together in a house with no television but plenty of alcohol. All the ingredients for a train wreck.

I left for Faísca after the show ended. The restaurant lay within walking distance of the hotel. The place was packed. People clustered near the entrance, waiting to get inside, while servers in bright-blue shirts rushed back and forth though the crowed patio area.

I entered the alley behind the restaurant. A tan Podengo stepped out from behind a dumpster. My first instinct was to keep my distance, in case the dog had rabies or was feral. Then I noticed a messenger bag strapped to its back. I also noticed its eyes. They were brown, almost humanlike, and sparkled with intelligence.

You've got to be kidding.

"Hello, *Senhor* Jones," said the dog in a man's voice.

Its mouth moved in a very human fashion.

"Blindside?"

"In the flesh, or should I say fur?"

"Okay. Two questions. How can you talk? And how can you use a cell phone without thumbs?"

"Daedalus," Blindside replied. "And with difficulty."

A talking Podengo. I guessed it made more sense than engineering the world's smartest goat.

"Thanks for clearing that up," I said.

"*Obrigado.* I have a few things for you. Check the bag."

I did. Inside, I found a manila envelope. It contained

information about Hernandez: his work schedule, his home address, a list of some of his favorite haunts, and a picture of him.

Hernandez had a round face, jolly cheeks, and short black hair. His eyes were brown. The right one was glass. He'd lost the real one to a firecracker when he was a kid. He wasn't smiling, but still looked friendly. He had a wife and two small children, giving me another reason to spare his life.

"Any questions?" Blindside asked.

I caught myself frowning as I skimmed through the materials, and then forced my expression into one of disinterest. "No, I think I'm good."

"Then I'll take my leave. *Foi um prazer conhecê-lo, Senhor Jones.*"

"Nice meeting you, too. Where're you headed?"

"Rio."

"Another assignment?"

"A vacation. Louis gave some time off."

"Ah," I said. "Well, have fun doing whatever dogs do on vacation."

Which probably involved lots of mating, napping, and butt-sniffing.

"I will. *Tchau, Senhor Jones,* and good luck."

And with that, Blindside trotted out of the alley, his tail wagging happily.

Lassie, eat your heart out.

Hernandez worked at a meatpacking plant in one of the *favelas.* Before setting out, I equipped my Five-seven. I didn't plan on using it, but I'd rather have a gun and not need it than need one and not have it. My watch, smartphone, and most of the contents in my wallet stayed behind.

I still had no idea what I'd do upon encountering Hernandez. But I'd come up with something. I had an extremely vivid imagination.

I picked up a dirt bike from a neighboring rental center and headed into the *favela.* Massive in scope, the hillside community resembled a staircase. Crumbling tenements were arranged in ascending rows, their paint long faded, and intersected by a network of alleys and walkways. I rode down a busy thoroughfare, past open-air markets, food carts, and restaurants. Citizens flowed up and down the sidewalks in great waves—mostly human, with a spattering of satyr and minotaur. They watched me as I passed. My being an outsider might've had something to do with it.

Don't mind me, folks. Just your average, everyday double agent.

The meatpacking plant was deep within the *favela.* The sun had set by the time I got there. Windowless and made of red brick, the building reminded me of a block from a game of *Super Mario Bros.* Unlike the game though, there probably weren't any gold coins inside. A single chimneystack belched smoke into the atmosphere.

I rode to the employee parking lot and found a car that matched the description of Hernandez's. A green Chevy sedan. I parked beside it and waited.

Fifteen minutes later, a whistle sounded. The factory doors boomed open, releasing a stream of workers in navy coveralls. They trudged, zombielike, into the parking lot, Hernandez among them. He wore a white baseball cap smudged with dirt and carried a metal lunchbox. As he neared his car, I moved forward to cut him off.

He stopped when he saw me.

I gave him my friendliest smile, a look that said, *Don't be afraid. I'm not here to brutally murder you.*

"Hi," I said in Portuguese. "You're Miguel, right?"

Hernandez said nothing. His eyes shone with alarm. He seemed to know that I was here on behalf of the MLF.

"My name is Brick," I said. "Got a minute to talk?"

Hernandez flung his lunchbox at me and broke into a sprint. I dodged it and gave chase.

I guess that's a no.

I pursued Hernandez out of the parking lot and into a narrow alleyway. His co-workers watched and pointed, but no one tried to help him. So much for workplace solidarity.

I followed him over a fence at the end of the alley, and onto a congested sidewalk. Pedestrians hurried out of the way. Hernandez ran into the street, dodging cars and bicycles to a cacophony of horns, screeching tires, and curses. He was remarkably spry for a man his size. But he'd run out of gas before me. I had to keep him in my sights until then.

Hernandez reached the opposite sidewalk and raced up a narrow flight of stairs. Upon reaching the top, he shouldered open a door to his left. I went in after him and found myself in a minotaur strip club. Bathed in red light, females danced onstage to bass-heavy music while hordes of slavering males tossed money at them. Everywhere I looked, there were flopping udders. I didn't want to think about what went on in the champagne room.

Remarkably, no one seemed to notice the two humans running through the middle of the floor. I trailed Hernandez through a door at the back of the club. It emptied us into a narrow corridor that slanted upward.

Hernandez veered down an adjacent street and entered a basketball court where a party was going on. Strings of holiday lights burned overhead as Brazilian house music bumped from huge speakers on either side of the DJ table. Unfortunately, I didn't have time to admire all the scantily clad beauties shaking their derrieres.

I waded through the crowd, bumped and shoved from all sides, struggling to keep a bead on Hernandez. In the dying light, his dark clothes appeared black. If not for his white cap, I might have lost him.

By the time I reached the end of the basketball court, Hernandez had lengthened the distance between us. But his pace had slowed down. He jumped into a drainage ditch and scrambled up the opposite side. A construction yard lay ahead. No workers or equipment were present, just half-finished tenements fringed by mounds of rubble.

I gained on Hernandez. He didn't look back, but must have sensed the walls closing in. I followed him up a ladder to the roof of one of the construction projects.

"I just want to talk," I shouted.

Hernandez kept running. He took a flying leap toward the adjacent rooftop but came up short. He managed to catch the edge. His body swung forward, bashing against the side of building. He fought to pull himself up but didn't appear to have the strength.

I cleared the gap and grabbed Hernandez's forearms with both hands. I used the remainder of my strength to pull him over the edge. We both rolled onto our backs, gasping and pouring sweat.

"If you're going to kill me," Hernandez wheezed in his Ecuadoran accent, "just hurry and get it over with."

"Who said I wanted to kill you?"

"Don't bullshit me. I know Louis sent you."

"He did. But I have other plans. Ones that involve keeping you and your family alive."

"You know about . . ." Hernandez abruptly stopped talking.

"The MLF knows everything about you." I got up and offered Hernandez a hand. "But they don't know everything about me."

He allowed me to help him up.

"I want you and your family to leave this place," I said. "Tonight."

Hernandez nodded vigorously.

"But steer clear of Rio," I advised. "And don't trust any dogs or goats."

Hernandez's brows gathered in confusion, but he nodded regardless. "Whatever you say."

"Good man."

"Why are you doing this?"

"I have my reasons."

That explanation seemed to be enough for Hernandez.

"Is there some way I can repay you?" he asked.

"Actually, there is. You tried to sell information to the OBI about Louis's operation. Tell me what you told them and we'll be even."

Hernandez glanced around, then gestured for me to come closer. "It was about the MLF's funding. Louis has a number of businesses that bring in ridiculous amounts of money. But his most lucrative one involves the illegal sale of osmium."

"Where does he get it?"

"He owns several mines. But only he and Felix know where they are."

"How did you get this information?"

"I was in charge of distribution and billing."

That was new. Hernandez's file said that he worked in the R&D department. Convenient oversight or flat-out lie? You be the judge.

"After I told the OBI what I knew, they shut down the distribution center," Hernandez said. "But it was just one of many, or so I'd been told."

"Told by whom?"

"Louis."

"Did he tell you where the other centers were located?"

"No. He didn't want one person to have all the answers—other than himself and Felix."

"Why'd you jump ship?"

"I didn't agree with the way things were being run. Too much collateral damage. Louis says he's fighting for humans, but won't hesitate to shoot through them if they wander into the crossfire."

It was refreshing to finally meet someone with a conscience.

"You mentioned other businesses," I said. "What do you know about them?"

"Just that they exist. Like I said, only Louis and Felix have all the answers."

I found the lack of details disappointing. But saving a life more than made up for it.

"Thanks for being honest," I said.

"And thank you for sparing me. What are you going to tell Louis?"

"I'll tell him you're dead. That you had an unfortunate accident at a construction site. And that I put two in you for good measure."

I unbuttoned my shirt, drew my gun, and fired two silenced rounds into the ground. Hernandez flinched with each shot.

"I fancy myself a perfectionist." I winked at him.

"He'll want proof of my death."

"I was just about to bring that up." I holstered my gun and buttoned my shirt. "Mind if I take that glass eye off your hands?"

"Of course not." Hernandez plucked out the eye and gave it to me.

Blood from his hand smeared the surface—he must have injured his palm while hanging from the edge of the building. A nice touch.

I put the eye in my pocket. "Now it's time for you to do your part."

"Thank you again."

"No problem. And Good luck."

Hernandez ran home. I returned to my hotel room for a much-needed shower.

32

Before heading to the airfield, I bought a prepaid phone from a drugstore and gave Hermes an update. He confirmed Hernandez's story, having led the raid on the osmium distribution center—the OBI had yet to find the others. He criticized my decision to let Hernandez live. I, in turn, criticized his garish fashion sense. It evened out in the end.

I trashed the phone and hopped on Louis's jet. The eighteen-hour flight back to HQ gave me plenty of time to get my lies straight. I dropped off my luggage and headed to the intelligence department for debriefing. Louis and Felix waited for me in the office above and overlooking floor.

Time to put on my mask.

Felix seemed pleased to see me. Louis was harder to read. He always seemed to be scowling. Not once had I seen him smile. Did he even have the capability? Maybe he hadn't gotten enough hugs as a kid.

"How was your trip?" Felix asked.

"Hot," I said. "And not in a good way."

"Caught something nasty, huh?"

"I was referring to the heat."

"Oh!" Felix chuckled.

I shook my head. Felix King, master of international relations.

"Did you pick up any souvenirs?" Felix asked.

"Just one." I took Hernandez's glass eye out of my pocket and put it on the desk.

It still had flecks of dried blood on it. I gave him a fictional account of the assignment. Louis and Felix appeared convinced.

Louis handed the eye to Felix. "Have this analyzed."

"I'm on it." Felix hurried out of the office.

As the door closed shut behind him, I was visited by a sense of claustrophobia—as though I was now locked in a cage, bleeding and injured, with a starving lion. Thankfully, the feeling was short-lived.

"I'll expect a full written report from you by tomorrow evening," Louis said.

"Okay. Need anything else?"

"That's all for now."

I left the office and got on the elevator. Even as the doors closed, I could sense Louis's presence. He was still testing me. My going after Hernandez had been only the first part of the test. Confirming his death was the second and most important one. He wanted definitive proof of my loyalty—and he wouldn't be disappointed. Once he finished analyzing the blood on Hernandez's eye, his reservations about me would be laid to rest.

I hoped.

I finished my report the next day. The end product far exceeded my expectations. The lies contained within were so compelling and hard to disprove; they would've made even the most corrupt politician blush.

Around the time I submitted it to Louis, the lab results for Hernandez's glass eye came back. The blood was a match. Regardless, I expected the boss man to sit me down for a bonus round of questions—to remove any residual doubts. But he never did. Instead, he arranged a trip to Vegas for himself and the rest of the MLF's key players: Felix, Danny, Helena, Eric, and Stavros. He invited me as well. Perhaps my first successful field assignment put him in a good mood. Or maybe he just enjoyed gambling.

We loaded onto Louis's jet the following morning and departed for the United States. I'd visited the States numerous times. It was lot like Greece—a melting pot of races and cultures, living and working, laughing and loving, all connected by a mutual fear of their immortal overlords.

A couple of centuries earlier, Zeus had appointed his daughter Athena as President of the United States. The title was merely a formality. In regard to political affairs, the King of the Gods held all the cards.

Athena's popularity as a president was similar to that of her father's. Some people loved her, and others hated her, but none dared challenge her authority. Their methods of rule, on the other hand, couldn't have been more different. Zeus controlled through intimidation, while only pretending to be a nice guy—the type of guy you'd have a beer with while watching sports. But Athena took a kinder, gentler approach toward to politics, and her benevolence seemed genuine.

Seemed genuine.

I'd only interacted with her a handful of times, back in my OBI days, usually acting as part of Zeus's security team during his visits to the States. As if the King of the Gods needed protection. Each time, Athena had been a class act; warm, talkative, and surprisingly down to earth. She frequently donated to charities and inner-city schools and worked tirelessly to eliminate unemployment throughout the country. From time to time, she even volunteered to work the line at community soup kitchens.

I still didn't trust her, though, not completely. She was an

Olympian as well as a politician. Enough said.

We touched down in Nevada Friday evening, landing in yet another one of Louis's private airfields. This one was out in the Mojave Desert, miles away from civilization. We jumped in a white stretch Hummer that waited for us at the security checkpoint and set out for the Vegas Strip.

The sun had gone down by the time we reached our destination. A galaxy of neon lights burned away the darkness and dazzled the eyes. Taxis and limos choked the streets, picking up gamblers whose luck had run out, and dropping off those eager to lose their shirts. Humans and nonhumans alike moved in clusters along the sidewalks. The atmosphere was electric.

I found it impossible not to get caught up in the grandeur.

We rented all seven penthouse suites at the Basilisk Hotel and Casino. One for each of us. Before we disbanded, Louis told us to come by his room in one hour. He had a special treat for us. It sounded good coming from the boss, though I would have been nervous had I been the only one invited.

The bellboy carting my luggage showed me to my suite. The bedroom alone was almost twice as big my condo, and expensively furnished. A chandelier glittered overhead, tossing shards of light across marble floors and stainless steel kitchen appliances. Just outside the living room, the private balcony offered a breathtaking view of the strip.

I showered and changed clothes. Then I channel surfed until it was time to meet up with Louis and the others. Everyone had arrived, except for Helena and the boss man. Felix lounged in a recliner, chugging a large bottle of Jägermeister. Across from him, Eric and Stavros watched TV from the couch—a documentary about wolves. Danny stood near the patio entrance, his gaze fixed on the glittering cityscape.

"Plato Jones," Felix exclaimed. "Welcome to the party!"

I glanced at the bottle of alcohol. "Getting started early, huh?"

"You know it."

"Fellas," I said to everyone else.

"Yo," Eric returned.

Stavros nodded without smiling. Danny remained silent. He didn't even turn around.

"Don't just stand there," Felix said. "Get over here."

I sat on the vacant loveseat.

Felix raised the bottle. "Want some?"

"Maybe later," I said.

Felix took a drink big enough for the both of us. "Feeling good?"

"Pretty good. Yeah."

"You're about to feel even better."

Helena showed up. She wore a black dress—a short number with a deep V in the front. It showed a fair of amount skin while somehow retaining an element of class. In her left hand, she carried a snakeskin purse. Her jade bracelet adorned the right. Waves of black hair framed a face that, even without makeup, would have been the quintessence of perfection. My heart all but stopped. Then it soared when I noticed the green heels I had bought her.

"Oh me, oh my," Felix said.

Helena rolled her eyes. She sat beside me on the loveseat. Her perfume got into my lungs, heated my blood. She seemed too perfect to be real.

"You look nice," I said, trying to maintain a semblance of composure.

"Thanks," Helena replied. "You're not too bad yourself."

I smiled automatically.

"Aw, isn't that sweet?" Felix said. "You gonna invite her to the ice cream social?"

Helena and I both glared at him.

Shortly, Louis emerged from the bedroom, holding what looked to be a cigar tin. He stopped in front of the fireplace.

"Come here, everyone."

We gathered in front of him.

"Being a revolutionary can sometimes be a thankless job," Louis said. "That's why I want to show my appreciation for all of you. The sacrifices you've made."

He opened the case. It contained seven glass tubes—no bigger than fragrance samples—filled with fluorescent-blue liquid. They were individually labeled with each of our names. We reached in, one at a time, and grabbed the corresponding tubes. Louis placed the empty case on the mantle above the fireplace.

I examined the liquid. It didn't take a genius to realize it was some kind of drug. Perhaps one of Felix's infamous potions—or one of Louis's.

"What is this?" I asked.

"Whatever you want it to be," Louis said.

We removed the plastic caps from our tube. A smell similar to burnt sugar emanated from the liquid.

"I've watered down this batch," Louis said, speaking directly to me. "To ensure you don't lose yourself."

"This won't kill me, will it?"

"Not unless you overdose."

Well that made me feel a bit better—and by *a bit*, I meant not at all.

"You'll be fine," Felix said. "Trust me."

Trust him? I'd rather take a course on table manners from two stray cats fighting over a fish carcass. But snubbing Louis's offer might insult him—and I needed all the brownie points I could get.

So here I was, about to add recreational drug user to my list of recent accomplishments, alongside a convicted criminal and borderline alcoholic. If I'd been a good singer, I could have pursued a career as a rock star at this rate.

Louis raised his tube. "To the MLF. And to Plato Jones. Welcome to the inner circle."

We drank the liquid. It was thin and, despite the smell, had no taste. As it slid down my throat, "White Rabbit" by Jefferson Airplane inexplicably played in my head.

It seemed appropriate.

33

After our little powwow in Louis's room, we all split up to do our own thing. Helena planned to hit the hotel bar. I waited for her to invite me to come along. When she didn't, I asked her flat out if she wanted company. Shameless? Maybe. Effective? Definitely.

The hotel bar was on the ground floor, across from a ritzy seafood restaurant. The place seemed to cater to an older crowd with even older money. The men wore tailored suits, and the women sported dresses that wouldn't have looked out of place on a Parisian runway. I was, without a doubt, the worst dressed person there.

Dim lighting and polished wood created a tranquil environment, wholly at odds with the alcohol-fueled merriment going on outside. A pianist serenaded the crowd with smooth jazz, adding another layer to the ambiance.

At the suggestion of the bartender, Helena and I had ordered vodka martinis. I'd never been much of vodka guy. Gin, rum, and whiskey were more my speed. But tonight, I decided to class it up so as not to look completely out of place.

We found an empty booth in the corner of the bar. As we sipped our drinks, I waited nervously for the effects of the drug to kick in. At present, I felt normal—as normal as

I *could* feel given the circumstances. If the cards were in my favor, I wouldn't end up on the floor, half-dead and foaming at the mouth.

"I take it you like the shoes," I said.

Helena returned a somewhat playful smirk. "Did your keen powers of observation bring you to that conclusion?"

"Could be. How do they rank among your all-time favorites?"

"I'd say top five."

"Well how about that. Why'd you put them so high on the list?"

"Because you bought them," Helena said.

A smile forced its way onto my face. "Oh, really?"

Helena's eyes widened. "I didn't mean you in particular. I was referring to the act of picking them out. The thought that went into it."

"Gee, thanks."

"That came out wrong." Helena showed me her bracelet. "This belonged to my mother. My birth mother."

"You were adopted?"

Helena nodded. She started to speak but caught herself. I waited for her to continue.

"I was born in Sierra Leone," she said. "I didn't move to Russia until I was ten. Your government *acquired* my hometown because it sat on the largest osmium deposit in the region. The locals were relocated to a refugee camp."

"Refugees in your own country," I muttered.

"The camp was like the Wild West. There were no rules, and not much in the way of healthcare. There were regular food and water drops, but the gangs hoarded most of them and charged people for basic necessities. And if they didn't have any money . . ."

She left off the rest. I could fill in the blanks.

"Were people allowed to work in the mine?" I asked.

"Yes, but the pay was small, the conditions hazardous. Every day, you'd hear about an accident. Every day another wife became a widow, another child was orphaned. But it was either that or starve. Or give up your humanity and join a gang. My dad refused to become one of the animals, so he did things the honest way, and took a job in the mine."

Moisture rose in Helena's eyes. For the first time since we met, she looked vulnerable.

"You can stop if you want," I said.

Helena blinked back the unshed tears. She shook her head. "I'm fine."

"You sure?"

"Yeah." She took a deep breath, let it out, and continued. "My father had been working for a little over a week when my mother and I got the news. There'd been a cave-in at one of the sites. No one got out alive."

I was silent for a time. Though the moisture had gone from Helena's eyes, the vulnerability remained. I wanted to reach across the table, put my hand over hers. But she didn't seem like the kind of person who expected sympathy. Her reveal raised an important question, however. Stories like hers were usually reserved for close friends and family.

Did this mean we were friends?

"I can see why you aren't too fond of the Gods," I said.

"My father's death was a contributing factor. But that isn't my only reason for hating them. Every time a miner died on the job, the grieving family received money. Something to shut them up."

"Courtesy of Olympus."

Helena nodded. "It showed us how much the Gods valued humans. To them, our lives can be measured in credits."

I shook my head.

"Having to buy supplies from the gangs burned through our money pretty quickly. Within a month, it was all gone.

My mother tried to take a job in the mine, but only men were deemed fit for that kind of work. That left her with only one option." Helena paused. "To keep us from going hungry she . . . did things."

I understood the implication.

"Even as child, I could tell what was going on," Helena said. "I asked her to let me take her place. Begged her. But she wouldn't have it. She said it was her responsibility to put food on the table, not mine. Looking back, I should have fought harder to change her mind. But I didn't. I sat back and did nothing while she sacrificed everything. To this day, I'm still angry with myself."

"You were just a kid," I said.

"I know. But it doesn't change the way I feel."

"How did you end up leaving Africa?"

Helena looked down at her half-finished martini, but didn't touch it. "One day, a revolutionary group showed up. They wanted to take over the mine, cut a swath in the Gods' infrastructure—though it turned out to be more like a paper cut. The saddest part is that I don't think any of them knew about the effect osmium had on the Gods."

No surprise there. The Gods went to great lengths to keep their vulnerabilities under wraps. But little by little, people were catching on. I could only imagine what would happen once it became common knowledge. A ban on osmium, most likely. It would be music to the ears of every two-bit fencer and black marketer from New York to Tokyo.

"This group," I said, "was it ours?"

"No, but their goals were similar. Most everyone joined, including my mother. Kids like me weren't allowed to do much. But we were protected."

"How'd the gangs respond to all this?"

"The only way they knew how. With violence. But it didn't do them much good. They were outmanned and outgunned.

Those who fought were killed. The rest were given the chance to leave with their lives or join the revolution. None of them chose to stay. I guess after everything they put us through, they figured we'd try to get a little payback. They were right."

"I'm sure karma caught up with them at some point."

"That's what I tell myself. Anyway, it didn't take long for the revolutionaries to seize control of the mine. But they realized they couldn't keep it. Once the Gods found out what was going on, they'd send someone to investigate. So we took as much osmium as we could from the mine, as fast as we could, then blew up the entire excavation site. I thought seeing that place destroyed would give me a sense of closure, or something close to it. But it just reminded me of everything I'd lost," she finished. "Is that strange?"

"Not at all."

Helena smiled.

"What happened next?" I asked.

"We fled to Liberia. We knew the Olympic military would be looking for us. Our only chance was to lay low until they abandoned the search. It might have worked."

"*Might* have worked?"

Helena's expression grew dark. "We were betrayed by one of our own. I'm not sure what his reasons were, but he led the enemy right to our camp. The attack happened in the middle of the night. It was a massacre. Those who survived were taken prisoner. My mother and the rest of the adults were tried as terrorists and executed by firing squad. Their bodies were stripped naked and tossed into a mass grave. Like garbage. The children were all forced to watch. I was forced to watch. When it was finally over, the soldiers gave each of us a plastic bag containing our parent's personal effects."

Helena indicated her bracelet. "This was in mine. My father gave this to my mother on their tenth anniversary. It was her most cherished possession."

We sat in silence for an interval. I didn't say *I know how you feel* or anything of the sort. It would have been a lie. I had no idea how she felt. The Gods had screwed me over more times than I could count. But they had torn Helena's life asunder. I hoped my loved ones never experienced that kind of pain. I hoped Helena would never have to relive it.

"I'm sorry," was all I could say.

Helena nodded. "In the weeks following the attack, all of us children were shipped off to government-funded orphanages around the world. I was sent to one in Russia. I'd only been there a month when I was adopted by a British couple living in St. Petersburg. Because of them, I was able to find purpose. They reminded me that I still had the capacity for happiness, for love."

Helena's eyes moved from her drink to me.

At that moment, something came over me—some nameless, indescribable emotion. It made me glad to be on this mission. Helena was unlike any woman I had ever come across. I felt like my life was richer for having met her.

"Thank you," I said, "For sharing that with me."

Helena smiled again. It was sad. But within that sadness, I saw a glimmer of hope. We finished our martinis and ate the olives.

"That was good," I said. "Care for another?"

"Do you have to ask?"

"I'll be right back." I stood up and grabbed our glasses.

I had almost reached the bar when an explosion of adrenaline ignited in the center of my chest. It coursed outward—hot, electric, violent—crackling every vein and muscle fiber, infusing every cell. My heart began to beat rapidly, like the wings of a bird whose cage was being rattled. Intense heat engulfed me as the energy seeped from my pores. My body felt wrapped in flames. Yet goose bumps roughened my skin.

I started hyperventilating. The world around me hushed and disintegrated, leaving behind little more than darkness.

I was loosely aware of the glasses falling from my hands as all thought abandoned me, and my awareness slipped into oblivion.

34

STRONG WINDS PUSHED AGAINST ME. I OPENED MY EYES AND discovered myself plummeting though the night sky, high above the Vegas Strip. Below, pinpricks of light glittered against a black backdrop, millions of them, in every color. Panic gripped me. I thrashed about, groping for anything solid as the lights grew larger and brighter. Buildings and streets materialized in the darkness, followed by streams of cars and pedestrians.

I fell toward a building. As the number of feet reduced to single digits, I could see my shadow on the roof—rapidly expanding. I shut my eyes and braced for death.

But death never came. I opened my eyes again and found myself finishing off a gin and tonic in some flashy club. Humans and nonhumans packed the dance floor, raving to "I Remember" by deadmau5 and Kaskade. Water nymphs moved seductively in caged platforms suspended from the ceiling. Multicolored strobe lights reflected off their sleek, semitransparent bodies.

My fear and confusion had been washed away by a sudden and unaccountable flood of euphoria. The question of how I got here never entered my mind. I just went with it. As I put my empty glass on a nearby table, someone tapped me on the shoulder. I turned around to see Helena. She took my hand and led me to the dance floor. We ground against each other, our hands wandering, our gazes locked.

Being so close, I could now see her eyes fully. They called to me, deep pools steeped in predatory hunger. I became lost in them.

I reemerged in a small karaoke bar. I was on stage, performing "Human" by Human League. But the voice coming out of me wasn't mine. This one could actually sing. Helena stood next to me, providing backup. The sounds coming out of her mouth could have earned her top billing on Broadway.

At the end of our performance, the crowd exploded into thunderous applause. I gave a bow and left the stage. Someone in the crowd handed me a beer. I didn't look to see who. I drained it in seconds. As I lowered the bottle, my surroundings changed yet again.

I sat at a poker table in a casino, peeking over a wall of chips. Helena stood behind me, her fingertips resting on my shoulders. My opponents and I showed our hands.

I won. A straight flush.

The other players groaned as the dealer pushed more chips my way.

Behind me, Helena shouted, "*Ura!*"—which I somehow recognized as the Russian equivalent of hooray. I sensed her leaning forward and turned my head toward her. The kiss she gave me was more than a peck. Her lips were firm and wet against mine, her tongue probing. This should've come as a shock, but didn't.

A sound like crashing waves filled my ears, and the world

unraveled. When would this ride end? I would've been fine with never.

My next impression was of Helena and me in a dark alley. Across from us stood five extremely pissed off individuals: three humans, one minotaur, and one satyr. Their aggressive stances guaranteed that a fight would soon break out. I didn't try to diffuse the situation. Instead, I gestured for them to come at me, inexplicably excited.

One of the humans accepted the challenge, swinging wildly. His punches were mired in unnatural slowness. I avoided his attacks with ease and shoved him in the chest. He flew back several feet, crashing into a garbage can. Groaning and covered in filth, he made no attempt to rise. I stared at my hands. Did I really just do that?

The guy's buddies looked equally shocked. The satyr and one of the other humans ran off. The minotaur and the remaining human held their ground. They rushed me and Helena at the same time.

I swatted away the human with a backhand while Helena, still in heels, sent the minotaur whirling in midair with a jumping spin kick. With the attackers lying unconscious at our feet, Helena and I looked at each other. Her eyes told me we were thinking the same thing. She grabbed me by my shirt collar and pulled me into a kiss.

The next thing I knew, I was crashing through a wall. I landed on the bed in my penthouse suite, naked and covered in dust and bits of plaster. I felt no pain whatsoever. The light fixture swung overhead, throwing long shadows across holes in the walls and ceiling as debris scattered across the floor.

Helena suddenly appeared on top of me, as if out of thin air. She was also naked. Her hair fell in inky waves, obscuring her face.

I sat up as she straddled me and kissed her hard. She moaned deep in her throat, tore away, and pushed me flat against the bed. She draped herself over me, nipping my earlobes, sucking my neck, and running her tongue along my collarbones. All the while, her body gradually slid down mine.

35

I WOKE UP FACE DOWN ON THE FLOOR OF MY SUITE, ALONE and hung over. I eased onto my back and sat up. The room was in shambles. The dresser, door, and bedframe had indeed been smashed to bits, and the walls and ceiling sported more holes than a shooting range. Bits of glass and plaster covered the floor.

I struggled to remember the events of last night, but my thoughts lay hidden behind a fog of pain. No doubt about it; the blue liquid had been the source of Felix's and Louis's god-like powers. But what was it?

I scanned the room for my clothes, but found only my pants. I wrestled them on then stumbled out of the bedroom. The living room and kitchen had been destroyed as well. Sunlight poured through the shattered patio window, much too bright.

I lurched to the kitchen, across cracked marble, past overturned pieces of furniture, and around the flat-screen TV, which had been torn from its mount. Cracks snaked across the screen, forming a web. Thousands of crystal fragments glinted on the floor; they were all that remained of the chandelier. By some great miracle, the refrigerator had survived the night. I grabbed a bottle of spring water and sat on the only barstool still intact.

I wondered where Helena had gone. Back to her room, most likely. Thinking about her both aroused and terrified me. I wanted to see her again but dreaded the prospect. It was the uncertainty I found troubling. For me, sex with someone new required a period of reflection. I always asked myself, *Did I do the right thing,* and *would I be willing to do it again?* In Helena's case, it was yes to both. But there was a third question, one that only reared its head in times of extreme uncertainty: *What does this mean for us?*

I wondered if she felt the same way.

I heard a knock at the door. At first, I thought it was Helena. But as the knocking continued, I noticed it had a rhythm. The theme from *Green Acres.* I answered the door, half-relieved, half-annoyed.

"Mornin', champ." Felix peeked into the room. "Looks like you kids had fun."

So he knew about me and Helena. I imagined everyone else knew as well. Great.

"Was it everything you dreamed?" Felix asked.

I was too hung over to give a witty retort. I stepped back and let Felix inside. He went straight to the fridge.

"That stuff we drank last night," I said, crawling onto a barstool. "What was it?"

"I believe it's called alcohol."

"Don't play dumb. The blue liquid. What was it?"

Felix ignored me. He took a cartoon of eggs from the fridge, put in on the counter, then began scrounging through the cabinets.

"What was it?" I repeated.

Felix removed hot sauce, Worcestershire sauce, salt, pepper, and a drinking glass from the cabinets. The ingredients for a prairie oyster—a popular hangover cure.

"I guess there's no point in keeping it a secret," Felix said at last. "It was ambrosia."

My heart jumped into my throat. Ambrosia was said to be the most delicious concoction in the world, made by combining the juice from a golden apple with the blood of a God. But no mention had ever been made about it giving mortals superhuman powers.

On top of that, the existence of golden apples was questionable. I'd never seen one, no one I knew had ever seen one, and the Gods had never mentioned them. Suddenly, that visit to India made sense.

But even if golden apples did exist, how did Louis acquire the blood of a God? I thought back to the God-killer case. Had Lamia been in league with the MLF? Had she provided them with the blood of her victims? Or was there a traitor on Olympus? The possibilities were frightening.

I preferred the first explanation. But the second seemed more plausible, since Lamia—as far as I could tell—had been working alone.

Once again, the entire pantheon had made it on my list of suspects. I doubted Zeus or Hermes had a hand in this. They'd hired me to find the truth, after all. The idea of a criminal hiring someone for the sole purpose of exposing them seemed pretty dumb, even for the Gods. But the rest of them were fair game.

This job was just getting better and better.

"Ambrosia is the culinary equivalent of Bigfoot," I said. "How'd you guys get your hands on a batch? Did you make it yourselves?"

"Everything will be explained in time." Felix cracked one of the eggs on the edge of the sink and poured it into the glass. "Right now, we have other matters to attend to."

"Another assignment?"

"Yeah, but I'll let Dad give you the details," Felix slid the glass toward me. "Drink up."

I downed the prairie oyster. It was equal parts slimy, spicy, and salty. Revolting overall. And it didn't make me feel much better.

"You finished it all," Felix said. "You get extra dessert after dinner."

"*Ura,*" I said with all the fervor of a sloth on sleep aids, Helena's word giving me vague flashbacks from the night before.

"Congratulations, by the way."

"For what?"

"For taking that step," he said.

"Toward insanity?"

"No, no, no, no, no. Not that step. *That* step."

The pounding in my head increased. "Look, I don't have the energy to try and figure out what you're talking about, so do me a favor and speak like a normal human being. I know it'll be tough, but give it your best shot."

"Someone's grumpy," Felix said. "Are you angry because I didn't throw you a bachelor party?"

It took a moment for his words to seep into my brain. Even then, I didn't fully comprehend them. Ambrosia is one heck of a drug.

"What?" I asked.

Felix leaned forward, resting his elbows on the counter. "You really don't remember?"

That moment, some lonely, drug-addled brain cell fired up in my head. I looked at my left hand. A gold wedding band gleamed on my ring finger. I stared at it, confused. How could I have missed this? I felt like a robot that had been dipped in water. This did not compute.

"W-who?"

"Who do you think?" Felix said.

"No," I said. "No way."

"Yes way. I've got pictures."

Felix took out his phone and accessed a photo album. In the first pic, Helena flaunted an asteroid-sized diamond ring.

The next three showed the two of us standing at an altar in a wedding temple that looked more like a carnival funhouse. An Elvis impersonator performed the ceremony. The last shot featured Helena and me locking lips.

"Believe me now?" Felix asked as he put his phone into his pocket.

I leaned back on the stool, blown away. "How did this happen?"

"Easy. You walked into the temple, paid your fifty credits, and Elvis handled the rest."

"That's not what I . . ." I paused. "Helena doesn't seem like the type of woman who'd just up and marry someone. We're not even dating for crying out loud."

"You have me to thank for that."

"What did you do, Felix?"

"I spiked your ambrosia. And Helena's."

"Spiked it with what?"

"More ambrosia. Everyone else got the watered down version, but you and your girlfriend—I mean, wife—you two got the real deal, and then some."

I shot upright, knocking over the barstool. "You what!"

"It's a great way of getting rid of those pesky inhibitions. And when you mix it with alcohol, whoa, Nelly! No need to thank me. I was happy to do it."

"Thank you? I should kill you!"

"I'm sensing some anger. Not really the reaction I was expecting, but I'll go with it."

"Every time I think you can't get any crazier, you kick it up another ten notches. Does Helena know about this?"

"I told her about an hour ago," Felix said. "My jaw still hurts."

"Serves you right. What about Louis? Was he in on this too?"

"Dad?" Felix laughed. "Gracious, no. He knows about the

wedding, but not the particulars. Make sure it stays that way. It'll be better for all of us."

"Shit," I whispered. "I need to talk to Helena. We need to get this thing annulled."

"Annulled? I thought you wanted to be with Helena."

"I do, but this is a bit much. Leaving things as they are wouldn't be fair to either of us. I'm sure she'd agree."

"Love doesn't play fair, Plato Jones. It makes up its own rules. It's a renegade. Like me."

I didn't have the energy to keep arguing. Besides, no closure or understanding could be achieved with someone like him. I'd have better luck trying to paper train a pet rock.

"The assignment you mentioned," I asked, "when is the briefing?"

Felix checked his watch. "In about ten minutes. More than enough time to find the rest of your clothes."

Felix and I relocated to Louis's penthouse. The whole gang was there. The boss man and Danny stood at the bar in the kitchen. Eric and Stavros sat in the living room. Helena leaned against the far wall, her arms crossed. Our eyes met then quickly cut away.

Eric and Stavros grinned at me. I didn't have to ask why.

Felix and I joined Louis and Danny in the kitchen. Numerous documents, photographs, and blueprints covered the bar.

"Now that everyone's here, we can start," Louis said. "But before that, I'd like to congratulate the lovely couple."

If not for his humorless expression, I might've thought he was poking fun. Eric, Stavros, and Felix clapped. I felt my face turning red. Helena covered hers with her hand. Unlike me, she wasn't wearing her ring.

"The war is almost upon us, people." Louis tapped his

index finger against a photograph of a cruise ship. "It's time to set the wheels in motion."

I recognized the vessel. It was called the *Kraken*—named after the legendary sea monster that used to plague the waters near Greenland and Norway. One of Poseidon's pet projects, it was touted as the largest cruise ship of all time, almost as big as the Sea God's ego. It would make its maiden voyage three days from now, in California.

Louis spent the next hour going over a plan to flash-freeze the entire ship using a cryogenic bomb developed by Daedalus. He meant to rile up the public by implicating the Gods in the attack. Poseidon in particular, since he had the power to control water and ice—and since he'd be aboard the *Kraken* when it embarked.

The operation was a three-man job. Two men and one woman, to be specific. Danny and I would infiltrate the ship disguised as maintenance men and plant the bomb. Helena's part involved hacking into the *Kraken*'s security system and making sure we didn't show up in any of the camera footage.

Working with Danny wasn't my idea of a good time. But it gave me an opportunity to save innocent lives. I had to keep that bomb from going off.

36

In the morning, I stashed my wedding ring in the side pocket of one of my suitcases until I figured out what to do with it. Helena and I hadn't spoken since our "encounter." She seemed to be avoiding me. I couldn't blame her. I was doing the same thing, but sooner or later, we'd have to sort things out.

Danny and I took the jet to California. We landed in—you guessed it—another private airfield. A white maintenance van waited for us. There were three sports bags in the back. Two of them contained our disguises, blue coveralls and work boots, along with forged ID bracelets and documentation, radios, and silenced handguns.

Daedalus had equipped the bracelets with devices that could trick metal detectors and X-ray machines. As long as we wore them, any concealed weapons we carried would be rendered invisible. The OBI had a similar gadget. I couldn't begin to tell you how either of them worked.

The third bag held the bomb's components, which would be assembled onsite. The bag's inner lining produced false images when put through an X-ray machine. Ship security would see various clothes and toiletries rather than nuts and bolts. This too came courtesy of Dr. Daedalus.

Danny assembled the bomb then took it apart, to ensure every part was accounted for and worked properly. R&D had fashioned the parts, but Louis made the catalyst—a plastic orb, the size of a baseball, filled with a clear liquid. When detonated, the compound would flash-freeze everything within a two-mile radius.

Where does Louis come up with this stuff?

We drove to the docks and parked across the street in a lot reserved for the maintenance team. The *Kraken* was the biggest ship I'd ever seen. Completely white with countless windows and soaring towers, it could have been a floating city. I heard a rumor that the project had taken ten years to complete and cost well over a billion credits. I could see why.

When we got out of the van, Danny spoke to me for the first time since the mission began. "Don't get in my way."

"Wouldn't dream of it."

We boarded the ship and showed the security officer our IDs and papers, while our bags passed through the X-ray machine. Everything checked out, and we were allowed to enter. No muss, no fuss.

Danny and I stopped by our rooms to deposit our bags. We each had a private cabin. After assembling the bomb, we'd stash it in an air duct in one of the boiler rooms, then leave the ship. The bomb would be detonated remotely back at HQ.

We had two hours to kill before our shift started. The time gave us an opportunity to scope out the boiler room. It reminded me of the one in Tartarus, but much brighter and cleaner. A security camera monitored the entrance. The air duct where the bomb would be planted sat in the camera's blind spot.

It gave me an idea.

Danny and I split up after we finished looking around. He went to his cabin to start assembling the bomb. I had my own plans. I dropped off my smartphone in my room then paid a teenager to buy me a prepaid cell from one of the gift shops—to avoid being caught on the store's security cameras.

At some point during my wild night with Helena, I'd cashed in my poker chips. My winnings totaled over thirty thousand credits. I'd brought along five hundred. I left the rest back at the penthouse in Vegas.

I took my new phone to a restroom on the far side of the ship and called Hermes.

"Still alive, I see," he said.

"And kicking."

"Where are you?"

"Inside the *Kraken*. The ship—not the giant monster."

"Another vacation?"

"No, this is business."

"What do you want?"

I wanted to ask him why he had kept the existence of ambrosia a secret. But I already knew the answer. Fear, plain and simple. Fear of what mortals would do if they learned that the magical elixir was more than a myth. Fear so strong it wouldn't let him tell me the truth. Me—the guy currently pulling Hermes's supposedly omnipotent ass out of the fire.

"I have new information," I said. "Turns out, the MLF is using ambrosia to gain superpowers."

Hermes was silent for a moment. "Where are they manufacturing it?"

"I'm not sure. But I'll find out."

"You do that. What else do you have for me?"

"The coordinates of Louis's private airfields. I'll text them to you after I hang up."

"I'll have my men do some reconnaissance."

"Good."

"You still haven't told me what you're doing on that ship."

"I was getting to that." I looked around to make sure I was still alone. "Me and another guy are here to plant a bomb that freezes anything caught in the blast. People will mistake it for magic and blame Poseidon. And by extension, the rest of you."

"When will the bomb be detonated?"

"Tomorrow, when the ship departs."

"Where is it?"

"A vent in boiler room B. I'll contact you once it's been planted so you can send a crew over to remove it. Discreetly.

"Won't the MLF be a tad suspicious when the bomb doesn't go off?"

"Are you concerned about me?" I said. "That's mighty human of you, Hermes. Don't worry though. I have a plan. I need you to gain full access to the ship's surveillance systems. The guy I'm here with is named Danny Zhao. Get some shots of him. High resolution."

"Done."

"But be careful. The MLF have already accessed the system. Try not to cross the wires."

"Anything else?"

"One more thing. I need you to get a hold of whoever made that video for the trial."

Hermes chuckled softly. "Clever mortal."

37

The morning after Danny and I planted the bomb, Louis called a meeting. I hated leaving all those lives in Hermes's hands—he was a God, after all. And all the Gods were jerks. But it was my only option. For the sake of my soul, I hoped Hermes had come through for me just this once and removed the bomb as promised.

All the big leaguers: Felix, Helena, Danny, Eric, Stavros, and me—gathered in a conference room I'd never been in. A long, rectangular table took up the middle of the floor, and a hundred-inch flat-screen hung on the west wall. Every major news network would be covering the *Kraken*'s departure live. Louis wanted to witness the exact moment when the ship got iced.

Everyone except Helena sat at the table. My blushing bride stood, leaning against the wall. She and I exchanged fleeting glances. She wore a deep frown, but it didn't seem to be directed at me. Maybe she hated the thought of killing scores of civilians as much as I did.

"It's time," Louis said, from the head of the table.

He turned on the TV using a tabletop control. A news program covering the *Kraken*'s imminent departure appeared on the screen. My pulse quickened. I crossed my fingers under the table. My toes, too.

Please let this work.

An attractive female reporter interviewed Poseidon before an excited crowd. The God of the Sea gave her the rundown about how the *Kraken* had gone from concept to cruise ship. He sported a white tuxedo and held an unlit cigar in his right hand. Black-haired and blue-eyed, he looked almost identical to his brother Zeus—his full beard and larger build being the only features that set them apart.

We all watched in distaste as Poseidon patted himself on the back. Not once did he give credit to the engineers and builders responsible for putting the ship together. Like the rest of his family, he enjoyed taking full credit for other people's hard work.

When the interview ended, Poseidon boarded the *Kraken*. The program switched to a different camera, one that provided an aerial view of the docks. Ten minutes later, the ship raised anchor and began its departure. The crowd cheered. Balloons floated into the air. The camera followed the vessel as it slowly exited the dock.

Felix glanced at Louis, who nodded. He pulled out his smartphone.

I swallowed deeply.

Here we go.

Felix tapped his phone's touchscreen several times and put the device on the table. It displayed a large, red button.

"It's all yours, Plato Jones," Felix said.

I recognized the offer for what it was. One final test to prove my loyalty. Even at this stage of the game, refusal might raise suspicion. I hoped Hermes had done his part. Otherwise, I wouldn't just have innocent blood on my hands. I'd be drowning in it.

"You sure?" I asked.

"Yeah," Felix said. "Go ahead."

I knew better than to hesitate. For the first time ever, I put all my trust in Hermes. I tapped the button.

Time seemed to stop. We stared at the TV screen. Seconds passed. The *Kraken* drew farther and farther away from the docks. Everyone looked confused, even me—I hoped.

"Try it again," Felix said.

I pressed the button. Nothing happened. Felix tried it. Still nothing. Danny appeared to be the most mystified. He took out his phone and gave it a shot.

Nada.

Louis stepped up to bat. He tried to detonate the bomb using his tablet.

No dice.

"Someone had better start explaining," Louis said.

"I-I don't know what happened," Danny stammered. "I assembled the bomb correctly, made sure the detonator was functional. It should have gone off."

"But it didn't."

Danny shrank under Louis's disapproving gaze.

He pointed at me. "He must have sabotaged it!"

"Me?" I said.

"I knew there was something wrong about you from the very start."

"Don't try to shift the blame to me, pal. Maybe if you concentrated more on your job and less on shooting steroids in your ass, things would've gone smoothly."

Danny tried to leap across the table, calloused fingers reaching for me. Eric and Stavros moved to stop him while I jumped from my chair and shuffled backward. Felix did too, taking a position between my aggressor and me. Almost invisibly, Helena's right hand grazed her ankle, returning with a firearm, which she kept at her side.

Danny broke free of the hands that restrained him. He

fell over the edge of the table, shoved himself to his feet, and lunged forward, intent on powering through Felix. Felix reacted with the quickness of a viper on speed. His hand shot out, long fingers digging into Danny's thick neck.

Danny came to a sudden stop. His eyes bulged. His mouth opened, but no sound came out. He grabbed Felix's arm with both hands but couldn't break the hold.

"Relax, Danny boy," Felix said. "Don't make me rip out your throat."

Danny struggled. The muscles in Felix's arm tensed as he tightened his grip. Danny's face burned red. Veins bulged in his forehead and on his biceps. He went to one knee. His grip on Felix's arm gradually loosened.

"That's enough!" Louis shouted, his voice resounding throughout the room.

He had remained seated through the entire altercation.

Felix released Danny, who let out a chain of ragged coughs.

"You good?" Felix asked me.

"Yeah. Thanks."

"No problem."

Helena and I glanced at each other. She put her handgun back in her leg holster, concern etched on her face.

Eric and Stavros tried to help Danny to his feet. He pushed them away and rose on his own. His eyes burned with contempt, but he didn't come after me again.

"We're going to figure this out right now." Louis looked to Helena.

She moved to the head of the table. Louis gave her his seat. She fired up her tablet and used it to patch into the *Kraken*'s security archives.

Moment of truth.

A camera feed appeared on the screen, showing the entrance to the boiler room. Helena sped up the footage. Danny and I stepped into the shot. We entered the boiler room with the finished bomb and came out minutes later.

Helena sped up the video some more. Many minutes later, Imitation Danny crept into the shot. He stopped, glanced over his shoulder, and slipped into the boiler room. I had to give Hermes credit. The imposter looked just like the genuine article.

I looked at Danny. He hadn't returned to his seat. His reddened face betrayed a mixture of fear and disbelief.

Imitation Danny emerged from the boiler room, carrying the bomb in his arms. Three people stepped into the camera's line of sight.

Hermes and two men in black suits. OBI agents.

"That's not me!" Danny protested, hoarse from Felix's chokehold.

No one acknowledged him.

Imitation Danny gave the bomb to one of the agents. Hermes handed him a white envelope, presumably filled with money. The two of them shook hands and departed—Hermes first and Danny shortly after.

"I've seen enough," Louis said.

Helena logged out. The TV screen turned black. She got up and returned to the wall she'd been leaning against. Louis reclaimed his seat.

"This has to be some kind of trick," Danny insisted. "Louis, you know I'd never betray you or our cause. Not for anything! Please . . ."

Louis cut his eyes toward Felix, who drew his gun and trained it on Danny.

Terror flashed Danny's face. "Wait!"

Felix pulled the trigger.

Blood splattered as the round punched into Danny's forehead. He went boneless and collapsed. A pool of blood spread beneath him.

Felix holstered his gun.

I stared at Danny's corpse. Guilt trickled like poison into my heart. Helena, Eric, and Stavros seemed to be caught somewhere between anger and disappointment. If Louis or Felix had even a shred of remorse, I couldn't find it.

"Get rid of that trash," Louis said.

Eric and Stavros obeyed. They dragged Danny out of the room by his ankles, leaving behind a trail of dark-red blood. I felt ill.

To the rest of us, Louis said, "Leave me."

And we did.

38

THAT NIGHT, I SAT IN MY ROOM, WATCHING *MAGNIFICENT Kick*—an old Kung-Fu flick—but not really *watching* it. Danny occupied my thoughts. He had been scum of the lowest form, a murderer of women and children, and the world was a slightly safer place without him around. But he was still a human being, one whose death I'd helped orchestrate.

Over the course of my career, I'd taken out more people than I cared to remember. Bad guys—the worst society had to offer. Yet that didn't make killing them any easier. Murder is murder, no matter who the victim is or what that person's done. Only the insane took pleasure in it.

Someone knocked on my door.

I looked through the peephole. For some reason, I expected to see Felix. Instead, it was Helena. My throat tightened with dread. She had come to talk about one of two things: what happened in the conference room, or our marriage. I wasn't ready to discuss either. But running would only postpone the inevitable. Better to get it over now.

I opened the door. "Hey, there."

"Hi." Her smile looked forced. "How are you doing?"

"Fair to middling," I replied. "What about you?"

"The same."

"Come on in."

"Thanks."

I sat on the couch. Helena lingered near the door. She glanced at the TV.

"You watch a lot of Kung-Fu movies?" she asked.

"When I have time."

Helena nodded. I could tell she had something to say. Perhaps she couldn't find the words.

"Finished breaking in your new car?" she asked after a time.

"Not really."

"Want to go for a ride."

"Where to?"

"Around," she said. "I need to run some errands."

I didn't have to consider her offer. I needed to get out of here. I needed a distraction. Something to get my mind off the past few days. I took it Helena did as well.

"Let me grab my keys."

Helena's errands took us to one of the rougher sides of New Olympia. A predominately human community with high crime and poverty rates and a limited police presence. The kind of place that didn't exist in the eyes of the government, a forgotten echelon of society. Driving a Ferrari through an area like this might have exacerbated my guilt. But it wouldn't be mine for much longer, assuming I completed the mission.

The purpose of our trip was to donate money to those in need. We visited a homeless shelter, an orphanage, and a community center. Everyone knew Helena—by her real name—and seemed overjoyed to see her, especially the kids. The feeling appeared to be mutual.

It was nice to see the MLF finally doing some real good. The acts of charity did little to ease my guilt, but they were steps in the right direction. They showed what the organization could have been under different leadership.

Once all the money had been distributed, Helena and I drove back to HQ. On the way, we picked up a few beef empanadas from La Casa de Fernando—a twenty-four-hour taqueria—and drove to a local park. We grabbed a couple of sodas from a vending machine and sat at a table near the edge of the lake to eat. The moon and stars decorated the night sky.

"You like it?" I tipped my head at Helena's half-eaten empanada.

She had already finished her first. Despite her size, the woman could eat just as fast as I could.

"I love it," she said. "My hips don't."

"Your hips are fine."

Helena gave a sly grin.

"Does Louis do this a lot?" I asked. "Give money to the poor?"

"About once or twice a month."

"A modern-day Robin Hood."

"All he's missing is the tights."

"Thanks for putting that image in my head."

"Don't mention it." Helena winked.

"You've got jokes."

"Must be your influence."

"Go ahead, blame it on the new guy."

Helena chuckled.

"Why did Louis form the MLF in the first place?" I asked. "The Gods must've really pissed him off."

"He never told me."

"Did you ever check his file? Or Felix's?"

"There are no files to check."

"I thought we each had one."

"Not them."

Curious. "I questioned Felix awhile back, but he danced around the subject. Guy should audition for Broadway."

"No kidding," Helena said.

She went quiet then, staring thoughtfully at the lake.

"Something wrong?" I asked.

"Just remembering something."

"Good or bad?"

"Both."

"Want to talk about it?"

I expected Helena to decline, but she surprised me.

"I moved to England after graduating from college," she said. "I'd only been in the country for a couple of months before I met Peter."

"Your ex-husband?"

Helena nodded. It was the first time she had ever mentioned her ex by name.

"We lived next door to a park that had a nature trail leading to a lake like this," she said. "Every day, we'd wake up at dawn and take a jog before going to work."

"You worked at the same place?"

"No. He worked for a software company. I worked for Bolden-Greene."

I recognized the name. Bolden-Greene had been one of the largest pharmaceutical companies in the world, until the Gods discovered a secret plot to resurrect Typhon—a Titan so powerful he once defeated Zeus. They intended to use the creature to topple the government. But the OBI shut down the operation before it got off the ground, confiscating every scrap of evidence, and getting rid of everyone involved. The whole incident was covered up.

With its board of directors dead, Bolden-Greene's infrastructure collapsed, and the company inevitably went under. Luckily, I'd played no part in the shakedown. I'd been in China at the time, hunting down a man who was breeding pegasi without a license.

"What did you do?" I asked.

"I was an information security specialist, officially."

"And unofficially?"

"I was part of the company's cyber warfare division. My job was to keep an eye on our competitors and occasionally steal secrets. I also provided security for another project."

"The Typhon Initiative?"

Helena nodded. "I managed to get out before the bubble burst."

"You quit?"

"In a manner of speaking. I actually have Peter to thank for that."

"How's that?"

"Let's just say our careers put us on opposing paths."

"What did he do for a living?"

"He was a programmer for a major software company, or so I thought."

"He was a corporate spy?"

"You catch on quick," Helena said, still staring at the dark surface of the lake. "He was an undercover operative working for the OBI. His name wasn't even Peter. It was Waylon Mercer."

I'd heard the name but never met the man.

"Rumors of Bolden-Greene's experiments eventually reached Olympus," Helena said. "Waylon's orders were to see if they were true. Somehow, he found out about my involvement and tricked me into falling in love with him to get information."

"When did you find out the truth about him?"

"About a week before the raid. By then, he'd gotten everything he could out of me. I was a loose end."

I felt like I should have been shocked. But I wasn't.

"We were at home. I was in the kitchen, making dinner. That's when it happened: three bullets in the back. The last thing I remembered was seeing him walk out the front door. The man I loved, who I thought loved me, shot me and left me to die. But I didn't die. I woke up and went into hiding. When I was strong enough, I hunted Waylon down to settle up."

So that's what happened. I'd heard Mercer had been killed in action, but the killer had never been positively identified. Now that I knew the truth, I wasn't sure how to feel. But that changed when Helena looked at me with tears in her eyes.

"The Gods have taken away everything I ever loved," she said. "But never again."

The raw emotion on her face made it difficult to maintain eye contact. Though our goals had been different, Mercer and I were essentially the same. We both pretended to be something we weren't, manipulating a woman who had known only loss.

But unlike Mercer's, my feelings for Helena were genuine. Every trace of uncertainty had been eliminated. I needed to protect her, to shelter her from the approaching storm. At present, the means eluded me. But I'd come up with something.

I had to.

"Thanks for taking me out," Helena said, as we stood outside the door to her room back at HQ. "I needed it."

"I think we both did."

"I guess I'll see you in the morning."

"Yeah."

Neither of us moved.

"When we have a chance," Helena began, "we should probably do something about this predicament of ours."

"Predicament is putting it mildly."

She chuckled.

I shook my head. "Vegas."

"Vegas."

We laughed nervously. Helena reached into her pocket and pulled out her wedding ring. It sparkled in her hand. Looking at it should have required UV goggles.

"I should probably give this back to you," she said.

"Keep it," I said. "As a souvenir."

Helena stared at the ring. A smile spread across her face, as bright and flawless as any diamond.

"It *is* a nice ring." She put it back in her pocket.

"What can I say? I've got good taste."

"You have your ways. But don't go getting a big head."

"Trust me, I won't. I don't think my neck could handle the strain."

Helena chuckled. "Goodnight, Plato."

"Goodnight, Helena." I darted in and gave her a quick kiss.

She smiled.

I kissed her a second time. "See you tomorrow."

"Yeah."

Again, neither of us moved. *Aw, screw it!* I wrapped my arms around her waist and pulled her into a kiss. Within seconds, organized thought gave way to mindless passion.

We tore away from each other long enough for Helena to open the door. From there, we went straight to the bed, tearing away articles of clothing as we went, until we were both naked. I slid into her the instant we hit the sheets. She gasped.

I gripped the headboard, burying myself inside her. Helena's breasts heaved. Her fingernails raked against my back. Pleasure and pain mingled, compounding my madness. For the next hour, my mind reeled before some nameless, primal sensation.

Afterward, exhausted, I remained on top of her for a time. I couldn't remember most of what happened that night in Vegas, but this experience was one that would stick with me forever. I'd never felt so connected with another person, not even during my marriage. The feeling was indescribable. A taste of Elysium here on earth.

39

The next morning, I awoke to the sound of my smartphone ringing. I reached out and turned on the lamp. Helena was gone. But the lingering smell of her perfume suggested she had left only recently.

I rolled out of bed and stretched. Bared to the weak lamplight, Helena's room was clean and perfectly organized. There were no decorations, no personal touches, nothing that provided a glimpse into the woman who lay beneath that cool, emotionally detached exterior. It seemed that not many people knew the real Helena. I counted myself one of the lucky few.

I picked my pants up off the floor and checked my pocket for the phone. Felix had invited me to join him for breakfast but didn't say why. He probably had a new mission for me and wanted to go over the details. Not another assassination, I hoped.

I stopped by my room to wash up then went to meet up with him. The halls were silent, and there were only five other people in the cafeteria. All of them wore security guard uniforms. Where was everyone?

Three of the men turned their heads toward me as I entered. The other two continued to eat without missing a beat. The looks I received were neither nasty nor friendly.

Felix sat at a table near the back of the cafeteria, eating an apple. I didn't have much of an appetite, so I skipped the buffet and joined him.

"Good morning, Plato Jones," he said. "You look well rested."

"You wanted to see me?"

"Mm-hm." Felix crunched into his apple and proceeded to talk with his mouth full. "I have something to show you."

"What?"

"You'll see. You're not eating breakfast?"

"Don't have much of an appetite."

"Well, damn. Plato Jones. The whole point of meeting here was so you could get a little sustenance, replace those salts and proteins. I thought you'd need it after last night's workout."

So, Felix knew about my extracurricular activities. But how did he find out? I couldn't see why Helena would have told him. Had he been spying on us? I wouldn't put it past him. Pervert.

"That's mighty considerate of you," I said. "But I'm fine."

"Okay then." Felix finished his apple and threw the core over his shoulder. It sailed directly into the trashcan. He got up, wiping his hands on his shirt. "Let's go."

We got on the elevator.

As the doors closed, Felix said, "What you're about to see doesn't leave this facility."

I nodded. "Yeah."

Felix held out his hand, his pinkie finger extended. "Pinkie swear?"

"You have my word, but I'm not touching your little finger."

"Fair enough." Felix took a small brass key out of his pocket and inserted it into the keyhole under the button panel.

One sharp turn and the elevator started to move. The ride lasted nearly a minute, descending past all the floors corresponding to the numbers on the elevator buttons.

Felix removed the key from the hole and put it back in his pocket. "We're here."

The doors opened and we stepped into a large, circular chamber. Ultraviolet lights reflected off walls covered in silvery tarp. Aluminum stairs led down in the center of the chamber, which resembled a grassy meadow, complete with flowers and butterflies. Two heavily armed guards stood watch.

In the heart of the meadow was a single apple tree. The fruit hanging from its boughs appeared to be gold.

I blinked hard.

"This is our secret garden," Felix said. "Neat, huh? A secret garden within a secret room within a secret base. That's a lot of secrets."

I felt like a kid who accidentally saw his parents having sex. My mind rebelled against the image.

"Golden apples," I said. "The key ingredient in ambrosia."

"Yep. I hear they also make a damn good apple pie. Never tried it though. Maybe after the war."

"How long has this tree been here?"

"Since we got back from India. Can you believe it sprouted from one of those tiny little seeds? Nature is something else."

"Fast growth cycle."

"Yeah. Too bad they die just as quickly, unless you know what to feed them."

I took a guess. "The blood of a God."

"Right-e-oh. But even then, there's no guarantee the seed will take root. Out of the handful we bought from Majit, only one of them worked out."

"Where did you get the blood?"

"From a donor—duh."

"Willing?"

"It's complicated."

"Who is it?"

"I can't tell you until Dad gives the okay. But forget about that. There's something else I want you to see."

I followed Felix along the walkway to a metal door on the opposite side of the chamber. There was a panel beside it, containing a numeric pad protected by a clear, plastic cover. On the wall below that was another keyhole.

Felix inserted his key into the hole. The panel beeped, and the plastic cover flipped up. I memorized the four-digit code Felix entered: 8008—BOOB.

Felix King. So full of class, among other things.

The door slid open, granting us access to the ambrosia manufacturing plant. Gears turned, pistons pumped, and steam hissed. No workers were present. The place must've been fully automated.

"This is where all the magic happens," Felix said. "I'll give you a tour."

He showed me a machine that mashed up the apples and added them to huge vats of water. For some reason, the fruit pulp turned the water a dark shade of green. Another machine added the blood—just one drop per batch—which gave the ambrosia its distinctive bright-blue color.

I'd have to get a sample of the blood for the OBI to analyze—provided Hermes hadn't been the donor.

Felix climbed a flight of stairs and stepped onto a metal catwalk. It spanned a vat of ambrosia. From our vantage point, we could see the entire factory.

The MLF had enough ambrosia here to raise an army of superhumans. In an ideal world, the thought of humans becoming strong enough to go toe to toe with the Gods would be extremely attractive. But not everyone could handle that kind of power. Some would use it to protect the innocent.

Others would use it for personal gain. And then there were those who would use it to dominate, to spread chaos and misery just for kicks.

Not on my watch.

We moved toward a door at the end of the catwalk.

"Why are you showing me all this?" I asked.

"Because I like you. And my dad likes you. And Helena likes you. And you keep everyone laughing. Like back in Vegas, when you got into that rap battle with that parrot."

I assumed Felix was referring to another of my ambrosia-fueled escapades—one that, like the wedding, had been stricken from my memory. But friendship wasn't his only reason for opening up. Since Danny's death, Louis's private club looked more *Pac-Man* than inner circle. I guessed he expected me to fill the vacancy.

The door brought us to another catwalk overlooking a storage area. Dozens of wooden crates sat stacked on wooden pallets, wrapped in cellophane. A forklift was parked near the freight elevator.

We stopped near the middle of the catwalk.

"Ambrosia in those crates?" I asked.

"Yes," Felix said. "But this batch is special."

"How so?"

"It's highly explosive."

I cocked an eyebrow. "Highly explosive?"

"Yes."

"Ambrosia?"

"Yes."

"The stuff we drink?"

"Yes."

"I'm sorry, but I fail to see the intelligence behind this."

Felix patted me on the shoulder. "It's all part of the plan, Plato Jones."

"The plan to turn us all into walking pipe bombs? You

know, stuffing TNT down our throats would have been easier. Cheaper too."

"True. But this ambrosia isn't for drinking. It's fuel."

"For what?"

"For the fire we're about to start. After what went down on the *Kraken,* Dad decided to go ahead with the final stage of our plan, with a few last minute changes."

It made sense that Louis would want to rush things along. He probably thought Danny had given Hermes sensitive information about the organization—like the location of MLF headquarters.

"Helena's already out doing her part," Felix said. "It's time for us to do ours."

That explained where Helena was. What was she doing? Nothing dangerous, I hoped. "What is our part?" I asked.

"We're going to personally deliver this ambrosia to one of our research facilities in Antarctica. To make sure nothing goes wrong."

"Antarctica?"

"You might want to wear something warm."

I looked at Felix, waiting for an explanation.

"You have questions," he said. "I can see it in your eyes. No worries. I'll explain everything on the way. You're going to love this."

Famous last words.

40

WHILE FELIX AND I GOT READY FOR OUR POLAR EXPEDITION, my mind kept turning back to Helena. Curiosity became worry became fear as I contemplated both her skills and her courage. She could be anywhere, doing anything. She was that committed.

I later found out what her assignment had been—and just how well she had executed it.

According to her recounting after the fact, Colonel David Manolis of the OSDF—Olympic Strategic Defense Force—opened the door to a pizza he hadn't ordered. I couldn't help imagining he had done so in large measure because the delivery woman was gorgeous. I bet he was tempted to claim the pizza just to buy time looking at her.

Helena pulled out a tranquilizer gun and shot Manolis in the chest. She told me he fell unconscious almost immediately.

She put away her tranquiller gun and entered Manolis's house, closing the door behind her. She set aside the insulated pizza bag and dragged the Colonel by his ankles into the living room. "The house was something straight out of *Modern Luxury* magazine," she had told me, "lots of polished marble and hand-carved wood.

Helena had tied and gagged Manolis, grateful that she didn't have to fight him. I knew she was versed in numerous marital arts, but I also realized skill didn't always ensure victory. Sometimes, an opponent would get lucky.

Inside the pizza box was an empty syringe and a vial of purple liquid. One of Louis's potions. A particularly useful one, it turned out, and quite volatile.

Helena drew a small portion of Manolis's blood using the syringe, and added a drop to the vial. The mixture turned white. She drank the potion and immediately doubled over. She said she could feel her bones shifting, breaking, and mending. The pain had caused her to black out. When she regained consciousness minutes later, she staggered to the bathroom mirror. It was the Colonel who looked back at her.

"I have to admit, I was glad you weren't around," Helena said to me, pausing from her story. I guessed she figured if I saw her like this, I might not have been too eager to take her out for a night on the town. She was probably right. Fortunately, the transformation was only temporary.

I wondered where Louis had learned the art of potion-making—an art that sounded like the stuff of legends and fairytales. Only he and Felix knew the answer. But neither seemed willing to share it. Like me, she also wondered if the two of them were as committed to helping mankind as they claimed. Planting the bomb on the *Kraken* and now this. The end didn't justify the means.

But what could she do? If she defied Louis there would be no place on earth she could hide.

Helena donned the Colonel's uniform, grabbed his wallet and keys, and commandeered his silver Porsche Cayenne. Her own truck was parked several blocks away, near the neighborhood golf course.

It took Helena less than thirty minutes to reach OSDF headquarters. She removed the Colonel's ID from his wallet and showed it to the guard at the security checkpoint. Then the two of them had a brief chat—about their ex-wives—before she was able to enter the facility.

I hadn't known a thing about it at the time, but she had researched the Colonel for weeks prior to this mission, learning his habits, gestures, and speech patterns as well as the names and histories of his family and co-workers.

Seven large, nondescript buildings made up the bulk of the complex, with smaller structures scattered throughout the grounds. With so much going on, it would have been easy to get lost. But—no surprise here—Helena had obtained a copy of the blueprints by hacking the organization's internal network. She knew exactly where to go.

Helena entered the largest of the main buildings. The ground level looked no different from a corporate office. People were tucked away in cubicles, answering calls and working on computers. Many of them greeted her as she passed by. She took the elevator down to Satellite Control and headed to the maintenance room. Computers, monitors, and switchboards covered the walls, interspersed with thousands of blinking lights.

Helena was there to plant a bomb—of sorts. The memory stick she had smuggled in contained a virus she had personally created. For now, it lay dormant. When the time came, Louis would trigger it remotely. Once activated, the virus would shut down New Olympia's missile defense system. Then the final stage of their plan would commence.

I wondered whether she had hesitated. But I realized that, whatever her feelings, she'd had no choice.

Helena returned to the Colonel's house to gather her belongings and retrieve her truck. En route to HQ, she called Louis to tell him that she had accomplished her mission.

I kind of wish I'd been there for this next part, which would have been a sight to see. When she got back here, the potion had yet to wear off. The guards knew about her mission, but had been ordered to treat her as an imposter, just to be safe. They sent her to quarantine.

Less than hour later, she reverted to her original form.

41

PRIOR TO LEAVING FOR ANTARCTICA, I CONVINCED FELIX TO let me run a quick errand. Once alone, I called Hermes on another prepaid cell phone. I told him about the explosive ambrosia and my impromptu trip to the frozen south. I also begged him not to do anything stupid while I was gone, like storming MLF headquarters. He promised to proceed with caution.

But a promise from the Gods was worth as much as Monopoly money.

Felix and I boarded the cargo plane we used to escape the Ark Facility—it had been seized by the MLF and repurposed. About half the ambrosia I'd seen in the warehouse had been loaded into the hold. Louis was already in Antarctica, awaiting the delivery.

He'd texted everyone an evacuation notice, spurred by fear of a possible OBI raid. But that wasn't the only reason. Louis planned to fill two missiles with the explosive ambrosia and fire one at New Olympia and the other at Washington, D.C. So he'd ordered his people out of New Olympia in anticipation of the explosion there.

The ambrosia would vaporize upon impact, creating a blanket of gas. Those who breathed it in would be endowed with superpowers—if they survived the blasts. I also learned that the batch had been engineered to affect only humans—and that it contained trace amounts of osmium, enough to leave the Gods vulnerable to attack.

I knew how Louis aimed to get past New Olympia's missile defense system. Helena had taken care of it already—and that didn't sit well with me. Thousands of innocent people would be killed in the explosion. I couldn't imagine Helena was all right with that. But I'd been wrong before, especially when it came to women. I still chose to think the best of her, though I was probably setting myself up for disappointment.

We reached sunny Antarctica and exited the cargo plane. Louis's jet sat at the end of the runway. The barren landscape reminded me of a painter's canvas: featureless white for as far as the eye could see. The cold proved almost unbearable, intensified by dry, cutting winds that penetrated my heavy coat and thermal shirt. It caused my bones to ache and my teeth to chatter.

Layered with snow and ice, the base resembled a collection of children's blocks. A radio tower loomed in the distance. A red light blinked at its peak, a bead of color in the endless white. The chief science officer, Dr. Petros, came out to greet us—a squat man with a round face and glasses who looked like a ball of tin foil in his puffy silver coat. Four armed guards accompanied him, almost invisible in white camo.

"Doc, gimme five!" Felix said, raising his hand.

Petros left him hanging. "Always a pleasure to see you, Felix."

"Now, Doc, we both know that's bunk. But thanks anyway. This is Plato Jones."

"Hello, Mr. Jones," Petros said. "I've heard a lot about you."

"That can't be good."

We shook hands. The chill had gotten into my joints, stiffening them.

"Well, gentlemen," Petros said. "What do you say we get out of this cold?"

"Sounds like a plan."

The three of us went inside as Petros's entourage unloaded the ambrosia. The inside of the base reminded me of the R&D department back at HQ, full of bright lights, white surfaces, and shatterproof glass.

We moved down a long corridor lined with offices. Through the windows, I saw men and women working on computers and conducting various experiments. The toasty air streaming from the air vents made it uncomfortable to wear a coat, so I unzipped mine.

"Everything running smoothly?" Felix asked.

"Smoother than ever, thanks to your father. His presence has motivated some of our slower workers."

"He *is* a great motivator."

In the case of Louis, the words motivator and bully were likely interchangeable.

"How close are we to completion?" Felix asked.

"We should be ready any day now."

"Awesome."

"Would you like to see one of the missiles?"

"We're kinda in a hurry, Doc. Gotta get back to HQ and help with the evacuation. But I think we can spare a minute. How about it, Plato?"

I shrugged. "Why not?"

Petros smiled eagerly. I could tell he was proud of the death machines he and his staff were manufacturing.

"Wonderful," he said. "Come along."

We rode an elevator down to one of the base's sublevels then hopped on a tram that brought us to an underground silo. A team of scientists was running tests on the tallest missile I'd ever seen.

"Now that's a big missile," I said.

"That's what she said," Felix added, chuckling at his own joke.

"Your blow-up doll?"

"She has name, you know."

"Sorry."

A lift raised us to a catwalk near the top of the silo, where Louis was observing the scientists like a raptor on its perch.

"Why are you still here?" he asked without looking in our direction.

"Me and Plato Jones just wanted to check out the missile," Felix said. "And to say hello." He nudged me in the arm with his elbow.

"Hey," I said.

Still, Louis didn't turn to face us. His eyes remained anchored on the scientists below. He seemed different. Subdued. Maybe Danny's death had gotten to him. Stranger still, Felix acted less nervous around him than usual. What was up with these two?

"I guess we'd better head back to base," Felix said. "Make sure nothing important gets left behind."

Louis gave no indication that he'd heard him.

Weird.

Felix and I bid Dr. Petros goodbye and hopped in the cargo plane. Only when we were in the air did I feel comfortable enough to inquire about Louis.

"Did your dad seem a little different?"

"Different how?"

"I can't really explain. Just different."

"You're just being paranoid."

"Maybe you're right," I said.

"When am I not?"

"Is that a rhetorical question?"

"A *what* question?"

"Never mind."

Felix grinned. He'd been screwing with me. "I wrote something for you," he said.

"It's not a love letter, is it?"

"Of course not!"

Thank goodness.

"It's a song," Felix said. "About my best friend in the whole world."

"Samuel Adams?"

"No, no. Sam and I are merely acquaintances. You're my best friend."

"Lucky me."

Felix opened the overhead compartment and pulled out a . . . ukulele? He cleared his throat and performed the opening theme to the 1966 *Batman* series, replacing the word Batman with "best friends." It wasn't half-bad. I started to feel guilty about deceiving him.

First Lamia and now Felix. Why did I always find myself sympathizing with crazy people? I had no idea. Maybe I should schedule a meeting with Gabby, the MLF's resident psychologist.

Felix finished his song. He looked at me but said nothing, his eyebrows raised. I assumed he expected applause. I decided to indulge him.

"Bravo!"

Felix returned a knowing grin. "I figured you'd like it."

"You know me so well."

Felix tossed the ukulele into the empty seat to his right "Want a beer? I forgot this plane had a minifridge down in the lower cabin."

Not really.

After being out in subzero weather, the idea of tossing back a cold one had about as much appeal as being waterboarded.

I accepted the offer nonetheless. "Sure."

Drinking even when you don't feel like it. The sign of a lush.

Felix ventured below and returned with two beers. He tossed one to me. I cracked mine open and took a sip. It wasn't as cold as I had expected.

"How do you think the evacuation is going?" I asked.

"It had better be going good. After that shit with Danny, we can't afford any screw-ups."

"You never told me where we're evacuating to."

"I'm afraid you're mistaken, Plato Jones. I sent you a text while you were out running that errand of yours. You should check your phone more often."

A missed text. This was sad. And maybe dangerous. I checked my phone and found a message from Felix. It gave detailed directions to twelve safe houses strategically placed throughout New Olympia. He even included a handy-dandy map.

"We'll be going to the safe house on Old Shell Avenue," Felix said. "After the tree has been moved off site."

"What about the processing plant? Moving all that heavy equipment will take time."

"Daedalus will handle that. So don't worry your strangely shaped head over it."

The shape of my head isn't strange. Is it? "Does any of this bother you?" I asked.

"What?"

"Blowing up all those civilians."

Felix shrugged. "To make an omelet, you have to break a few heads."

"Eggs."

"Same difference."

Felix's indifference destroyed what little sympathy I had for him. I wanted to see another side of him, something to counterbalance the maliciousness. But maybe that was all there was to him.

Felix's phone rang. His ringtone was the theme from *Knight Rider.* He took the call.

"Talk to me."

I could faintly hear the person on the other end. But I couldn't make out what he was saying.

"Oh really?" Felix said. "Was he alone?"

He waited for a response.

"Get whatever you can out of him," Felix said after a moment. "I'll squeeze out whatever's left once I get there . . . Yeah. Okay. Bye."

He ended the call.

I felt a chill as bitter as the Antarctic wind. "What was that about?"

"It seems we have a houseguest."

42

Felix said a suspicious man had been caught snooping around the warehouse at HQ, and that he was currently being held prisoner. Easton fit the description. Hermes, that idiot. He just put the entire operation in jeopardy. Once again, I had to clean up one of his messes—and had to do it without blowing my cover. I'd have better luck trying to solve a Rubik's Cube with my feet while blindfolded.

Only a handful of MLF operatives remained at the base. Most of the computer equipment had been removed. Eric accompanied us to an interrogation room in the barracks and unlocked the reinforced steel door.

"I'll be right outside," he said. "Holler if you need anything."

The door closed behind us. A single light bulb burned overhead, casting weak light across stone walls caked with dried blood. A security camera watched us from the top right corner of the room. The air stank like a meatpacking plant. The smell coated my nasal cavity.

In the middle of the room, Easton sat bound to a chair, motionless, his head hanging. He had been stripped down to his underwear. Blood glistened on his chest and stomach, darkening his gray boxer shorts. Faint breaths whistled from his nose, the only indication that he still lived.

Felix walked in slow circles around Easton.

"So, you want to be the good cop or the bad cop?" he asked me.

I didn't know how to answer that. But I didn't have to. Easton let out a groan.

"You got something to say?" Felix asked.

Easton didn't answer. He seemed to have lost whatever shred of consciousness he clung to.

"Hey!" Felix grabbed a handful of Easton's hair and yanked his head back. "Don't check out on me yet. We've got a lot to talk about."

Easton's face was a bloody mask. He cracked open swollen eyes. His irises were brown, indicating that Hermes was not in control. The bastard had abandoned him to the wolves.

Felix grilled Easton while I watched, asking him his name, profession, and most importantly, his purpose for snooping around the base. Every question went unanswered. I wasn't sure if it was Easton's commitment to Hermes that had bolstered his resolve, or if was just too out of it to speak.

Occasionally, Felix punched or slapped him to loosen his tongue. Still, Easton gave him nothing.

At one point, Felix insisted I take part in the brutality. I realized that saying no might appear suspicious, so I slapped Easton across the face—hard enough to be convincing, but not so hard as to cause any significant harm. I felt sick afterward.

As the interrogation went on, Easton remained largely silent, only giving the occasional grunt when Felix struck him. The chance of his blowing my cover no longer concerned me. Whenever he looked at me, I saw no recognition in his eyes. No anger. No fear. Only vacancy.

I suspected that once Felix realized the pointlessness of the interrogation, he'd get rid of Easton. There'd be no point in keeping him alive.

I couldn't let that happen.

Felix eventually threw in the towel, his hands stained with blood. "Well, color me embarrassed. I'm usually a lot better than this. Want to give it a go, Plato Jones?"

I looked at Easton. Despite some fresh cuts and bruises, he seemed no worse for the wear. But that wasn't saying much.

"He's had enough," I said.

"You're no fun. You're right, though. We're wasting time. Kill him, so we can wrap up this evac."

"I'm not sure that's a good idea. He's clearly here for a reason. We need to find out what it is. Maybe if we let him rest for a while, he'll be more agreeable."

"I admire your compassion, Plato Jones. But I'm going to have to disagree. We're too short on time. Kill him, unless you want me to do it instead."

"I'll handle it," I said automatically. *Damn!*

"That's the spirit."

I aimed my gun at Easton. He gazed dazedly at me. The sclera in his right eye burned bright red. One of Felix's blows must have ruptured a blood vessel. I struggled to come up with a plan.

"Getting cold feet, are we?" Felix said.

Okay, Plato. How far are you willing to go to finish this mission?

Apparently, not far enough. I turned the gun on Felix and fired.

43

The round struck Felix in his right leg. He went to one knee without a sound, his eyes wide with shock and confusion. He reached for his gun. I kicked him in the face before the weapon cleared its holster. He tumbled into a clumsy sprawl across the floor, unconscious.

An alarm sounded. I anticipated Eric bursting into the room and moved to the right side of the door, just as it swung open. Eric rushed through, his gun drawn. I bashed him in the head with the butt of my Five-seven, incapacitating him. I dragged him away from the door, then patted Felix down. I stole his gun and elevator key—in case a chance to destroy the tree presented itself. For good measure, I also swiped the magazine from Eric's gun.

I untied Easton and hauled him to his feet. He couldn't stand on his own, so I draped his arm across my shoulder and helped him out of the room. In the hall, I heard Stavros's voice on the loudspeaker.

"Plato Jones is a traitor! He is to be shot on sight!"

I guessed my days of being Mr. Popular were over.

I led Easton down the hall. I had no idea where to take him. Anywhere but here seemed a fine choice. But I needed something more specific. Easton released a shuddering breath. His muscles tensed.

"You okay, buddy?" I asked.

Easton replied in voice that wasn't his own. "I'm just fine, Mr. Jones."

Hermes.

"About time you showed up," I said. "What were you thinking, sending him here?"

"I decided it was time to act. To do that, I needed someone on the inside."

"You already had someone on the inside. Me."

"Stop for a moment and I'll show you what I mean."

Against my better judgment, I did as Hermes asked—allowing him to support his own weight. He squatted and stuck two fingers down his throat. He gagged, and a stream of yellow-brown vomit sprayed from his mouth. With it, came a black device no bigger than a double-A battery. There was a button on the end of it.

"What's that?" I asked.

Hermes picked up the device. "Just watch."

He pressed the button. The lights in the hall went off, and the alarm fell silent.

A portable EMP. Clever.

The emergency lights kicked in seconds later, bathing the hall in a red glow.

"My men and I will be storming the facility shortly," Hermes said. "I suggest you stay out of our way."

"What about Easton?" I asked.

But Hermes had already relinquished control over Easton's body. The man teetered off balance. I caught him before he could fall. He mumbled incomprehensibly.

"Don't worry, Easton," I said. "I'll get you out of here."

What I didn't tell him was how. I still had to figure that part out. I heard an explosion coming from one of the upper levels. The OBI had launched its attack. Escaping the facility suddenly became a secondary objective. I needed to destroy the ambrosia facility, lest the MLF members decide to juice up. Even with superpowers, they'd prove no match for Hermes. But the rest of Jackass's team would be slaughtered.

I guided Easton to the laundry room. By some stroke of luck, we didn't encounter any MLF operatives on the way. I hefted Easton into a bin of dirty bed sheets and pillowcases. I forced Felix's gun into his hand and stuck the extra magazine in the waistband of his underwear.

"Stay here until I get back," I said.

Easton gave no response. He had lost consciousness. I grabbed an armload of laundry from another bin and heaped it on top of him. Not the ideal hiding spot, but it would do. He should be okay so long as he stayed quiet.

I left the laundry room and made for the elevator—the only means of accessing the facility's sublevel. Or the only one I knew of. Along the way, I stopped by the armory to pick up a few things. Three MLF members rushed out the door, armed to the teeth.

I dipped around the corner before they could spot me. They hustled down the opposite hallway. After their footsteps had dwindled to silence, I hurried forward. The armory shelves had been picked clean for the most part. But enough remained to suit my needs. I grabbed a tactical vest, an FS2000 assault rifle, four extra magazines—two for the FS2000 and two for the Five-seven I'd given Easton—and an incendiary grenade.

Once I had geared up, I exited the armory, only to come face to face with Helena. We raised our guns. For me, the reaction had been instinctive. I couldn't say the same for her. She glared at me, rage and sadness blazoned across her face. This was the moment I'd feared.

"Is it true?" she asked. "Are you a traitor?"

"Yes."

Helena said nothing. Tears welled in her eyes.

"I want to see Zeus dethroned just as much as anyone

here," I said, lowering my assault rifle. "But not at the cost of innocent lives. You understand?"

Helena continued to point her gun at me. "So it was all a lie?"

"Not all of it."

Tears rolled down Helena's cheeks. She gradually lowered her gun.

"Come with me," I said.

More tears fell as the anger faded from her face, leaving only sadness.

"Helena . . ." I stepped toward her.

Her rage reignited. Helena pulled back her fist and punched me hard across the jaw. I reeled under the blow but stayed on my feet. Before I could recover, she grabbed the back of my head and pulled me into a fierce kiss.

She tore away suddenly, leaving us both breathless. "Go."

"Come with me," I repeated.

"We both know that's not possible. I've done too much."

"I can help you."

"No one can help me, Plato."

Gunfire rang out from an adjacent corridor, eclipsing her words.

"Damn it, Plato, get out of here!" Helena shoved me.

There was no arguing with her.

"I'll find you," I said. "I promise."

Helena nodded. Tears still flowed from her eyes. I forced myself to run away, and didn't stop until I reached the hall that ended at the elevator. There, I saw three OBI agents: two humans and one satyr. Garbed in black combat gear, they stood over the lifeless bodies of two MLF operatives. I recognized them from the armory.

The satyr caught sight of me. "Freeze!"

I raised my hands as he and his teammates aimed their guns at me. They lowered them once they realized who I was. I didn't recognize any of them, however. They must have joined the OBI after I quit.

"I'm glad to see you guys," I said. "We've got wounded in the laundry room. Easton Green."

"We'll handle it, Mr. Jones," said one of the human agents. He then regarded the satyr. "Escort Mr. Jones to the extraction point."

"Yes, sir."

"I'm not going anywhere," I said. "Not yet."

The lead agent opened his mouth to reply.

I cut him off. "We need to destroy the ambrosia factory before these clowns go super."

The other two agents looked to their leader.

"I said we'll handle it," he said.

"The plant is locked down tight. Good luck getting inside without me."

The lead agent pursed his lips. He sighed after a moment.

"Secure Easton," he said to his men. "I'll accompany Mr. Jones."

The two agents hustled down the hall.

I called out to them. "Hey!"

They paused.

"There are still hostiles on this floor," I said. "Two of them are unconscious in the interrogation room. They may have woken up by now, so stay on your guard."

The agents nodded and moved on.

I hoped they wouldn't come across Helena. But she was resourceful. Somehow, I knew she'd survive this.

The lead agent and I got on the elevator. As the door closed, his radio crackled. He put it to his ear.

"Simms here."

I heard the person on the other end say the laboratory had been secured. My first thought was of Daedalus. I hoped he hadn't been hurt or worse. Though he was technically one of the bad guys, he didn't strike me as an evil person. Just misguided. My second thought was of getting some backup. Who knew what kind opposition awaited us on the lower level? It wouldn't hurt to bring along a few extra guns.

"Good," said Simms. "Keep me posted."

He put away his radio.

"Before tackling the plant, we should pick up some extra guns," I said.

"Good idea."

I pressed the button that would take us to R&D. The elevator began to move.

"Crazy day, huh?" I said. "You said your name was Simms, right?"

"Yeah, Darren Simms."

"Nice to meet you, Darren."

"Likewise. You're a bit of legend around the office."

"Is that so?"

"Yeah. I've read some of your OBI case files. Impressive stuff."

Well how about that? And here I thought I was only a legend in my own mind. "What's the rest of the OBI up to?" I asked, assuming Hermes hadn't been dumb enough to commit all his forces to this one assault.

"Some are attacking the MLF's safe houses," Darren said. "Others are going after the organization's foreign partners."

By foreign partners, I assumed he meant Majit and his hired goons. "Sounds like you guys have got things under control."

"We couldn't have done it without you."

I smiled. "Thanks."

The elevator stopped and we stepped into the lab. Daedalus and several members of his staff sat against the wall, handcuffed. Gabby stood at the end of the line, staring into space. It seemed the good doctor had taken my advice and given her a pair of glasses. Four OBI agents guarded the prisoners while four more searched the lab for intel. I was relieved to see no dead bodies or blood on the floor.

I could feel Daedalus's eyes on me. I avoided looking at him. I imagined he was pretty pissed at me. But it couldn't be helped.

"I need two volunteers," Darren said.

A pair of guards joined us at the elevator. I inserted Felix's key into the slot under the control panel. The doors closed, and the elevator began to descend.

"Is there anything we should know going into this?" Darren asked me.

"The tree is probably being guarded. But the factory seemed fully automated. Even so, be on your guard. Humans hopped up on ambrosia are nothing to play with."

"You hear that, guys?" Darren asked. "We might be in for some freaky shit. Don't get distracted."

"Yes, sir," both men said in unison.

The elevator stopped and the doors opened. Two MLF guards with shovels stood in the meadow below, uprooting the tree. Across the way, I caught a glimpse of two figures leaving the room through the door that led to the manufacturing plant. I couldn't make out the person who had gone through first; I saw only a body obscured by a tall figure in hooded black robe.

"Freeze!" Darren shouted.

The remaining robed figure paused and looked at us, eyes flashing like flecks of tin. The rest of the person's features lay hidden beneath the hood's cast shadows. He—she—whatever it was turned and went through the door. It closed behind him.

The MLF guards dropped their shovels and went for their handguns. Darren and his men peppered them with bullets. I knew the killing had been necessary—they would have done the same to us. But that didn't make me feel any better about it.

Darren and his men took a long look at the tree.

"I didn't want to believe it," Darren muttered.

I took out the incendiary grenades.

"What are you doing?" he asked.

"Making sure those apples don't fall into the wrong hands."

Whether those hands belonged to mortals or Gods.

I pulled the pin and tossed the grenade into the meadow. No one tried to stop me. The tree went up in a red-orange blaze. Wood crackled. Leaves and apples withered and blackened, turning to ash.

Darren and his men frowned. They probably would have preferred to keep the tree alive until Hermes could decide what to do with it. But Jackass was their boss, not mine. Too many lives had been lost because of those apples. But the cycle of death would end today. I'd make sure of it.

We ran to the plant entrance. I slid the key into the panel—to gain access to the keypad—and entered the code: 8008. Nothing happened.

I tried it again.

Still nothing. *Damn! Someone must have changed it.*

"What's wrong?" Darren asked.

"I'm not sure."

Maybe Felix hadn't changed the code. Maybe I just remembered it incorrectly. Either way, I couldn't afford to waste time. I had to get into the plant—and I knew just how to do it.

"I need you to keep this room secure," I said.

"Going somewhere?" Darren asked.

"Yeah."

Darren didn't ask any more questions. Good man.

I returned to R&D. Daedalus and the other prisoners were gone. They must've been carted away. Three OBI agents had replaced the two who joined Darren and me. I jogged to the case containing the locust eggs. Only one remained on display. What happened to the others was anyone's guess.

Two agents were examining it. I squeezed between them.

"Pardon me, gents."

"What do you think you're doing?" said one of them.

"Just grabbing my spare key." I plucked the orb from its case and stuffed it in my pocket. "When your boss is done powdering his nose, tell him to join me downstairs."

I got back on the elevator. I turned the key, removed it from the slot, and tossed it into the lab before the doors closed. Hermes would figure out what to do with it. The tree still smoldered, and the flames had turned the grass black. Apple-scented smoke clouded the air. As I made my way to the plant entrance, splashes of blood on the floor and walls caused me stop. Darren and his men were missing. The hair on the nape of my neck prickled.

The door to the plant stood open. A crimson trail led inside. I should've gone for backup or waited for Hermes to get there, but a weak plea for help coming from inside the plant demanded immediate action. An image of Admiral Ackbar from *Star Wars* popped into my head, shouting "It's a trap!" I cast the warning aside. Turning my back on those in need was something I had never been able to do. No point in breaking tradition now.

I crept into the lab, my heart racing. My eyes swept across the scene of a massacre. Limbs and entrails littered the immediate area, glistening with blood. The severed head of one of Darren's men looked up at me with an expression of horror.

Further ahead, Darren lay in a pool of blood. His left arm and both legs were missing, as though he had stepped on a land mine. He saw me and reached out weakly before succumbing to his injuries. I moved toward him, scanning the area for the two figures from earlier. I suspected they were responsible. But how could they have taken out three highly trained OBI agents? I would have said ambrosia, but the long, deep gashes in Darren's back were consistent with an animal attack.

I checked Darren's pulse. Gone. I hung my head.

"Sorry, son," said a voice from behind me. "I don't think he's gonna make it."

I whirled around to see Felix standing across from me.

44

FELIX'S EYES SHINED WITH MAD GLEE. BLOOD COVERED HIS nude body from head to toe, and the leg I had shot earlier seemed to have healed.

"Surprised to see me?" Felix asked, his teeth blindingly white against the red blood. "I would be too."

I pretended not to be freaked out. "Where are your two friends?"

"There's no one here but us, Plato Jones."

More of Felix's patented bullshit. On to the next question. "What are you?"

"Your best friend—or so I thought. But don't worry. I'm not angry with you. I'm actually embarrassed. You really had me fooled. Had all of us fooled. You're almost as good a liar as me."

"Give up, Felix. Make it easy for both of us."

"I've never been a fan of the easy way." Felix took a step forward.

I fired a shot from my rifle. It whizzed past his head.

Felix halted.

"The next one won't miss," I said. "Stay where you are."

"Plato Jones, convicted criminal, MLF operative, and certified badass is nothing but a puppet for the Gods." Felix shook his head. "That's a secret if there ever was one. But I've got my own secrets. For starters, my name isn't Felix. It's Fenrir."

Felix put emphasis on the name, as if he expected me to be familiar with it.

"Fenrir, huh?" I said. "Sorry. Name doesn't ring a bell."

"I suppose it wouldn't. But don't worry. This next reveal is guaranteed to blow your socks off."

"If it's all the same, I'd like to keep my socks right where they are. And the rest of my clothes."

Felix glanced down at his nakedness and laughed. "Good one, Plato Jones. Even in the face of death, you're still able to keep your cool. I admire that about you."

"It's a gift."

"Do you remember our fight with Achilles?"

"My body does."

"Do you remember when I told him to watch and be amazed?"

"Not really."

Felix frowned. "Just pretend you do, okay? You're ruining my big reveal."

"Fine."

"Thank you."

I wasn't sure how Felix—Fenrir, or whoever he was—managed to take out Darren and his men, or how he recovered so quickly after being shot. If he were some kind of inhuman creature, the osmium round would've had a more lasting effect. Maybe ambrosia was to blame after all. At any rate, I needed to keep him talking long enough for Hermes to arrive.

"You still haven't told me what you and your dad have against the Gods," I said.

Felix shushed me. "I need total silence for my big reveal."

Well, so much for prolonging the conversation.

Felix blinked, and his dark eyes suddenly turned amber. The blood on him bubbled and evaporated, producing a foul steam. I could feel the intense heat radiating. Thick black hair sprouted from his pores. His muscles stretched and grew larger, and his limbs snapped into unnatural positions. I winced at the wet crack of bone. He collapsed onto the floor, thrashing about as his body continued to distort and reconfigure itself. His fingernails lengthened and curved into hooks. An inhuman roar exploded from his mouth.

A shape-shifter. I didn't know what Felix was turning into, and I didn't plan on finding out. I opened fire. A few rounds managed to pierce his flesh but had no noticeable effect. The rest just bounced off. I held down the trigger until the rifle clicked empty. At that point, instinct told me to run. I surprised it by listening.

I sprinted toward the door but didn't get far. Clawed hands seized me and flung me through the air. I landed on my back, near Darren's body. The impact knocked the wind out of me, causing me to drop the rifle. Spots of light danced before my eyes as I pulled myself off the ground.

In front of me stood a creature every bit as monstrous as Cronus. Growing up, I'd watched movies about werewolves. I'd read comics about them. But I'd never seen one in person. Not even a shape-shifter that could turn into one.

In his man-wolf form, Felix stood over eight feet tall on two slightly bent legs. Midnight-black fur covered his hugely muscled frame and intensified the gold color of his eyes. His gaze contained only a faint glimmer of humanity. Drool trailed, thick and viscous, from a mouth filled with fangs designed to rip flesh and crush bone.

"Incredible," I said.

Felix returned a wolfish smile, literally.

"I thought you couldn't get any uglier," I added.

He growled.

The chances of me surviving this encounter were nonexistent. Might as well go out with a one-liner.

Felix rushed at me. There was no time to react. He crashed into me, knocking me back several feet. He appeared over me the instant I hit the ground. His jaws snapped shut around my waist. Fangs the size of steak knives punched into my skin, separating muscle, breaking bones, puncturing organs. Pain ravaged my body, unimaginable in scope. I tried to scream but could produce no sound. Blood gurgled in my throat.

Felix shook me like a chew toy. I could hear more of my bones snapping. He then tossed me into the air like a ragdoll.

I landed on the catwalk overlooking the plant. The world spun out of control, growing dim. I couldn't feel my legs. But I could feel my back—like it was on fire. I gasped, fighting for air. A burst of pain answered each breath, as broken ribs sawed into flesh. Time seemed to slow to a crawl, and I became aware of my own faint heartbeat.

Through gaps in the metal grating, I spied a vat of ambrosia down below. A thought entered my brain, like a light in the impeding darkness. I clung to it. With the last of my strength, I removed the locust egg and yanked out the pin.

The device released a cloud of gray smoke. Millions of tiny nanobots sought out and consumed anything metal. The catwalk rapidly disintegrated beneath me. I blacked out for a second. When I came to, I saw the pool of ambrosia rushing up to meet me. It was the most beautiful shade of blue I had ever seen.

45

I AWOKE WITH A GASP AND DISCOVERED MYSELF STANDING. Drenched in the blue liquid, my body was completely healed. The nanobots had consumed both the catwalk and the vat, and were now expanding to other parts of the plant.

Energy raced through my veins like current. But my heart beat at a relaxed pace. The world around me appeared brighter, more vivid. Sounds and smells had been magnified. Even the smallest details—slight imperfections in the stone walls, the buzzing of a gnat, the reek of a burned out light bulb—arrived with preternatural clarity.

Felix stood more than twenty feet away. He went to his hands and knees, about to lap up some of the spilled ambrosia.

No, you don't!

I ran to stop him. No. Not ran. More like teleported. One second, he and I were on opposite ends of the plant. The next, I was tackling him. The impact produced a boom that shook the air, and we went flying through the exit. We smashed in the guardrail, bending it, and tumbled into the smoking meadow. Our landing charred grass and roused a cloud of ash. We scrambled to our feet, covered in soot.

Felix snarled and went on the offensive. His clawed hands slashed wildly, blurring in the smoky air. No humanity remained in his eyes. Instinct seemed to have taken over, an animal's desire to kill. He searched for the one blow that would end the fight. He wouldn't find it.

I anticipated his every move. I bobbed and weaved, avoiding strikes that—under normal circumstances—would have been impossible to evade, and countered with a right cross that could shatter boulders. Felix flew back, smashing through the tree's blackened trunk and into the wall. He landed on all fours and charged.

I was ready for him.

We kept our fight confined to the meadow, kicking up a storm of ash. The more shots I landed, the slower and sloppier Felix's attacks became. I poured on the punishment, chipping away at his defenses, not giving him a chance to recover.

I could only imagine how many people had fallen victim to his fury. Darren and his men would be the last. I'd make sure of it.

I jumped clear of a strike intended to impale, and countered with an elbow to Felix's face. The hit dazed him. He threw a desperate backhand to prevent me from pressing my advantage. I dodged it like all the rest. But the diversion served its purpose.

Felix recovered and redoubled his efforts to kill me. He lunged, snapping his jaws. His fangs found only air and ash.

I answered with a lightning-fast barrage of punches and kicks that drove Felix back. I delivered each attack with surgical precision, targeting sensitive areas: the eyes, the nose, the temple. He took a swipe at my throat. I sprang backward and kicked ash in his face. He covered his eyes, roaring in pain and outrage.

Time to end this.

I tackled Felix to the ground and hammered his face with punches. Blows rained down on him with unbelievable force. One final shot put him to sleep. I rose, looking down at my opponent, watching the rise and fall of his chest. Gradually, he reverted to his human form. The compulsion to finish him gnawed at me. I suppressed it.

Animals kill the weak and defenseless. Men show them mercy.

The elevator doors opened as if on cue, and Hermes stepped out. The real Hermes. Somewhat subdued in his attire today, he'd matched a black suit with a dark shirt underneath. Five agents accompanied him.

"Hello, Mr. Jones." Hermes looked at Felix. "It seems I'm late to the party."

"That's nothing new."

The agents behind him entered the meadow to apprehend Felix.

"Careful with him," I warned. "He's a shape-shifter."

"Really?" Hermes said, his voice betraying more interest than I'd expected.

"Yeah. He turns into an eight-foot man-wolf."

"Curious."

"Turns out his name isn't Felix. It's Fenrir."

Hermes narrowed his eyes. "Fenrir."

"You've heard of him," I said. It wasn't a question.

"No."

Hermes was lying. I could sense it, more so than usual. But I didn't have the patience to finagle the truth out of him.

"Were your men able to get Easton out safely?" I asked.

"He's being taken to the hospital as we speak."

"Good."

"You should head there too," Hermes said. "Overdosing on ambrosia can be hazardous to your health."

So he knew about my dip in the blue stuff. That came as no surprise. Even without his heightened senses, he could have smelled the sweet, slightly burnt aroma coming from me.

"We can worry about me later," I said. "Right now, we need to concentrate on stopping those missiles."

"I've already dispatched a team to Antarctica."

"They'll never make it in time."

"I suppose you have a better idea."

"I usually do where you're concerned."

Hermes brushed the insult aside. "What do you have in mind?"

46

I ROCKETED THROUGH THE CLOUDLESS SKIES ABOVE ANTarctica, shattering the sound barrier, and drunk off the sensation of speed beyond imagination. Far below, the snowy flats stretched thousands of miles toward distant waters. Hermes flew beside me, his silver hair streaming in the wind. The cold had no effect on us, even as ice crystallized on our clothes and skin.

It took us less than two hours to reach Antarctica. Unlike during my first experience with ambrosia, I maintained full control over my mind and body. I also gained a rudimentary understanding of the energy surging through me. Earlier, Hermes had told me that the blood of the Gods was not only infused with power, but knowledge as well—properties that could be unlocked only when combined with juice from a golden apple.

Cool stuff. But I still couldn't see why someone would wear a five-thousand-credit suit to a raid. I guess there are mysteries mere mortals just aren't meant to comprehend.

Once the base appeared on the horizon, Hermes zoomed toward it at an extreme downward angle. He crashed through the roof of the central building like a torpedo, creating a huge hole. I couldn't lie. The move looked awesome, but too excessive for my taste.

I flew in through the hole and landed beside him. We stood in a dark corridor, shrouded in a cloud of dust, rubble at our feet. Jackass's dive-bomb maneuver must have knocked out the lights. But the alarm still functioned. It started to wail.

"Would it have killed you to exercise just a smidgen of subtlety?" I asked.

"Mr. Jones, there's a time for subtlety and a time to—as you humans say—wreck shit."

"I guess I can't argue with that. Can you at least try not to kill anyone?"

"You've got to be joking."

"Do you see a smile on my face?"

A squad of guards with assault rifles appeared at the end of the hall. Hermes was unarmed, and I had left my FS2000 back at the MLF headquarters. I still had my Five-seven, but with my newly acquired strength and speed, I didn't need it. The ambrosia bath and subsequent freezing had probably rendered it useless anyway.

"Hands up," yelled one of the guards. "Both of you!"

None of them seemed the least bit intimidated. I couldn't help being impressed. They may not have remembered my face, considering how brief my last visit had been, but surely they recognized Hermes's. And yet they stood their ground. That took a lot of guts.

And stupidity.

"Be careful," I said to Hermes. "They're probably using osmium rounds."

"I know how to handle myself in a fight. I wasn't born yesterday."

"That much is obvious. The crow's feet are a dead giveaway."

Hermes narrowed his eyes thoughtfully, as if taking the comment seriously.

The guard spoke again. "If you don't comply in five seconds, we will open fire. Five . . ."

"Four, three, two, one," Hermes chanted along.

The guard cursed under his breath. "Fire!"

He and his teammates unloaded on us. Hermes and I dodged the hail of gunfire while advancing toward our attackers. For me, the bullets appeared to be suspended in midair. I reasoned it was the same for Hermes, but to a much greater degree. We reached the gunmen in less than two seconds and dispatched them with punches and kicks, using only a fraction of our strength—knocking them down rather than into the air or through the walls.

I had to commend Hermes. Not a single kill. I hoped the good behavior would persist.

Hermes put his foot on the chest of the only guard who was still conscious, pinning him to the floor. "Tell me where I can find your boss, or I'll pull your teeth out one by one, slowly."

"I've seen him do it," I lied.

The guard cracked easily.

"Th-th-the war room," he stuttered. "He's in the war room. In the control booth."

"And where is this war room?" Hermes demanded.

"The basement. The elevator at the end of the hall will take you right to it."

"Your cooperation is greatly appreciated." Hermes stomped on the man's face, just hard enough to knock him out.

Could it be that Jackass had finally grown a conscience? I supposed I'd have to wait and see.

We breezed through another group of guards before reaching the elevator. I pressed the down button. It didn't respond.

"It's locked down," I said.

"Not a problem." Hermes pried opened the door with his hands and jumped down the shaft.

I went in behind him. It was a fifty-foot drop, straight to the bottom. The fall should have turned my bones into talcum powder. But with ambrosia in my system, it proved no more perilous than a game of hopscotch.

The inside of the shaft existed in near-total darkness. But my enhanced vision allowed me to see my surroundings in perfect clarity. I sensed guards outside the elevator doors. Ten in all. I could hear them breathing. I could smell the oil on their guns, the polish on their boots.

Hermes seemed aware of them as well. "Shall I do the honors?"

"No, I've got this one," I said. "Our casualty rate is zero. I intend to keep it that way. Besides, there's something I want to try."

"Then by all means."

I focused my awareness, assuming control of the energies streaming through me. As if they were threads, I pulled them to a single point, then reached into the wellspring, grappling with ancient power. The power of the Gods. I drew out a small piece—not even a pinch—and thrust my hand at the elevator doors. A shock wave exploded from my palm and smashed into them. They crumpled outward as easily as tissue paper. The blast sliced through the room beyond and hit all ten guards head on, tossing them aside like wooden dolls.

Its purpose fulfilled, the energy dissipated.

Hermes and I climbed out of the elevator shaft and entered the war room. A gigantic monitor covered the entire north wall. The screen was black. The guards lay scattered across ascending rows of seats. Three of them writhed in pain while the rest lay motionless, slumped over guardrails, and sprawled across desks. I could hear their heartbeats. They were all alive.

"And you were worried about me going overboard," Hermes said.

"Hey, I didn't kill anyone," I argued.

He had a point though. I put a little too much mustard on that last attack. Ambrosia should come with a warning label.

"Let's wrap this up," Hermes said.

We levitated into the air and floated toward the control booth at the top of the risers. Through a viewing window there, I saw Louis hunched over a computer console, typing furiously. He glanced at us. There was no fear in his eyes.

Hermes held out his right hand and unleashed a telekinetic blast. The window shattered into a cloud of sparkling mist. Caught in the backlash, Louis flew backward and slammed against the far wall. We drifted into the booth and landed in front of him.

Dusted with pulverized glass and bleeding from myriad cuts, Louis smiled wickedly at us. His teeth were stained red.

I expected him to turn into some monstrosity. He and Felix were father and son after all. But in the end, it made no difference. Shape-shifter or not, Hermes and I had him outnumbered.

"He's a cheeky one, isn't he?" Hermes commented.

"The cheekiest," I said.

"No, I believe that honor belongs to you."

"I'll take it."

Louis let out a wheezing laugh. It was strange to see him in such a vulnerable position. Surreal.

"I have to commend you, Jones," he said. "You're quite the actor."

"I keep hearing that. I almost wish I'd gone into politics."

Hermes scoffed.

"You think you've won, don't you?" Louis asked.

"Looks that way," I said.

"You know what they say about looks . . ." Louis pulled his gun from his chest holster, put it to his temple, and pulled the trigger.

Blood, bone, and brain matter splattered against the wall. Louis's head sank. The gun slipped from his fingers.

I stood frozen, my mouth agape.

"Pity," Hermes said, looking disappointed. "Now I'll never find out what they say about looks."

"They're deceiving," I muttered, turning away from Louis's bloody corpse.

I turned back as Louis's wristwatch beeped three times. *Bomb* was the first word that came to mind. The truth however, turned out to be far more terrifying. A huge monitor turned on above Louis's body. It displayed a camera feed from one of the silos. The missile was launching. A small box in the right corner of the screen showed another silo; the second missile was also taking off.

The screen then changed to a digital map of the world. Two white blips represented the missiles. Each moved toward its designated target—marked by a red circle. New Olympia and Washington, D.C.

"That was unexpected," Hermes said.

"Detonator must've been wired to his heart."

"Yes, I gathered that much on my own."

"Any ideas?"

"Just one." Hermes typed a text message on his phone and received a reply within seconds. It brought a smile to his face.

"What's going on?" I asked urgently.

"We're in the green."

"What does that mean?"

"It means relax and enjoy the show." Hermes put away his phone.

I suddenly realized what was happening. Less than a minute later, the white blips vanished from the digital map. The OBI must have removed the virus Helena had uploaded into the missile defense system. Relief washed over me.

"Some show," I said. "I don't think it's going to get picked up for a second season."

Hermes gave a partial smile. "My men should be arriving

shortly. In the meantime, we should do a sweep of the facility, round up as many miscreants as we can."

"I'm game. But before we head upstairs, there's something I'd like to do."

"Make it quick."

"I intend to." I rammed my fist into Hermes's face.

The air shuddered as the impact sent the Messenger of the Gods zooming backward and crashing through a wall.

"You have no idea how long I've wanted to do that," I said.

Hermes emerged unscathed from the hole he had created, brushing the dust off his suit. "Was it worth the wait?"

"Oh, yeah."

Hermes grinned. "Ready to get to work?"

"Lead the way."

47

I HAD ACCOMPLISHED MY MISSION. BUT MY WORK WASN'T done. Dismantling the MLF had produced a mountain of figurative rubble that needed to be sifted through. I spent the two days that followed the raid in quarantine at OBI headquarters—until the ambrosia had completely passed through my system. During that time, I found myself subjected to numerous debriefings. Having to relay the same information over and over again made me wonder if Hermes was giving me an insanity test.

Before releasing me, the bureau's resident doctor gave me a thorough checkup. He issued me a clean bill of health, but wanted to see me again in three months. He said that in rare cases, ambrosia poisoning unfolded in a delayed reaction. Only after I committed to an appointment did he allow me to leave.

True to his word, Zeus granted me a full pardon. No apologies though, from him or Hermes. Even worse, the OBI confiscated all the goodies I'd picked up during my stint as a hardened criminal. But they did slide a few credits my way. And most importantly, I was a free man.

That weekend, my mom organized a barbecue at her house and invited all my friends and associates—the ones who weren't psychopaths or Goddesses obsessed with turning me into a sex slave. She even invited Alexis—and Calais . . .

goodie. Unfortunately, Geno couldn't make it. No sooner had he recovered from his bout with worms than he contracted a mild case of conjunctivitis—pinkeye. Poor guy couldn't catch a break. I planned to get him hammered as soon as he got better.

After the festivities had gotten under way, Herc pulled me aside, wanting to hear all about my adventures as an international man of intrigue. I revealed more than I probably should have. Blame it on the beer.

"I still can't believe you got married," Herc said, shaking his head in disbelief.

"Neither can I. Do me a favor and keep it to yourself. The last thing I need is for Alexis to find out. She'd never let me hear the end of it."

"You got it."

"Thanks."

"Helena Jones," Herc said. "I like the way that sounds."

I did too, as crazy as it seemed.

"Did the OBI catch her?" Herc asked.

"I don't think so. I checked the arrest records from the raid. Her name wasn't on any of them."

"Well, here's hoping she got away." Herc raised his beer can and took a sip, as did I.

Though he had never met her, it seemed that Herc had taken a liking to Helena—and not just because I smiled at the mere mention of her. During one of my debriefing sessions, I asked Hermes about the virus that corrupted the satellite defense system. He told me that there was no virus, meaning Helena never uploaded it. That moment earned a place among my happiest memories. It was one of those instances that reaffirms your faith in inherent goodness.

"Think you'll ever see her again?" Herc asked.

"It'd be nice."

"Maybe the two of you could invite Alexis over for dinner."

"Uh . . . no."

Herc laughed. "What happened to the rest of the MLF?"

"Eric and Stavros were both arrested and sent to Tartarus."

"And Felix? Oh, I'm sorry. Fenrir."

"Hermes claims he's in custody. But he's real close-lipped on the subject. He's hiding something. I know it."

"Did he say anything about Cronus?"

"Just that the 'problem has been resolved.'"

"What in Hades does that mean?"

"No idea." I shook my head. "I have a feeling that this is the start of something big."

"Well, Jonesy," Herc said as he raised his beer can. "Here's to your being wrong."

"I'll drink to that."

Night had fallen by the time I left the barbecue. On the way home, I stopped by the cemetery to say hello to Claude—and to apologize for not being able to save him. He probably didn't blame me for what happened. But the admission made me feel better. It also reminded me of what truly separated mortals from Gods. It wasn't everlasting life, or limitless power. It was mankind's capacity for forgiveness. To let go of the past and make the best of what little time we have on this earth. That was something the Gods—the undying—would never understand.

At home, a manila envelope waited in my mailbox. There was no return address. Inside, I found Helena's wedding ring and copies of the wedding pictures from Felix's phone. They smelled of women's perfume.

A dull ache rose in the center of my chest. I smiled through it. Despite the gesture, Helena was probably pissed with me, and I couldn't blame her. I had deceived her and abandoned her during the raid, when she needed me most. But what could I have offered a fugitive on the run? Sheltering her from the wrath of Olympus would have been impossible with Zeus keeping tabs on me. And would she even have accepted my help? I couldn't answer that.

For now, Helena's future seemed cast in shadow. And some crazy, naïve part of me wanted to walk beside her, wading through the darkness. Maybe I'd get my chance one day.

I put the items on my nightstand.

I went to the kitchen and opened the fridge. I reached for a beer but stopped myself, grabbing a soda instead. Refreshment in hand, I sat down in front of the TV. As I prepared for some much-needed me-time, Mr. Fancy Pants emerged from that secret place cats go when they don't want to be bothered. In his case, it was under the loveseat. He leaped into my lap.

"Okay, hairball," I said, scratching behind his ear. "Just for tonight, me-time will be *our* time."

Epilogue

Hermes entered Zeus's office in a hurry, carrying a file folder bearing the OBI's official seal. He dropped it on his father's desk.

"The results?" asked the president.

Hermes nodded grimly. "Yes, sir."

Zeus opened the file folder and flipped through the pages within. His electric-blue eyes scanned the information with preternatural speed, processing it within seconds. Though his expression remained calm, a sudden gathering of storm clouds outside his window insisted that all was not well.

"Are you certain these are accurate?" he asked.

"Yes, sir," Hermes said. "I ran the tests myself."

"Hephaestus." Zeus leaned back in his chair. "Even in death, you're more trouble than you're worth."

"What do you need me to do?"

"Nothing. Continue your search for Cronus. He can't be allowed to roam free. We'll discuss other matters once he's back in Tartarus where he belongs."

"What about Jones?"

"Leave him be for now. He's earned a rest."

"Understood."

"Do you have anything else for me?"

Hermes hesitated, but only for an instant. He knew better than to keep things from his father. He pulled two photographs out of the jacket's inside pocket and placed them beside the file folder.

Zeus leaned forward. One of the photos was of Louis King prior to his autopsy. The other was of a creature that the King of the Gods—in his countless years—had never seen before. A reptilian humanoid covered in dark-green scales. It had two slits where a nose should have been, and a gaping mouth filled with small fangs. It appeared to be dead, bearing a gunshot wound to the head.

"This isn't . . ." Zeus didn't finish his sentence.

"It is," Hermes said. "The coroner and his assistant claimed the body transformed before their eyes."

"Louis King."

Thunder rumbled beyond the office window, and somewhere in the distance, a bolt of lightning split the sky in two.

ABOUT THE AUTHOR

A fan of thrillers, fantasy, and science fiction, Robert B. Warren has been writing stories ever since he could hold a pencil. In 2009, he received a Bachelor of Arts degree in English and creative writing from the University of Alabama. He currently lives in the South.

Previous Plato Jones Books
Murder on Olympus

More Plato Jones books are coming soon.